THE UNBOUNDED

THE SUNDERING SERIES
BOOK 2

D RAE PRICE

DRaePriceBooks

Book Cover Design &
Illustration © Tom Edwards
TomEdwardsDesign.com

Library of Congress Control Number: 2022921478

ISBN 979-8-9852043-5-3 (paperback)
ISBN 979-8-9852043-6-0 (e-book)

First Edition December 2022

Published by: DRaePriceBooks, Concord CA, USA
Contact: DRaePriceBooks@gmail.com

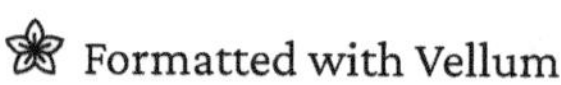 Formatted with Vellum

For my Family

CONTENTS

The Sundering Series

By D Rae Price

Published by DRaePriceBooks

Book 1: The Sundering
(Published in August 2022)

Book 2: The Unbounded
(Published in December 2022)

Book 3: The Harbingers
(Published in April 2023)

Book 4: The Convocation
(Published in August 2023)

For printable maps and diagrams:
https://www.draepricebooks.com/maps-diagrams

LAGRANGE POINTS

Not to scale

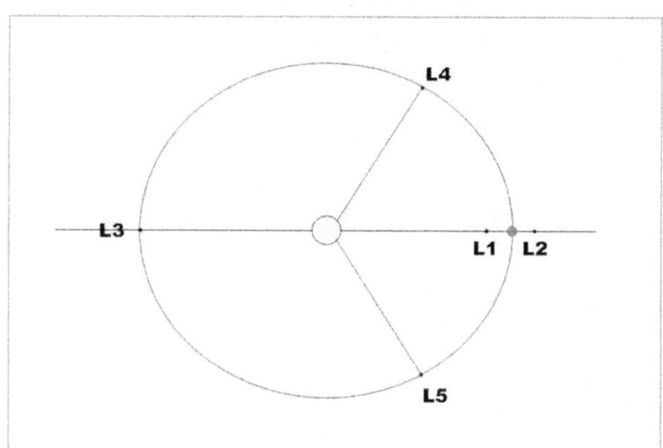

In space, for a planet orbiting its central star, there will be five places, called Lagrange Points, where gravity balances. A small object, such as a space station or asteroid, could be placed in those spots and stay there. This also works for some planet and moon systems. These points were discovered in the late-1700s by the mathematician Joseph-Louis Lagrange.

Three of these points, L1, L2, and L3, are "metastable." It's similar to a ball balancing on top of a hill. A small push will send it down the hill.

However, the L4 and L5 points are stable, as if the ball were inside a bowl. A little push will make the ball roll around in the bowl, but it won't get out. In fact, there are asteroids that ended up in the L4 and L5 points of many planetary orbits, especially the bigger planets like Jupiter. These asteroids are called Trojans.

To see maps and diagrams, go to:
https://www.draepricebooks.com/maps-diagrams

The Bahá'í Faith
The Bahá'í Faith is a real religion, founded by Bahá'u'lláh in the mid-1800s. The quotes used are real quotes from the Bahá'í Faith. For more information: https://www.bahai.us/.

The Badí' Calendar

The Badí' calendar, used by members of the Bahá'í Faith, is also a real calendar. New Year's Day is set on the spring equinox on Earth. It has 19 months of 19 days and 4-5 intercalary days, known as Ayyám-i-Há, so the calendar will match the solar year. The day begins and ends at sunset.

Names of the Months

(On Earth, dates vary slightly with the equinox, but these "set" dates are used in the sectors.)

- Splendor: Mar 21 - Apr 8
- Glory: Apr 9 - Apr 27
- Beauty: Apr 28 - May 16
- Grandeur: May 17 - June 4
- Light: June 5 - June 23
- Mercy: June 24 - July 12
- Words: July 13 - July 31
- Perfection: Aug 1 - Aug 19
- Names: Aug 20 - Sept 7
- Might: Sept 8 - Sept 26
- Will: Sept 27 - Oct 15
- Knowledge: Oct 16 - Nov 3
- Power: Nov 4 - Nov 22
- Speech: Nov 23 - Dec 11
- Questions: Dec 12 - Dec 30
- Honor: Dec 31 - Jan 18
- Sovereignty: Jan 19 - Feb 6
- Dominion: Feb 7 - Feb 25
- Ayyám-i-Há: Feb 26 - Mar 1
- Loftiness: Mar 2 - Mar 20

WHERE WE LEFT OFF AT THE
END OF BOOK 1:

<u>Heading back to Earth:</u>

Oatah—Special Agent of Sector 1 Council, in charge of Project Restore and Project Contact

Reeder—Oatah's assistant

<u>On the *Drumheller*, inbound to Redrock Station:</u>

Beezan—Captain of the *Drumheller*

Jarvie—Former teen runaway, now Beezan's adopted son

Iricana—Deputy of Oatah, relaying his orders to Captain Beezan

Katie—Doctor

Sky—Beezan's black podpup, sister of Star

Star—Jarvie's white podpup, brother of Sky

The first part of *The Unbounded* backtracks to Dominion 1082 (February, 2926 CE) when the Harbor a-rings were destroyed, possibly by an alien ship. What really happened there?

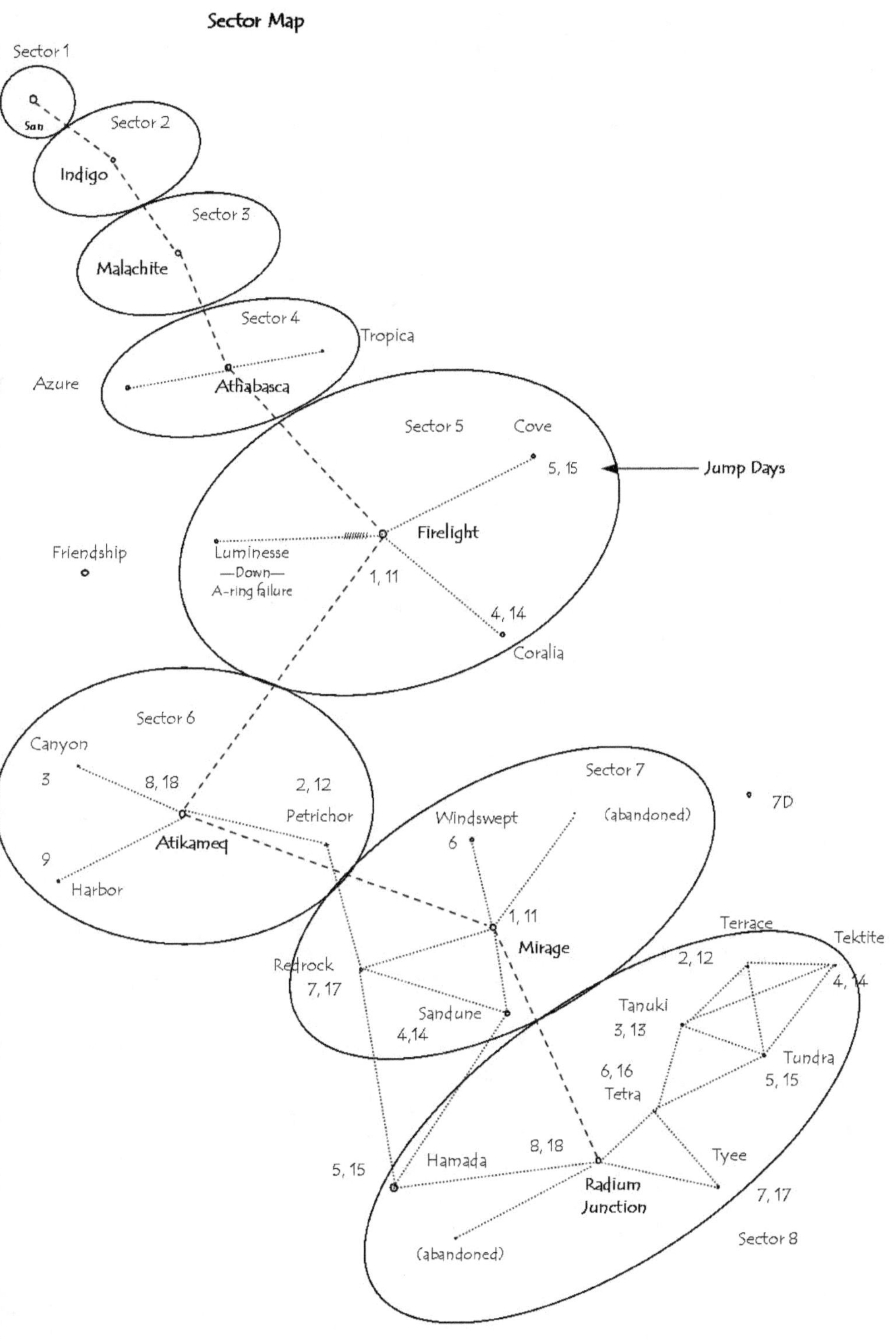

Sector Map
Jump Days
Sector 1
Sun
Sector 2
Indigo
Sector 3
Malachite
Sector 4
Athabasca
Tropica
Azure
Sector 5
Cove
5, 15
Firelight
Friendship
Luminesse
—Down—
A-ring failure
1, 11
4, 14
Coralia
Sector 6
Canyon
3
8, 18
2, 12
9
Petrichor
Atikameq
Harbor
Sector 7
(abandoned)
7D
Windswept
6
1, 11
Mirage
Redrock
7, 17
Terrace
Tektite
2, 12
4, 14
Tanuki
3, 13
Tundra
5, 15
6, 16
Tetra
Sandune
4, 14
5, 15
Hamada
8, 18
Tyee
7, 17
Radium
Junction
(abandoned)
Sector 8

1 / NO ESCAPE

Date: 3-Dominion-1082

Harbor Station

A young man, 27 years old, outer-sector thin, circled furtively on the Harbor Station TopRim. His cold hands were tucked nervously under his poncho, holding a red packing box. He had medium brown skin and dark eyes that darted constantly, as if he were on the run. But if others noticed anything, it was the expensive alpaca wool of his brown and tan poncho, an uncommon show of wealth. Although he wasn't wearing a pilot's jacket, his intense demeanor was enough to identify him and keep strangers away.

Lanezi stopped abruptly, realizing he was pacing in circles. Poncho swirling, he turned and made himself pace in a line— but then he had to retrace that same line—so it was still a circle, no matter how flat he made it. There was no escape.

Circles. He had walked TopRim four times today: giant circles of nowhere to go. Now he paced in his flat circles, outside the art gallery, waiting for the buyer to pay him. The owner was concerned about Lanezi's request for a cash slider, but since

Lanezi was a sector-famous artist, as well as a respected pilot, it had been arranged. The gallery had already hung one of his paintings, "To Atikameq." A cluster of people gathered around it, seeing in the painting what only long jumpers could see in life.

Lanezi circled away to avoid the crowd, so the buyer had to come out to pay him. Finally, slider in hand, Lanezi hurried to the cargo agent to put his box on a ship out of Harbor.

Lanezi hesitated outside the cargo customer desk. The gears of his circling mind ground to a stop. He was about to ship a package that would change his life. Before he lost his nerve, or his hope, he took a breath and went up to the desk.

He said a prayer for the smaller box within the red packing box, the engagement ring for Katie. It carried his hope for a future with his own family, a spouse and children, a future where he would no longer be cycled from family to family, ship to ship, just to be cycled on, in indifference, in practicality, in tragedy and more tragedy. Surely he had had his share.

Lanezi scolded himself. Life in the outer sectors wasn't easy. He wasn't the only one struggling. Better times were ahead. He would break free of the circles. Katie would get the ring and they would be married, and someday Jarvie might even catch up and be his shipmate again, his surrogate nephew, the co-survivor of Lanezi's latest cycle of loss.

Lanezi was so, so grateful that he had not been separated from his few remaining loved ones in the Sundering, the tragedy that had recently rocked the outer sectors.

As far as most people knew, Firelight System, in Sector 5, had lost its a-rings in an accident. Lanezi, on Thayne's top-secret team, knew that aliens were attempting to jump into human space—and every time they tried, there was a terrible accident.

Of all the possible losses, Firelight, the one transit point between the inner and outer sectors, was the worst. Now separated from Earth, Lanezi feared that the outer sectors could not survive much longer.

But the Sundering had not been personal. He had only two people in his life, Katie and Jarvie. Katie was part of Thayne's team, on Redrock now. And Jarvie—Lanezi fervently hoped that Jarvie was on his way to Harbor and would soon arrive.

He watched until the box disappeared down the sorter, then took another deep breath and sighed, relieved that it was finally done. He'd been off the ship all day. Thayne was too sick to notice, luckily. Thayne, as leader of their secret mission, "Project Restore," and Captain of the *Cheetah*, could command Lanezi not to go to the station, as Thayne usually did. Today Lanezi had been able to take his paintings and get out without anyone even knowing.

Lanezi had a little pang of guilt. Thayne would have been able to jump last month and the month before if not for Lanezi's secret stalling, hoping that Jarvie might arrive. Now Thayne was too sick. The weakness of Thayne's body and the storms of his mind combined to disable him, sometimes dangerously.

Lanezi started back toward TopRim, not as fast as his moment of guilt might have driven him. Thayne had an Earth-born personal doctor, a genius engineer, and the best data hunter in the outer sectors, along with assorted ship robots to support his every whim. Lanezi could be free for a day. Free from the constriction of circling around Thayne.

Lanezi was not jealous. His own unusual jumping skills were an undeserved gift. If Thayne wanted to use him to augment the mission, Lanezi was happy to help, for the sake of the sectors. But Thayne was work, not family.

Lanezi meandered along TopRim, savoring his last circle of freedom, before heading back to the *Cheetah* to see what Thayne's latest mental firestorm had launched. His p'link beeped again. He ignored it, for the twentieth time, and concentrated on staring into the nearest shop window.

"RESCUE" The sign caught his eye, but it wasn't a teen training sign. Lanezi was staring into the Podpup Nursery. The "available" sign advertised seven pups and one rescue. The seven pups were right in the window, tumbling about and ignoring all else. Back in the corner, an adult podpup in a pink knitted sweater cowered inside a box. Lanezi bent down to see better and she, seemingly on guard, looked up and met his eyes. They stared at each other. *What happened to her? Was she abandoned? Was it possible she was mistreated?* Lanezi had never heard of that happening, but the way she cowered in the box was heartbreaking. *I haven't been mistreated, but I feel that way sometimes.*

Go! We don't waste our time on podpups! a voice insisted in his mind, but it was only the echo of Thayne invading Lanezi's conscience. Lanezi ignored it and read the sign again.

"RESCUE. Female, 8 years old. Former Locator."

A locator! Locators were specially trained to find people or bodies after a disaster. She was a rescuer herself, and now she needed rescuing. Lanezi shook himself. He had people to worry about. He looked back down at her. She was still staring at him with hurt and beseeching eyes. He needed to go, but he felt a great surge of sympathy. She had been torn from her former life and family just as he had. "Goodbye, little one," he whispered and turned quickly away.

He had not gone three meters when he was overcome by a

heart-rending sound, a keening that seemed to strip the blood from his veins. He dropped to his knees in shock and pain. He could see others cover their ears and look around, but they were not struck down as he was.

Several people were coming to help him when it happened again. Now his heart was on fire. Heat pulsed through his body and engulfed his brain. *What is happening?* He turned on his hands and knees to look behind him where the sound was coming from.

A tall, very dark-skinned man ran out of the Podpup Nursery and paused in the rimway, his fierce eyes scanning the stunned people. "Bring him!" he commanded as soon as he saw Lanezi on the deck. Two green-banded teens hovering beside Lanezi grabbed his arms under his poncho and dragged him into the Podpup Nursery.

"What is it?" One teen asked the other.

"The death cry. The last cry of an abandoned podpup."

"No," Lanezi feebly shook his head. "I just looked in the window."

"There," commanded the man, pointing to a reclining chair.

The teens hauled Lanezi into it.

"He says he was only looking in the window," one reported.

The man leaned down to look Lanezi in the eye. "I am Dr. Obala. Do you deny you are bonded to the podpup?"

"I was just looking in the window," Lanezi repeated. "I haven't had a pup since I was a child."

"Go," the doctor told the teens. "Restore order outside."

"Yes, honor." And they were gone.

Another cry started and Lanezi thought he would faint in the chair. He was gasping for air.

"Look at you!" The doctor had a tinge of desperation in his

voice now. He yanked Lanezi's poncho off. "The cry is killing you. Somehow you have bonded with her."

"I . . . just . . . looked . . . in—"

"You were chosen." The doctor turned and signaled to his assistant, a purple-banded teen with tears streaming down her cheeks. "Bring her. Perhaps it is not too late."

The doctor looked on sternly as the assistant put the podpup, in her little pink sweater, into Lanezi's shaking arms.

Lanezi held her against his chest, but did not feel any relief, on his part or hers. If she cried again, he feared for his life. There was a rumbling in her chest and Lanezi let out an involuntary sob.

"Where is that human med team?" Dr. Obala demanded into his s'link.

The rumbling was building. "No, no," Lanezi begged her. "I'm here. No more crying. I didn't know." Lanezi couldn't keep the panic out of his voice. "I won't leave you." The rumbling reached a roar inside the pup and she uttered a cry that shook Lanezi to his core. He heard himself scream the same strangled wail as if they were crossing through some crucible together, and then she collapsed against his chest, expiring her last breath.

Lanezi was vaguely aware of the doctor holding his shoulder, hard. The assistant was sobbing while trying to comfort the seven pups. Other medical people were suddenly around him. They had his p'link. *Supposed to be secret*, his foggy mind fretted.

"Lanezi. He's that famous artist."

"He's a long jump pilot," the other said. "We may be able to save him."

"We must save them both," the doctor declared, sliding a resus pack around the podpup's chest.

Lanezi said a parting prayer as he faded from the world, but he was not afraid. Whether they saved him or not seemed of little consequence. The rumbling had stopped. If he never heard that sound again he would not care if he lived or died.

Lanezi awoke with a start. The same people hovered around him. It must have been only moments later. The resus pack was still on the pup. Resus pack. Green light. She was alive. He heaved a sigh of relief and almost fainted again. His chest felt crushed and burned out even though the weight of the little pup was nothing. He feebly felt her, sliding his hand under the sweater as they took off the resus pack. He could feel her heart beating. She was breathing. Her head rested on his chest. Lanezi opened his mouth to talk, but the pain in his throat stopped any sound from coming. He tried again. The medical people sprayed something down his throat, momentarily panicking him.

"That should help," they reassured him, afterwards.

"Alright? Will she be alright?" He croaked.

"That depends on you," the doctor answered. His eyes took Lanezi's whole being into consideration, and he was unsure.

"I didn't mean to—"

"You walked away, even as she bonded with you."

"I didn't know!"

The doctor continued his scrutiny. "Within *you* is the conflict, the reaching out and the walking away. There must be no hesitation now. You are entrusted with a being who has sacrificed much for humanity."

Dr. Obala looked at Lanezi as if he thought Lanezi might be incapable. Then a stray thought seemed to cross his mind. "It doesn't appear that expense is the problem."

"No. No." Lanezi shook his head and winced. "My boss-he won't like it."

"Your duty is with the pup. If your employer objects, leave him."

Leave Thayne?

It was a thought from outside Lanezi's realm. *Walk away?* Like he walked away from the pup? Surely, Thayne was worth more to humanity than a podpup. And Project Restore was classified, so he couldn't even explain it to the doctor.

Centuries ago, a mysterious alien race had linked up the human stellar neighborhood with an intergalactic transportation system. In the L4 point of one planet in each planetary system, the aliens had built a contraption that allowed ships to jump from one star to another. The acceleration rings, or "a-rings," were more like short tunnels held in place by a central gravity ball. By steering a ship through the tunnels, receiving extra acceleration from each tunnel until the ship reached jump velocity, a specially trained jump pilot could see paths resonating between the stars and drop into one, sending the ship on a jump that was sanctified from normal spacetime. The ship and passengers, if they survived the acceleration, would arrive unharmed, light years away, in mere minutes. The a-ring system was a gift.

But it had its price. The aliens were no longer around to fix anything and humans were not yet able to. If one ring segment was damaged, it could be towed out, the remaining five reset, and the system could still be used. But if two segments were damaged, or the central gravity ball destroyed, the whole system would shut down. No ships could leave the system. The people left behind would be completely cut off, from people, ships, supplies, and even communications.

The search for a fully habitable planet had exhausted the resources of humanity. Barely operational space stations teetered on collapse. Completely domed greenhouses barely kept them alive. No planetary system in the outer sectors was self-sufficient, despite the frantic work of the Solo Journey pilots, trying to deliver key supplies and equipment. Any system with failed a-rings was doomed.

Born into this challenging time, the greatest genius that the outer sectors had ever produced, 30-year-old Thayne Melika Rexan Tetra was entrusted with the most important mission in the outer sectors—repairing the a-rings. His was the only human mind with a hope of comprehending an advanced alien technology. The future of humanity was at stake. The burden on Thayne was great. It was an honor and sacred duty for Lanezi to serve him. How could Lanezi even think about abandoning Thayne?

Even if he wanted to.

Lanezi's mind flitted from one thing to the next. The pup was still breathing. People hovered around him, but he didn't want to meet their eyes. Dr. Obala was arranging podpup supplies to be sent to the *Cheetah*. Lanezi cringed. He was supposed to keep a low profile. Thayne would be livid that the name *Cheetah* was even mentioned, let alone linked with Lanezi's name and a story that would circle Harbor Station at lightspeed.

If Lanezi had nurtured a hope that the story would not cross over to the docking ring, where the ships were, and that Thayne would not find out, that hope was dashed when he heard Dr. Obala actually talking to Dr. Tenshi on the *Cheetah*. *I am in trouble.*

"Your doctor can't come for you," Dr. Obala explained. "She doesn't want you to go to the Med Center. She says you have two shipmates on station already who will escort you back to your ship."

The med people frowned slightly and glanced briefly at the

doctor. "You know," one said, "you can go to the Med Center anyway if you want to."

"No," Lanezi assured them, now worried about how much trouble he would be in. "We have a good Med Bay. I'll be fine."

They all frowned. Dr. Obala took Lanezi's p'link again, saying he would load special podpup instructions.

Suddenly, there was a commotion at the door. One of the green-banded teens returned, dragged in by two younger twins that he was trying to hold back.

"Honor," the teen addressed Dr. Obala, "these two say they were sent—"

At that moment, the twins saw Lanezi and broke free—flinging themselves to Lanezi's sides and grasping his arms in alarm.

Dr. Obala, the med techs, the green-banded teen and the assistant, with seven pups in her lap, all stared in awkward puzzlement at the strange identical twins fussing over Lanezi. They were small, looking no older than 8 or 9, but wore the white armbands, meaning they were really 15. There was no need for the additional thin red armbands on top. The two were obviously not part of the regular teen training program. Besides their shiny, almost metallic dark skin and elfish looks, they were childlike in behavior, innocent and sincere in their concern for Lanezi. They patted the podpup gingerly, muttering "hurt, gentle" to themselves. They even patted Lanezi's arms and stroked his forehead asking plaintively if he was alright.

"This is your *escort*?" Dr. Obala breathed in surprise.

The boy on Lanezi's right, Io, who was closest to Dr. Obala, straightened up and turned to the doctor. "No harm shall come to Lanezi while Euro and Io are near!"

Several people stifled snickers at his dramatic announcement, but Dr. Obala considered Io carefully, nodding. Dr. Obala, the podpup expert, could see that if podpups were people, they would not be so different from Euro and Io.

It took two more hours before Lanezi was stable enough to go. Meanwhile, the twins made friends with the assistant and helped calm and feed the seven terrified pups until they were their rambunctious selves again.

Lanezi walked a bit, testing the podpup carrier, while Euro collected his poncho.

"Ready?" Dr. Obala asked.

"Yes, Doctor," Lanezi answered, as Euro and Io took their posts at his sides.

"I will be in touch," the doctor added, but it sounded more like a warning than reassurance.

Lanezi, Euro, and Io walked a long way without speaking. They went along TopRim as far as they could to stay in the artificial gravity. Since leaving, Euro and Io had become very serious and agitated. Lanezi just wanted to get to the shuttle dock before he collapsed. Finally they reached the lift to the inner rims. Lanezi let the twins hold on to him and guide him as they lost gravity. They were nogee experts and he was losing his strength quickly.

They seemed so nervous, Lanezi tried to reassure them. "I'll be alright. It's not much further. Thank you for coming to help me so fast."

A look, like lightning, flashed between them. "We were already here," Euro whispered, even though they were alone on the lift. "They sent us to find you."

"Why?" Lanezi asked, suddenly worried that something had happened on the *Cheetah*. *I should have answered my p'link.*

The lift stopped and they floated out. Euro and Io helped Lanezi along. "They thought you had gone," Euro whispered again. "We mean—run away."

"What?" Lanezi said in astonishment. He couldn't believe they would think such a thing, even as *leave him*, the words of Dr. Obala, echoed in Lanezi's mind. "Besides," Lanezi said, wondering if maybe the twins had misunderstood, "why would they send you to make me come back?" The small twins, two of a quad actually, could hardly pull Lanezi along when he was willing.

They floated to a stop, glancing around. "They thought you would trust us," Euro explained. Io nodded nervously. He maneuvered closer to Lanezi.

"You can," Euro whispered.

I can . . . trust them? Lanezi puzzled over their behavior. They didn't always see the world as everyone else did. "Of course," he reassured them, "I've always trusted—what did they ask you to do?"

"They said something was wrong with you," Euro whispered so low, not just for fear of being overheard, but from the worry of saying it. "Something is wrong. They are all—angry—about something. They won't say what. They just said we had to find you because you might be afraid to come back. We're supposed to tell you to come back. They promise to help you. They said you would trust us."

"Euro! Io! I wasn't running away. I just got caught in this podpup thing," Lanezi whispered desperately, but his throat pain reliever was wearing off and he didn't think he would make it to the shuttle dock if he had to argue any more. *What could the crew possibly be so upset about? That he'd left the ship without telling them? Not answered his p'link? He'd done that before without causing all this alarm. Something else must have happened.* He was suddenly anxious to get back.

He started towards the dock but they didn't follow. Lanezi turned, floating backwards to look at them. Their subtle hand messages flashed between them faster than Lanezi could catch.

"What?" he prompted them. They caught up with him and grabbed a holdbar, stopping the three of them in the junction.

"We are with you, Lanezi," Io stated in his dramatic way.

"Yes, thank you for coming to help me."

They looked up at him as if he were missing the obvious.

"If you are running away, we will not stop you," Io continued.

"We will go with you!" Euro added.

"*What?*" Lanezi said too loud, in his shock.

"Captain Ryan is hiring in the crew lounge," Euro explained in the quietest possible voice, pointed with his head down the rimway to the right. "He would hire you and you could fix it for us."

"Twenty minutes left," Io said, looking at his p'link. "Then Captain Ryan is gone."

Lanezi gripped the holdbar, pain surging through his body again. The pup whined in the carrier. Her heart was pounding. Lanezi's heart was pounding. *Leave him.* His mind was foggy. Were they suggesting what it sounded like?

Suddenly, Euro darted off toward the lockers, returning with four large packs. "We brought our stuff. They are so busy with Captain Thayne they didn't notice."

Lanezi shuddered. He could leave. Only his oath and sense of duty kept him with Thayne, but the twins would be runaways. And they'd be running away from their doctor.

"No," Lanezi whispered. "I can't. YOU can't."

"You could fix it," Euro suggested, now uncertain.

"We are ready to do as you say," Io proclaimed.

Lanezi stared at them, then stared down the rim to the left, to the shuttle dock and the ride back to the demanding Thayne and oppressive life aboard the *Cheetah*, then stared down the rim to the right, to the crew lounge, to escape. *Leave him.*

Another wave of pain washed over him and he sagged in the air. It was an insane idea. "Listen," Lanezi let go of the bar to take them each by the shoulder. "I really wasn't running away. I'm in no condition now anyway."

They gave small nogee nods, accepting his word. "But promise—," Euro said.

"Yes, promise," Io continued. "If you ever go, you will take us with you."

"I'm not going!" *Leave him.*

"Promise," they echoed together, eyes trapping him from both sides. Lanezi was starting to shake badly.

"Yes, yes, I promise. If I go, I'll take you with me." *So now I really can't go.*

Then they turned down the rimway to the left, towards the life of no escape.

2 / *CIRCLE OF LIES*

Harbor Station Shuttle Port

An hour later, Lanezi, exhausted, put his poncho back on and struggled to strap himself into the shuttle seat without squishing the pup. While the twins were stowing their luggage and greeting the other podpups on the shuttle, he pulled out his p'link to check the messages he'd ignored. He started at the beginning, in the morning, just minutes after he had left the ship.

```
To: Cheetah Crew Announce
From: Dr. Tenshi, Cheetah
Thayne  having  mindstorm.  Melawn,  Lanezi,
Zahar, please report to the Med Bay as soon as
possible.
```

```
To: Lanezi, Cheetah Pilot
From: Zahar, Cheetah Med Assistant
Can you come to the Med Bay, please?
```

To: Lanezi, Cheetah Pilot
From: Dr. Tenshi, Cheetah
Come to the Med Bay right away.

To: Lanezi, Cheetah Pilot
From: Melawn, Cheetah Science, Special Assignment
Lanezi where are you?

To: Lanezi, Cheetah Pilot
From: Nkiroo, Cheetah Engineer, Special Assignment
Lanezi, please respond. We know you have left the ship. Thayne is making bizarre accusations. M needs information from you to reason with him.

To: Lanezi, Cheetah Pilot
From: Dr. Tenshi, Cheetah
LANEZI, CALL ME.

To: Cheetah Crew Announce
From: Melawn, Cheetah Science, Special Assignment
LANEZI IS ORDERED TO RETURN TO THE CHEETAH IMMEDIATELY. UNAUTHORIZED CREW CONTACT WITH LANEZI IS FORBIDDEN. ORDERS PER CAPTAIN THAYNE.

Lanezi closed his eyes. A wave of sickness threatened to overcome him. Bizarre accusations could only mean one thing. Thayne had figured out that Lanezi was stalling. Thayne would be furious. The crew would be angry. He knew he could never explain, that they would not understand. He looked up at the shuttle door. Closed. The secure light was on. Too late. He could not escape now.

Cheetah at the Harbor Docking Ring

After arriving at the docking ring, Lanezi, Io, and Euro took the express belt to Bay 18 and made their way to the *Cheetah*. Lanezi had the twins leave their extra bags in the delivery bin at the bottom of the gangway. No sense getting them in trouble.

It'll be Melawn waiting for me. Although both Melawn and Nkiroo were sector-famous scientists, they'd also been Thayne's personal assistants for 10 years, since they were hand-picked at age 15. Besides the data and engineering, they listened to his wild theories and nursed him through the mindstorms. They did whatever Thayne asked, even wore the fancy clothes he told them to wear. But when it came to conflict, even mild, family-style conflict, Nkiroo would disappear.

So Lanezi was prepared to meet Melawn at the entry hatch, but surprised to see Nkiroo floating shyly beside him, worry and sorrow creasing his dark face. Nkiroo tapped each of them on the shoulder, as always, to make sure they were real. "Come," Nkiroo whispered to the twins, with a toss of his head toward the kitchen.

Io and Euro didn't budge from their handholds.

"It's okay," Lanezi said, choking on the last word. "Go."

Euro handed Lanezi his water bottle before following Nkiroo. Both twins floated past Melawn without a word.

Euro and Io were not normally shy with Melawn, they loved him. Although he was brilliant, his humility made him univer-sally likable. His wavy golden hair tumbled over his bronze features. Glinting golden-brown eyes further entranced the younger twins to idolize him. Lanezi was amazed that the twins had even considered leaving him.

"*Cheetah*," Melawn said, "codelock the hatch for Captain Thayne's s'link only."

"*What?*" Lanezi gasped and the pup stirred on his chest.

"Yes," Melawn said, rotating away. "Thanks to you, we're all locked in now."

No escape! How bad could it have been today? "How is he?" Lanezi asked.

"What do you care? You disappear all day and don't even reply to *urgent* messages?"

"I'm sorry. I just had to get away. You know how it is."

"No. I *don't* know how it is to *get away*. And now we've been taking ten times the heat. Thanks to you." Melawn's usually polite and cooperative nature obviously battled with his stress and anger. And Lanezi couldn't blame him. "And a podpup! Just to push him over the edge?"

"I didn't mean to—" Lanezi lost his voice again and struggled to swallow a drink of water.

A flash of concern crossed Melawn's face and he took a second look at Lanezi. Frowned. "I'm commanded to ask you some questions." With a determined breath, he looked past Lanezi's shoulder and asked, "Did you, Lanezi, send false data about the fuel converter to Captain Thayne on 3-Sovereignty?"

Lanezi had never expected to be found out. He hung his head and whispered, "I wasn't ready to jump. I just thought it would save Thayne from the stress of an argument."

"You do not deny it?" Melawn asked.

"No," Lanezi admitted. *No sense making things worse.* "I was stalling."

Melawn let out an angry breath. "In that case, I am ordered to place you under arrest."

"*What?*"

"Captain's orders."

"That's crazy! It's completely overreacting!" Lanezi was so stunned, he was practically shouting, but his throat couldn't take it. His hand went to his neck trying to stop the pain.

"Lying and *falsifying data!*"

Lanezi tried to object again, but began coughing, which made the pain almost unbearable and disturbed the pup.

"I'm taking you to Med Bay. You're to remain under supervision. And you have to turn over your s'link."

Lanezi couldn't take it in. *Arrested?* Every breath he took was like fire in his throat. He just wanted to sleep, to make the pain go away, to make the hurt in Melawn's eyes go away. He felt faint, but he knew he had to hand over his s'link willingly. He reached under the poncho, struggling to get it from under the podpup carrier. He yanked it out and stared at it a moment. The symbol of his status aboard the *Cheetah*. Slowly, he held it out to Melawn. "Take it," he whispered.

At the top of the stairwell, Melawn grabbed a holdbar and paused, giving Lanezi a moment to wipe his eyes and compose himself. Then the door opened, exposing the Med Bay. Everyone inside froze in place as if in a theater scene. Even the rats, in their two Enriched Environment Habitats, floated transfixed except for their twitching whiskers.

The Med Bay was a model of what Dr. Tenshi thought it should be: sterile, efficient, bright, and all business. The same could be said for Dr. Tenshi: her uniform, her short black hair, and especially her bedside manner. Anything that distracted from her main medical work was dealt with quickly and unsympathetically. Occasionally, she would show a glimmer of interest in a highly unusual problem. She was floating with Zahar, heads bowed over a pad, but now she looked up and frowned at Lanezi as if he were the cause of all the inconvenience in her life.

Zahar, their 16-year-old reluctant medical assistant, was obviously frazzled, her brown hair frizzing out. Eyes squinting as if she had a horrible headache, she took a breath to brace herself. She glanced at the back of the Med Bay, where Thayne's special alcove was.

Thayne floated, cross-legged, meditating. He was 30, thin in a sickly way, pale in a sickly way, with red-rimmed eyes. He looked exhausted, but had his calm, beneficent demeanor. Then his eyes opened, brilliant black eyes, angry. His calm exterior was merely a cage. Inside a lion paced, pressing against the bars, waiting.

Lanezi froze, instinctively fearful of Thayne's anger and rejection. "Doctor," Melawn addressed Dr. Tenshi, but glanced repeatedly at Thayne, "this patient will require supervision." She nodded gravely, looking Lanezi over.

"You really are hurt," Zahar said, about to move towards him, but didn't when Tenshi spoke.

"And you really did bring a podpup aboard," Dr. Tenshi said disapprovingly.

"Yes, sorry, I had to," Lanezi croaked, too stubborn to stop talking. "Didn't you believe Dr. Obala?"

"We didn't know what to believe," Dr. Tenshi said pointedly, as they all nodded.

"I'm sorry," Lanezi paused as Melawn pulled him toward an exam bed. "I wasn't running away," he appealed to them, but Dr. Tenshi did not look any less stern. "I just had a little trouble," but his voice ran out and his whole body started to shake.

"So I heard," Dr. Tenshi commented, finally coming over to check on Lanezi, who would have been swaying on his feet if not for the nogee. At her movement, Zahar jolted to action, powering up the exam bed and helping Lanezi out of his poncho. "The podpup doctor presumed to explain this condition to me," Dr. Tenshi said with annoyance. She glanced down at the pup. "Lanezi! This creature is half starved! She'll be lucky to survive the week."

Lanezi gasped and hugged the poor shivering pup. The thought of losing her now was unbearable. Dr. Tenshi reached to take the pup away, but Lanezi instinctively pulled back.

"Lanezi! How am I supposed to work here? Zahar! Take the pup and . . . disinfect it."

Zahar gently pried the pup from Lanezi's fingers, whispering, "I'll take good care of her."

Dr. Tenshi pulled out her med pad. "Symptoms?" she snapped.

Lanezi swallowed and winced, pointing to his throat. "Throat? That's not an indicative symptom."

He closed his eyes in exhaustion. *Please can't I go to sleep and wake up without all this pain?* But when the scan came up, he peeked at Dr. Tenshi. She blinked and stared at it. Her frown changed from bothered to concerned and her manner changed completely.

"Yes," she said, nodding, with a touch of sympathy even, "you've certainly experienced a systemic event." She shook her head. "Podpups. No end of trouble. I'll get you something for your throat." She glanced at Melawn, "Further discussion will have to wait."

"Yes, Doctor," he answered, rotating to leave.

"Doctor!" Zahar exclaimed, "All her hair fell out!" Lanezi's heart pounded in alarm, but he could not move to look.

Melawn floated over to investigate. "This sweater is insufficient. Nkiroo can design a better one for the knitter."

Zahar was wrapping the limp, naked, scrawny pup in a blanket. "Thank you. We have to help her. She's part of the crew now."

"Of course," Melawn said.

"Yes," came a determined and dangerous voice. They all started. Thayne had moved silently to float in the archway. His exhausted black eyes pounced around the scene.

"You must save her, or I really will lose Lanezi, and I need him—for now—despite his disloyal, lying behavior, his disloyal—" the others gasped as Thayne choked over his angry words. He seemed to be burning from the inside. His small weak body convulsed as the doctor gently pulled him back to his bed.

"Save that pup!" she mouthed over her shoulder to Zahar.

Lanezi had had enough. Thayne had declared him disloyal, but the crew was taking care of his podpup. The bad and good extremes were too much. Lanezi's mind circled from one to the other in a frenzy of panic and relief until exhaustion took him into a jittery sleep.

After a few hours, Lanezi woke up, still shaken from his ordeal. Excuses, defenses, and denials aligned themselves in his mind. Arresting him was so . . . so . . . unnecessary, so overblown. It wasn't as if stalling was against the law.

The pup, now in a beautiful blue sweater with white snowflakes, was sleeping soundly by his side. He still didn't feel a bond with her. He almost felt as if she too were rejecting him. They had accused him of lying. *Lying?* He had admitted that he had stalled, had sent some false data, just to protect Thayne, to save him from the stress of an argument. *". . . lying is despicable . . ."*[1] They would not have understood his real reasons. *"If we meet with lying, faithlessness, and deceit, we are miserable."*[2] It was for their own good, mostly. *"We should at all times manifest our truthfulness . . ."*[3] *Lying and stalling are not the same thing!* *"Without truthfulness progress and success, in all the worlds of God, are impossible for any soul."*[4]

His life-long reading of 'Abdu'l-Bahá's Writings came to him unbidden, as if his soul and mind battled over the truth of what he had done. A terrifying thought came to Lanezi. If he managed to excuse away the lying, did that mean that his mind had won? His soul would lose?

Lying. *I must face it. I have done an evil thing.* More excuses rose up. He was not to blame, he was stressed, he lived with turmoil, *I was forced . . .* but he knew now that he could not allow his lower instincts to win. True life was the life of the soul. No more excuses. No escape. *I lied. I must beg God for forgiveness. I must let my soul win the battle for myself or I am lost.* *"I beg Thy forgiveness, O my God, and implore pardon after the manner Thou wishest Thy servants to direct themselves to Thee."*[5]

3 / BROKEN CONSTRAINTS

4-Dominion

Cheetah at the Harbor Docking Ring

A full night's sleep did not ease the pain in Lanezi's chest or in his heart. The hurt in his chest would go away, but what of the misery of lying? Lying, **"the very foundation of all evil . . . no more evil or reprehensible quality can be imagined in all existence."**[1] The shame of it swirled around Lanezi. *Why now? Why did I not feel the pain until I was found out? Why didn't I feel it when I was lying, if lying itself was the evil?*

Now the whole crew knew. Lanezi could tell by their small movements in the busy Med Bay. He could detect a difference in the attitude toward him.

The twins had come early to help Zahar feed the rats, as always. But they did not come to pat the podpup or greet Lanezi. Their fearful glances usually flung in Thayne's direction were now coming Lanezi's way.

Thayne was still resting in his alcove. Melawn was floating next to him praying quietly and murmuring reassuringly to Thayne. Both of them were pointedly ignoring Lanezi.

The doctor seemed to be building up to a difficult task. As she was usually the one who facilitated their consultations, Lanezi knew what was coming: the big consultation to restore unity. It would focus on Lanezi, the weakest link in their chain that kept Thayne surrounded and manageable. Now, the circle of containment had been broken.

Only Zahar seemed unchanged, or at least unsurprised, by the turn of events. Since she was aboard the *Cheetah* reluctantly, she probably expected the worst from all of them.

"Incoming call for Dr. Tenshi," the *Cheetah* announced. The doctor winced at the loud voice.

"*Cheetah*, send it to my s'link."

Much quieter on the s'link, Lanezi could just make out Dr. Obala inquiring about the pup. Tenshi frowned and answered, "Thank you for following up, doctor. They are both improved this morning. The pup is eating well. Her hair fell out completely, so we're keeping her warm. She is sleeping with Lanezi now." Over her shoulder, Lanezi saw Thayne maneuver so he could see better. The doctor went on with the medical details. Lanezi couldn't hear Dr. Obala clearly, but Dr. Tenshi suddenly stiffened.

"Visit?" She whirled in the air and signaled Thayne for any suggestions. "Our Med Bay is a class 4 facility. I hate for you to spend your valuable time, doctor, coming all the way from the station. Of course. Two hours."

They all waited a beat to make sure he was off.

"He's coming," she said simply to Thayne. "What could I say?"

"Nothing," Thayne agreed. "It's not your fault," he added, flashing an angry look at Lanezi. "How perceptive is this Obala?" Thayne asked the doctor.

"He sounds suspicious, but more as if he thinks we couldn't manage to take care of a podpup than anything else."

"We must put him at ease. Where is Nkiroo?"

"Kitchen duty," Dr. Tenshi answered.

"Kitchen? It's a waste. Others should do that work." He signaled Melawn to stay behind. "I assume everyone remembers what we do here?" he said to the twins.

"Yes, Captain," Euro answered timidly.

"Genetic research," Io added innocently. "And radiation research. And cargo."

Thayne nodded and floated down the stairs. The pup hid her face from him as he passed by.

"A quick clean up in here, please," Tenshi said nervously, half looking like she might go after Thayne.

The twins finished with the rats, scratching each one in turn so that they would not feel slighted. Lanezi got a clean blanket for the pup and made sure pink formula drips were wiped off her furless chin.

"Dr. Obala coming!" Lanezi thought that might illicit some response from the pup, but she just looked up at him.

Lanezi had washed up and made himself semi-presentable when they were all stunned by the *Cheetah* making a loud announcement.

"Attention: Code Blue. All crew prepare for reorientation. Attention: Code Blue. All crew to blue zones."

"*What?*" Dr. Tenshi exclaimed.

"God protect us," Nkiroo breathed, just coming up the stairs. "What is he doing?"

"Thayne!" Dr. Tenshi warned over her s'link. "Leaving will only make Obala more suspicious!"

"All crew to blue zones. Five minutes."

"Five minutes?" Nkiroo repeated, unbelieving. They looked at each other in panic.

"He wouldn't," Lanezi started to say, but then he felt the precision pulsing of the docking engines.

"Yes he will. He's been pushed over the edge," Melawn warned, launching toward the stairs.

"No, Melawn, you can't make it to the Command Bay in five minutes," Nkiroo objected, reaching for Melawn's arm. But Melawn twisted in air to avoid him and headed down the stairs.

"Confirm blue zones!" The *Cheetah* was ordering. There weren't even six safe spots in the Med Bay, unless they pulled down the other beds. And they couldn't get far in the four minutes they had left. Whoever wasn't in a blue zone could be injured or killed, depending on the acceleration.

This is insanity. Lanezi took a breath to countermand the order, but it would make Thayne storm beyond anything they had yet experienced. Lanezi locked eyes with the doctor.

"Containment. Maintain rationality," she whispered.

"There's nothing rational about this!"

"Placate him until he calms down." she suggested. But Lanezi knew Thayne wasn't just undocking to avoid Dr. Obala. Thayne meant to join the jump group.

"He'll take us to the a-rings!"

"Then we'll have five days to deal with him!" the doctor insisted.

Lanezi looked at Nkiroo. "I do not believe we can stop him," Nkiroo cautioned.

"Three minutes! Confirm blue zones."

Lanezi had a sudden fear that Nkiroo was warning him that he would not even be able to countermand the *Cheetah*. And he didn't have his s'link. They must be ready or risk their lives. "Euro! Io! Get to your cabin and strap!" Their cabin was the closest and they were fast in nogee. They could make it in three minutes.

"Thayne!" The doctor called. "Melawn is on his way to you. Wait for him!"

The doctor ordered Nkiroo and Zahar to the extra exam beds and she headed for Thayne's special bed. Lanezi strapped back into his exam bed, securing the podpup carrier to his sore chest.

"Confirm blue zones!" The *Cheetah* announced again.

The doctor raised her hand to silence them. Although they were all strapped, she held her s'link, waiting to hear from the twins.

"Tenshi confirm." Thayne himself was now doing the confirms.

She held her silence.

"Nkiroo confirm."

"We need a few more minutes, Captain," Tenshi explained as calmly as possible. "The twins have gone to their cabin."

"Euro, Io, confirm."

"Confirmed," Euro announced breathlessly, "both of us."

"Tenshi, Nkiroo, Lanezi, Zahar, confirming blue zone," Tenshi reported.

"Attention: Prepare to undock." The bed turned 90 degrees so 'down' would now be flat against the wall.

There was a jolt and Lanezi knew they were free of the dock. He used his p'link to activate the big screen and bring up the scene in the Command Bay.

No sign of Melawn, yet Thayne had already started to maneuver.

"Thayne," Lanezi croaked into the p'link, knowing he would be ignored. "Thayne, I'm in no condition. I can't jump. We have plenty of time to get to Nocturne and come back next month. Iricana said she was delayed. There's no rush." No one else said anything. "I'm sorry. I'm so sorry for stalling. For . . . lying. Please don't . . . Captain," he begged. He felt the others' eyes on him. *Please listen to reason.* "I won't be ready in five days." Lanezi was shocked when Thayne glared back at him over the screen.

"Yes, you will. You will jump. You owe it to me, you . . ." the ship lurched and Thayne was talking to the *Cheetah* again. Melawn burst into the Command Bay, but made no attempt to stop Thayne. Strapping into the co-pilot seat, he humbly nodded to Thayne. "Blue zone confirmed, Captain."

Lanezi tried to think straight. There was no reason to panic. Thayne could order the *Cheetah* through docking maneuvers. He could order the trip to the a-rings, but no ship could jump without a pilot. Thayne could not leave Harbor system without Lanezi. And all his fuming couldn't force Lanezi to do anything that wasn't safe. Dr. Tenshi had warned Lanezi many times that part of their job of circling around Thayne was to stay rational.

Who am I kidding? If they made it to the rings in time for the jump, Thayne would guilt Lanezi into going.

The boosting schedule came up on the main screen. Dr. Tenshi couldn't see the screen so Nkiroo read it out. "Nine hours boosting at 1.2 gee."

"Nine hours!" Zahar complained, "With only three breaks?

"Three ten-minute breaks," Nkiroo confirmed.

It was barely enough time to go to the facilities and grab some food. Thayne was taking his anger out on all of them.

Lanezi got food for the pup during the first break so he was starving by the second break. He spent the hours worrying and trying to talk to the pup. They turned off the main screen so they didn't have to see Thayne.

He said prayers to himself and some to the pup. She seemed

to relax a bit and even stretched her little paw out of the carrier and pressed it against Lanezi's chest. He almost cried. He kept reassuring her that everything was fine and he would take care of her. She had no way to know that his turmoil was with Thayne—and himself.

The others tried to sleep and talk a bit, but worry over what would come next kept them from any true rest. After the third break was over, they had just started accelerating when there was a spronging noise. Something dropped onto Lanezi's leg— and scampered away.

"The rats!" he called out. The mutated rats' EEHAB door had sprung open and several rats had jumped or fallen out. They weren't back to full acceleration yet so the drop didn't kill them. But the door was still open and others were teetering at the brink.

Lanezi grabbed his p'link. "Cancel the acceleration! *Cheetah*, cancel boosting! Thayne, the rats! The door is open. They're falling out. They'll be killed!"

"Thayne, stop." Dr. Tenshi said simply, "We can't lose the rats."

"We're not stopping."

"Thayne, Captain, my work, the twins."

"You can breed more. We're not stopping."

"They'll come back," Zahar said.

"We have to stop," Nkiroo argued, sounding more panicked than Lanezi had ever heard him. *"We can't let them loose on the ship!"*

"Are you afraid of a few rats?" Thayne scoffed.

"Thayne, you don't know, you've never seen a ship infested, it's horrible—you don't know," Nkiroo when on. He was not sounding so rational himself. Lanezi didn't know Nkiroo's whole story, only that he'd been orphaned and alone on a ship for a long time. But *rats?*

They were at full acceleration now. Lanezi tried to watch where the rats went, but they scrambled out of sight. Nkiroo was reaching for his straps. "Kiro! Don't unstrap; we can't get them while we're boosting!" the doctor ordered.

"They'll come back!" Zahar insisted. "They always do. They love their treats."

The mutant ones were so small—just like the twins whose mutation they were bred to study. The remaining rats in the EEHAB seemed to understand their danger as they stayed back from the door. One in particular was pushing the others to safety.

"Lanezi, what's happening?" the doctor called.

"There's still some in the EEHAB, but they're staying back. At least five fell out, but they all got up and ran away."

"Thayne," the doctor pleaded, "I know how much you want to get to the a-rings, but we can take a break now and boost later. We'll only add on a few minutes."

"No breaks. You can find them later." Lanezi recognized the imperious tone of Thayne at his most unreasonable. There was no point in arguing. Proof that staying rational was sometimes no help.

"No," Nkiroo sobbed.

At last, the boosting was over. In nogee now, Lanezi unstrapped his tense, aching body. The doctor checked on Nkiroo, who needed help unstrapping, he was shaking so badly. Melawn came zooming up the stairs to Nkiroo's side, putting an arm around him and assuring him everything would be alright.

"Where's Thayne?" Lanezi whispered to Melawn.

"Went to his cabin to sleep."

"Thank heavens," Zahar whispered so only Lanezi could hear. "Maybe he'll wake up as a human being."

As unhappy as Zahar was with being part of their team, Lanezi had never heard her be so harsh with anyone. *We're all reaching our limits.*

Tenshi checked the cage. "Five missing, four males, but only one female."

"ONLY ONE!" That's 10 pups per litter—"

"Shhh," Melawn tried to calm him. "We'll find them."

The pup stirred in Lanezi's arms. She was looking around the room intensely. "Find."

"She spoke!" Lanezi said. "Whispered, anyway."

"Find! She said find!" Zahar said excitedly.

"Yes! She's a locator!" Lanezi slipped her out of the carrier. "Can you find the rats?"

"Please," Nkiroo murmured.

The doctor, peeking into every crack in the Med Bay, on the verge of tears, looked over. Lanezi wasn't sure how it was done, but they hung, waiting for the pup to take the lead. She closed her eyes. The others dared not make a sound, although as far as Lanezi knew, podpup hearing was no better than human hearing, and what would she listen for, a snoring rat?

She hung there, turning slightly. The pup tilted her head, eyes still closed. For a second, Lanezi felt the fire in his veins again and a surge of fear overwhelmed him. But it passed quickly this time. Suddenly, she pointed with her naked little finger.

The doctor gently guided the pup towards where she was pointing until she touched a small panel door that wasn't shut properly. "Nothing could squeeze in—" Tenshi popped open the panel and sure enough, a sleepy rat was curled up inside. In a flash, the doctor had the rat. She turned with astonishment to the pup, her skepticism gone. "Good girl!" she praised. "Oh you are a treasure!" The pup wiggled in happiness at the first sign of acceptance from the doctor.

"Oh, little one," Zahar cooed and patted her. "Can you find more?"

Within minutes, all the rats were safely back in the EEHAB, with only one minor injury. The crew was giddy with relief.

"Lanezi, you have to name her," Zahar insisted.

"Whisper," Lanezi thought aloud. "She only whispers."

"Yes," everyone agreed, including Whisper.

A small burden of worry dropped away from Lanezi. Whisper had spoken. The rats were found. The ship would not be infested, and the race against time experiment to save the twins' lives would not be delayed. Best of all, Thayne would sleep for two days.

Two days of peace to heal, both his body and the break in unity he had made by lying to the crew. Of course, it would take more than two days to fix that, but a head start without Thayne was a blessing.

Whisper looked up at him. "Rats sick" she said. "Die anyway," just as Io and Euro came up the stairs looking tired and pale.

4 / FRACTURING PATHS

5-Dominion

Cheetah, en route to Harbor a-rings

The next day, Lanezi was feeling so much better and so relieved, he thought maybe he would be able to jump—or was that just the guilt talking?

He was back in the Med Bay for Whisper's daily check up. The doctor dispensed with him after a quick scan. "You'll live." Then she fussed over Whisper as if she were a human baby.

Nkiroo, who was on duty in the Command Bay, called Lanezi's p'link. "Urgent packet for the *Cheetah* from Harbor Outbound Authority."

"For me?"

"Thayne's asleep."

Lanezi dived into the alcove and whispered, "But I was arrested, so I'm removed from the command order, right?"

"Oh." Nkiroo said, "I'll just play it for everyone."

"*Cheetah,* this is Harbor Outbound Authority. Your request to jump cannot be granted at this time," a formal voice read out.

"You must first fulfill your obligation to Relay Readiness. You are assigned as Relay Standby Ship starting 9-Dominion until the next jump on 9-Loftiness, when you may resubmit your jump request. As your relay turn has already been waived three times, no further exceptions are possible under the jurisdiction of H.O.A.

"Your flight path should be corrected within the day to allow the current relay ship to stand down. Please confirm. H.O.A. out."

The crew stared at each other in surprise. "Well," Dr. Tenshi said, "that solves that problem."

"What problem?" Io innocently asked.

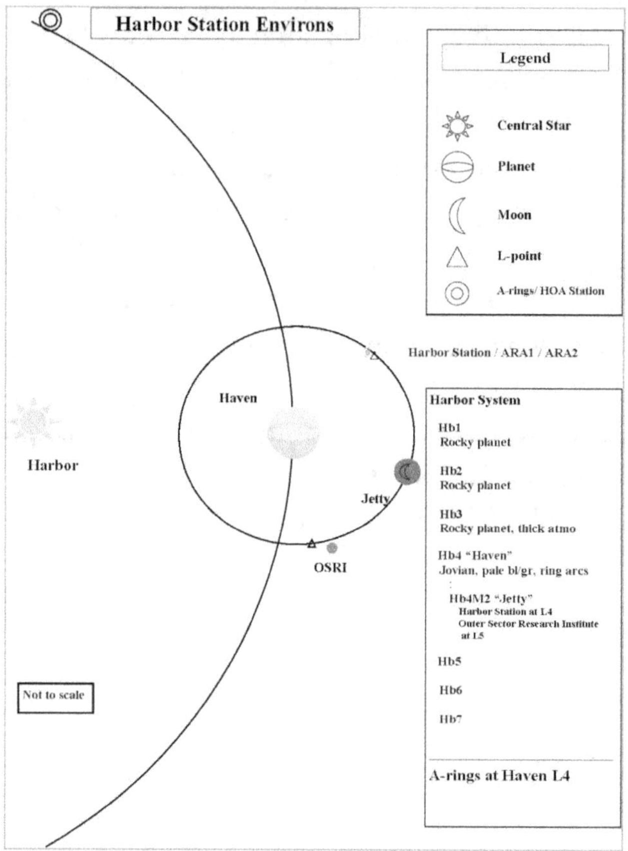

Dr. Tenshi scowled. Most of the crew tried to protect the teens from the difficulties of dealing with Thayne, but Dr. Tenshi believed in straight talk.

"Captain Thayne was eager to jump, even though Lanezi is not recovered, but now we can't jump anyway, because we have to do our relay turn."

"What's that?" Euro asked. Lanezi sometimes forgot they weren't from the outer sectors.

Melawn steered them to the screen and pointed out a picture of Harbor system, tracing an imaginary line from Harbor Station to the L4 point where the Harbor a-rings were. "In case Harbor needs to send an emergency message, one ship has to wait here, at the H.O.A. Station, next to the a-rings, at all times. That way, you don't have to waste five days waiting for a ship to get to the a-rings and jump."

"So it's our turn to wait," Lanezi added. "We can jump next month, which gives me more time to be ready." He said it in the most casual way, but the twins were not fooled. They could see the crew was relieved.

"Come hold the rats. I just put trackers on them, so they need some calming down," Dr. Tenshi interjected, distracting them from any further conversation.

Lanezi floated out after Melawn and headed to the Command Bay to meet Nkiroo. Lanezi was technically second-in-command, but on the *Cheetah*, there was really only Thayne-in-command.

"Should we wake him up and tell him?" Nkiroo asked. Lanezi would have tried to get the doctor to forbid them, but he couldn't suggest that in front of Melawn.

"I hate to disturb him," Melawn agreed, "but he'll be angry if we change course without asking."

"We don't have a choice, so we'd only be aggravating him," Lanezi argued.

"Yes," Melawn agreed, "but he's already mad at you—so we must make the appearance of asking his permission."

Nkiroo nodded, deferring to Melawn, who understood Thayne better than anyone. Both Melawn and Nkiroo had been with Thayne for ten years, but Nkiroo was unaccustomed to dealing with bad behavior, supposedly due to his odd upbringing. Lanezi was just as happy to let Melawn deal with him.

While Melawn went to Thayne's cabin, and Nkiroo stayed in the Command Bay, Lanezi went back to the Med Bay to get Whisper. Just spending a few minutes without her already seemed strange.

He crashed into the doctor in the stairwell.

"You should have warned me you were waking him up!" she said, pushing off Lanezi to get by.

"Sorry—what's wrong?"

"He's in no better temper."

Lanezi heard doors closing in the rimway and went back down with the doctor.

Melawn was rocketing down the rimway away from Thayne's cabin, toward them. He was holding his hand to the side of his face.

"Melawn!" The doctor called, "What happened?"

He yanked his hand from his face and grabbed a holdbar.

"How is he?" the doctor specified.

Melawn, so forgiving and charitable to Thayne, seemed severely rattled. He cleared his throat and shook his head slightly. Trying not to cry, Lanezi realized. Lanezi had been there with Thayne many times, so he didn't blame Melawn, but the sharp-eyed doctor reached for Melawn's chin and turned his face. A red patch blemished his bronze cheek.

In a voice like ice, she asked, "Did he hit you?"

"No! No, Doctor. An accident. I startled him. Just an accident."

The doctor's eyes narrowed and she scowled. Of course, in Melawn's mind, anything bad Thayne did would be an accident.

Suddenly Lanezi's p'link went on. Nkiroo, still in the Command Bay, had put his to broadcast. Thayne was now in the Command Bay ordering Nkiroo out of the pilot seat. Thayne was obviously in a rage again.

"Oh, no," Lanezi whispered.

"No one is going to change course," Thayne hissed.

"Captain," Nkiroo reasoned, "it's required. We can't get another waiver."

"I am not doing relay duty!"

"It's the law. H.O.A. said they couldn't change it—that it was outside their jurisdiction." Nkiroo's voice was shaking.

"Well, I'm outside H.O.A.'s jurisdiction, so we'll just tell them."

"Okay," Nkiroo whispered. "You tell them."

Lanezi switched off his p'link. "Now what?"

The doctor frowned. "It doesn't seem as if he'll calm down enough to change course today. Lanezi, maybe you could talk to H.O.A. privately and tell them we'll be delayed."

"Don't delude yourself, doctor. We don't have any private packet capability with Thayne around," Lanezi said more harshly than he meant to. Tenshi was taken aback and glanced at Melawn.

"It's useless," Melawn said. "He won't calm down. He's going to jump. He said no one could stop him."

"Well, that's ridiculous. He has to obey the law," Dr. Tenshi said. Lanezi wasn't so sure Thayne would agree with that.

"He has higher orders," Melawn said.

"If he does, H.O.A. would know," the doctor insisted.

"He's going to file a waiver anyway," Melawn said.

"Well, for all our sakes, I hope they deny it—orders or not. If Thayne is losing his ability to control his temper and we are losing our ability to moderate him, we cannot jump to the middle of nowhere by ourselves."

"Sitting at the relay point is almost the middle of nowhere too," Lanezi pointed out.

"Not as bad as Nocturne. We can still get packets here. We might be able to get Thayne—*and you*—some treatment. And if I could recommend, arrange for a back up pilot!" She whirled off to the Command Bay, giving orders over her s'link. "Zahar, take the twins to the kitchen and keep them there. Lanezi, take Melawn to his cabin. He needs to *rest*."

"Yes, doctor."

Melawn rolled his eyes, but there was no ignoring the doctor. Lanezi casually went with Melawn to his cabin. He did seem frazzled.

At his cabin, Melawn's p'link started broadcasting the doctor's arrival in the Command Bay. Melawn turned it off. "I don't want to hear."

"Will you be alright if I go?" Lanezi asked.

"Yes, it's nothing really. I surprised him and he knocked me away. He would never hurt me."

"Seems like he did hurt you-"

Melawn's loyalty to Thayne flared. "I just happened to be there! He hasn't hurt us the way *you* have!"

"I've never hurt you," Lanezi protested in shock.

"You think lying doesn't hurt? You think all this anger is for no reason? Thayne thought *I* knew you were lying! He thought *I* was in on it. And then he said I was *stupid* for not seeing through you! And I forgave you! And I prayed for you—and I'm still taking the heat—for you! And you have the nerve to be judging him?"

Lanezi was shaking his head, stunned. He hadn't realized the extent of Melawn's hurt feelings. Melawn suddenly stopped, seeming to realize what he was saying. He turned away from Lanezi, grasping the back of a chair for stability.

"I'm sorry." Lanezi felt a desperate need for Melawn at least to understand. "I was wrong. I shouldn't have lied. I didn't see any other way. I just wanted to give Jarvie a chance to get here."

"What?" Melawn asked, turning back to Lanezi, wide-eyed with concern. "You're stalling for your old shipmate? The teenager?"

"Yes," Lanezi whispered, "I know how bad it sounds."

"But do you know how bad it really is?"

"It's not—"

"If he leaves school, he's a runaway. If you've told him where you are—*you've broken your oath!*"

"It's not like—"

"What else did you TELL HIM?" Melawn demanded in a panic.

"It's okay, he—"

"IT IS NOT OKAY! OUR MISSION IS A SECRET!" Melawn stared at Lanezi in horror, probably imagining panic in the sectors if word of alien ships got out.

"Melawn," Lanezi reached out and gripped Melawn's arm, "listen to me! Jarvie already knows. He was at Luminesse. He knows about the aliens."

"He was unconscious. Drugs were confirmed in his system."

"No. He knows. He's probably *already* a runaway. All I'm trying to do is get him here before they catch him and start asking questions."

Melawn did listen and seemed even more alarmed. "You should have told Iricana! She could track him down faster."

"I did! But she didn't believe me. She insists that he was under and knows nothing. I know Jarvie. I know better."

Melawn shook off Lanezi's hand. "I'm so tired of people who think they *know better*."

Lanezi bolted from Melawn's cabin, shaken. Then he didn't know where to turn. He felt the absence of Whisper and figured that she was in the kitchen with the twins. He would have to face the rest of the crew and apologize sometime. It wasn't a confession. They all knew what he had done. He had harmed them all by his lying and it was up to him to start the healing process.

He went slowly to the kitchen, letting his heart calm down from the encounter with Melawn. The twins and Zahar smiled stiffly when he came in. They had made hummus rollups and were happily eating. Whisper was hooked between the twins, snoozing.

"We fed her!" they both assured Lanezi, as soon as he slid in beside Euro.

"Thank you."

"Why are you sad?" Euro asked.

Zahar gave him a warning look, but he had no intention of telling them about Thayne. "I've come to apologize—to all of you."

Zahar nodded cautiously.

"Remember two months' ago, when I was too sick to jump?" Lanezi asked the twins, who nodded. "I wasn't really that sick. Then last month," Lanezi took a calming breath, "when I told Captain Thayne the fuel converter was giving anomalous readings . . ." he looked down at the table, ashamed, "I lied."

The twins gasped. Lanezi cringed inside. "I sent the readings myself, because I wanted to stall. I'm sorry. It was wrong of me and crazy. I'm sorry for how much hurt and anger I've created. I'm sorry I've caused trouble and hurt Melawn and I hope you'll forgive me. I hope God will forgive me," he whispered.

Zahar nodded with approval. "I forgive you Lanezi," she said formally.

"Thank you," Lanezi breathed, grateful that she did not grill him further.

The twins were looking down at Whisper. "Was that your only lie?" Euro asked hesitantly.

Lanezi was startled. "Of course—" *Was it?*

"You will stand by your promise?" Io insisted.

Promise? To not leave without them! Lanezi gripped Euro's shoulder. "Yes, I will keep my promise. No more lying. I just . . . I know it will be a while before anyone can trust me again," he admitted.

Io straightened, even in nogee, as he always did when about to quote Bahá'u'lláh. ***"Forgive the sinful, and never despise his low estate, for none knoweth what his own end shall be."***[1]

As was their way, if one quoted Bahá'u'lláh, the other would quote 'Abdu'l-Bahá. ***"If someone commits an error and wrong toward you, you must instantly forgive him,"***[2] Euro added with a nod.

Tears came to Lanezi's eyes. Their pure spirits and forgiving natures were a great consolation to him.

8-Dominion

Zahar often ate breakfast in her cabin, but since Thayne was sleeping, she hung out at one end of the kitchen table, updating the ship schedule on her pad. Melawn and Nkiroo were tethered at the other end of the table in their fancy clothes.

One of Thayne's rules, so he'd be more "in tune" with the universe, was to surround himself with beauty. *Too bad he doesn't surround himself with kindness.* But thanks to the beauty order, Melawn suffered a gold and white uniform that made him look like a comic book hero, stunning but fake. And Nkiroo had designed his own black uniform with metallic geometric shapes, as if a blueprint of ship parts got mixed into the textile printer. Thank heavens Tenshi didn't tolerate such nonsense. She and Zahar could just wear regular medical uniforms.

It all went against the One Ship-One Uniform guidance. In Zahar's monitor training, when she was in touch with a ship, she would note if pilots or crew had unmatching uniforms. Laziness, poverty, or disunity were all signs of trouble aboard.

She was also trained to hear every nuance of voice. Right now, Melawn and Nkiroo were talking about some diagram on Nkiroo's pad, relaxed and with an undercurrent of their brotherly affection, forged when their short internship with Thayne turned into a life sentence.

Zahar went back to her schedule. Today's project would be prepping chairs for the jump. Even though no one else expected to jump, Zahar's reading of reality was that Thayne almost always got his way.

The door slid open and she tensed, but it was just Lanezi. He hesitated, but Zahar waved him in. "God is Most Glorious," he said quietly, and they all answered. Whisper was in a pink carrier and Lanezi didn't have his poncho on. Zahar made a note to get a fancier unpink carrier and make sure Lanezi's uniform was beautiful enough without the expensive poncho.

Whisper squirmed out of the carrier and pushed off to Zahar while Lanezi got his breakfast. "Oh," he said, surprised, no doubt finding Whisper's breakfast and bottle that Zahar had set out. "Thank you," he said to Zahar as he tethered across from her. Zahar had already set a tiny holdbar on the table. Whisper hooked herself on while Lanezi stuck her box of small crunchies and little squeeze bulb by her. "I guess I better read up on feeding podpups."

Zahar gave him a look. Besides that it had been *four days*, "Everyone knows about feeding podpups."

He looked startled. "They do?" He appealed to Melawn and Nkiroo for help.

Nkiroo shrugged. "Holographic podpups don't actually eat."

"Huh," Melawn said. "Real ones eat all day—that's what you need to know."

"All day," Zahar agreed.

"All day," Whisper confirmed with a crunch.

"The twins have been feeding her," Zahar explained.

Lanezi tapped the bottle. "Sorry, I was so young when I had a podpup before. Where'd we get the food?"

"Dr. Obala sent a year's supply. I got it out of the bin just before we left."

"A year?"

"Perceptive person."

Whisper tried the tiny squeeze bulb at the same time Lanezi tried his. "Good!" She declared.

"What is it?" Lanezi asked.

"Smashed pumpkin—lots of it in the garden."

"Arggg," Lanezi slapped his forehead. "The garden wasn't secured when we undocked and boosted."

"Right."

"God help us," he whispered.

"We need to help ourselves," she whispered back more fiercely than she'd planned. "The twins and bots are cleaning up in the garden and they could use some help." He nodded, but Whisper gave her a stern look. "No worries, sweetie. The bots won't bother you. I gave them strict orders."

Whisper shyly turned to watch Nkiroo and Melawn. "You can go meet them," Lanezi suggested, as she had not been offi-cially introduced. She hesitated, but then took her little squeeze bulb for fortitude and coasted over to Melawn.

"I Whisper," she said quietly.

He held out a bit of oat bar for her. "I'm Mel-LAWN."

"Good Melawn." She crunched while she looked at Nkiroo.

"En-KEER-oh," he said, stealing a bit of oat bar from Melawn and giving it to her.

"Kiro good." She crunched more, then took a hold of his

finger. He gently gave her a ride in a big circle. She huffed in excitement as he and Melawn smiled and laughed, full of friendliness and charm. *Is that how they would be all the time, if not for Thayne?*

Lanezi had just started to relax, as it seemed the crew wasn't particularly mad at him, and Whisper was having fun, when Melawn's special wrist link chimed. "He's coming," Melawn breathed, straightening up. Nkiroo gently sent Whisper back to Lanezi. Sensing tension she dived back into her carrier, then reached back out to grab her crunchies.

Zahar looked ready to bolt, but there was no polite way out. They gave each other sympathetic looks. The door slid open and Thayne floated in, in benevolent mode, serene and smiling. No one relaxed. "God is Most Glorious," they chorused, and Thayne responded.

"Good morning, Captain," Melawn said as he coasted over to make Thayne's breakfast. Lanezi forced a neutral expression as Thayne approached him, Zahar deftly offering her spot and escaping to the food prep area.

"Ready for deceleration today?" Thayne asked him, something he normally would have no interest in.

"Yes, honor. How are you?" Lanezi responded.

"I am completely recovered and ready to jump. You're looking much better too." Thayne seemed sincere and caring—and he probably was. Lanezi was just nervous of Thayne's mercurialness.

"Yes, Captain. I'm feeling much better."

"Good." Thayne nodded at Melawn, who stuck Thayne's breakfast tray to the table in front of him. Then he fished around in the pocket of his sleek black and tiger-gold uniform and pulled out Lanezi's previously confiscated s'link, handing it to him.

"Thank you," Lanezi breathed, hardly hoping to believe what it might mean.

"We were so overwhelmed with our firestorms; some things just got out of control. I was just about to tell Melawn that I *never* would have arrested you. It was just a little madness."

Lanezi couldn't hide his sigh of relief. He quickly stashed his s'link in his pocket. "Thank you, Captain. I am very grateful. I'm so sorry for lying. I hope you can forgive me. I never meant to cause you pain. You know I wouldn't . . . and I have vowed to never lie again."

Thayne nodded. "Of course we forgive you Lanezi," Thayne gripped Lanezi's arm gently. "We know you will do better. I only regret that we could not have been to Nocturne and back faster. Too bad you're not well enough to jump now. I'd really be pleased to go tomorrow, when our waiver gets through."

"I'm much better," Lanezi heard himself saying. Relief and a great desire to please combined to take over his mind. "I could jump by tomorrow—if the doctor cleared me."

Thayne's face lit up with a sincere smile. "You are a wonder, Lanezi. Dr. Tenshi has already cleared you, actually, and I'm sure our waiver will come through. So we'll plan on the jump then." And Thayne twirled and left the kitchen, leaving his breakfast untouched and the crew stunned.

Melawn and Nkiroo flashed smiles. Anything that made Thayne happy made them happy. But Zahar had the *What were you thinking?* look.

What was I thinking? I am insane. What if he gets the waiver?

. . .

That evening, after cleaning up from their garden work, Lanezi, Io, and Euro joined Zahar and Nkiroo for dinner. "Do you want to see who is jumping tomorrow?" Nkiroo asked the teens.

"Yes!" They loved it when Nkiroo talked about the ships. The list came up on the main kitchen screen.

OUTBOUND ORDER:

DESTINATION ATIKAMEQ

- *STREAMER*
- *SPRING TIDE*
- *MAHARI*
- *LEE*
- *EAGLE FLIGHT*
- *MARS FOREVER 7*
- *ECHO BLUE*

"Why is it called *Mars Forever* with a seven?" Euro asked Nkiroo.

"The *Mars Forever* ships seem to have a bit of bad luck—not that I believe in luck, but six of them were destroyed."

"I believe in luck," Io informed them, "and that's bad luck."

"Why don't they give it a new name—to change the luck?" Euro asked.

The rest of the crew, except Io, laughed good-naturedly.

"What would you name it?" Zahar asked.

"*The Good Luck Now!*" Euro declared.

The crew laughed again, until Nkiroo added, "Too late."

"What?" Lanezi asked in alarm.

Nkiroo pointed to the screen. "*Mars 7* just got bumped to relay duty."

"But that means . . ." Lanezi trailed off.

The new jump order came up. Captain Ryan's ship, *Echo Blue* had moved up to the number 6 spot. The last spot now listed the *Cheetah,* no destination.

"Looks like we're jumping after all," Nkiroo said. And Lanezi's heart dropped into his stomach.

9-Dominion Eve

Lanezi had thought that midnight in the Observation Bay would be a private place to say his last long set of prayers before the jump. But he should have known that Thayne would come looking for him. He should have stayed in his cabin.

"Lanezi, I'm not asking you to do anything different. I know you're still recovering, and I am so happy with you for jumping, but if you could just indulge my one passion."

Lanezi's pre-jump serenity seeped right out of him, and he hung limply by the window.

"No! No need to be discouraged!" Thayne said in his comforting voice. "You won't fail me, because there is nothing to fail. I just want you to look." Thayne gestured out the window with his other hand, as if gazing across the universe. "Just notice. That's all."

Lanezi shook his head no.

"You can do it. I know other pilots need all their attention just to find the one jump path they are looking for. But Lanezi, you, you're so brilliant, such a natural jumper, you could spare five seconds to check for another path. Think what it would mean for humanity!"

"What?" Lanezi interrupted the pep-talk. "Plenty of pilots have claimed to see alternate paths, and it hasn't done them or humanity any good."

"Some become seers!"

"A rare few, but most get knocked off course, turned into wanderers, or lose their sanity."

"No. Those are ignorant rumors."

"No they're not!" Thayne recoiled slightly at Lanezi's outburst. "I've known people. Pilots."

"So have I," Thayne argued and continued in a conspiratorial tone. "I've been talking to them, a lot, at the Pilots' Retirement Station at Harbor, and they are not crazy!"

"They're lucky then! Because my parents went crazy!" Lanezi hadn't intended to ever mention it. In the last jump he had taken with his parents, when he was four years old—they had become completely detached from reality. And Lanezi never —*ever*—looked at the mysterious ways that led their minds away from him.

Thayne was shocked but persistent. He floated close to Lanezi and put his arm around him. "I'm so sorry. I had no idea. But if your parents saw the paths—Lanezi—they were not insane."

He stayed with Lanezi for a minute, full of concern and sympathy, and didn't say any more. And Lanezi didn't say any more, because he knew that it wasn't seeing the paths that made pilots insane. He saw them all the time. It was *indecision*. All those paths calling you, splitting your mind in a hundred directions. That's why he focused on only one path.

9-Dominion

Cheetah at Harbor a-rings

Lanezi sat in the Command Bay, brackets and helmet on, cocoon sealed. *I am ready. I AM* ready*!*

Once the administrative details were out of the way, Lanezi would be fine. He loved to jump. He did not remember a time when he did not know how to jump. The pathways had shown themselves to him when he was an infant. He had never been in a failed jump. He'd never come in further out than eight weeks. If there was one thing he could do right in life, it was jump.

Lanezi pushed against the brackets as if the ship were holding him back. Nocturne. He could almost see the path now.

"Crew ready," Tenshi advised. "Seven people, one podpup."

"Confirmed. P&P is eight. Thank you doctor," Nkiroo answered. Tenshi was passenger monitor. She would remain awake in the Passenger Lounge until they jumped. Io, Euro, and Zahar were put under voluntarily, Melawn only after Thayne insisted. Melawn's curious mind and interest in jumps could sometimes interfere, but Lanezi had learned to gently guide him along. Melawn could be a pilot if he didn't devote his life to Thayne. This time, though, Thayne insisted that Lanezi not be distracted. Thayne and Nkiroo, although not pilots, had extremely disciplined minds and never disturbed Lanezi. They sat in the Command Bay with him, their helmets ready, waiting only for the roll call.

"Jump ships, H.O.A. God is Most Glorious. Stand by for roll call."

Nkiroo, who was acting as monitor, sent the ready code.

"Roll call in twenty," Nkiroo announced quietly. They all snapped their helmets on. "Doctor?" Nkiroo asked.

"Ready."

"Captain?"

"Ready."

"Robots secure," Nkiroo confirmed. "To you, Lanezi."

"Thank you." *Eight souls.*

"Jump ships, H.O.A. Commencing roll call: *Streamer?*"

"*Streamer* ready."

H.O.A. knew perfectly well that *Cheetah* was going to a classified location. Captain Ryan unknowingly carried an extra packet, a private communication from one sector authority to another, known as a PS packet, which kept the councils informed.

Pilots and monitors all understood this system to keep sensitive work from spilling out into the public and causing crazy speculation or outright panic.

"*Cheetah?*"

"*Cheetah* ready," Lanezi answered, a bit breathlessly.

"Jump ships, H.O.A. God be with you all. *Streamer*, proceed."

Once in the rings, Lanezi immediately relaxed into his element. His burned-out chest pained him some, but he also felt the comforting nearness of Whisper, in a padded box attached to his chair.

Lanezi said prayers to himself until they reached half jump velocity. Then he toggled through his screens, verifying that each crew member was okay before shutting down those feeds. All ship functions were excellent, of course. *Cheetah* was one of the few ships in the outer sectors that was in superior condition, and less than 300 years old.

Lanezi brought up the graphic of the a-rings. The *Cheetah* was guiding them through each tunnel-like segment. The surges, as the segments accelerated the *Cheetah*, were getting harder. As they exited each segment they felt the bump of the Path Adjustment Thrust. Then there was a short rest until the next a-ring segment.

Surge, bump, rest. As they built up speed, the surges got shorter and harder, the bumps sharper, and the rests so brief it was all Lanezi could do to take a few big breaths and align his mind to the next segment.

Most pilots would say their favorite prayers, building up to a spiritual crescendo of certainty to help them locate the resonant path, but Lanezi had learned the paths before he learned the prayers. He could hear the harmonies of the stars in his soul. Circling through the a-rings was a winding up of the material substance of the ship, his body, and his being into one compressed will that would suddenly spring free to ride the resonant path to Nocturne.

Almost there. Lanezi no longer heard the H.O.A. monitor's voice. He heard the humming of the ship and the stars. Seven laps to go. As the ships approached jump velocity it was like a hundred orchestra instruments joining in one all-powerful tuning note. Soon it would be perfect. Lanezi heard each ship as it approached JV. *Streamer* was so close. But one ship was completely off. Was a ship dropping out? Lanezi flicked his consciousness back to the monitor's voice. He glanced at the graphic. All seven ships were near JV. *What is that off-tune humming?* A sudden fear formed like a block of ice in his stomach. *I've heard that before.*

His rational mind fought the idea. He sorted through all the harmonies, *Streamer, Spring Tide, Mahari, Lee, Eagle Flight, Echo Blue.* They were all near JV. Did some other ship join the jump? Did *Mars 7* go crazy and join? Was the *Cheetah* vibrating?

Lanezi tried to think clearly. The others would not dare disturb him unless he said something first.

"Nkiroo?"

"Yes?" came a surprised but calm voice.

"Do you feel a vibration?"

"No. Checking ship functions."

Another surge took Lanezi by surprise and sent his mind into a frenzied catch up. The PAT bump left him speechless for a moment.

"Nothing wrong with the *Cheetah,*" Nkiroo reported worriedly.

The vibration was getting stronger. He only felt it in his head, in his implants. It was not a vibration; Lanezi forced himself to face the facts. It was resonance. It was happening again.

"*Cheetah*, private to H.O.A."

"Ready."

"H.O.A., Lanezi here. I feel a resonance wave." He could not control the fear in his voice.

"*Cheetah*, H.O.A. No other reports. Talk to me," the monitor answered, not yet convinced of a problem.

Surge, bump.

"There's an incoming ship!" Lanezi tried to keep his panic

down. He had felt this before, at Luminesse, right before the accident. He had been knocked out seconds later by the abort burn.

Surge, bump.

"Jump ships, H.O.A. Report any abnormalities." The monitor seemed calm. Lanezi realized that the monitor might not take him seriously, might think he was flashing back to his earlier disaster.

"*Cheetah*, H.O.A. Remain calm. You may abort if you wish at any time since you are last. We have no flags."

Lanezi was paralyzed now with fear. Two laps left. Abort now and save the ship? Or jump before the Harbor a-rings were destroyed? And he realized with another surge of panic that he'd have to jump for Atikameq, not Nocturne, as there was no other way out of Nocturne except through Harbor. His mind whirled. All his visualizing the Nocturne path was too strong to let go. He'd have to follow the other pilots to Atikameq.

The other ships were on communications now, concerned about the strange humming they were just starting to feel. The pilots were confused. Only the *Cheetah* crew would fully understand what was happening. Other pilots only knew that there had been accidents at Firelight, Hamada, and Luminesse, but top-level scientists knew they were all caused by the same thing—incoming ships appeared and crashed into the a-rings during a jump. And Lanezi knew that the ship would be alien.

"Incoming ship!" *Mars 7* reported. "We have resonance waves! Incoming ship!"

They feel it at the relay station! Lanezi thought. *It must be coming in from the relay point side.*

"Jump ships, H.O.A. Trying to calculate trajectory—stand by to abort!"

"No," Thayne commanded.

Could they even reach jump velocity before that ship dropped into their space? A flashing red line appeared on Lanezi's helmet screen. "Possible intruder trajectory." He gasped. They must cross the line to jump. They were risking a direct collision.

Streamer and *Spring Tide* were already across the line.

"*Streamer, Spring Tide,* Go! All others abort! *Mahari* abort!"

Mahari made a burn down to get below the plane of circling ships. Lanezi's implants were buzzing painfully. He could feel the fear and the discipline of the crew. There was no time to talk to the *Cheetah.* He would have to abort manually, right after the next segment. They were going so fast he would only have a second or two.

"*Lee* abort!"

But *Lee* did not abort. The humming suddenly stopped and Lanezi gasped. "Where is it?" he called to Nkiroo.

A red icon appeared on his screen on top of the line, just crossing the a-rings.

"Lee abort! You are—" It was too late. *Eagle Flight* and *Echo Blue* went up and down in desperation, *Eagle Flight* nicking the edge of a segment. Lanezi had no choice. Fire bloomed before him and a silent stream of wreckage flowed towards the *Cheetah.* Lanezi aborted, spinning off to the right, just missing a segment, hoping their speed would eek them ahead of the flying wreckage. They would be on a similar trajectory with the intruder, almost side-by-side.

Lanezi fought to control the *Cheetah,* canceling their wild spinning and easing it away from the path of the wreckage. Their speed had not been enough. Two huge pieces tumbled past them. He had to make repeated corrections away from the wreckage before he realized—"We're being pulled toward the wreckage!"

"Gravity ball!" Thayne exclaimed. "In the bigger piece. Follow it, Lanezi!"

"*What?*" Follow the huge, venting, tumbling, debris- flinging, destroyed piece of alien ship? Every crazy thing Thayne had ever said paled in comparison.

"Wake the passengers!" Thayne ordered.

"Stay in your chairs!" Lanezi added. "*Cheetah!* Increase particle and radiation fields!"

There was chaos over the ship link. A hundred voices sounded in Lanezi's head—some of them echoes of the Luminesse accident. He tried to focus only on a safe trajectory for the *Cheetah*, parallel and slightly behind the two biggest pieces. "Kiro, can you sort it out for me?" Lanezi asked.

"On it."

Most of the voices disappeared as Nkiroo routed com traffic to his headset. Lanezi had two screens up, one showing the danger ahead, the other showing the destruction behind.

"*Lee* is hit," Nkiroo said quietly. Lanezi could hear in his voice both despair and the determination to be calm.

"It's off now," Thayne said, as if Nkiroo had not spoken. "See, the gravity ball has turned off! The other piece is no longer attracted to it."

Lanezi could not fathom why Thayne was so intent on that rather than what was happening back at the a-rings.

"Orders?" Lanezi asked.

"Not for us yet," Nkiroo answered. "*Mars 7* is trying to help the *Lee*. *Streamer* and *Spring Tide* got away. *Eagle Flight* has damage and venting. No communications from the *Lee*."

"Where's *Echo Blue*?" Lanezi's tactical was a mess of trajectories. A blue dot started blinking to the left and above. They were headed the other way.

"Where are the tugs?" Thayne asked. "We need them for the wreckage."

"They won't have any to spare, Captain," Nkiroo warned him.

"All passengers awake," the doctor reported. They would have to make a decision about where to go. They were speeding away from the a-rings and away from Harbor station.

"It might be hours before they get to us," Nkiroo said, as if reading his mind. "We may have to make our own orders."

"What about survivors in the wreckage?" Zahar asked, voice surprisingly clear after just waking up.

"Zahar," Nkiroo said calmly. "There are no rescue shuttles to be spared."

"What about the doctor's shuttle in our hangar?"

Lanezi gasped. "Us? You want *us* to do search and rescue? We can't even get near it! How would we detumble it?"

Lanezi sent the main view to everyone, showing two huge tumbling pieces of wreckage, now moving away from each other.

Zahar persevered, "We can detumble! We have rock relocators and PSTs."

"Those are for asteroids!" Lanezi argued, "And we don't have SAR training!"

"I do!" she answered determinedly.

"We do too!" insisted two identical voices.

"We have an obligation to check for survivors," the doctor agreed.

"We are going after the gravity ball on that wreckage. Stop distracting Lanezi," Thayne complained.

"Captain," Zahar persisted. "We did this in teen training. We can stabilize it, take Dr. Tenshi's rescue shuttle over with a robot repair team and bubbles, and search for pockets of survivors." She sounded as if she were reading from a textbook.

"I don't see how there could be survivors," Nkiroo reasoned. "It's just a couple of chunks, not a damaged ship."

Melawn hesitantly chimed in, "There were smaller chunks at Hamada, and there were intact places in that wreckage."

That's right, Lanezi remembered. Melawn had been aboard one of the alien ships. And he obviously didn't want to go into another.

"We can't risk the *Cheetah*" Nkiroo reminded them. "In our hold, we have the only prototype a-ring segments in existence."

Lanezi closed his eyes and tried to focus on calm. "We're stable for a few minutes if people want to get up." Cocoons unsealed immediately. Melawn, Tenshi, and the teens all crowded into the Command Bay, rubbing their arms where they had pulled off their brackets. Thayne was intent on nothing but the big piece with the gravity ball. Melawn was now furiously giving orders to the *Cheetah*. "Strap, please," Lanezi asked them, "except, Io, can you get Whisper out, please?"

There were just enough seats in the Command Bay for everyone. Euro pulled out a bottle for Whisper, who launched herself toward it before he could hand it to Io. They strapped in the back, Euro hooking Whisper onto the chair.

"We should try to eat if we have a few minutes," Dr. Tenshi suggested.

Lanezi couldn't possibly eat. "Orders?" he asked Nkiroo compulsively.

"Not yet."

"*Cheetah!* H.O.A. Report your status."

Nkiroo answered calmly, "We are undamaged. We are tracking two large pieces of the intruder vessel. Sending trajectories. Can you confirm status of a-rings? Awaiting orders."

There was a pause and a different voice came on. *"Cheetah? Thayne?"*

"This is Thayne," he answered, completely unsurprised that he would be asked for.

"Captain Thayne, I am Farzad, Special Assistant to the Sector Council at H.O.A. Two a-ring segments have been destroyed."

The crew gasped. Without them, no ships could leave Harbor.

"What about the gravity ball?" Thayne asked.

"Just missed."

"Lanezi!" came a fierce whisper from behind him. Io and Euro knew better than to interrupt such a high-level communication for anything less than an emergency, so the whole crew turned to look.

Straining against her tether, half-full bottle set adrift, Whisper was staring out the window. Her little paw came up and she pointed to the chunk of wreckage on the right. "Find . . ."

They stared, the Special Assistant left hanging. *"Cheetah?"*

Whisper was clearly pointing to the piece on the right, not the one with the gravity ball. Lanezi looked at Thayne, who swallowed in resignation. Thayne turned back to the panel. "Honor Farzad, we have a retired locator aboard with a find on the intruder vessel."

There was a shocked pause on the other end. *"Cheetah . . . do you volunteer for search and rescue?"*

"We can do it!" Zahar insisted, the twins nodding.

"We must try," Nkiroo added.

"Find!" Whisper declared in a louder, more insistent voice, but she was no longer looking out the window. She was staring at Lanezi, and he felt the fire in his veins.

Melawn suddenly reached for the mute button and turned to Thayne. "If we can save them, they can send a message to stop crashing into our a-rings, and they will know how to operate the gravity balls."

"Yes," Thayne agreed, signaling for Melawn to switch off the mute.

"*-tah?*"

"H.O.A., *Cheetah*," Thayne replied. "We are commencing SAR."

Lanezi could not imagine any successful outcome except to claim that they tried.

6 / NEW TRAJECTORY

Cheetah near Harbor a-rings

"We need a plan," Lanezi said as he tried to eat a protein pack with two big chunks of wrecked ship tumbling outside.

Zahar jumped in. "We'll launch the portable swivel thrusters and rock relocators. Nkiroo can do the remote detumble. Lanezi will pilot the *Enkindler* with a robot repair team, Melawn, Io, Euro, and me." The doctor tried to object but she cut her off. "Doctor, you need to make an airtight environment in the Med Bay and supervise decontamination protocols. Give us a sensor to send environmental data from the alien ship."

Thayne pushed out of his chair. "Who are you to be giving orders?"

Zahar blinked, surprised, and for the first time Lanezi had ever seen stood up for herself. "I have the most search and rescue training!" She tapped a pin on her yoke.

"Well, I'm the Captain in case you forgot. And Melawn is not going with you."

"He's been in the alien ships before. We'll need his help

inside." She said it calmly and logically, but Thayne just got angrier.

"Enough! Nkiroo's been inside too. He can advise you verbally from here. Melawn is coming with me to secure the gravity ball, as soon as the high-speed tug gets here."

"Survivors are more import—"

The twins looked on wide-eyed as Zahar talked back to their Captain. But Lanezi gave a shake of his head and she stopped.

"Let's go," Lanezi said, tugging on her arm, "before it's too late."

"I'll brief you while you suit up," Nkiroo called after them.

Lanezi was in the rimway when Whisper spoke up. "Whisper go."

They turned to look at her. "How?" Lanezi asked.

"In box," she answered as if anyone could figure that out.

"There was a strange pressure box in the stuff Dr. Obala sent. It's in storage," Zahar told them.

"I'll get it!" Io said and pushed off.

It's been three hours. Any survivors are probably not going to make it, Lanezi thought, as he kept Tenshi's shuttle, *Enkindler,* as close as he dared to Wreck 1, as they called it now. Lanezi glanced at his second screen. Thayne and Melawn had already set out to Wreck 2 in the *Chinkara.* The tug was just about to latch on and slow it down. Whisper insisted that there were no survivors there. They were looking for a gravity ball. Lanezi shut the screen off; he didn't want to be distracted.

Nkiroo proved to be a detumbling genius. Wreck 1 was now stable enough to approach in spacesuits. Lanezi hated that their three youngest crew were doing the most dangerous job, although admittedly, they were the best trained for it. He also had a pang of anxiety over Whisper being outside the ship.

The robot repair team came into view, approaching the wreck first. Lanezi stared at the big screen, transfixed. Zahar and the twins, in their suits, Euro carrying Whisper in her box, followed the robots. Sharp edges and venting were major hazards, dealt with by the robots. There was no need to find a hatch or figure out how to open one. They had preselected a hole in the side that they could easily fit through. From there, they would follow Whisper's instructions, relayed by a lit arrow on the top of her special finder box.

Zahar landed feet first on the wreck, next to the hole. The robots had layered a sticky rubbery blanket over the side to cover any sharp edges. Followed by the twins, Zahar carefully climbed in. The changing camera views were disorienting, so Lanezi glanced away until Zahar's light illumined a partial rimway. Io flash-bolted a holdbar to the inner wall so they could all hook onto a tether. Pushing away from the wall, they continued down the rimway.

Euro held Whisper and watched the arrow on top of her box. "Straight. She's pointing ahead."

They worked their way through another hatch where a single door was open.

"No pressure here," Zahar reported, studying the air monitor.

"She's blinking left," Euro directed.

Lanezi despaired. How could they even find their way around?

"Zahar," Nkiroo's voice came over the link, "to get through the door, look for a picture of a tree."

"I see what looks like a tall skinny bird."

"Oh."

"Different artistic theme?" Lanezi suggested.

"For the tree, we pressed the trunk." Nkiroo had far more knowledge of alien ships than Lanezi had imagined. He must have helped Melawn secure Thayne's gravity ball from the wreckage at Hamada. The enormity of that mission now sunk in and amazed Lanezi.

Standing in front of the bird picture, Zahar reached out and pressed the wing firmly. A blazing orange light with a yellow streak appeared in the bird's eye. Without even waiting for Nkiroo's advice, Zahar pressed the eye with her suited finger. The light changed to flashing muted orange.

"It probably needs confirmation because you don't have pressure," Nkiroo surmised.

"What if we're risking their last pockets of air?"

"You may come to that. Be prepared for a blast. Let's hope there's a double lock somewhere."

They moved to the side as Zahar pressed the button again. A full-length door slid open, but there was no air. They quickly went in. Zahar turned to an obvious picture of a small bird to shut the door.

"No!" Euro reminded her. "Leave a quick exit."

"Right!" They turned again. Their headlamps caught the etchings on the walls, bringing the glinting pictures to life. "It's so beautiful," Io whispered.

"Don't get distracted," Nkiroo reminded them sympathetically. "Their ships are like art museums."

Lanezi wished he could see an intact one.

"Which way?" Zahar asked.

"Right, 25 degrees."

Lanezi could feel Whisper's urgency as if she not only knew where survivors were, but could sense that they were running out of time.

The next lock had a window. "It's a double lock, but we'll have to squeeze in. Zahar took the compacted bubbles from the robots and ordered them to stay. Io flash-bolted another hold and they ended their first tether there. This time the door opening did release a small rush of air.

Inside the lock, the door shut. "Wait a moment," Nkiroo said. "Is it pressurizing?"

"Yes, I think so. There's a colored bar indicator increasing."

"I can't believe it's still functional," Nkiroo whispered. "Such contingency engineering. Proceed," he advised after a moment. "They won't lose air."

This time, after pressing the bird symbol only once, the door opened. Io installed another holdbar and they snapped on. Zahar was looking at her air monitor. "Good pressure!" She sounded pleased. "Sending you air sample analysis, doctor."

"Ahead," Euro moved into the lead with Whisper, compelled by her urgency. After the next intersection, there were two corridors, one leading left and the other right. Doors lined both. But Whisper still pointed straight ahead.

"It must be this door." Zahar bolted another holdbar outside a door slightly to their left.

"Ready?" She asked the twins.

"Yes," they answered in unison.

They entered quickly, flash-bolting another hold, hooking their tethers, and letting the door close. "She's blinking green!" Euro called out.

"It's hard to see," Zahar wavered around.

And then lights came on.

The only thing that was immediately clear from the camera view was that a suited human-shaped figure was moving towards Zahar. Nkiroo and Lanezi both shouted to her to be still, but she ignored them, grabbed some kind of table and moved toward the alien.

She pointed to the door, then pointed to a small screen on the front of her suit. "Lanezi, feed me a picture of the shuttle!"

Lanezi sent a diagram as quickly as he could. The alien watched her suit screen, seeming to understand, although a bar of light on ziz suit shone a steady white.

Ze was hesitant, looking between them and the shuttle picture. Then ze noticed the box. Ze maneuvered to look and Euro came closer. Whisper put her paw right up to the side and gazed up at zir. Ze slowly touched the place where her little paw was. Whisper's light went from blinking green to steady.

The alien made a decision. Ze took Zahar gently by the arm and turned. "It's okay," she shouted over the link to the worried crew. Ze pulled her toward a chest-like box with a clear lid. Her shocked voice came through before the camera view. "Oh my God! Babies! Two of them. They look almost human, except purple, with headbands of light."

They could see from Euro's view that the alien was pointing to the babies and to the picture of the shuttle.

"Io! The bubbles," Zahar said. "We'll need one for each baby." Euro came to help too, hooking Whisper on a cabinet handle. They unfolded a collapsed bubble and pointed to the pad at the center that provided handgrips. The whole thing wavered in nogee as if floating in a gentle wind. The alien did not seem to understand. Zahar made a motion like the bubbles expanding and closing over the babies.

The alien's color bar flashed yellow and then went back to white. Ze unsealed the baby chest and pulled one out. The baby was screaming now; they could hear it over the suit pickups. The other started screaming when the first was taken away.

The alien placed it on the bubble pad and then held ziz hand on the baby's colored forehead as if saying prayer, or saying goodbye.

Zahar pressed the activate button and the bubble inflated around the baby, capturing the native air and resealing double.

Quickly, they did the same to the other baby, including the sad parting.

"You must concentrate now," Tenshi reminded them, "air is limited and they are screaming."

"I wonder if there are others," Zahar said, looking at the alien.

"Maybe," Euro answered. "Whisper is intent on something on the other side."

The alien had now floated over to the other side of the big room exactly in the direction Whisper was looking. Ze was taking some time to gather something up. Lanezi began to feel very pressured when the alien finally picked up another bundle and launched himself back towards Zahar and the third bubble.

"Podpups! Baby ones! Different colors." Zahar exclaimed, activating the bubble before anyone could object.

"Can you manage the bubbles?" Nkiroo was asking.

"I'll join them together," Io said, busy with the tethers.

Meanwhile, Zahar was gesturing to the alien to come with them. Ze wouldn't need a bubble since ze had a suit. Ze held out ziz hands as if pushing her away.

"I don't think ze wants to come." The alien started pointing to the door, urging them to go. Zahar again gestured come along, but ziz colors started flashing lime green and ze backed away.

"You may have to leave zir, Zahar," Tenshi said gently.

"Thayne wanted an adult to stop the accidents," Lanezi added worriedly.

"She can't drag zir, and we don't have time to persuade," Tenshi argued.

"But ze'll die," Zahar despaired. "We can save zir."

"You must save the babies. There's no time to delay."

Zahar clasped her hands together as if begging. The alien came forward and touched her hands. Ze slowly tilted towards her until their helmets touched.

The crew could hear Zahar stifle a sob. "I think ze's a woman. She's old! She won't come," Zahar whispered.

"Go then," Tenshi urged.

"Ready," Io braced and carefully tugged on his string of bubbles. Euro checked Whisper one more time, who continued to show steady green, despite leaving a living being behind.

Does she understand? Lanezi wondered

Zahar left the other equipment. "God be with you," she whispered, and waved a sad farewell.

Lanezi, also suited up, floated at the inner hatch, trusting the *Enkindler* to pilot itself. Robots had gone to the back storage area. The two bubbles with the babies were inside the airlock; the decontamination procedure was running. As soon as the light turned green, Lanezi opened the door and wrestled the bubbles into the ship, quickly closing the door.

"Zahar and the pups next," Tenshi insisted.

"And Whisper!" Euro added. "They will fit."

The twins were radiation resistant, so they would come in last. While the decontamination was running, Lanezi hooked the bubbles onto an exam bed. The strange babies were frightened out of their wits after the open space crossing. The screaming would use up the air fast. He tried not to get distracted looking at them. The strange, lighted headbands almost seemed to be skin and were pulsing red and black.

Zahar pushed Whisper's Box out, quickly followed by the bubble full of the alien podpups. "Six of them! They're going wild!" Not with fear, but with familiar podpup craziness and curiosity. Lanezi strapped them to a second bed while Zahar secured Whisper's box and the twins got in the lock.

"How's her air?" Lanezi asked.

"Fine. She's got four more hours." Zahar switched off the finding light. "Maybe she'll nap."

The twins tumbled out of the lock. "Secure! We're going!" Lanezi ordered as he dove for his pilot seat.

"*Enkindler,* to me."

"Secure."

"Secure."

"Secure."

"*Cheetah*, shuttle *Enkindler*, ETA 13 minutes."

Despite the disaster, Lanezi felt a strange exhilaration. Purple alien babies, and wonder of wonder, alien podpups. But then a suppressed realization struck him like a hammer and he almost couldn't breathe. *We are stuck at Harbor.* He was separated from Katie. And Jarvie. He had lost another family.

10-Dominion Eve

Cheetah en route to Harbor Station

Four hours after dragging the near-lifeless babies to the Med Bay, Zahar leaned against the wall in her cabin, still breathing heavily. Her heart was beating hard, but that was good. It was the pounding of action, not fear, action she had not taken in two years of living with these *Cheetah* people.

Two years of waiting and wasting. Tiptoeing around the brilliant but frustrated Thayne, staying out of Dr. Tenshi's way, not bothering the senior crew, not 'bossing' Euro and Io, not even getting the education she was supposed to. Two years of aggravating inactivity. Two years too long for a person of action.

Zahar didn't get into the special monitor training program at the age of 14 from sitting around. A take-charge leader with her little sisters and cousins, 9-year-old Zahar had saved 12 people from a depressurization accident. Her farm colony trusted her. But still, she'd been quarantined from the day the *Sunburst* jumped in from Luminesse, sending a classified packet with the one word that hijacked her life.

'Aliens,' the word Zahar had the misfortune to overhear, had stifled her in quarantine for two years now. It was supposed to be temporary. But then Thayne wanted to keep her. *Why?* On a creepy ship, with a secret mission she wasn't even fully briefed on, with a crew of geniuses that saw so much complexity in every problem they could hardly find their way to the kitchen.

The babies had barely survived the journey to the Med Bay, and their long-term survival was questionable. Zahar kicked herself for not telling Dr. Tenshi to meet them in the Entry Lounge with refills for the bubbles. Any sensible person would have thought of it. Zahar, raised with a go-to-action family and schooled in the first waves of teen training rescue work, was often caught off guard by the abstracted crew of the *Cheetah*.

With the tremendous resources of his mind, Thayne would spiral around a problem, looking at it from every angle, circling closer and closer until he reached a nova-like burst of understanding that would dazzle the others and leave Thayne reverberating from the shockwave. Other times his mind would just spiral in and crush him.

Melawn seemed to be the only one who could ride the final waves of destruction and bring Thayne back to some form of everyday sanity. And how Nkiroo, who obviously needed competent mentoring, ended up with Thayne was mind-boggling.

Lanezi was another case, confused, unfocused, and prone to lying—an extreme form of confusion in Zahar's mind. However, he had bonded with a podpup of obvious maturity and he did manage to see the clear path whenever he jumped. Maybe he was only focused in jumping; his jump art was extraordinary by anyone's judgment. Returning to regular space somehow clouded his vision.

Dr. Tenshi was actually very focused, but on only one thing, finding the key to helping humans live in dangerous radiation environments. Such was the force of her will that she convinced parents to loan out two of their four sons. As much as Io and Euro yearned for adventure, they had not bargained on being separated from their family for so long.

Zahar missed Katie, the crew's doctor. *Why did Thayne send her off? Just to get at Lanezi?* Tenshi was actually Thayne's personal doctor and probably took this classified job on the *Cheetah* to have time to work on her radiation project. She had no interest in aliens, a-rings, or gravity balls. Even in an emergency, part of Tenshi's mind was somewhere else, not a good quality for a ship's doctor.

Zahar let out a frustrated sigh. Emergencies would have to be her job. During the rescue she had relayed all the key information about the babies and number of podpups to Tenshi, but environments were not prepared when they got to the Med Bay. Zahar had to take charge to isolate the pups.

She clicked on the Med Bay view on her main screen. Both babies were stable for the moment. Six podpups were in spare rat EEHABs, testing different human air environments—Zahar's project. She had claimed it. No one overrode her for once.

And after her shower, a snack, and some sleep, she was going to go back to claim the babies too—before Tenshi made a mess of things. A brilliant researcher, yes, but substitute parent? Not ever.

10-Dominion

At four in the morning, Melawn gave up trying to sleep and pulled out his pad. Back when Thayne's cargo team had discovered the first gravity ball in the alien wreckage at Hamada, Melawn had gone aboard to oversee its extraction. It wasn't easy, but there had been no bodies. He hadn't given it a second thought, until yesterday.

The images of dead aliens floating in the dark flashed before him all night. While he was on the wreck, he had tried not to look, but could not help seeing. He tried not to remember, not to dream, and not to recall his dreams. He pushed negative thoughts away with stronger positive thoughts. He chanted prayers for the departed. He reassured himself that the images would fade if he did not dwell on them, but for the moment, it left him shaken.

Underground on the mining outpost, where he grew up, he was always afraid of cave-ins. When they moved to the dome at the launch site, he worried about crashes and dome failures. He suspected that inside every space-faring human was a deep-denied fear of the void, of the unmerciful nothingness held back by feeble human-made walls. Now that his fear was unearthed, would he ever be able to bury it again?

To occupy his mind, Melawn checked on his data collection program. Back in the alien wreckage at Hamada, Melawn had salvaged what looked like receivers and transmitters. From them, he figured out the range of frequencies the aliens might be using. Then Nkiroo built receivers that they positioned at Hamada, Harbor, Atikameq, Canyon, Redrock, Petrichor, and on the *Cheetah*. Yesterday, it paid off. They captured some unusual transmissions. He'd started working on them last night, wanting to process everything before presenting it to Thayne.

Melawn's mind cycled to Thayne automatically. He glanced at his wrist p'link, habitually checking the coded icons that told him Thayne was still in his cabin, vital signs stable. Sleeping. *Good. Like I'm supposed to be.*

Melawn looked over the new transmission data, organized and processed by the *Cheetah* AI per his instructions. He verified the automatic cleanup that *Cheetah* had done, double-checking that discarded information was actually human-generated or other known natural sources. He scanned outliers, separated, and saved them. He confirmed the timeline of events with Harbor Outbound Authority and overlaid the data.

"Yes!" There were three unknown, possibly alien transmissions. Two were packets, short layered bursts, but so different from human packets that Melawn didn't know how to unlock the data.

"*Cheetah*, research programs to decode packets and summarize."

"Confirmed."

The third transmission came from the part of the wreck with the gravity ball after the ship had broken apart. It was on a different frequency, one never used by humans, but captured on the new receivers. In fact, the only other blip on that frequency was a small outlier. It came from the opposite direction from the ship. *Partial echo?*

There was an almost inaudible tap on the door he shared with Nkiroo. "Open," Melawn, said.

"What's happening?" Nkiroo asked, completely unsurprised to find him up.

"Three possible transmissions. I've got the *Cheetah* processing."

"Great!" Nkiroo, in his black thermals, plopped down in the chair next to Melawn, giving him the customary tap on the shoulder. "You look . . ."

"Terrible. I know. I kept thinking about the bodies." Nkiroo nodded sympathetically. "The whole time, I was shaking, and Thayne was so . . . composed."

"Determined," Nkiroo said.

"He just pushed a body out of the way," Melawn added.

"Single-minded."

"He was right to be. Now we have a gravity ball *and* a control panel."

"I can't wait to get a look at it."

"It could be the break we needed." Melawn sat back in his chair, legs stretched out next to Nkiroo's. "Ten years."

"Yeah, I expected to be building ships by now."

"I expected to be home by now." Melawn said.

"You were never going home," Nkiroo chided.

True. He hated that place. "Okay, but I did expect to see my parents again." And then he felt bad for saying that. Nkiroo was never going to see his family again. Only because Nkiroo's "rescuers" stopped at OSRI for repairs had Nkiroo come to Melawn's attention. A teen his age, with a pad full of ship designs. Melawn alerted Thayne, who snapped Nkiroo up, giving them both a real live brother.

"Hey, we promised Tenshi we'd be at yoga today! Let's get some breakfast first." Nkiroo jumped up.

"You promised. I don't like yoga."

"I know. So Earthcentric. *Mountain pose*. It won't kill you. Come on."

So Melawn stuck his pad in his backpack, pulled on his uniform, and followed Nkiroo.

Zahar peeked in the Med Bay. Tenshi was nowhere to be seen and the red light above the door of her lab was on. Probably doing another autopsy. Zahar checked on the rats. One in particular glared at her. *That old rat never dies, no matter what. She's outlived generations of others. Zombie rat.*

Zahar scowled. Animal experimentation was outlawed in Sectors 1-4 and only allowed in the outer sectors under very strict conditions if there was no other choice. It was the worst part of the Med Bay work.

The twins quietly came in. They'd finally shed their old Saturn jackets that were getting way too tight despite the drugs to slow down their development. They now wore two-colored sweaters with podpup pouches, gray and coral for Io and gray and ivory for Euro. Probably made by Nkiroo. Who would have thought their engineer was a fashion designer?

Zahar dredged up a smile. It wasn't the twin's fault that the rats were medical subjects. And if they could save 500 people from Gas Giant Environment Syndrome, maybe that made it okay? Otherwise, Io and Euro and all the other GGE sufferers would die when they reached adulthood.

Lanezi had spun up, so the babies would have gravity, and it would be easier to care for them. The baby in the ordinary human air was doing as well as the one in the reproduced alien air. Of the six podpups, two were lavender, one was light blue, one was pink, one yellow, and the male was light green. All pastels, as if they had been designed that way. All had purple eyes. They were small and fuzzy so they had to be young. They were adorable. She couldn't wait to hold them.

"We had to bring Whisper," Euro explained. "She needs to check on the babies and pups."

"And Lanezi is in the Prayer Room," Io added. "So we must care for her."

Zahar nodded, letting Euro hold Whisper near each baby and podpup to observe, which she did long and carefully.

"They're ze?" Io asked.

"The babies, yes," Zahar answered. "We know from autopsies from the other accident at Hamada that most of the children were not gender specific." The two of them nodded.

"Also," Zahar volunteered, "the purpose of the forehead membrane was unknown."

"But now we know it's for light!" Euro said.

"But what's the light?" Io asked.

"That's the big question," Zahar answered, watching as Whisper continued to study the pups.

Based on the pups' reactions and what Dr. Tenshi had been able to figure out from the babies, they were slightly altering the atmosphere in one baby's environment, acclimatizing zir to human air. The changed air didn't seem to hurt zir, but ze didn't seem to be doing so well to start with. The other baby was no better. They were lethargic and their purple color had faded to a sickly gray-lavender. Their headbands of light had gone from frenzied flashing to dying embers of reddish pink.

Zahar attached a medical shelf to the observation window so Whisper could sit and observe without Euro holding her. The twins made a nest for her and settled her in. Then they took their time feeding and patting the rats. Finally they sat down at the table. Zahar joined them.

The three of them were almost the same age. In another life, they would have been friends, having fun. But Zahar felt ancient and they seemed like kids. Their commonalities were sad things, like they were all separated from their families. *And* they had to deal with difficult adults.

"Not the adventure you planned on?" Zahar asked sympathetically.

"I liked our adventures in the solar system with Dad better," Io admitted.

"But if we'd stayed home on S-Tro base, it would be so boring," Euro said. Zahar filled in the unspoken part. *If you're not going to live long, you have to take your adventure where you can.*

"Well, I hope we won't be stuck here too long," Zahar told

them. "The Harbor Council is in session. In a few days they are going to tell us the plan. We know that no one can leave Harbor because we can't use the a-rings anymore."

"Will we all die?" Euro asked.

"I don't think so. The Council is gathering the facts. They're counting how many ships we have and how many passengers they can take."

"You mean we are going to jump without the a-rings?" Euro asked.

"Evacuation is the only option. Well," Zahar considered, "no one has said this; it's just obvious that Harbor is not self-sustaining. The greenhouse isn't big enough. As far as I know, there's no seed vault here. We must leave. Either they must build a-rings, which Thayne is working on, or we must find a gravity assist. Meanwhile, everyone has to report how much food and fuel they have so it can be rationed."

Whisper suddenly turned to them. "Bad," she said.

Zahar frowned and got up to pat her, talking partly to the twins and partly to Whisper. "I know, but we don't know what to do. We think the air is okay. Dr. Tenshi came up with a formula to feed them and she is really smart about those things. We don't know if they are just scared or if it's a physical problem."

"Can we feed them?" Io asked.

Zahar had to smile. "Well, not yet. We have to keep them quarantined until all their microbes can be identified. The robots are feeding them." Zahar looked at the babies. "We don't know what they need . . . besides their parents, their people, but we can't give them that. Is there some trace element? Different gravity? A mental telepathy field? Colored lights?"

"They need love." Zahar wasn't even sure which of them said it, but Whisper looked up at her.

"Need pup," Whisper murmured and nodded once in self-confirmation.

"Yes!" Io and Euro exclaimed with excitement.

Yes! Echoed in Zahar's mind. *They are not quarantined from the pups.* "We didn't think of that."

Just then Tenshi came out of the lab, looking defeated. She collapsed in a chair and frowned.

"Doctor," Zahar said, "I'm going to put a pup next to each baby."

Tenshi nodded with resignation, as if she didn't think anything could save them. "Fine, I'm heading over to the gym." But she just sat there.

Whisper turned to the pups and studied them. "She's picking!" Io said.

Zahar froze. Whisper did seem to be considering. Then Whisper pointed to one lavender pup and then to the baby in the alien air. She pointed to the other lavender pup and pointed to the other baby.

"Got it!" Zahar said excitedly. "Thanks, Whisper."

They had to sedate the pups in order to let the robots handle them. They had the same crazy fear of robots as human podpups did. In fact, Whisper had to be held and consoled during the whole process. When the pups were finally transferred there didn't seem to be any immediate change.

"Maybe when the pups wake up," Zahar suggested.

The twins nodded. "These things take time," Euro added.

They all stood watching. "We got to meet aliens," Io said.

"Yes, what more adventure could you ask for?" Zahar asked, smiling.

"God protect! Don't say that," Tenshi said, making the deflect gesture.

. . .

Melawn shed his warm outer clothes and sat down on his yoga mat. He tried to calm his mind as Thayne and Nkiroo sat and a stressed-looking Tenshi started the music. It was music with 'nature sounds' to help create a meditative mood. This one was the sound of a river running over rocks. Sounded like broken pipes in the mine. Melawn peeked to his right at Nkiroo, but his detached and disciplined mind was undisturbed.

Melawn closed his eyes and started the deep breathing. His brain immediately focused on the data screens he had been studying. He hardly needed a pad; it was so vivid in his mind. He could hear Tenshi saying to let go of their work for a few minutes; to cleanse the mind was to strengthen the mind. He realized he was behind and stood up for the famous mountain pose.

The outlier—the possible echo—kept coming back to him. He pushed other data out, but that one returned.

"Set aside your cares," Tenshi was saying.

. . . set aside . . .

Tenshi must have sensed that he was so preoccupied. "You will have all the time you need to do your work and keep your body and spirit strong."

. . . time . . . He slowly followed the others into tree pose, paying almost no attention to his body.

. . . 55.7 seconds . . . Where did that come from? Melawn stopped listening to the doctor, his mind now chasing the 55.7 seconds. *Timeline, intervals . . . set aside . . . data set aside . . . from Hamada?* There had been an outlier there too, a similar echo. Melawn had used it to help formulate the new receivers.

"Melawn?" The doctor asked, but he held up his hand to stop her. He could feel the force of Thayne's consciousness come to focus on him. He opened his eyes and turned, looking around the gym in confusion. Where was a panel? He crossed the room quickly to his pack and pulled out his pad.

Soft music could have no effect on the sudden pounding of his heart. Of course he still had the Hamada data loaded.

"What?" Thayne whispered, he and Nkiroo cautiously waiting.

"55.7 seconds between the outlier echo at Hamada and . . ." Melawn waited for the timeline to come up. "The shutdown of the gravity ball."

He sat down on the deck, flicked that data away and pulled up the new data with the new timeline. He reset the distance of the receiver to adjust the time and then asked for the interval between that echo and the gravity ball shutdown.

'55.5 seconds' flashed on the pad. He turned the pad to show Nkiroo and Thayne.

"God in heaven," Nkiroo whispered.

"It's not an echo; it's a shutdown command," Melawn said. His voice was shaking. His whole body was shaking.

"A command from where?" Nkiroo asked.

Melawn looked up at Thayne, who nodded. "Yes, from the big gravity ball."

Nkiroo gasped. Tenshi had stopped the music and joined them. "You're saying the big gravity ball—the one with the a-rings, sent the little gravity ball—the one on the ship, a message to turn off?"

"Yes!" Thayne nodded in excitement.

"Why?"

"Probably a safety feature of some kind," Nkiroo surmised. "They may not be made to operate so close together."

"Well that's interesting," the doctor said.

The three of them turned to look at the doctor in complete astonishment. *"Interesting?"* Melawn repeated in disbelief.

"Doctor, we now know the frequency that gravity balls use to communicate."

"We will be able to command the gravity balls," Thayne said in awe, reaching down and gripping Melawn's arm, pulling him to a standing position.

"Well, what good is that?" the doctor asked. "You're not going to turn the big one off."

"No doctor," Nkiroo smiled, "we're going to turn the little one back on."

"You don't have the 'on' command."

"Yes we do!" Melawn explained. "The control panel in the gravity ball room of the alien ship is intact this time. One of those commands will turn it back on."

"And one might blow it up."

"Doctor! That's old science fiction," Thayne argued. "No one programs self-destruct commands."

"Well," Nkiroo qualified, "no humans do."

"We must decode that command packet—top priority," Thayne told Melawn, who was already nodding and planning. Then Thayne turned to Nkiroo, grabbing his arm with his free hand, linking the three of them together. "Make sure the OSRI engineers finish more a-ring segments by the time the gravity ball arrives. Lanezi has done us a favor after all. None of our a-ring segments were ever delivered to Nocturne." Thayne's eyes were shining. "With the little gravity ball, we'll be able to build our own working a-ring system right here."

Melawn's heart swelled with joy. After all that the three of them had been through together. He would have hugged them, but the doctor stood there scowling. "Doctor," Melawn entreated, "what if you had just discovered the key to your research after all these years?"

"I'd be careful," she said somberly, "very, very careful."

16-Dominion

Cheetah at Harbor Station

Two more hours. An exhausted and depressed Lanezi steeled himself to make it. He knew Nkiroo or Thayne or even the *Cheetah* itself could bring the ship in for stationkeeping, but he wanted to do it. It was a symbolic moment. It was the last Harbor ingathering. Only six more ships remained after the *Cheetah*. Two damaged ships limped in behind them from the a-rings, and still weeks away, three ships approached on their long incoming runs. Last of all would be *Raincloud*, a large passenger ship full of teens returning to the Teen Training Center, their semester-long separation from their families now indefinite. There would be no more incoming ships as news would have reached Atikameq to stop all jumps.

All the ship crews were now Harbor Citizens, their fate to be shared, their family their stranded companions. Lanezi's duty to bring in the *Cheetah* might be his last as a pilot.

They could not dock as they were quarantined. He would rendezvous near ARA2, and then they would wait, wait to see if the *Cheetah* crew died from contamination, and wait for the Council's plan for their future. Would it be to stay on a dying station and hope for rescue? To make a feeble attempt with untested a-ring repair? To risk an exodus by gravity assist?

"Okay?" Nkiroo asked quietly.

Lanezi shrugged, bringing up a picture of the Harbor Station environment. Although built in the latter times of fast and functional, Harbor Station was a throwback to better times, when stations were great works of art and engineering.

The main station was built to look like a gleaming gas giant, the rays of the ordinary yellow star reflecting golden-hued bands and belts. Visual artists had created spots and storms, clouds and moon shadows that enhanced the effect. Two Artificial Ring Arcs, reflecting glittering white, orbited the equator of the station. Four small satellites acted as 'shepherd' moons, completing the model of a miniature gas-giant family.

Artificial Ring Arc 1, ARA1, was the major ship dock. The other, ARA2, was a combination Teen Training Center and Pilot 'Retirement' Center. The teens lived on the main station, where they had artificial gravity, but their nogee training took place on

ARA2. Although the idea behind a nogee Pilot Retirement Center was in anticipation of making them comfortable in their old age, Lanezi knew that many were not old. 'Retirement' was a polite way of saying 'incapacitated.' He shuddered. He did not want to go anywhere near there. But when quarantine was lifted, they would dock, as ARA2 had an advanced Medical Bay, and it was another level of quarantine from the main station.

3-Ayyám-í-Há

Six days later, Zahar sat on a stool, with her guitar, facing the camera that wasn't turned on yet. She wore her new dress uniform, which in Sector 6 was a gold-trimmed buttoned coat, split below the waist, with a wide gold belt. Very fancy. Her coat was burgundy. Io and Euro stood calmly next to her, similarly dressed in royal blue and emerald green. They each had sleek new black pants and boots, all gifts from Melawn and Nkiroo.

Part Ayyám-í-Há gift, part consolation prize, she thought, and then reprimanded herself. *Be thankful and positive.* They were very generous to give such beautiful and expensive gifts, and it helped ease the embarrassment of appearing on the broadcast without anyone from the senior crew.

Expecting to be at Nocturne, they already knew they would be away from their families during Ayyám-í-Há. But she couldn't help being sad. She missed her family, the parties, the food, the whole colony. And she could see that Io and Euro were trying to be brave and upbeat.

Zahar had reminded the crew to get gifts in advance. She'd purchased special food and planned a party. But charity was a big part of the season, and all ships were expected to do some form of charity for the station: school visits, loaning specialists, donations of supplies, performances, etc.

Thayne refused to *waste time* on such things, especially performances. He wouldn't even support the required social arts aboard the *Cheetah.* So Zahar and the twins had done the only thing they could do, practice singing during their mentoring circle.

And the BIG THING at Harbor was the live show of the retired pilots. The Teen Training Center and ships with talented crews put together small performances, professional level ones, and then the retired pilot orchestra would play. It was a huge deal. The recording was sent all over the outer sectors.

"One minute," Nkiroo, their last-minute director, whispered.

Zahar and the twins straightened up. They had nowhere near the skills needed, but as the *Cheetah* was quarantined and had nothing else to offer, they were allowed to participate by singing the opening hymn. The whole show was on a ten minute delay to sync up the feeds, and give them a second chance if necessary.

Of course, it wasn't necessary. They sang *Benediction,* the eternal song. Io and Euro's voices soared from their hearts, almost making Zahar cry.

"We're off," Nkiroo whispered. "Beautiful." They all smiled in relief. They watched the rest of the show, the twins entranced as if their souls were starving for it. They were sad when it was over. But Zahar smiled at them.

"Ready for a party?" she asked.

"Yessss!"

They had to go to the Med Bay so they could keep an eye on the babies. Nkiroo had worked overtime making sweaters for all seven pups and blankets for the babies. The robots had slipped them on while they were sleeping.

"You love that knitting machine," Zahar laughed.

"I do. It's so logical."

Melawn had 3D printed colored balls for Whisper. Now she was happily playing a rolling game with Io.

Giving gifts could be challenging when people had everything, or nothing, or had no room for anything, but generally in the outer sectors, any small treat was appreciated. Zahar had long ago purchased real Earth chocolate bars. "Oh, my God," Tenshi said, breathing in the smell. "Thank you, Zahar."

Lanezi had painted space scenes for them, small enough to put on a necklace or attach to your fancy dress uniform. Io and Euro were especially happy with theirs, scenes of their namesake moons. In return, the rest of them gave Lanezi paints and all their art supply ration sliders.

The party had started out stiff and formal, but slowly, the food, the gifts, and Whisper's playfulness seeped into them. They sat down, relaxed. Thayne eventually joined them and handed out new soft shoes for everyone. Zahar stifled a laugh: they all knew how much Thayne hated the noise of the skates.

"I have not properly thanked this crew for your hard work," Thayne said. "This pit stop at Harbor will not keep us from our mission. We're on the verge of a great breakthrough." They all nodded, and Melawn and Nkiroo smiled, eyes shining. "During this Fast, your first," he nodded to the twins, "let us rededicate ourselves to our task, the reunification of humanity."

Maybe there was hope for this crew after all.

4-Ayyám-í-Há

Lanezi sat with the crew, except for Dr. Tenshi, at the conference table in the Consultation Hall, waiting for the special news conference to begin. He glanced casually at Thayne and Melawn, sitting together. Since the accident, they had been in constant contact with Harbor monitors as well as Farzad, the stranded Sector Assistant. Their anxiety over Wreck 2 and the gravity ball would not dissipate until they had it docked at the OSRI research station.

The Harbor Council had inventoried ships, pilots, supplies, including food, medicines, fuel, and cargo. Some ships had already offloaded cargo. *Cheetah* was scheduled to wait, first for the babies' quarantine, and then again, after they had exposed themselves to the babies and podpups. Lanezi prayed the babies would survive, but then what? Lanezi felt for them. He'd been passed from family to family as a child, but at least they had been human. What would it be like to be raised by aliens? Or worse, not even raised in a family like regular children, but studied in a laboratory like . . . aliens? And then he noticed Nkiroo staring at the babies. Nkiroo, raised by an AI, obviously worried about them. "Maybe someone can take them back," Melawn whispered. *Jump into alien space? I wouldn't want that job. Or would I?*

It was a great test for Thayne to wait for the quarantine when there was so much to be done. The good news for Lanezi was that Thayne, Nkiroo, and Melawn seemed to have completely forgiven him. Lanezi was grateful, knowing he didn't deserve so much understanding.

The screen flashed on.

"Message from the Harbor Council:"

"God is Most Glorious."

All nine members of the council stood humbly in their meeting chamber against a wall of screens. The central member chanted a prayer for protection.

The member on the left stepped to the side of her screen and it activated, the *Cheetah* screen automatically switching to its feed.

"Universal Survival"

"Friends of Harbor, the Council reassures you of its daily prayers during this difficult time. We offer our deepest sympathies to those who have lost their loved ones in the accident and to those now separated from their families, as well as prayers for the departed of our people and the beings on the alien vessel.

"The Council has spent the past two weeks in crises management, fact gathering, calculations, consultation with experts, quiet contemplation, and beseeching prayer. A plan has been formed and carefully checked. It is now time to share that plan with all of you, the citizens of Harbor, and to put its elements into action."

The second council member took over the narration. "As you may know, the current population of Harbor, including all inbound ships, is 2725. There are 31 functional ships." The speaker paused to let people do their own math. Eighty-eight people per ship, Lanezi thought, but of course, they would not be divided equally. *Cheetah* had a big cargo hold, but small Passenger Lounge. They wouldn't be able to take more than forty. "This plan has one goal," the speaker continued, "Universal Survival."

In the corner of the screen a number went up, +14, the number of days since the accident, Lanezi realized.

"Harbor Station has not yet reached self-sufficiency. Our only survival option is evacuation." Lanezi sighed in relief, as did Zahar. Thayne and Melawn nodded as if they already knew, and Nkiroo had no reaction, as if no other option were reasonable so he had not had a second thought about it.

The third council member took over. "The Council, after careful deliberation, has decided against using any untested a-ring segments." Lanezi was taken aback. Why not? If they didn't try the a-rings, that meant a gravity-assist. Lanezi's suppressed fear welled up in him. On his previous g-a, he'd killed half the people on the ship. No one had ever accused him. He had only done what he needed to do, and yet so many had not survived. And he owed guilt-filled gratitude to Canim for saving another 17 people.

Lanezi refocused on the screen. The number in the corner updated to +767. The council member was now talking about a gravity-assist convoy, about all the ships going together, about how it was an especially favorable alignment, about having time to plan and execute carefully.

"Our jump date, 3 Splendor, 1085, 767 days after the accident, will bring us into Atikameq—"

Two years?

They talked about rationing, redistribution of resources, refitting ships with passenger chairs, about how they had more than sufficient supplies and no one need entertain "any sacrificial notions." All would travel together for the 767 jump date except one ship, which would be dispatched earlier on a much more difficult g-a. "This ship will carry news and plans to Atikameq as well as a small number of special personnel.

"Let us dedicate ourselves, on the eve of this Fast, to a detachment from worldly concerns, to patient resolve, and to the unity of our people."

15-Loftiness

Cheetah, near ARA2

To: Lanezi, Cheetah Pilot

From: Nkiroo, Cheetah Science, Special Assignment

Please join us for the morning briefing. N.

Lanezi frowned at Nkiroo's message in resignation. Back to business. Lanezi and most of the crew were struggling with being separated from their loved ones. Since he had not yet recovered from the sickness of his lying, he felt especially unsteady dealing with the loss, even if he told himself it was only temporary.

At least they let me get through a couple weeks of the Fast, he reminded himself. He scooped Whisper off the bunk, smoothing her just-long-enough-to-be-soft fur. It wasn't gray as it had been when she was a rescue. It was the color called silver mist. It shimmered when she moved, giving her podpup cuteness a bit of glamour. She wasn't old and feeble as Lanezi had first thought. She was healthy and, Lanezi knew now, strong inside and out.

She looked up at him with love and acceptance, not the blind trust of an adoring baby podpup, but the understanding of one who knew he was doing his best. Her eyes flashed with a hint of Dr. Obala and Lanezi laughed. She leaped against his chest and squirmed under his poncho.

"You can't come to the meeting you know," he chided her.

"Blah meeting," came her muffled voice as he went up the stairs. "Play twins."

"And rats."

"Rats naughty," she said sternly.

Lanezi laughed again. Maybe a podpup was what he needed to get through life for the next two years.

"*What?*" Lanezi objected without any thought to propriety.

One podpup was what he needed, not seven.

"You are the logical person," Tenshi insisted. The morning briefing hadn't been a routine one to ease him back into ship work. It was his undignified demotion from pilot to podpup sitter.

"We're lifting a level of quarantine," Dr. Tenshi explained. "Two people need to go into the Med Bay quarantine zone *with* the aliens. For at least two weeks. We'll take every precaution, but of course, there may be danger of untreatable sickness. My work with Io and Euro can't be compromised and Zahar can't take care of two babies and six podpups alone."

"Why not?" Lanezi interrupted with an apologetic glance to Zahar, who looked like she preferred to be without him anyway. "The robots took care of them."

"We must stop using the robots as they are stressing the

podpups and the babies. They need people. You are experienced with podpups and you don't have any pressing work."

So much for the untouchable status of pilots. What can I say without seeming like a coward? Lanezi sat back. His mind flew over the recent news packets. 31 ships. 52 pilots. Yes, he was expendable from that point of view.

"You can also help interface with the doctors at ARA2," Tenshi continued.

Lanezi was too humiliated to even meet their eyes, but he could sense from their body language that they had agreed in advance. "When?" he asked meekly and they nodded in approval.

"This afternoon. Bring everything you need," Tenshi finished.

So he did. He brought his paints and his podpup. Whisper was both excited and worried, peering through the glass at the sickly babies. Lanezi had no second thoughts about exposing Whisper, knowing that if he died, she would die anyway.

The twins came to say "good luck," not "goodbye" to Whisper, but hugged Lanezi fiercely.

"We'll be okay," he whispered to them.

"Where is everyone else?" Euro asked.

Zahar shrugged.

"They are not worried?" Io asked.

"It isn't good luck if you don't worry," Euro explained.

"Well, then, we have plenty of good luck right here," Zahar joked.

At the door of the makeshift airlock, Zahar whispered to Lanezi, "Don't forget about the camera feed."

He glanced around for cameras. "Not general broadcast?" He asked in dismay.

"No, the public doesn't know about survivors. Direct feed is going to the Council and ARA2 doctors."

He nodded grimly.

"Think of it as an opportunity," she said with a raised eyebrow—and then the lock unsealed them to their fate.

Lanezi fought the instinct not to breathe. Zahar took a deep defiant breath.

Opportunity? For getting some alien disease and dying with people watching?

Zahar went straight to "Baby 1", so Lanezi cautiously approached the other.

The purple podpups snuggled close to the babies, but looked up worriedly as the humans came near.

"It's okay, sweetie," Zahar said to either the baby or the podpup. Lanezi wasn't going to be caught talking baby talk on the feed, no matter how overwhelming the instinct.

Zahar, without any hesitation, picked up the baby gently and cradled zir. Zahar's defiant look disappeared, eyes looking up to Lanezi with one obvious thought—*too late*.

Lanezi, gingerly, with far less practice than Zahar, picked up Baby 2. Ze was skin and bones. Ze didn't squirm or cry. Ziz skin was a horrible gray as if ze were already dead. Lanezi held zir against his chest and remembered Whisper dying in his arms—and coming back. He feared this time there would be no coming back.

After Zahar did more medical tests on the babies than Lanezi could stomach, they sat on a fold-down couch with the babies and prayed. They fed them, or tried to feed them, but had to put them back in their med beds to be force-fed.

To distract themselves they made a big nest for the podpups, moving the two purple ones in first. The two pitiful pups greeted each other as if grief stricken, huddling together.

Lanezi caught some of Zahar's determination then. They opened the EEHABS and pulled scared pups out. The light green baby boy whined until plunked down in the center of the girls. Their reunion seemed to perk them up and podpup treats were devoured with new energy.

By unspoken agreement Lanezi and Zahar went back for the babies, determined to hold them to the end, even if that was all they could do.

16-Loftiness

The next day, Whisper sat on the couch, disdaining to mingle with the pups in the pile. She sat between Zahar and Lanezi, worrying over both babies.

"Which pup do you think is the leader?" Zahar suddenly asked. Usually, one of the elder females was leader.

Lanezi looked down at Whisper, who didn't seem to have an opinion. "They're so young, maybe they don't have a leader," Lanezi answered.

"They need names," Zahar declared.

"I thought Tenshi wouldn't let us name them," Lanezi answered, fearing insubordination.

"We can't name the babies. She didn't say anything about the pups."

"Oh," Lanezi said. "Well, I guess we can't just call them 'pink one' or 'green one.'"

"You name them," Zahar decided.

"Why me?"

"You always have nice titles for your art."

"Oh." Lanezi had no idea anyone on the *Cheetah* even looked at his art.

He slid down off the couch so he was sitting on the deck by the podpup nest, still carefully holding the baby. He studied the pups' behavior, looking for clues for their names. The two lavender ones were sleeping now, exhausted from their vigil with the babies. The others, freed and fed, now explored their new play area. They frolicked around like furry paintbrushes, leaving the occasional floating piece of fluff, bound for the filter.

The yellow one came over to Lanezi once he got down. The pink one dutifully followed. They sniffed and gurgled at him like any other podpups, but kept looking up at him. They seemed puzzled.

"Is it because we're not purple, like the babies?" Lanezi asked Zahar.

"I don't know. It's almost as if they are looking for something."

The green one, whining and then forcing himself to follow the others, slowly came up to Lanezi. Lanezi shifted the limp baby so he could scratch the podpup, who promptly curled up right next to him, with no sign of puzzlement.

The blue one ignored them, curling into a ball, like a giant fuzzy–

"Blueberry." Lanezi said, pointing to her. She looked up at him with a stunned expression, then immediately rolled back into a ball.

They laughed quietly. "Oh it's cute," Zahar reassured the pup.

"Well, podpup names can't be too serious." Lanezi looked down at the green one. "What's a food that's green and fuzzy?"

"Something in the back of the fridge."

He smiled. "I know," he tapped the boy, who looked up, "Kiwi!"

"Lanezi! What station are you from? Kiwis are brown and fuzzy on the outside."

"Kee—WEEEE" the little green one repeated.

They laughed again. "Too late to change," Zahar admitted.

Lanezi curled his free hand around Kiwi, who looked up at him adoringly. He felt a little tug on his heart and sighed. Bonded already.

"Okay," Zahar must have felt his distraction. The little pink one whined next to Zahar. "She wants a name too."

"Um, well, strawberry?"

"That's red. She's pink."

"Radish?"

"Red."

"Cherry?"

"Lanezi! You're a jump pilot and an artist! Don't you know your colors?"

"Okay. Cotton Candy?"

"Eww, too sticky. You know how they can live up to their names. Maybe a non-food name?"

"I have some great paint colors: Island Sunrise, Flamingo, Ballerina, Salmon, Dusky Rose."

"DUS-TEE," the pup perked up.

"No, Dus-KEE," Zahar corrected.

"Dus-TEE, Dus-TEE," the pups chanted. Then the pink one puffed out her fur and sneezed. Lanezi and Zahar stifled a laugh, not wanting Dusty to repeat the gesture for life.

Zahar shook her head at Lanezi. "We should have figured this out when they weren't around."

They skipped naming the sleeping purple pups as their

people should name them, someday. Then they turned to the yellow pup, who was waiting for her name with such an expectant, trusting look, Lanezi couldn't hold off. "Well, let's see. I have a yellow paint called 'Sprinkle of Summer.'

"Summer!" Zahar said quickly. "That's a perfect name."

"Great!" Lanezi summarized. "Dusty, Kiwi, Summer, and Blueberry, who will end up being called Blue and then everyone will think we have no imagination."

Whisper chose that moment to jump down from the couch into their midst. Without a beat of hesitation, Summer sat down in front of Whisper and bowed her head. The other pups, even the aloof Blueberry, immediately sat and bowed, following Summer's lead. Whisper nuzzled them each on the head, hierarchy established.

Then Blueberry, still in a ball, with little arms sticking out, rolled over to Lanezi. He laughed, Zahar laughing with him. The alien pups made the same puffing noise that human pups made when amused. The laughing startled the baby that Lanezi was holding. Ziz eyes flew open.

"Sorry. Sorry, little one," but the baby's eyes suddenly focused and tracked to Lanezi's face, searching. Zahar knelt down next to him.

"Ziz color—it's slightly better."

Then the alien eyes found his, and Lanezi's breath caught in his throat. As in a jump, when his mind first found a new star, saw its essence, felt its spirit and leaped across the lightyears, Lanezi's heart now reached out of his human experience and connected with the alien baby, finding another soul, struggling and afraid and looking to him for hope.

17-Loftiness

Melawn got up from his panel in Consultation Hall as if coming out of a daze. He had been working feverishly, side by side with Nkiroo and Thayne, for days, eating and even sleeping in the Consultation Hall. When it was time to eat, food would be there. If he felt sticky, he would go wash up quickly.

The main screen behind him went on for the big meeting. He was ready. He had tweaked the packet-decoding program as much as humanly possible. It was up to the *Cheetah* AI now.

He had only a moment to stretch before sitting at the big conference table, making a mental run-through of the five hundred prayers he knew by heart to decide on something appropriate.

They would be consulting with Kanika, the manager of Nkiroo's engineering team at OSRI, the Outer Sector Research Institute in orbit around Haven, the same planet that Harbor Station orbited. Kanika was investigating the recently damaged a-ring segment. She was a thorough, no-nonsense scientist who never wavered after her pronouncement of the facts. She had led the same team at Hamada, but the only segment they had been allowed to touch there was badly damaged.

At the entrance to each tunnel-like a-ring segment, there was a circle of location lights. But at the exit end of each a-ring segment was a torus, made of a strong clear material. While the a-rings were in operation, the tori would pulse with a glowing light. They had tentatively decided that the tori were empty when not activated. All their work hung on this issue. Nkiroo had designed the replacement segments based on the theory that the gravity ball would somehow create or transport particles into each torus to pull the ships along with small pulses of extra gravity, before decaying.

There was not enough information in the glow to decide what the original particles were, but it didn't matter. If the tori were already filled with some exotic material, humans would probably not be able to build their own segments. Everything Thayne had been working for hinged on the information. Thayne was pacing the room in extreme anxiety. Melawn rubbed his eyes to surreptitiously read the icons on his wrist p'link. Thayne was not dangerously upset, yet.

"You've reminded everyone about the extra delay for security," Thayne told Nkiroo compulsively.

"They all understand," Nkiroo said soothingly.

They would also be getting updates from Jamez, Nkiroo's construction manager at OSRI. Jamez was precise, brilliant, a good delegator and best of all, good at explaining things. He had already built two collapsible a-ring segments based on the preliminary data from Hamada. They were still in the cargo hold of the *Cheetah*. He was mostly done with four more segments at the OSRI hangar.

Thayne had asked for an update from the tug captain, the one bringing in Wreck 2, with the gravity ball. She was an eccentric known as Swooper, but tuggers were not known for their punctuality at meetings, or anything else.

The screen blinked on at precisely 10:00. Kanika must have anticipated the delay. "Vacuum confirmed," she announced, not wasting words. All thoughts of proper greetings or prayers left their minds. Thayne practically collapsed in a chair. Nkiroo jumped out of his chair in excitement. A wave of joy passed through Melawn, but he had no idea how to express it, especially as Kanika was still talking. "There was absolutely no damage at that end of the segment. There were no cracks in the torus. We sterilized the surface and checked with multiple methods before we opened it in our vacuum chamber."

Jamez had joined the call and was obviously thrilled and relieved. In the background they could hear his team cheering.

After thanking and congratulating Kanika profusely, Thayne turned to Jamez. "We'll need a total of eight segments. Can you build two more by the time the gravity ball arrives?"

"I just need clearance for the materials," he said, smiling and shushing his people. "We're in rationing now."

"Send me a list; I'll take care of it," Thayne reassured him. "Nkiroo, we're agreed then, the object on top of each a-ring segment is a stationkeeping receiver and transmitter. Whatever goes on in the torus must be completely controlled by the gravity ball."

"Yes. As soon as we have the codes and set up the mini a-ring system, we can test it." Nkiroo hadn't sat down. He seemed ready to jump back into another 40 hours of work.

"So all we need now is a pilot—" Thayne was cut off.

"Hey Cap! Swooper here. Reporting as ordered with nothing to report! We're on our way. See you at the hangar. You better have chocolate! This crew doesn't haul alien gravity balls for just sliders you know." She cut off laughing.

Nkiroo, Kanika, and Jamez looked after her vanished image as if *she* were some kind of alien. Melawn had a hard time keeping a straight face as they signed off. She reminded him of every ore hauling pilot he'd ever known.

"My new shuttle, the *Frontier*, is ready at OSRI and I've got a second shuttle being rigged, so we can have two shuttles to test our a-rings," Nkiroo said. "So as you were saying, all we'll need is a test pilot."

"Maybe Swooper would volunteer," Melawn said jokingly.

"God forbid!" Nkiroo complained. "They seem to think that tugging, slinging, and catching things in-system is just a giant pinball game."

"No," Thayne said calmly, the far off thinking look settling in. "Someone from the retirement center. Someone with . . . vision."

"The retirement center?" Nkiroo asked, concerned. "They were retired for good reason you know."

"No, I don't think so. Besides, the Council will never let us have a working pilot."

Melawn was surprised by a little twinge of doubt. Those pilots would be desperate to jump again. They would volunteer for anything, regardless of the risks. Thayne suddenly turned to look at him. "Melawn, don't you trust me? It will be as safe as any other jump."

"I know," he whispered, embarrassed.

"Oh, Melawn," Thayne, sighed, squeezing Melawn's shoulder gently. Then Thayne glanced back at the screen, concerned. "Just in case, better round up some chocolate."

10 / OUT OF SYNC

1-Splendor-1083 BE

Cheetah, near ARA2

Hot. So hot. Lanezi was sleeping on the deck in the quarantined area. He reached to throw off his blanket, but he didn't have one. *Careful!* his mind reminded him. *Whisper. And Kiwi . . . and . . .*

"Are you okay?" Zahar asked from their makeshift kitchen in the Med Bay.

"Hot."

"Well, no wonder, you've got five podpups sleeping on you."

Lanezi propped himself up on his elbows, sending colored furballs rolling off his chest onto the deck.

Zahar turned to look at Lanezi. "Happy New—" she froze.

"What?"

She took a calming breath. "You have a rash." She drew her finger across her nose. Lanezi reached up to his face. There were bumps across his nose that itched fiercely as soon as he touched them. Zahar pointed to the exam bed. "We need to scan. Dr. Tenshi, come to the Med Bay please."

. . .

14-Splendor

It had been a long and boring two weeks. Lanezi watched anxiously through the window as Tenshi checked the blood of the other crewmembers to make sure the vaccine had taken.

"A few more minutes before it'll be safe to let you come out," she told Lanezi.

"Thank you," he turned and walked away, pretending not to care. His gaggle of podpups tripped over themselves meandering after him. A gaggle or a pod? Or a pack? No. Nothing that organized. More like a mess. He scowled down at them. They all looked up adoringly at him. Maybe there was no official word. After all, who would be so crazy as to bond with five podpups? *I'm destined for a life of fuzz.*

His sickness had added two weeks to their quarantine while Tenshi worked on the vaccine. In those two weeks, Zahar had ended up taking care of him, seven podpups, and two alien babies, who were now in the purple of health. Zahar never got the alien rash, and somehow managed to avoid bonding with a single podpup.

Euro and Io decided to stick around after the testing, as anxious to get in as Lanezi was to get out. After only a few minutes, Lanezi heard the twins cheer, the door opened, and they were beside him with quick hugs and perfunctory requests for permission. Each little pup gurgled in excitement with more hugs, more playing, and more love to go around.

Lanezi collapsed on the couch with Whisper, harboring a hope that a couple pups might rebond with Io and Euro.

"They knew, Lanezi," Io said, looking over at him in innocent amazement.

Lanezi, confused, glanced at Euro. "Knew what?"

"That you needed a family, of course," Euro explained.

Stunned at the thought, Lanezi sunk further into the couch, the weight of years of responsibility on him. His life would be consumed.

3-Glory

Zahar had lived in the Med Bay for weeks, but now that Thayne was having one of his mindstorms, she decided to get out—and take the babies with her.

The twins came along as official babysitters. True to their word, they were good at feeding. They were also good at rocking, playing, crawling on the deck talking nonsense, and even smooching little purple cheeks. The babies ate it up. They gained weight. They got loud. They started rolling around. Most encouraging of all, their headbands glowed with astonishing colors.

Zahar pointed out that the colors were consistent with what they were doing or feeling and that both babies ran the same colors when, apparently, they felt the same. The ARA2 doctors agreed to observe and study the matter. Dr. Tenshi was skeptical, but the twins had no doubts.

"White means 'I'm going to cry until I get what I want,'" Io explained.

"Yes," Euro agreed. "Pink means 'Play with me.'"

"White with a brown streak is hungry and pink with a purple streak is happy," Io continued, making a streaking motion across his own forehead. Zahar just wrote down whatever the twins said. And she worried. Every day of quarantine that passed meant they would be docking soon. The babies would certainly be transferred to the 'experts' on ARA2. Zahar warned Io and Euro, but nothing would stop them from loving with all their hearts.

15-Glory

Nearly two weeks later, Lanezi went to the kitchen early to feed the podpups so he could at least sit down with the crew for a few minutes of dinner. He was demoted to the junior crew table anyway, the furthest possible seat from Thayne, so that the Captain wouldn't be bothered by the pups' inevitable visits to the table.

Lanezi didn't mind the company of teens; he liked them all very much, but he felt completely left out of operations. He missed the more professional talk of the adults.

Zahar had prepared the food, which meant they had protein cubes with choices of brightly colored sauces. The twins took turns guessing the flavors until a drift of conversation from the other table caught their attention and they were simultaneously quiet.

"You think they'll make you turn over the DNA data?" Melawn was asking Dr. Tenshi.

"Of course. Once they get around to it. They're aliens. We have no treaties, no research agreements, nothing. We'll want our record to be clean before we start negotiations."

"But no one has said anything yet?" Melawn asked.

"No, we still have the babies. Once we turn them over, I expect a cleaning crew."

Zahar, Io, and Euro exchanged sad looks.

"What tests are you running, Doctor?" Nkiroo asked.

"Anything related to radiation resistance."

"But you'll have to turn over the data too," Melawn commented.

"Yes, that's why I'm focusing on the most important thing. If I learn anything, even the slightest hint, I can apply that to the rat project, even if I don't have the data."

"How is the research going?" Thayne asked, with no regard for the patients sitting right there, perhaps because he knew that Tenshi was always open with them.

"Mutant rat life expectancy has been increased 20%. I believe I can increase that to 60% or better in the two years we'll be waiting for the jump convoy. I'll have to find immediate passage back to Sector 1 for myself and the twins."

"Doctor, there is no guarantee that a workaround for Firelight will have been found by the time we get back," Nkiroo cautioned.

"We'll have to find something. I promised to return the children."

There was a beat of silence as everyone stared at the Doctor, the twins in perfect innocence, the others in appalled shock. *Obviously*, Lanezi thought, *Tenshi is not from the outer sectors.*

"How could you promise?" Melawn whispered.

"I have every intention," Tenshi replied, insulted.

Nkiroo leaned forward to whisper to Tenshi. Lanezi only knew what he was saying because it was what any of them would say. "This is the outer sectors, Doctor. Tomorrow is not a promise."

Dinner petered out, weighed down by the news that the babies were leaving soon. Lanezi stayed to help Dr. Tenshi with cleanup duty. Luckily, the teens took all the pups so they wouldn't be in the way.

"Doctor, I'm feeling much better. Do I have to have an exam to be cleared for full operations?"

Tenshi stopped her work to gaze sternly at Lanezi. "You have not been removed due to your physical health issues."

He blinked in surprise.

"You must complete your therapy before you can be officially reinstated to the command order," she continued.

"Thayne said the arrest was all a mistake."

"It may have been. But you admitted to lying. You must complete the Truthfulness Therapy."

"Why didn't you tell me?" Lanezi asked, embarrassed.

"It's all in your medical instructions, didn't you read them?"

He hesitated. He hadn't really gone past the first page, assuming it was all the usual.

Tenshi continued, "Certainly you have studied your options in the release document?"

Lanezi shook his head slowly.

Tenshi fully rounded on him now. "Did you think an infraction of this magnitude would just disappear?"

"Well . . . no. I guess I've been distracted."

"Yes, we've had some distractions, but you have a serious problem you need to confront—and speaking of distractions!" She turned back to her work shaking her head. "Even if you complete the therapy, I don't know how you are going to go back to operations with five podpups."

"I'll have plenty of time, and the teens help me take care of them."

"It's not the time! You don't have any work to do! I have to do more research on this, but there is some clinical evidence that too many podpups can affect your mind."

"*What?*"

"Especially five! Some psychologists claim even one."

"It sounds like a myth. Maybe we could just ask Dr. Obala."

"We cannot ask anyone! The fact that we have alien podpups aboard is classified!"

"Oh, right."

Tenshi was glaring at him now, probably wondering what else he just didn't get. "When can I start the therapy?"

"It's all in your file. You should have started immediately." She turned and went down the stairs, clearly done with him.

At breakfast with Zahar, Euro, and Io, Lanezi commented that the doctor had said that pups affect your mind. "Especially five pups." Lanezi grabbed an empty bottle Summer had thrown. "No throw!" he interrupted himself.

"That's ridiculous," Zahar scoffed. "People have five children and it doesn't 'affect their minds.'"

"Maybe it does," Io said, tilting his head in contemplation.

"Our parents have seven children," Euro added.

"They do get confused sometimes."

Lanezi smiled in sympathy for the distant couple with four identical boys. "Well, it's not the same" he objected, "because people get bonded to the podpups."

"People get bonded to people too," Io said, as Zahar rolled her eyes.

"Not the same way. It's like I always know where they are, what they're feeling and, God help me if they're hungry."

Zahar laughed, but the twins seemed puzzled. "I always know where Io is, what he's feeling and if he's hungry—" Euro suddenly seemed sad.

Io, downcast too, said, "We used to know where Calli and Gani were too."

"But now . . ."

"It's like there's space . . ."

"Like a dark void."

"You can't see."

"You can't feel."

Zahar put a hand on each boy's shoulder. "I'm sorry you're so far from home. Have hope. For now, the *Cheetah* is your home."

But they scowled at that. And Lanezi did too. And Zahar bit her lip. *Sunburst* had been a home, Lanezi thought. *Cheetah* was ...not.

14-Beauty

Finally, another two weeks of quarantine passed with no sickness. But the crew was grumpy in the morning because they had to give up gravity for the near future. Once they were docked at ARA2, they would not be able to spin up.

Lanezi kept an eye on the screen, allowing *Cheetah* to bring in the ship and dock. Some pilots liked to do it manually, but it was really much safer to let the computers work it out—and that's the way the ARA2 docking monitor wanted it.

"Ten minutes to docking burns. All crew, signal secure," Nkiroo announced.

"Secure!" Euro and Io practically shouted from right behind him. He'd allowed them to ride in the Command Bay for the docking. Nkiroo was there too, acting as monitor. It was overkill. Io could have brought in the ship with the computer's help. But Lanezi had enough respect for the unexpected not to go that far.

He received secures from the rest of the crew and Nkiroo officially ordered them to stay in place. The computer link was established and *Cheetah* started the first of several planned burns. Docking was more unnerving to Lanezi than jumping. It always seemed at the last that the ship was coming in too fast. He glanced at the screen and then at the quickly growing dock lights. *Something . . .* "Kiro . . ." Lanezi murmured nervously, embarrassed to let it get to him.

And then he couldn't stand it. Some red alert system in his brain snapped into overdrive. Lanezi flipped the manual override switch, but nothing happened. In a panic, he glanced at his s'link, already in the slot. Level 6 flashed on the side. *Six! Thayne demoted me!* An alarm sounded and 'computer sync failed' flashed on the screen.

"Kiro! I need level 3 to override!" Even though Nkiroo was quick and coordinated, it took agonizing seconds for him to get his s'link in the slot.

"*Cheetah*, manual override!" Nkiroo ordered.

Lanezi burned 1g back, sending the thrust right at ARA2. He glanced down at the screen for deceleration numbers, but they were scrambled and blinking. Better to waste fuel than ram them, but he had no real-life experience doing it without the numbers. Simulations from his training days came flooding back to him; the feel for the mass and thrust, the last seconds of panic approach before the simulator screen would flash 'failure,' the doing it over and over until those last seconds seemed like a slow motion never-ending float. He burned back again, 2g this time.

"Estimate 3g, 16 seconds for full stop!" Nkiroo shouted.

"We don't have 3g on the forward thrusters!" Lanezi objected, but Nkiroo would know that.

"Give it all you've got," Nkiroo said in resignation, pulling the *Cheetah* vent alarm.

Lanezi did it, going for the full stop instead of the match. ARA2 was on comms, venting alarms going in the background. For 30 seconds no one on the *Cheetah* could move. They almost scratched the paint when they finally slowed and then moved slightly back. Lanezi kept it up another 20 seconds before letting off. Then they lurched forward in their seats. Lanezi was gasping for air and trying to think straight. "Do you have forward motion?" he shouted to Nkiroo.

"No," he said.

"*Cheetah*, auto track sideways to stay with our port!" Lanezi looked out the window to see how close they were to the next ship. They needed to stay in their docking lane. Smooth thrusting started to the right.

"Are we okay now?" Euro whispered.

"Yes, but we need to dock." Nkiroo cut the venting alarm, not that anyone had been able to prepare, and spoke to the whole crew. "Sorry everyone. Sync failure. We are currently out of danger. Please stay secure while we sort it out."

Lanezi flicked through the screens, hunting for the one his instincts told him to look at. "Computer capacity – 93%." He looked at Nkiroo. "That can't be right."

"Sync speed failure—that's what ARA2 is telling me."

"*Cheetah*, display computer use," he ordered.

Nothing happened. "Nkiroo . . ."

Nkiroo ordered the computer to comply.

Four huge programs were running, taking over almost all the resources of the computer. "What are you people *doing?*" Lanezi complained. The *Cheetah* was the most advanced ship in the outer sectors. That it should run out of thinking power was unthinkable. One program had Melawn's name, one had Nkiroo's name and two had no name. They were marked classified. Nkiroo immediately stopped his program and called Melawn to stop his. "We're still at 54%," Lanezi said. "Get Thayne to stop his programs while I reprogram the dock."

A few seconds later, one more program stopped.

"He says he can't stop the last program," Nkiroo whispered.

Something more important than not crashing the ship?

· · ·

Cheetah docked at ARA2

When it was all over, when the *Cheetah* was safely docked, when ARA2 was stabilized, when Nkiroo had apologized and explained, when an inquiry was officially opened and the ARA2 commander had interviewed Lanezi, Dr. Tenshi, Thayne, and Nkiroo and closed the inquiry with a reprimand against all four of them plus a point put on Lanezi's record, his first, Lanezi zipped himself into his sleeping sack and cried. He could have killed someone, which happened, during jumps, not docking! Pilots were not permitted to fly without their level 3 clearance and he had not thought to check or run it up during the dock. He was also responsible for checking the computer, something he never did on the *Cheetah* as it had always seemed so unnecessary. Dr. Tenshi, Thayne, and Nkiroo were all reprimanded for allowing Lanezi to fly without full operations clearance. All the crew except Thayne had come to the Command Bay to check on each other and support Lanezi. Nkiroo had quietly promoted him back to level 3. "Promote him or replace him immediately," had been the order of the ARA2 commander.

The next morning, Lanezi stared at his latest painting in progress. It was nothing like all his other work. It was . . . fuzzy. He opened the computer capacity screen and checked it. They were using 91% again. He opened his medical file and read through the requirements of his therapy. Since Nkiroo had promoted him, he felt honor-bound to finish as quickly as possible. He determined he would not leave his cabin until he was done, so he worked day and night, with breaks for exercise and food that was delivered.

As part of the therapy, he had to come to terms with his 'situation', to choose the pathways to hope, to commit to honesty, and to do right by every person he met. He accepted the responsibility of the podpups, deciding that God had some reason and that five podpups were not a particularly burdensome test anyway. He embraced being their protector. He gave them more attention, trained and exercised them, brushed them himself, even if the teens did it again later, and talked to them, not just silly podpup talk, but real talk, from one being to another. They flourished. He prayed. He painted. He worked on his therapy. The twins visited him every morning and had their lessons with him. Every evening someone else in the crew visited. They seemed to have planned it out. Except Thayne never came, of course. And Lanezi was just as glad.

10-Light

"Lights," Zahar said as she floated into the Med Bay. "Lanezi!" He was floating by the empty baby cribs. "You startled me."

"Sorry. They're gone?"

"Yes, a medical team came for them. The purple pups too." She drifted over to join him. "Last night. Thayne wouldn't let us call you. It's been over two weeks. It's good to see you." A look of pain crossed Lanezi's face. She wasn't sure he was hurt that he didn't get to say goodbye or that Thayne had prevented it. "You can visit them on ARA2 maybe."

The door opened. Lanezi tensed.

"Oh—Lanezi," Dr. Tenshi said. "Do you have an emergency?"

"No Doctor. I'm here for phase two of my therapy."

Zahar floated away and occupied herself as the doctor approached, looking puzzled.

"The mentor part," Lanezi clarified.

"Oh," she seemed taken by surprise. "I'll have to be your mentor."

"It has to be someone I've never lied to. So I thought of Dr. Obala," Lanezi said.

"What?"

"He's a senior medical professional. I've never lied to him. I can take a shuttle over to Harbor station."

"I'm sure Dr. Obala is a busy man."

"He's on the mentor list."

"Lanezi, are you clear on the fact that you couldn't take the pups and you can't tell him anything about our mission, even the slightest accidental hint?"

"I've been thinking a lot about that."

Dr. Tenshi looked alarmed.

"I mean about the difference between lying and not telling," Lanezi clarified.

"And what have you decided?"

"That they could be the same thing." Tenshi frowned. "Especially if a person needs to know something."

"Lanezi, there's a big difference between not admitting you broke the cookie jar and doing classified work."

"Sure, I'm not crazy. I understand that some work might need to be kept quiet for short periods so as not to cause panic. But I also think, the more mature the society, the less the need for classified work."

"Do you think our society is sufficiently mature for *anything?*"

He hesitated a moment. "No, not quite."

"So what's the problem?"

"Have you noticed all the news about the gravity ball?"

"Which gravity ball?" The doctor wasn't one to follow the news.

"The one in the alien ship—the mini gravity ball. It's all over the news that a tug is bringing it in and a team of scientists will investigate it."

"So? No secrets there," Tenshi said.

"Except a Council member was quoted as saying we'd never discovered a small gravity ball before."

Dr. Tenshi looked puzzled.

"And" Lanezi tipped toward Dr. Tenshi, "we know perfectly well a mini gravity ball is on its way to us from the other wreck at Hamada."

"Are you accusing a Council member of lying? Is this some mental exercise to make your own crime seem less?"

"Doctor!" Lanezi was thrown off and flustered.

"Perhaps that Council member just didn't know," the Doctor continued.

"That would mean that Councils are keeping information from each other! I don't think that's possible."

Zahar frowned to herself. Lanezi had a point.

Tenshi shook her head. "We are way off the subject. You can't have Obala for a mentor. Thayne would probably not rescind his order that you can't leave the ship. I'll have to be your mentor, so no secrets will slip out."

"Doctor," Lanezi almost whispered, "doesn't it just feel like we are surrounded by secrets?"

Yes, Zahar thought. *Too many secrets, but whose secrets are they?*

11 / AN EXTRA VARIABLE

4-Mercy

ARA2 Station

Zahar, Io, and Euro were escorted out of the ARA2 Med Bay by a friendly nurse. Their visits to the babies were getting shorter and shorter.

"We have an hour before Thayne is done at the Pilot Retirement Center," Zahar told the twins. "Let's visit the juice bar." They pulled down the rimway, but when they got to the juice bar, Zahar hesitated. It was crowded with boisterous teens. "They all know each other," she said, worried about their red armbands.

"That's okay," Euro said.

"Soon they will know us!" Io added.

Inside, Io and Euro went ahead of Zahar, got juice, visited podpups, and worked their way to the middle of a big group, making room for Zahar to strap next to them. The teens were friendly and excited, swapping stories of the "EVA Emergency" that they had practiced that morning. Someone mentioned their new "ship teams."

"I don't understand," Zahar said over the general hubbub. "You're all from the Teen Training Center. What are ship teams?"

The other teens had no doubt already taken in the fact that Zahar, Io, and Euro were all red-banded, but had politely not asked their posting. "Oh, you're on a ship already," the blue-banded boy across from Zahar figured out.

"We are being put into teams for the convoy," a purple-banded girl next to him answered. "You know, one medical assistant, one monitor, one mech, one cook, a younger one, and a team leader. The list is supposed to be posted to leaders in two minutes!"

"Wow, that's planning ahead," Zahar said, impressed. "Are there enough teens?"

"Well, some ships don't need as many and some teens are coming off ships soon to make more teams," the girl explained.

"Got it!" A green-banded leader announced.

"Share!" the others shouted. And suddenly, they were tapping their p'links together for hard links, bypassing the station network. Zahar, prepared for this moment for months, quickly added her p'link to the mix. Not only would she get the ship list, she'd get all the other junk news with it.

"My team's going to *Echo Blue*!" The boy said, sounding a little like he was bragging.

Zahar retrieved her p'link and smiled at the twins. Junk news was just that. Rumor, conspiracy theory, wild talk about aliens, lost ships, podpups, and wide-ranging opinion on every subject. It was the people's free-speech mode. A lot of it was nonsense, but a careful reader of junk news could often filter out the truth, and truth was Zahar's new mission.

And while everyone was reading and announcing their ships, Zahar, Euro, and Io slipped away.

. . .

5-Mercy

Cheetah, docked at ARA 2

When she had a free moment the next day, Zahar hooked her foot under the holdbar at her cabin workpanel. On the big screen, she'd opened the junk news and was looking at the tags. The teen training list of ship assignments was there. *Cheetah* was listed, along with all the other ships, but next to *Cheetah's* name it said, "Compliment Filled." Probably they didn't want to expose any more teens to classified work. *Good.*

There were tags about the accident and alien wreck, the small gravity ball, and alien bodies. Another tag was *smoldering eyes.* That was about a strange man visiting the Pilot Retirement Center. *Thayne, of course.* He'd be unhappy to know people were watching him. The Thayne entries were followed by wild speculation that a seer pilot was needed to jump back to alien space, that the aliens were trying to warn humans about an invasion, or that it was already an invasion and the retired pilots were going to be mobilized to find the alien star system. Or in alternate schemes, pilots were going to attempt a long jump all the way to Earth. From the credible to the crazy.

18-Mercy

There was a knock at Lanezi's door and the pups went wild, bouncing off the walls to be the first to greet the visitor. It was Melawn. Since Lanezi had finished phase 1 of his therapy and come out of his cabin, the other adults had stopped visiting, but Melawn still came sometimes.

"Hi, Melawn, come in."

It wasn't that simple, of course. Each pup insisted on a two hand greeting with eye contact and name. Melawn had to crook his arm around a holdbar. "You must go nuts with all this . . . activity."

Although Lanezi had had his arguments with Melawn, they seemed to be past that. Lanezi truly liked him. Usually Melawn was friendly and humble, but lately, it almost seemed as if he were channeling Thayne. "So what's up?" Lanezi asked before any awkwardness could set in.

"Actually, it's about the four pups." Lanezi stiffened in alarm and then had to grab his chair. "Nothing bad," Melawn reassured him. "It's good actually. We just got official word that they'll be able to remain here with you."

Lanezi suddenly felt weak. "I didn't know there was any question."

Melawn nodded. "They wanted the pups, but Thayne intervened, explaining that he needed you and you were in a secure place."

Lanezi took a deep breath. *A near escape, and I didn't even know.* Melawn scowled, maybe expecting that Lanezi would be more grateful to Thayne. Looking closer, Lanezi noted how stressed and tired Melawn looked when he wasn't smiling. "Thank you for telling me. I'll thank Thayne later. Are you okay?"

Melawn sighed as he unhooked his arm from the holdbar. "Thayne is more agitated than usual. He has so much work. So much depends on him. But he'll be relieved to get back to working on the gravity ball. He'll be able to start testing some of his more important theories. So things should calm down."

"Did Thayne stop that computer program?" Lanezi asked.

"The big one? No. He said it's vital."

"Did you know that the computer sync speed was off by over one second?"

"Impossible. Capacity trouble wouldn't slow it down that much."

"Did you know our packets are delayed by several micro seconds?"

"That's security."

"Docking operations can't be run through a security delay like that."

"I'm sure Thayne will take care of it." Melawn seemed completely unconcerned.

"What happened to the first gravity ball from Hamada?"

Melawn shook his head at the change of subject, but seemed unconcerned about that as well. "It didn't get here before the jumps were cancelled. Probably still on a ship at Hamada."

"Do they know what to do with it?"

"Iricana will take care of it. They'll just have to park it somewhere safe."

"Do they even know they've got it? Does Iricana know?"

"Of course!"

"Did you tell them?"

"*I* didn't. I wasn't aboard. I was doing the salvage work. Thayne arranged the transport."

"So do you know for sure that anyone knows about the gravity ball?"

"Lanezi! Of course they must know. Special arrangements would have been made."

"Did you ask Thayne? Did you check through operations records?"

"He doesn't need to be bothered by *unnecessary* questions, and I don't go spying on his records. Why are you so suspicious?"

Lanezi hesitated, feeling like a nag, but also compelled by his truth therapy to press the issue. "So," he asked calmly, "how did Thayne know that the gravity ball wouldn't blow up or disturb the a-rings during the jump?"

"Because it didn't 'blow up' on the alien ship. And Thayne already calculated the g-forces from the wreck at Hamada to make sure our own ships could handle it if it went on."

"There were only three minutes of data," Lanezi said.

"How do you know that?"

"I've been looking into this."

"Why?"

Lanezi shrugged. "What else have I got to do?"

Melawn scowled, almost like Thayne. Lanezi worried that he might soon be a lot busier.

"Well, you don't need to worry," Melawn continued, taking a breath and feigning detachment. "The ARA2 people did enough work on the babies and the suited body to verify that this gravity ball was not stronger than .97 gee, nothing our ships can't handle, even if it turned on in the cargo hold."

When the discussion had become a little heated, the pups had hidden in their box. Lanezi glanced down at them. "It's okay," he assured them.

"Yes, everything is okay, Lanezi. Try to trust Thayne. He can feel your mistrust. You'd help us all if you could get along better."

"It's not that I don't trust him, it's just that I have questions."

"Well, how trusting is that?"

18-Words Eve

Cheetah at ARA2

A month later, Lanezi was trying to eat his dinner, supervise the pups, and listen to Thayne and Nkiroo at the other table discussing the extra passengers they'd be assigned for the convoy. "How many more passenger chairs?" Thayne asked.

"Twelve," Nkiroo said. "Added to our already existing fifteen chairs, planning on the eight of us in the Command Bay, we should expect twenty-seven new people by convoy time."

"Twenty-seven?" Tenshi repeated, surprised. "They can't possibly expose twenty-seven more people to classified level."

"No doctor. In fact, I assume we will be getting those already cleared, such as Council members."

Nkiroo was looking down, not at Thayne, so he couldn't have seen the look of surprise, possibly even alarm, cross Thayne's face and then disappear under a casually interested look. But Lanezi saw, and quickly looked away.

"Lanezi," Thayne called him. "We're going to OSRI day after tomorrow." The entire crew, Nkiroo, and Melawn included, looked at Thayne in surprise. *They didn't know. Or he just now decided.* "We'll get there soon after the gravity ball. We'll leave after I pick up our two pilots at ARA2 tomorrow."

"We need to wait for the chair installers, 10 more days," Nkiroo reminded him.

"No, we've waited long enough. And no one wants strangers on the ship. Euro and Io can install the chairs."

The twins bounced around in excitement again as Nkiroo hesitated. "Perhaps. With my supervision."

"Good. Have them load the parts immediately."

"We get to do the chairs?" Euro asked.

Nkiroo nodded slowly.

"Can the pups help?" Io asked Lanezi. "They are good at catching things in nogee."

"I'm sure they'd be happy to work with you," Lanezi answered.

"Good. Sounds like an efficient use of talent," Thayne agreed.

18-Words

ARA2

The next day, Thayne dropped Zahar, Euro, and Io off to say a quick goodbye to the babies. "Meet me at the Retirement Center desk in thirty minutes," was his last order. Thayne wanted them to help escort their two new passengers.

When they got to the Retirement Center, there was no sign of Thayne. They were directed to a 'waiting room' with no screens, no food, and few holdbars. They were sad about leaving the babies. Zahar figured they would never see them again.

Like a mind reader, Io asked, "What will happen to the babies after the convoy?"

"I'm sure a ship will be selected to take them home," Zahar reassured them. "Well, that's what I would do anyway."

"Yes," Euro agreed. "They should go home."

"Where did they come from?" Io asked.

"We don't know," Zahar answered, "but a sensible way to find out would be to send a bunch of ships out to possible locations to check. When they find purple aliens, they can come back for the babies."

"That's what I would do," Io agreed.

"It would be fun, to go on a search ship," Euro added, "a big adventure."

"Haven't you had enough adventure?" Zahar kidded Euro.

"Well, sometimes the future seems like an adventure-"

"And the past seemed like an adventure-"

"But the now seems like . . ."

"... hanging around, waiting for adventure?" Zahar laughed as they nodded.

Zahar heard Thayne's voice, stressed mode. They pushed to the door to help.

Thayne was at the desk, checking out three people, not two. Zahar and the twins exchanged knowing glances. Thayne's plan, whatever it had been, had not gone his way. And who was clever or powerful enough to thwart Thayne?

The crew held back, waiting for their cue to help. Of the three people with Thayne, Zahar discerned who the unexpected member was, a woman in her seventies. She was the color of coffee with a splash of cream. Her hair was dyed all black and straightened. She had it combed out and back, making her seem a couple of inches taller. She didn't need it. She was an imposing woman with permanent frown lines and sharp brown eyes. She carried a long crowbar with a blunt end. Zahar couldn't suppress a twitch of a smile, although Io backed behind her, wary of anyone who could have their way with Thayne.

As soon as Thayne glanced around, Zahar, Euro, and a reluctant Io came to his side, floating in a line, at attention, as if they were in some teen training inspection. The sharp-eyed woman gave the slightest nod of approval. The other woman was surprised to see them, and the man ignored them completely.

After a beat of silence, in which the retirees took in Io and Euro's strange looks and the red arm bands, Thayne decided to introduce people. "The junior crew: Zahar, Euro, and Io, special assignment. They'll help with the luggage."

"Alesta Eve," he nodded in the direction of the senior woman. "Long jump pilot."

Not any more, Zahar thought.

"Evan," Thayne indicated the man. He had dark, translucent

skin, like rootbeer candy. No more than 40, he had dark ringlet hair. Unlike Nkiroo's stiff twists, Evan's hair was swinging short in the front and tied in a pilot's knot in the back. He had strangely packed pockets and his dark brown eyes were staring at a spot on the ceiling—or—Zahar realized, past the ceiling. He wasn't even paying attention. Evan was a major wanderer. Zahar had been taught the signs when she was a monitor for incoming ships. But Alesta Eve wasn't a wanderer. *Why is she retired?*

Evan's wife, Caspia, turned out to be a doctor, not a pilot. Caspia had a reddish tinge to her dark brown skin. Her hair, too, had a hint of red and all the tiny curls were captured high in the back, bouncing like her husband's. Of the three, only Caspia seemed at all friendly, smiling at them.

Thayne had signaled them to get the luggage and they were moving along. In the lift, Io and Euro smiled shyly at Caspia's attention, maneuvering toward her and away from Alesta Eve, who pulled herself along by hooking her crowbar around the holdbars.

"Euro and Io? Where are Ganymede and Callisto?" Caspia asked in jest.

"On S-Tro Base, doctor," Euro answered politely.

"Oh," Caspia was taken aback, but then smiled kindly. "You two are far from home, aren't you?"

"Yes, doctor," they nodded sadly.

As the lift descended to the shuttle hangar, Alesta Eve pressed a button in the curved handle of her crowbar. A recessed trigger popped out. Then the crowbar unfolded into two halves, attached by a bar across the center.

"An air jet walker?" Io whispered.

Euro smiled, like he thought it might be fun.

"Well, we've been here two years. I'm glad to be leaving," Caspia continued, speaking to the twins, "Big Adventure!"

Zahar noticed Thayne nodding unconsciously. *What adventure was he scheming?*

On the *Cheetah*, Lanezi in his dress clothes and pilot's jacket joined Melawn, Nkiroo, and Dr. Tenshi at the lift airlock to greet the new crew. He steadied the pups against the wall by the holdbar to make them seem more orderly. That lasted five seconds.

"There will be three new crew," Melawn quietly warned them.

"Three?" Nkiroo repeated. "Did he sound happy about that?"

"No," Melawn said and frowned. "We were cleared for two, a recently retired pilot named Evan and his wife, Caspia, a doctor."

"Do you know what her specialty is?" Tenshi asked.

"Nanosurgery, implants," Melawn answered. "She helps the retirement center remove implants. Except Evan still has his implants. They believe there is hope for him. Caspia also works at the Teen Training Center installing implants. Of course, there's not much need for that now, so she can join us."

"Who is the third?" Lanezi asked.

"He didn't say." Whenever Melawn or Nkiroo said just 'he' they meant Thayne, as if there were only one 'he' in the universe.

By this time, the four pups had drifted back up the rimway. "They don't seem to like it here," Lanezi murmured to Whisper, who was in his chest pocket.

"Too far from the kitchen," Nkiroo suggested. They snickered. Then the outer lock clanged and Whisper shivered. *The noise*, Lanezi realized, and decided not to call the pups back.

The door opened. Io and Euro sprang out, split apart and swung to the sides like some parade escort. Their expressions were unreadable, but they steadied themselves against the wall as if a cargo launcher were behind them.

With good reason, Lanezi discovered, as a person with a propulsion contraption jetted past them, zoomed several meters down the rimway, did a full flip and twist to come to a standing position facing them, the contraption suctioning itself to the deck with a slurp and a clunk.

Whisper dived deeper into Lanezi's jacket. Lanezi and Melawn grabbed each other to steady themselves after their instinctive recoils.

Thayne calmly, politely, as if infinite patience had been his life-long virtue, indicated the woman, "Alesta Eve will be joining us."

After a beat of stunned silence, there were introductions and attempts at small talk while the teens secured the luggage outside the lock.

As commanding as Alesta Eve was, Lanezi could not take his eyes off Evan. He was overstuffed. The many pockets of his big coat, vest, and cargo pants bulged. Evan seemed to go from dreamy to slightly-focused-but-slow, tentatively shaking hands. *A wanderer*, Lanezi thought, *but not crazy, not like my parents. Why?* Lanezi cleared his tightening throat to greet Evan.

"Lanezi," Evan said in a soft voice. "I know you," but they had never met. Evan smiled down at Whisper. "Here," he said, producing a podpup treat from one of his pockets, even though he had no podpup of his own. Whisper nodded approval anyway and took it.

"Good Evan," she whispered.

Alesta Eve radiated impatience as they all worked their way to her and proceeded up the rimway. "When are we leaving for OSRI?"

"Tomorrow," Thayne assured her.

"Why not now?"

"We have dinner prepared for you," Thayne said politely. She didn't look like she was going to accept that when Nkiroo jumped in.

"Also some last minute cargo,"

"And we need to have our classified briefing," Melawn added.

"First thing in the morning then?" she insisted.

"Yes, of course," Thayne soothed.

Evan had floated ahead and run into the four pups, who headed straight for his pocket of treats. He greeted them joyfully, "Look at their colors. How did you do it?" he asked Lanezi. *How does he know they're all bonded to me?* Then Evan opened his jacket and pulled a fan of color cards from an inside pocket, spreading it out and holding it up to the pups.

"He likes colors," Caspia said.

"Always stuff in the pockets. He's insane," Alesta said, not so quietly. "See what the wandering does."

"Actually, he was like that before," Caspia said gently.

Alesta Eve switched subjects. "You didn't color those pups," she declared. "They're alien pups from the wreck."

"Yes," Lanezi confirmed.

"You went aboard the alien ship."

"Yes," Nkiroo answered.

"You better get to the briefing fast, Captain. We have no time for dinner."

Lanezi glanced back down the rimway. Zahar and the twins had not budged. "Coming to dinner?" he asked.

All three gave terrified shakes of their heads.

"Luggage," Zahar pointed.

"Luggage," Io and Euro repeated.

"We're on it," Zahar gave a tight smile.

"Lanezi!" Alesta Eve barked.

He jerked and tried to cover the awkwardness with a more graceful turn.

"Yes."

"Brief me on the ship while we go."

You're not touching the ship. "Yes, honor."

Whisper crawled out of his jacket and launched toward the teens, the four pups shooting after her.

Alesta Eve grilled them through the whole dinner. Lanezi managed to excuse himself early. He had a reason she approved of, to be ready for a morning departure. He stayed awake though, and sure enough, later, Melawn called him to come to Thayne's cabin.

An amazingly calm Thayne hung in his sleeping sack while the rest of the original senior crew strapped to chairs and hold-bars in his large Captain's cabin.

"Sorry about the surprise, but it will work to our advantage," Thayne said. "I had thought to use Evan as a test pilot, but we can use Alesta Eve instead. She's focused all of the time."

"She's focused all right," Tenshi agreed. "Was she retired for age?"

"At 75? Of course not." Thayne hesitated. "The various reasons for retirement are confidential, but due to our special project, I was allowed to see limited records. Evan was a mid jumper inappropriately pressured by his captain into making a long jump. They believe he will have a full recovery. Most new long jumpers have a wandering stage. Evan's is the longest on record. However, it seems he was somewhat eccentric to start with." The others nodded.

"Alesta Eve was retired for recklessness. She jumped from RJ to Harbor—"

Lanezi and the others gasped. "Impossible," Lanezi objected.

"True fact, confirmed—and confidential of course."

"She made a successful jump between Radium Junction and Harbor? That's longer than the desperation jumps after Fire-light." Lanezi was incredulous.

"Successful is probably not the best term. Alesta Eve and the ship arrived in one piece. All crew and four passengers recessed but lived. No one knew she was going to try it. She is unre-morseful and angry about being grounded. It was Caspia who recommended her. Alesta Eve fears nothing."

"Sounds dangerous," Tenshi cautioned.

"I agree, but useful for our purposes. We need someone who believes in the unbelievable. And don't worry, I gave her a level 7 s'link."

"How did she take that?" Tenshi asked.

"She was pleased. Well, as pleased as I think she would ever admit. They don't have any s'links at the retirement center. I believe she thinks she will work her way up."

Lanezi frowned. "Did you give Evan a s'link?"

"Not yet."

Tenshi went wide-eyed. "You're going to?"

"You haven't seen him in his rational stage. The wandering is only 30% of the time. He's perfectly sensible otherwise. You'll see."

There were nervous looks all around.

"Meanwhile," Thayne glanced at the doctor, "I've suggested a project to Caspia . . . that she investigate tuning the implants to alternate frequencies, so she'll need a clean lab."

"I'd recommend Arc 6 or 9," Dr. Tenshi said. "The furry ones don't go past the lift lock or the Command Bay."

"Investigate?" Lanezi questioned as Melawn threw him a please-be-less-suspicious look.

"Yes, it's our theory that pilots could find jump paths at higher or lower harmonics."

"But you need a person to find them," Lanezi said, alarmed.

"Yes," Thayne assured him. "Evan has agreed to feel out the paths."

"Evan isn't in his right mind," Tenshi objected.

"Doctor, we didn't ask him while he was wandering. Wait. You'll see."

"Still . . ."

"Doctor, no harm can come to him from just listening or feeling for the resonance waves while we increase in speed. We will have Lanezi to rely on for the actual jumps."

"I thought you were building a-rings," Tenshi objected.

"We have several projects, doctor," Thayne said mysteriously. "The future of the outer sectors is at stake. Evan and Caspia understand that."

. . .

19-Words

"Blueberry! In the box!" Lanezi pointed to the jump box in the Command Bay where the other four podpups had obediently gone. Blue rolled around in mid air, pretending to be oblivious. *I don't have time for this. Alesta Eve will be storming about any delay. Thank heavens no one is around—*

"Hi," came a soft voice at the airlock, startling Lanezi.

"Evan."

"Sorry, I didn't mean to . . ." He trailed off.

Lanezi waved him inside. Hesitant, he maneuvered gracefully into the Command Bay. Lanezi could see that he was focused and rational, just as Thayne had claimed. Taking in the situation instantly, Evan pulled treats out of his pocket and rewarded the four pups in the box. Blue made a squeak as if her feelings were hurt and reached out for Lanezi, who allowed her to grab his finger.

"Blue good," she claimed as Lanezi towed her gently to the box and her treat.

"Thanks," Lanezi said to Evan and then realized why he would have come. "Did you want to . . . join us for the trip?"

"Yes! Please! I mean, if it's okay."

Lanezi couldn't help smiling as he indicated the co-pilot chair.

"Oh, thank you, thank you," Evan gushed. He strapped in. His pockets were arranged to fit between the straps. *I'm surrounded by eccentrics*, Lanezi thought. But it was comforting to have Evan there. He had not had a co-pilot since Bennezi— actually Lanezi had been the co-pilot for in-system flights.

"By-the-book today," Lanezi explained to Evan as Nkiroo came in and they verified that the extra computer programs were suspended, except, of course, the super mysterious one. The undock was uneventful and the ride to OSRI was long and boring, just as Lanezi had hoped. Evan sat quietly, not interfering, but soaking it all in.

OSRI was part giant hangar, part manufacturing plant and had a small habitat where Jamez and about 60 workers stayed. It was cluttered with miscellaneous shuttles and ship sections. The hangar was bigger than the ship-building hangars in Sector 2. It had to be in order to build a-ring segments, which were bigger than ships. Grand plans had once existed for Harbor.

"Did they ever even build ships here?" Evan asked Nkiroo.

"No. Just repair. And our classified work. But it may achieve its ship-building potential yet. If we can successfully build a-ring segments, this will be a valuable asset to the sectors."

The hangar itself was a huge curved lattice, with rails and piers so small by comparison that they looked like lines etched on the surface. The bright hangar lights overshone any starlight that may have peeked in from behind the lattice.

"How many ships can dock?" Evan asked.

"Ten big ones. Or a couple hundred shuttles. We should have plenty of room, even if Swooper hangs around," Nkiroo said.

As they drew closer, Lanezi focused on the docking procedure and Evan and Nkiroo were mesmerized by the scene at the hangar. It was mind-boggling, even for those who had been up close to the a-rings. Jamez had an a-ring segment, fully built and expanded, illumined as if ready for christening. He must have arranged the display for Thayne. It was stunning.

"You said . . . you had two . . . aboard the ship," Evan puzzled.

"Yes, collapsed," Nkiroo said modestly.

"Nkiroo's engineering," Lanezi explained. "Our a-ring

segments don't have solid walls like the alien ones. They have lattice walls that collapse into a quarter-cylinder and then collapse telescope-like into a large quarter-circle. Once at the location, it's all expanded. The torus for the particles is manufactured on the spot with grown crystal."

"Incredible. Amazing."

"But Evan," Lanezi took a chance that Evan wouldn't be offended, "it won't fit in your pocket."

Evan laughed gently and turned to Nkiroo. "Maybe a small model?" Nkiroo laughed, but Evan was completely earnest.

4-Perfection

Cheetah at OSRI

The next day, Swooper brought in the wreck with the alien gravity ball. Lanezi was invited to "document" the interior. Surprised and pleased, he went with Melawn, Nkiroo, Jamez, and two of Jamez's assistants. Aside from the bio cleanup crew, Thayne had forbidden anyone else, especially Swooper's tuggers, to go aboard. They wanted full documentation, but Thayne made it clear to Lanezi that his job was not scientific, it was to photograph for "posterity." Thayne even provided an expensive camera. *He plans ahead.*

Melawn told Lanezi that when he had been aboard immediately after the accident, there had still been emergency power and lighting. Those had long since ceased to function. The biohazard crew had only used head lamps, reporting that it was extremely dark and spooky. *Especially when you're looking for bodies.* Lanezi had a little shudder. He was happy that Thayne had agreed to let Jamez go in yesterday and set up lighting. Jamez was obviously enthusiastic about lighting.

Melawn led them straight to what he called the Gravity Ball

Chamber through a propped-open airlock. Lanezi had imagined a powerful, majestic, mysterious, gleaming black gravity ball floating free in the center of an immense cavern, but when Jamez turned on the lights Lanezi was disappointed, even disturbed. The chamber, although beautifully finished, was hardly bigger than the gravity ball. The gravity ball itself was suspended in a giant dull black net, actually, layers of interlocking nets, which held it prisoner in the ship.

"Captured," Lanezi murmured.

"What?" Thayne asked curiously.

"The purple people didn't make the gravity ball—they captured it and now hold it prisoner to do their bidding." The others were stunned and silent. Finally Melawn said, "I think you're right. I didn't see it that way before, although the technologies are obviously different."

"What kind of people would stick an alien gravity ball inside their ship?" Nkiroo asked. "But I think you're right."

"Yes," Melawn was looking at the netting. "And of course, the netting was destroyed at the Hamada wreck, so I had a different impression."

"The netting was gone?" Jamez asked.

"No, ripped to shreds. I didn't even know what it was for. The chamber itself was half-gone. The gravity ball was almost free."

Free.

"So the Hamada gravity ball was damaged?" Jamez asked.

"Not that we could see."

"But it must have taken a severe hit."

"Yes, it must have. They are apparently very durable."

"But we don't know about internal damage then?" Jamez continued.

"No," Melawn admitted. "We don't know about internal anything."

"That's why it's such a confirmation of our work to get this pristine one," Thayne said.

Confirmation?

Lanezi floated around, at first taking obvious 'artistic' and 'historical' type photos, then slowly getting a feel for the scope of the chamber, the beautiful machinery of the purple people, and for the restrained and shrouded gravity ball.

Thayne hung in place, gently bobbing on his tether while the others worked to measure, document, and investigate. He seemed to be in deep contemplation, so Lanezi was slightly startled to hear his private channel click on and Thayne's voice. "Yes, Lanezi, you are right. Such a majestic entity should not be held captive here. Soon, very soon now, we will set it—and all humanity—free."

17-Perfection

Cheetah at OSRI

Zahar was heading up the stairs to the Med Bay when Caspia found her. It had taken a couple weeks to set up a clean lab for Caspia's work in Arc 9. Caspia didn't want to be anywhere near the "fur and fuzz zone," as she called it.

"So what are you up to this morning?" Caspia asked.

"I have to feed the rats first. The twins usually feed them, but Thayne has them on some special work this morning."

"They haven't finished the passenger chairs."

"I know, but we're not going to use them for more than a year, so it doesn't matter."

Caspia scowled. Although Caspia was friendly when Zahar first met her, she now frowned with disapproval half the time. Was she unhappy on the *Cheetah*? Was it not what she expected? Or did she just not approve of her?

"What is Tenshi doing that requires *animal* testing?" Caspia asked. More disapproval.

"She uses the rats to model Euro and Io. She's trying to find out what makes them radiation resistant and why that shortens their lives. They have GGE Syndrome."

"Oh. How are Io and Euro doing?"

"No signs of premature aging—yet. Dr. Tenshi checks the rats' genes, their brains, growth, and aging symptoms. Sometimes she blasts them with radiation. Sometimes they don't come back."

Caspia nodded sympathetically. "It's hard to work in medical research."

Zahar tried to hide a wince. "I know." But she didn't tell Caspia that she wasn't here by choice.

The rats only had numbers, except in Zahar's mind, #12 was Zombie. Zahar tried hard not to notice their individual markings, their diverse personalities, their attachments to each other or how the mutant rats were so much sweeter and gentler, like Io and Euro. She tried not to notice when they disappeared and she tried not to notice when they looked into her eyes, asking for their lost ones.

She opened the EEHAB door. Although they were adapted to nogee, they would still climb all over people. They scampered out, clinging to Zahar's sleeves and uniform front.

"These are the mutant rats." Zahar scooped one up and gently transferred it to Caspia.

"They're small."

"Yes, small, dark shiny skin, blackish-green fur, slightly pointed ears. Elf-rats. Very much like Euro and Io."

"Reduced life-span?"

"Yes. They are born small and don't grow much, but they don't show any signs of premature aging until after reaching maturity. Dr. Tenshi has been working on two angles, trying to lengthen the adolescence, and trying to identify and separate the radiation protection from the premature aging."

"And she hasn't figured anything out yet?"

"Well, I don't know the details, but she's had some progress stretching the adolescence."

"That's not going to help for long."

Zahar shrugged, not knowing if Caspia was disapproving again or just being a doctor. Caspia handed the rat back to Zahar. It dove into her sleeve and scurried up to her elbow to hide. "They get one treat and then go into the nogee exercise module."

Zahar peeled one rat off her shoulder, gave it a carrot slice, which it devoured in four seconds, and let it go in the play zone. Once all the rats got in, it was a riot of movement. The rats had no trouble in nogee and even seemed to enjoy launching themselves into each other and tumbling around. Caspia laughed, her disapproval disappearing faster than the carrots.

Lanezi burst in the door with his parade of pups, clearly agitated. "Where's Tenshi?"

Zahar pointed to the lab.

Caspia was already grabbing a med kit when Tenshi came out. "I'm right here. What's wrong?"

Lanezi turned on the main screen while the two doctors and Zahar floated over. "I can't believe you gave Io and Euro permission!"

They stared at the screen, Zahar comprehending the scene and Lanezi's anger right away. The twins were doing an EVA on the newly-freed gravity ball. Not near it. On it.

"I didn't send them out there," Tenshi said, puzzled.

"Thayne did!"

"Well, they are certified EVA workers," Tenshi argued. "And they're 15 now, so they don't need permission from their caretaker."

"No one—" Lanezi stopped to calm himself. "No one really

knows much about the gravity balls or how dangerous they might be."

"I'm sure Thayne wouldn't send them out there if it were not safe," Caspia said. *She doesn't know Thayne.*

Zahar reached over and turned up the audio. Io was sprawled face down on the gravity ball, his excited voice saying "I can see inside!"

"The camera's not getting anything," Thayne was saying. "What do you see?"

Euro joined Io and held his big light right above the surface of the gravity ball. Nothing reflected back. It was as if the light soaked right in.

"It's empty," Io said.

"Empty?" Everyone repeated.

"Well, there are some small shadowy things in the middle," Euro clarified.

"I'm sure this has been done before," Tenshi said. "Lanezi, they sound fine. Let them have their adventure." *While they can.*

"Maybe there are exotic particles you can't see." Thayne mused.

"Maybe it's full of 8th dimension!" Io agreed.

Lanezi threw up his hands, losing Whisper in the nogee. "God help us. Next he'll tell them to cut a doorway in it."

"Well, wouldn't that make sense?" Tenshi asked.

"No!" Caspia, Lanezi, and Zahar all answered together.

"Tamper with an alien device?" Lanezi protested.

"Just because it's alien doesn't make it dangerous. No one has ever been hurt by a gravity ball—aside from flying into one, of course. Look!" Tenshi pointed to the pups, who had undone the latches of the play area and joined the rats, colorful furry giants among the small dark mutants. "You're not worried about the podpups and they're alien."

Lanezi shook his head sharply, grabbing the desk for stability. "No," he objected. "*God* made the podpups. *Aliens* made the gravity balls."

Aliens that are long gone.

8-Names

Since Katie had left the *Cheetah*, Lanezi only had the feeling of work, not family, of toil and stress, not love and acceptance. Things were exciting sometimes, but not in a good way. Now, since the gravity ball had been set free, the whole atmosphere of working on the *Cheetah* changed. It was almost as if Thayne had been freed along with the gravity ball. Thayne, Nkiroo, and Melawn were in their element, their individual and united genius pulsing with ideas, discoveries, and pure number crunching, theory-building power.

Evening meals were alive with the latest news and discussions. Everyone on the crew was on the same program. Even Alesta Eve, although she kept up her disgruntled exterior, would follow the daily events with excitement-fueled impatience. If they hadn't been classified, daily breakthroughs would have been headlines.

Jamez had finished the six a-ring segments and placed them around the mini-gravity ball that they took from the ship. The model a-ring structure was stationed at a safe distance. The segments were lit like jewels, surrounding the nearly-invisible gravity ball.

From his position in the Observation Lounge, with his nose pressed right up to the window, Lanezi could only see the black silhouette where the gravity ball blocked light from the background segment.

The gravity ball frequency and packeting format had been

broken by Melawn's program. The icons on the control panel had been tentatively interpreted, and the possible commands related to each button proposed. They had reached the stage of testing the command codes. And it was here that Lanezi, despite all the excitement and camaraderie, found himself stepping back, as if from a flimsy guardrail at the top of a work tower.

"Jamez agrees," Melawn announced at dinner. "Ten hundred, we'll test the control panel on the mini gravity ball."

"Tomorrow?" Euro and Io bounced around in excitement, setting off the pups.

"About time!" Alesta Eve glowered, but Thayne only smiled.

"Yes," he agreed. "Jamez will have his people clear, but ready to stabilize manually if necessary."

"We should celebrate," Io suggested, angling for ice cream, as usual.

"Maybe we should see what happens first," Lanezi suggested quietly.

The others dismissed his caution.

"No," Thayne agreed, "Lanezi is right. We stand on the eve of all possibilities. Tomorrow we can celebrate our actual success."

9-Names

Lanezi was stationed in the *Cheetah* Command Bay during the control panel test. Evan, in full focus, was with him. Everyone in the OSRI environs was in a secure place, 'Everyone ready for everything,' as Jamez had ordered. Lanezi was on the live link with Jamez at the OSRI hangar, Thayne and Nkiroo suited up at the alien control panel, still inside the alien wreck, and Melawn in an observation shuttle *Rhim*, with Alesta Eve piloting.

Zahar stood by in the *Cheetah* hangar, ready to escort patients. She had wanted to be on the medical shuttle, but Jamez insisted that he had faster mini-shuttles. The rest of the *Cheetah* crew, including pups, watched from the Observation Lounge.

Lanezi studied the screen showing the alien control panel. Thayne and his team had decided that the large green button at the top was a master shutoff. Thayne and Melawn had done experiments on the alien podpups, wondering if they retained any memory of the color instincts of their people. There was a strong reaction for them to stop what they were doing with a green flash. The twins also reported that the babies would flash green when they didn't want something.

Underneath the master shutoff, there were 18 circles all colored the same, pink on the left, green on the right. As the top master button was green, the crew surmised that these 18 were on/off controls. But why have 18 on/off buttons?

Next were six square orange buttons with what seemed to be a gravity ball in the center of each, larger for each button. The last two of those buttons were encased in a locked transparent cover. Obviously, the aliens did not want to use those accidentally.

Underneath those was a black circle, presumably a gravity ball, with three parentheses next to it. They speculated that this was a "Send the signal" button, but had low confidence. Next was a gravity ball surrounded by six segments. For this, there was high confidence that it would turn on the a-rings.

Under that was another locked button with, despite Thayne's skepticism, what looked like a destruct icon: gravity ball exploding or gravity ball becoming a star. Either way, Lanezi was grateful the aliens had locked up the dangerous buttons, giving the humans a bit more confidence to press the others.

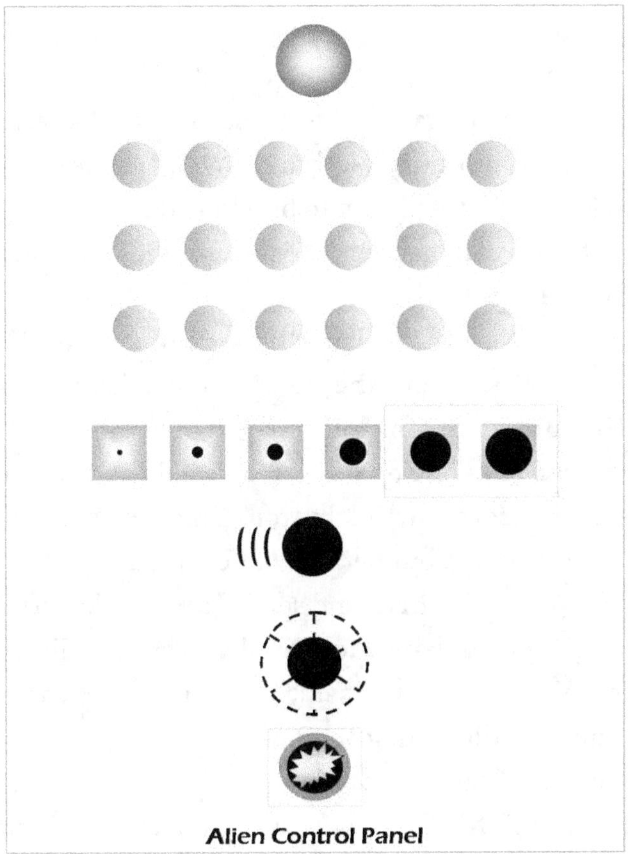

Alien Control Panel

"Skipping master button. First square button," Nkiroo warned them. Evan and Lanezi had ten screens up. Scanning them quickly, they shook their heads at each other. "Nothing," Lanezi said.

"Detecting your signal, but no sign of response," Melawn reported from the *Rhim*.

"One minute," Nkiroo reported. They waited a full twenty minutes before going to plan B.

"First pink semicircle," Nkiroo announced.

"No reaction," Melawn reported.

Twenty minutes.

"Send command button," Thayne ordered.

Since they really had no idea what it was, Lanezi held his breath. Twenty minutes. Nothing. "Well," Lanezi whispered offline to Evan, "this could get to be a long day."

"Something will happen," Evan assured him, eyes never leaving the screens.

Proceeding with their plan, Nkiroo moved on to the second pink semicircle, skipping the green semicircles unless all the pink failed. After each pink button, he'd press the 'send' button. After the third pink button, they shortened the wait time to 10 minutes. By the seventh pink button, Lanezi was hoping they'd shorten it to 1 minute, but he tried to be patient.

"Eighth pink semicircle, and send button," Nkiroo said.

Lanezi imagined that he felt the slightest little dip.

"Something," Melawn said, hesitant. "Mixed readings. Sensors showing different g-forces—"

"It's moving!" Jamez broke in.

"Off button!" Nkiroo announced. Lanezi was scanning his screens. The gravity ball had moved toward the source, the alien wreck. *Cheetah* was far enough away not to be in danger.

"It stopped," Melawn reported, "Full stop, velocity zero."

Sighs came over all the speakers. "Clarifying," Nkiroo reported. "That was the matching green semicircle, not the master button, which stopped it."

"God in Heaven," Thayne was saying. "No sign of thrusters. It must have moved by changing the gravity field around itself. Incredible."

"The gravity ball is still on," Melawn reported. "Sensors on all sides now read .015g. Recommend 1st square button."

Lanezi had been about to recommend a break.

"No stopping them now," Evan sympathized.

After a brief consultation, Thayne agreed.

"First square button, again."

Only a second later, Lanezi definitely felt a dip, as if he were in a lift that had dropped an inch and settled.

"Did you feel that?" Thayne asked.

"Yes," everyone answered.

"We didn't press the send button," Nkiroo reported. "And the gravity ball is not moving this time."

"It's not a send message button," Evan said a bit sternly. "It's a *come here* button. You better not press it again."

There were several moments of silence while they contemplated that. "Agreed," Thayne said.

"*Cheeta*h, stationkeeping on screen 7, priority monitoring," Lanezi ordered.

"No adjustment needed at this time."

"That last increase was to .15g, tenfold increase." Melawn reported.

"So the pink turned it on, the parenthesis called it over, the matching green button made it stop and then we were able to use the square button, once it was on. But why have so many on/off pairs?" Jamez asked.

"Could there be eighteen kinds of gravity balls?" Melawn speculated.

"Well, we know there are two kinds," Thayne said.

"If we've interpreted this correctly," Nkiroo continued, "the second square button will give us more gravity."

"*Cheetah*, be sure to use the Harbor beacons for stationkeeping," Lanezi ordered.

"Second square button."

Another dip.

".45g, a threefold increase."

"So we can't predict what the next one will be," Nkiroo warned.

"Third square button," Thayne had taken over. Determination rang in his voice. Lanezi was thankful those other buttons were locked.

Another dip.

".75g."

"Standby for stationkeeping burn."

Evan and Lanezi were now distracted from the button pushing by double-checking the *Cheetah's* position. In the back of his mind, Lanezi could hear Thayne and Nkiroo discussing whether to try the next highest gravity or go for broke and push the suspected a-ring activator.

"Jamez here. Segments need to be repositioned and stabilized. Fifteen minutes."

"Melawn," Nkiroo advised, "we want you to back up to position two."

"They're going to try it!" Evan whispered.

"Well, everything is working. Nothing bizarre is happening . . ." Lanezi trailed off. He didn't sound so convinced himself.

It was a good 25 minutes before Jamez was satisfied that the segment positions were exact. "Ready."

"Lanezi?"

"No problems here," he reported.

"Pressing a-ring activator."

Another dip. Again, Lanezi and Evan were distracted by checking beacons.

".91g, standard gravity ball," Melawn advised, "from all sensors."

"Feedback from segment A—" Melawn reported.

"Segment A is moving!" Jamez called. "It adjusted by 1.7 meters and stopped."

"The other segments are adjusting by similar amounts," Melawn reported.

It's going to work!

"Test objects moving!" Jamez announced.

Lanezi could see the slight glow in the tori indicating that the a-rings were really working. Then the torus of Segment B broke off the front of the tunnel segment, sending both parts careening out of control.

"Shutoff button," Thayne ordered.

The glowing stopped immediately.

"Clarification:" announced Nkiroo, "that was the specific shutoff button, not the master shutoff."

"All stopped except B torus, B segment and 3 test objects," Melawn reported. "All sensors report .015g. That seems to be the base level."

"Radiation?" Thayne asked.

"None that we can detect." Melawn answered.

"I'm going in for the parts," Jamez announced. Mini-shuttles rocketed out of the hangar wall.

"It's going to work!" Thayne exulted.

Lanezi hung stunned in his seat. Humanity had commanded a gravity ball. He looked at Evan, who looked puzzled. Were they all thinking the same thing? *Thayne wasn't crazy after all?*

Cheetah at OSRI

Zahar was pleased that everyone enjoyed the celebration she set up, even if it only consisted of ice cream, chocolate, and replays of the test objects shooting around the a-rings. Jamez declared he would find a better way to attach the tori to the a-ring segments and would be ready in six days. Alesta Eve scowled and complained that five should be enough.

"It was a successful day," Thayne remarked, "but our mission is to save Luminesse and reunite the sectors. This is just the first step."

"Blue!" Zahar lost the rest of the conversation while getting the ice cream back from the pups.

10-Names

The next morning, Caspia finished moving to the clean lab in the Arc 9 Med Bay, taking most of the med bots with her. Zahar was relieved she wasn't going to be assigned over there.

Even though she didn't like the rat experiments, she didn't want to miss out on the daily activity in Arc 1.

Evan's implant surgery was scheduled for the next day. They were just moving a last load of equipment when Zahar asked Caspia about the surgery. "We're not going to move the implants—that's the dangerous part of the surgery. We're just adding a variable resonance wave sensor and some nanobots for special procedures."

"Nanobots?" Zahar asked. "In his brain? What if they get away?"

"This type," Caspia explained, "can only escape into a machine environment. That's why we must monitor the clean room, but they can't operate in an organic environment, so they're limited to the implant."

From the rat play area, Euro spoke up. "Callisto had nanos."

"He did?" Zahar asked.

"The organic-operable kind," Tenshi clarified.

"Why?" Zahar asked.

"It was just an experiment, to see if his brain would track a little better," Euro said.

"But it didn't work," Io added.

"Why not?"

"The implants bothered him," Euro said.

"He said they talked too much," Io said with disapproval.

Caspia's stunned and unbelieving look didn't bother the twins. Apparently they were used to it.

Tenshi took a practical approach. "What do nano-brained robots have to talk about?"

"Callisto wouldn't say," Io answered.

"Their existence is minimal, insignificant," Tenshi said. "They are nano!"

"Well, in the big scheme of the universe, we're all insignificant," Euro reasoned.

"And we talk!" Io concluded.

"We are not nano!" Tenshi insisted in her no nonsense way.

"Maybe they just do math at each other," Zahar suggested.

"Maybe," Euro agreed. "Calli was good at math."

"Maybe he had help," Io said to Euro.

"That's why he wouldn't tell us," Euro agreed and they nodded in unison.

Caspia slowly nodded her head with them. Zahar smiled. If Caspia married Evan, the pocket person, she could accept the twins and their eccentricities. Although, Zahar had to admit, many times, Io and Euro seemed wiser than anyone.

13-Names

Two days after the surgery, Evan was transferred to Arc 1 and became Zahar's patient. Caspia stayed with him most of the time, so Zahar really had no work.

"What's that?" Zahar asked, as Caspia pulled a bulky blanket out of Evan's things.

"His pocket blanket." She floated it over Evan. Zahar grabbed one side to hook it down. It was covered with pockets, all full and zipped shut.

"He has more stuff?"

"No, it's the same stuff. He puts it in the blanket at night. I thought we should put it on him since he's been waking up more often."

"Was he always like this—with the pockets?"

"Since childhood."

"Was he an orphan?"

"No. No trauma anyone knows of."

Evan groaned, "I'm asleep."

"Yes, dear," Caspia agreed, patting his hand.

Evan patted one of the pockets and faded back to sleep.

15-Names

Evan was a pleasure to have in the Med Bay. When he was wandering, he was mellow and had a sense of spiritual meditation around him, which Zahar found very peaceful. When he was focused, he read, enjoyed visits from the twins, held the rats, or quietly looked at his pocket things.

"Can we see?" Io asked innocently.

"Of course." And as much as Zahar scolded herself for being drawn into a material thing, she couldn't resist. Evan was truly loaded with treasure.

In addition to the podpup snacks, and practical items like sliders, a pencil, pocketknife, tricky little tools, p'link, his color cards, first aid kit, headset, small notes, scarf and gloves, breather, sector map, magnifying glass, sample bag, and flashlight, he had very personal and odd things. He had a prayer book that was overstuffed with added prayers and notes. He had small colored rocks, a lacquered box that played music when opened, compact games and cards, a small book about vegetables with seeds taped in it, a prism, a magnet, a piece of art he called a dream catcher, and the most stunning thing, a long hexagonal crystal that showed six views of Earth.

Zahar and the twins rotated it in wonder. Each of the six scenes looked so real. Snow fell on a forest of green trees, a great blue-green sea lapped at a sandy shore, brilliant pink flowers flowed over rolling hills, red towers of rock rose from a purple desert, the yellow orange sun of Earth set behind a field of waving golden grain, and a multi-colored bird took flight in a deep green jungle, flicking a spray of water from the disturbed branch. There was an intensity to it that Zahar had never seen in movies, triggering something that those movies never had, a longing to see Earth.

16-Names

"Good," was Alesta Eve's hardly-considered comment about Nkiroo's masterfully designed shuttle, *Frontier*, after a short shakedown flight.

Good? echoed in Melawn's head. It was the most exquisitely engineered shuttle in human history. It was the only shuttle in the outer sectors built in the last 30 years. It was beyond machine; it was art with a propulsion system.

"It'll fly—that's all I need. When do I—we—get in the a-rings?"

"Tomorrow," Thayne answered, surprising her for once, "but only five laps."

"Five?"

He gave her a warning look.

"Fine. Five."

Melawn wished he could pilot a shuttle, at least beyond basic flying. That way, he could do whatever Thayne wanted and he would appreciate the honor of such service.

18-Names

"Slowly and carefully, but with a purpose," Thayne was saying. Melawn listened intently and glanced at Nkiroo, who was nodding in acceptance. "Alesta Eve will pilot the shuttle. Evan will ride with her, open to any impressions. We'll start with ten to fifteen percent of jump velocity, then increase by about a tenth JV every four days. That should give them enough time to rest."

"Whether they like it or not," Nkiroo added.

Thayne rolled his eyes. "They are both most energetic, if differently expressed. I'm setting the goal to proceed through the speed test and the two-shuttle tests in 40 days. We should have all the information we need by then."

"Forty days?" Melawn asked, wondering if Thayne had picked it for its religious significance.

"Yes," Thayne nodded, "We will then embark on our great journey."

Melawn floated back to his cabin, attempting to dodge Lanezi and the five pups in the rimway, who insisted on pestering him no matter how much he remained aloof. In the seclusion of his cabin, he picked multicolored fuzz off his clothes and rolled it into a pea-sized ball. *The filters must be clogging. We could sell it for quilts.* It was fortunate they had Alesta Eve, as Lanezi was too obstinate and distracted for the work.

Forty Days. It reminded him of his hero, Mullá Husayn, who before setting off on his great search, fasted and prayed for forty days. Suddenly, Melawn was filled with a soul-stirring idea. He would fast for forty days. Mullá Husayn had then set out on his quest—the quest which ended in the most dramatic moment in history—his discovery of the Promised One.

What will we discover? Melawn knew that Thayne's ambitions extended far beyond the stated goal of saving Luminesse and reuniting the sectors. Understanding the gravity balls would give them the freedom of the galaxy. Thayne, Nkiroo, and Melawn were in complete agreement with Alesta Eve on one issue: that longer jumps were possible. But Thayne has some other great mission on his mind. *The builders? Making more a-ring systems? Finding more gravity balls?*

As Melawn set in mind the goal of fasting for forty days, he also puzzled over why Thayne didn't tell him. It wasn't that he questioned Thayne. It was the slightest little hurt, something he thought he was above, yet he could not help wonder why Thayne did not confide in him, his most trusted, most loyal servant.

4-Might

Keeping his fast a secret was not difficult for Melawn. Their work schedule was hectic. Dinner was always late, after official Harbor 'sunset'. And he was often out in the observation shuttle, *Rhim*, following the tests.

Melawn had asked Jamez for a pilot rather than deal with Lanezi. Jamez had assigned two young women, 20-year-olds by their armbands. One was a pilot, the other a monitor, but they were so alike that at first Melawn thought they were sisters. Both had the dark dark skin that reminded him of Katie, *Cheetah*'s former doctor, but they were as towering as Katie was tiny. Their hair was done identically in long thin braids with beads and bells on the ends. They chattered and snacked all day. They clapped and chanted, both songs and sacred Writings, shaking their many bracelets in time. *They will never sneak up on anyone.*

When Melawn had asked if they were sisters, "We are all sisters," they proclaimed.

"We are fruits of one tree."

"We are leaves of one branch."[1]

"We are waves..."[2]

And then it was a chant and then a song, but the panel

would beep and they would pause, and with a shake of the bracelets, serenely turn to business.

Oddly enough, their voices were completely different. Pongola, the pilot, had the deep mellow tones of a tenor sax, while Magadi had a sweet birdsong of a voice, perfect for a monitor. Gola and Gadi, they called themselves. Sisters of the shuttle, Melawn called them.

The .10-.15 JV test went exactly as planned, with no trouble reaching the velocity and no trouble with the tori. Alesta Eve veered out of the rings at exactly .15 JV and flew in a wide circle while Evan meditated at that speed. The problem was, they had to use their own fuel to decelerate as the a-rings did not work in reverse. At .15 JV that wasn't a problem, but they would not be able to test more than .5 JV. Even that would be a difficult and dangerous deceleration.

"We're making a supply run," Gola said when they were done observing. "Do you want to come?"

"Oh, no. Thank you," Melawn said, thinking it was too bad they couldn't just send Alesta Eve since she had built up all that speed.

"We've got to get Kosi's new song," Gadi reminded Gola.

"Yes!" And the bracelets went dancing on the way back to OSRI.

8-Might

Days later, after the second test, Melawn stayed with Thayne for his debriefing of Alesta Eve and Evan. It was Evan that Thayne showed more interest in, closely questioning him about the .25 JV laps.

"Nothing," Evan was saying. "Even if I run the tuner up and down a bit. It all seems like normal space to me."

Alesta Eve was bored. "Why all this *slow* testing? It works. Let's just go for the jump."

"Patience," Thayne advised. "After all, I haven't acquired a spare ship, part of the problem with the convoy, and you can't go jumping in a shuttle."

"They're going to give you a ship?" Melawn asked, impressed.

"The need will become obvious. Nkiroo," Thayne turned to him, "do you think a tug could be modified?"

Nkiroo smiled in commiseration, but shook his head. "No. We need cargo room for supplies. It's not the jump. It's the possibility of a long run in on the arrival side."

Thayne and Alesta Eve both scowled, but for once, Alesta Eve didn't argue.

12-Might

The trouble with this fasting, Melawn thought, now that he was on his 13th day, was first, that it would not be over on the 19th day, like the annual fast, and second, he wasn't doing the praying that went with it. He was either working or sleeping or observing with the shuttle sisters. They had long ago given up offering him food. They devoured spicy crackers which grew more pungent the longer he fasted.

Alesta Eve and Evan tested up to .35 JV with no problems and no breakthroughs. Melawn hardly paid attention.

16-Might

Alesta Eve and Evan made it to .5 JV, with an anxious Thayne accompanying Melawn in the *Rhim*. Thayne insisted that Alesta Eve do several big laps at .5 outside the rings so Evan could have a long time, especially after he reported, "Something. No more than flickers, maybe my imagination."

Thayne went back to the *Cheetah* discouraged, but the day was saved with the news that Jamez had finished refitting a second test shuttle, the *Spring Azure*.

"You're going to let Evan fly alone?" Melawn whispered.

"Of course not," Thayne said. "Lanezi will have to do it."

"Does he know?"

"The need will become obvious."

1-Will

Melawn was tired. It was the 21st day of fasting, longer than he had ever fasted before and just over the halfway mark— the days of doubt, he reminded himself. *Persevere* . . .

He floated down to the hangar bay with Lanezi, Evan, and Alesta Eve. "We're wasting time," Alesta Eve scolded. "We're just starting over for no reason."

"The test with two shuttles is important to determine if we've got a real a-ring system, and to test the strength of the tori," Melawn practically quoted Nkiroo. He glanced between the scowling Alesta Eve and the scowling Lanezi and just could not comprehend how they did not take joy in this service.

During the test, Melawn paid close attention to the trajectories of both pilots. Surprisingly, Lanezi was the smoother of the two, especially outside, decelerating the *Spring Azure* without the severe step-breaking method that Alesta Eve favored.

Again, everything worked as hoped and Jamez reported no problems after his inspection. Melawn had the feeling that things were going too well. His fasting had not yet given him any great insights. If anything, he began to have doubts and questions. *Questions come before answers*, he reminded himself.

. . .

9-Will

Melawn was late. He'd overslept his alarm. The fast had become too much. He was a determined and disciplined person, but he was also a mathematician. He predicted that he could not complete the forty days and maintain his work schedule. As the fast was not required, he accepted its end without guilt, but with some disappointment that nothing had come of it.

He called Thayne and said he'd be late, but Thayne was supportive, giving him the day off from observing as Alesta Eve, and Evan wanted to leave early anyway. They had some theory about retuning Evan's implants near an a-ring segment. Melawn could not figure out what difference that would make. Thayne was indulging them. *Well, he's indulging me too.*

When he was finally ready, Melawn joined Thayne and Nkiroo in the Command Bay, right when the plan went off course. "She's past .5 JV. Now .53," Nkiroo reported. "Lanezi's out as ordered."

"Lanezi, get clear. She missed her exit," Thayne warned him.

"Understand." Lanezi immediately looped way out on the opposite side of the test a-rings. All Jamez's people were grounded during the test.

"*Frontier*," Nkiroo called, "report."

"It's okay," Alesta Eve answered. "Evan thinks he has something."

"At .53?" Thayne whispered, excited.

But Nkiroo frowned. "She's at .56 now." He turned back to the panel. "*Frontier*—do not exceed .6. Acknowledge."

".6. Understand."

"Where's Lanezi?" Thayne asked.

"I'll monitor Lanezi." Melawn floated into a chair, strapped, and activated a pop-up. "He's far." *He doesn't trust her.*

".61," Nkiroo whispered. "*Frontier!* Time to exit."

"He's got something!" Alesta Eve responded quickly.

Nkiroo glanced at Thayne who still looked hopeful.

"*Frontier*, time to exit, now," Nkiroo said, as if talking to an unruly podpup.

"I hear you. Let me calculate."

Suddenly all the fasting and hoping for insight came crashing down on Melawn with a terrible realization. "She's going to jump!"

Thayne and Nkiroo turned to look at Melawn as if he were insane. "Melawn," Nkiroo answered patiently, "she's in a shuttle with no supplies. She's not crazy. Besides, Evan is with her."

"Evan!" Melawn's alarm turned to horror. She would separate Evan and Caspia. He looked frantically back to his screen. "She's at .67. She's accelerating faster than she should be able to!"

Nkiroo's hands froze on the panel. "She's using the power booster we designed for the deceleration."

"No," Thayne objected. "That would be far too dangerous in the rings, even for an experienced pilot."

Nkiroo and Thayne looked back at their panels, then at each other. Thayne's hopefulness turned to suspicion.

".71," Nkiroo whispered.

"God in heaven," Thayne hissed.

"Alesta Eve!" Nkiroo started.

"Wait—" Thayne grabbed his arm. "Are you on a secure channel?"

"Yes," Nkiroo answered. No other ships or s'links could hear.

"Alesta Eve. Leave the a-rings immediately. This is a direct order."

Melawn reached for his own panel, switching to *Spring Azure's* private channel and warning Lanezi. Alesta Eve was no longer answering.

"They can't have more than a week's supply of water aboard," Nkiroo fretted.

"Alesta Eve! Answer me!" Thayne demanded and then changed tactics. "Evan! You are authorized to take command. Evan, get out of the a-rings."

"Jamez calling," Melawn relayed to Thayne.

"Fill him in privately. Does he have an override code for the shuttle?"

They waited with fingers clenched. Melawn tried to tell himself that there was hope, that Alesta Eve would come in close at Atikameq and they would be saved and Evan and Caspia would only be separated for two years instead of by death.

".83 JV. She's using the power booster almost continuously."

"She'll crash," Thayne declared.

"She may. She's not that good. Code received. Trying to override," Nkiroo said.

Melawn shook his head. Override codes were intended for disabled ships, not . . . what was the word? *Hijackings.*

"No," Nkiroo shook his head. "She's shut down the receivers."

They sat in stunned silence for another twenty minutes as the *Frontier* whirled through the rings, sometimes coming so close to the segments that Melawn held his breath.

"Is the Atik trajectory clear?" Thayne asked.

"Yes," Nkiroo answered.

"What will they do?" Melawn asked.

"At Atik? If both of them survive? Depends. I suspect Alesta

Eve could come up with some story that would hold until another ship arrives."

"But Evan would never go along with it," Melawn said.

"It just doesn't make any sense," Thayne said.

".97," Nkiroo updated them. "She's out! But going the wrong way . . ."

"Maybe she's aborting," Thayne said with a surge of hope.

"No, she's still accelerating."

Melawn said a silent prayer for Evan and Caspia.

The view of the shuttle wavered. "Gone," Nkiroo whispered, a deathly finality in his voice.

"NO!" Thayne had his head in his hands, breathing hard. "No, no, *no*! I hoped, at the last minute, that maybe she was just trying to prove a point."

Melawn worried that Thayne might suddenly have another breakdown, but he took a great, determined breath. "Melawn, bring in Lanezi. Nkiroo, get Tenshi up here. We need her to tell Caspia. *Cheetah*, where did the *Frontier* jump?"

"No regular jumps on that trajectory."

"Nearest known human colony on that path?"

There was a very long pause. **"Sector 1."**

"No," they all whispered, distraught. No one had ever attempted such a jump, even in a well-supplied ship. There was virtually no chance for them.

Thayne shuddered. "You couldn't have known," Melawn sympathized, grasping Thayne's arm. "No one could have guessed she would try such a reckless thing."

But yes, Melawn remembered. She had been retired for "recklessness." Someone had known. *We just didn't listen.*

Tenshi burst in the door with a med kit. "What's happened?"

"It's Evan," Nkiroo started to say, but the *Cheetah* interrupted.

"Priority call."

Melawn unstrapped to talk to Tenshi quietly when a familiar voice, polite but worried, came on the speaker. "Umm, sorry, could someone pick me up now?"

Stunned, the three of them grabbed the nearest support. "Evan?" Nkiroo asked, hardly keeping his hope in check.

"Yes."

"Evan! Are you alright?"

"Well, I'm running out of air. She told me radio silence, but I didn't know she would be so long."

"Your beacon is off. Where are you?"

"Torus D, like I was supposed to be."

Thayne looked like he might scream, but Nkiroo focused on the priority. Within seconds, two of Jamez's rocket-like mini-shuttles were on the way. Zahar's days of waiting in the hangar bay would finally pay off.

"What happened?" Tenshi asked in confusion.

"We thought we lost him." Melawn explained. "We thought he was on the shuttle with Alesta Eve."

Tenshi went ashen. "What happened to the shuttle?"

"She jumped." Tenshi stared at him, not understanding.

"Alesta Eve jumped. In the shuttle. To Sector 1."

Tenshi swallowed. "Is there any chance she'll make it?"

"We have no idea," Melawn said. "It's never been tried. Lesser jumps have failed, but at least Evan is safe."

"He's been on the activated segment all this time?"

"Apparently," Melawn answered, smiling in relief. But Tenshi was not smiling.

"Possible direct exposure to unknown radiation. He may have been better off in the shuttle."

. . .

"No sign of any type of radiation damage—at least nothing we know to look for," Tenshi reported to Melawn and Thayne in Thayne's cabin. "Only time will tell. For now, I'm more concerned about his mental state."

"Why?" Thayne asked, holding his head and squinting. Melawn recognized the signs of the headache that usually preceded a mindstorm.

"Well, first," she answered, "his wandering seems to have doubled, and second, he lost all his pocket things."

There was a general gasp of empathy. "Except his prayer book," Tenshi clarified. "Alesta Eve told him Thayne wanted him to observe from the torus and had him suit up on the *Frontier*."

There was a buzz at the door. "Open," Thayne called. Zahar stood, momentarily wondering if she should come in, but Tenshi waved her in. "I've had Zahar check the stores," she told them.

"It's just as you thought, doctor," Zahar reported. "Supplies are missing. We know for certain because we've had to keep a close inventory for the convoy. And it's exactly the sort of stuff you'd take for emergency shuttle supplies. I also checked the robot logs. There are several times where the log is blank, but the charge logs on the niches don't match. And Evan says he saw lots of water stored in the suit lockers.

"Why didn't he report that when he saw it?" Nkiroo asked.

"He says Alesta Eve commented that she had supplies in case they had trouble decelerating and that it never crossed his mind that she would jump."

"Clever," Nkiroo scowled.

"Sneaky, dangerous, betraying, disloyal—" Thayne started choking.

"Breathe," Tenshi said.

Thayne nodded and calmed down. "Well it's done—and we know for certain that the a-rings work. We no longer need to procure a spare ship to test it. We can proceed to the next step, but we'll have to move quickly."

"Why?" Tenshi asked.

"We have a chance to bump up our schedule. We'll jump with the advance ship, rather than waiting for the convoy."

The others turned to Thayne in surprise. He continued quickly, "Nkiroo, have Jamez turn off the gravity ball and break down the a-rings. We'll need it all loaded by as soon as possible."

"Wait," Tenshi said, confused. "You're not loading the gravity ball."

"Yes doctor. We're taking it all to Luminesse as planned."

"What about Harbor?"

"Jamez can make segments for Harbor. They'll be jumping again way before schedule. Luminesse cannot survive much longer. It has always been our primary mission to save them first. This is the break we needed."

"But you can't put a gravity ball aboard the *Cheetah*."

"Of course we can, doctor. Be at ease. The aliens did it. We can do it."

It was only on the way back to his cabin that Melawn realized they could have turned off the gravity ball to prevent Alesta Eve from leaving—or they could have tried. Both Jamez and the Cheetah now had the ability to send the alien control signals.

Why didn't I think of it? Why didn't Thayne or Nkiroo think of it? Or did they?

13-Knowledge

Cheetah, at OSRI

Zahar consulted her checklist. She was almost finished with the process of opening 19 new cabins, along with the kitchen and other crew areas in Arc 5. Jamez was sending a specially trained group aboard, Team OSRI. They would travel to Luminesse with the *Cheetah*, reconstruct the a-rings, make the tori, and set it all up with the new gravity ball.

Zahar had command of an entire bot family to open, clean and inspect cabins, repair equipment, replace filters, tune up life support, restart plumbing, check seals and lights, boot up kitchen equipment, allocate and transfer supplies, and generally make Arc 5 safe and civilized.

This was her kind of work, so she planned to do an extraordinary job. It would have been a lot more fun with the twins, but they had to finish the passenger chairs after all, as they would be needed for Team OSRI. Melawn was using the *Spring Azure* to pick up last minute equipment.

Her p'link beeped. "Zahar?"

"Yes, Captain."

"Stop what you're doing and get the robot team to the hangar to unload supplies. Melawn should be back in 20 minutes."

"Yes, Captain."

Zahar marked her spot in her extensive checklist. "Robot 1: Pause program. Save. Your team will come with me to hangar three now."

The *Spring Azure* entered the small passenger hangar, which was pressurized, so Zahar was able to go in and supervise the bots. She morphed them into an assembly line and got into the shuttle to code the supplies herself. As she worked her way from the back to the front of the shuttle she could hear the voices of the pilot and monitor. They sounded young.

Junk news. It would be her last chance. Melawn wouldn't approve, but he'd already left, pausing only briefly to say goodbye to the crew. As the robots took the last few items, the two women were revealed. Zahar smiled.

"Hello little sister!" The songbird one said.

"Hi, I'm Za—"

"Shuttle *Spring Azure*, prepare to depart," came Thayne's voice. *Is he listening?*

"Negative! *Cheetah* command," said the monitor. "Closing checklist is not complete."

In a hurry, Zahar grabbed her p'link and tilted it back and forth in the youth-understood signal for junk news.

"Oh, a music lover, yes," said the pilot, taking Zahar's p'link and connecting it to her own. Zahar smiled and nodded. Many people traded songs as part of the junk news. Zahar wasn't giving them any songs in trade though. She glanced at the robots, now reforming to their standard nogee config.

"Number 3, supply bag please." The robot jetted gently over. Luckily, she had leftover chocolate from the gifts she had left in the new cabins. She passed it to the pilot in exchange for the junk news.

"*Spring Azure*, prepare to depart," Thayne insisted.

Zahar waved and dived out the back. "Robot 3: close the shuttle." No one else could have unloaded that shuttle any faster. It was as if Thayne didn't want them to talk to each other.

17-Knowledge

Lanezi no longer felt guilty about leaving Harbor early. With Jamez working on replacement segments, it was likely that no one would have to convoy now. It would just be a matter of installing and testing the a-rings to the Council's satisfaction.

And, the sooner they left Harbor, the sooner Lanezi could contact Katie and the sooner he could leave the *Cheetah*. He knew he could not leave the classified program now that he had the pups. He planned to be assigned to explore alien space with another team. The fact that Katie was a doctor would probably secure them both assignments on a mission. Provided that she agreed to marry him. *She will.*

Of course, Thayne would take it as a sign of personal disloyalty, but Lanezi wouldn't be around for the fallout. Getting the twins and Tenshi to come along was going to be the hard part. But he had promised Euro and Io to take them with him.

It's still a long way off, he reminded himself. They had weeks before they'd even be able to jump. He had to focus on the gravity assists. He had gone over the trajectory and burns carefully. He would be continuously piloting for twenty days, swapping with Evan at night. Zahar, thank heavens, had requested their schedules and arranged meals for them, and help for the pups, all without being asked.

18-Knowledge

Zahar waited in the Passenger Lounge with Dr. Tenshi, ready to seat the 19 Team OSRI people. There were four scientists and 15 EVA workers. Kanika, Thayne's engineer, was the team leader, leaving Jamez behind to supervise the rebuilding of the Harbor a-rings.

Zahar went about checking the passenger chairs, assisting Dr. Tenshi. All Team OSRI's equipment, including a portable manufacturing plant and collapsible a-ring segments, had been loaded in the cargo hold, along with the nerve-wracking transfer of the deactivated mini gravity ball. It had been aboard for two days and they were still alive.

Shortly, Io brought in the first group, and handed them off. "OSRI Team Leader Kanika, *Cheetah* Dr. Tenshi."

"Thank you, Io," Dr. Tenshi said matter-of-factly.

Kanika, equally matter-of-fact, greeted them briefly and handed over the medical files to Dr. Tenshi. A friendly-looking woman reached around to shake Zahar's hand. "Jasine, Jamez's assistant." Zahar greeted her, as well as Kanika's science advisor, Ghanta, and her top engineer, Lovell. They were just getting situated when Euro arrived with the fifteen EVA workers.

Zahar told herself not to stare. Kanika, Jesine, Ghanta, and Lovell all seemed like serious engineer and science administrative types. But the other fifteen looked like they'd walked out of an adventure movie. They were all young and strong, with a 'we're here' attitude. They had especially glittery patches on their suits that said Team OSRI. Zahar found it hard to believe they were handpicked by the serious, hard-working Kanika or the easy-going, machine-loving Jamez. Melawn peeked in the door and was totally puzzled by the big smile Zahar gave him. Melawn outshone the lot of Team OSRI, but without the attitude.

They were friendly enough, as though they expected everyone to like them, and the twins did work their usual charm, socializing until Tenshi and Caspia signaled them to go to their assigned seats. They didn't need to use the cocoons today, just suit-up, and strap in the chairs.

The flashiest of the 15 OSRI workers, the one the others deferred to, named Zap, approached his chair, grabbed the arm and did a little side flip into the chair. Zahar had a flash of Alesta Eve flipping in the corridor. *Reckless.* "Hey, my chair arm is loose," he complained. *Maybe you broke it.*

Tenshi rolled her eyes and ignored him, but the ever-helpful Io went to look at it. "Oh, no! Missing a bolt."

"I'm sure I checked all those," Euro said, worried.

"Yikes," Caspia said, pulling out her s'link. "This is the P.L. We need a sweep for a missing bolt."

"Be right there," Nkiroo answered.

Zap was settled, except for his visor, when Nkiroo came in and told them to hold on to their p'links. He turned on the finder, and caught two bolts and a small clip. A deeply disappointed frown crossed his face.

"Pretty sloppy," Zap commented, and the team laughed.

Io and Euro's eyes filled with tears. Io hung his head and Euro formally said "We apologize, Nkiroo."

"Let's just do a quick check while I fix this one."

He coasted over to Zap's chair, hooked on and started to work when Zap said, "Hey, I know that name—Nkiroo."

"I don't think I know you," Nkiroo said mildly.

"Yeah, I mean, my mom was on the ship that found you, like ten years ago. You're the 'Raised by Robots' kid. You thought all those holograms were people," he scoffed. A couple workers snickered but everyone else froze.

Oh my God. Our Nkiroo. Zahar knew that story too—only the name of the kid was never released. He'd been found aboard an abandoned ship. For eleven years, he'd been alone, raised by the AI with the help of robots and 40 holograms. He was rescued when he was 14. The ship had trained up its own engineer to fix itself, but it couldn't train him to be a pilot.

Fire in her eyes, Tenshi, the Earthborn, did her own flip over a row of chairs, grabbed Zap's chair, hissed "Not your story," and slammed his visor down. With a swipe of her thumb on her pad, Zahar muted him.

And then a wave of compassion for Nkiroo came over her, for his ordeal and his attachment to Melawn. She understood Thayne's protectiveness and Nkiroo's tapping people on the shoulder—*to see if they're real*!

Nkiroo was frozen, eyes down. She reached out and tapped him on the shoulder. Caspia, eyes widening in understanding, coasted over and did the same. Tenshi reached across and tapped his hand. "Someone's got a screw loose." She jerked her head at Zap.

Nkiroo nodded and finished up, getting tearful hugs from Io and Euro on the way out—behind the backs of Team OSRI. "Okay, back to your chairs," Zahar urged them. She couldn't wait to send Team Uppity back to Arc 5.

After the long day's boosting, when Thayne found out what happened in the Passenger Lounge, he actually asked how long it would take to turn back and drop Zap off. Lanezi shook his head in horror. Thayne's dark eyes glittered, Zahar assumed with thoughts of sending Zap back in a shuttle. Alone. But Kanika apologized profusely and promised to keep Zap and all the rest of them in Arc 5 until the jump.

"I'm okay," Nkiroo insisted, putting his arms around the twins. "Someday I'll tell you about it."

Scientists calculated that Luminesse had already passed the point at which all would survive. *Cheetah's* rescue mission would be distressing, even if it were ultimately successful. Zahar had a twinge of guilt. *Cheetah* could probably use a medical assistant, but she had already decided not to go on to Luminesse. Her oath was expiring soon. She was determined to get off at Atikameq, classified information in her head or not. She had not told anyone on the *Cheetah,* of course. She would miss the twins and the podpups, but sneaking around the sectors with gravity balls was not what she had planned to do with her life. All these people could be rescue heroes without her. She could do SAR if she had to, but she preferred the less glamorous planning-ahead-to-prevent-problems approach.

Meanwhile, they had to brave 27 days on a strenuous gravity assist. Fortunately, the first few days would be the worst as they caught up with the already boosting advance ship, the *Cashmere.*

Cheetah, outbound from Harbor System

Lanezi was tired. Their first day of boosting had been a strain, whipping around the planet Hb4 itself, with multiple corrections, trouble with slow communications, and the OSRI person telling Nkiroo's story. Poor Evan, trying to sleep through that.

They were heading inbound, to swing around an inner planet, Hb3, back around Hb4, inbound again to Hb2, and finally out to Hb5 for the jump. In between, they would have many hours of serious boosting. *Good thing that Team OSRI is young and healthy.* He completely understood why the Harbor Council had planned to wait so long for the more sedate gravity assist using the outer planets.

Lanezi was in the kitchen, feeding the pups. They were especially whiny from being cooped up all day. Even Whisper seemed disgruntled.

"Hungry," Blue pouted.

"No more. You had food."

"Hungry," Dusty complained.

"Rationing—it means only so much food every day."

The pups floated around him, puzzled at the long sentence. He felt bad for them, not understanding, but until they found out what the situation was at Luminesse, they had to conserve.

Melawn quietly came in, looking as tired as Lanezi. He'd missed dinner, but Lanezi had saved him some. He pointed to the covered tray.

"Thank you." Melawn stuck it in the warmer and then floated to the table in a daze. The eyes of the little hungry pups followed him.

"Stop it," Lanezi whispered as he brought Melawn a sandwich.

"Stop what?" Melawn asked, becoming alert.

"Sorry, not you."

Whisper was helping Lanezi, but the four little pups pushed over to Melawn. "Hungry," Summer said, in her most pitiful voice.

"Summer, you had your food. That's Melawn's food. No pesting."

"They're hungry?" Melawn asked.

"They're always hungry." Lanezi had meant to sound more firm, but he was sympathetic. "They just don't understand about the rationing. Eat. I'll send them out." They whined. Whisper ticked at them.

"Oh, it's okay," Melawn said, carefully tearing up half of his sandwich.

"Melawn—" Lanezi objected, but Melawn shook his head. Lanezi got Melawn's soup from the warmer, grabbed two tea bulbs, and tethered across from him. Meanwhile, Melawn gently handed a piece of sandwich to each pup. He held one out for Whisper, who disdained it.

"Whisper share," she said nobly.

Melawn barely cracked a smile. He divided her part into four tiny bites and carefully handed them out. After eating, the pups tugged on Melawn's clothes and patted his hair saying "Good Melawn" and "Melawn, friend."

"Okay, let him eat," Lanezi said, sipping his tea. Whisper curled up in Lanezi's shirt while the pups drifted off to sleep. Lanezi felt a renewed bit of affection for Melawn and determined to try harder to be friendly. "Why so tired?"

Melawn took a long breath and closed his eyes briefly. "It's Thayne. Before, he would have periods of energy and then crash. Now, it's like he never sleeps. He's so excited, ideas are pouring out. Nkiroo seems to be able to detach himself, but I feel like Thayne needs me to talk to, bounce his ideas off of, not that I understand all of it."

"Well, maybe you could borrow a pup for him to talk to."

"They are very sweet," Melawn admitted. "He just doesn't like them."

"Thayne bad," Whisper piped up.

"Whisper!" Lanezi objected. "He's not bad just because he

doesn't like you," but she looked up and scowled. Another long sentence.

Later, in his cabin, Lanezi was still bothered. Although podpups could have their opinions, logical or not, it was shocking that Whisper had spoken out so strongly against Thayne, especially in front of Melawn. Long sentences confused them, but relationships didn't. Whisper certainly knew that Melawn was a loyal friend of Thayne's. *Maybe she's just showing her loyalty to me. Or maybe . . .*

Lanezi checked that the younger pups were asleep in their box. Yes, snoring away. He carefully shifted the sleepy Whisper out of his shirt and into the box.

With a tinge of guilt and a ton of rationalization, he told himself he would resolve his trouble with Thayne once and for all.

He put his s'link in the command slot and ran it up to level 3. It would have to do. He began methodically checking every order from Thayne, looking at packets, double-checking packets from the council, which legally had to be stored in *Cheetah's* shared database, checking Nkiroo's shared files, *Cashmere's* public orders, OSRI packets, Jamez's orders, even transmission from the *Spring Azure*.

He checked every news subject he could think of relating to OSRI, a-rings, or the *Frontier*. Among the things he didn't find was any mention of Alesta Eve's jump, but that made sense, as it would be classified above his level 3 rating.

Every single message checked out. Lanezi searched and read. He didn't send a request directly to the Council because they were on packet silence, and he wouldn't want to bother the Council anyway.

After six hours, he admitted that everything was in order. He had been suspicious for no reason. Thayne was doing exactly as ordered and stated in the mission instructions. *I should have read this stuff before.*

Lanezi hoped he wasn't just holding a grudge against Thayne for calling him out on his lying. He considered his therapy and determined to let it all go and start over, no suspicions. Thayne was an exceptional, brilliant person with a difficult mission. *And I've only made it harder for him.*

7-Speech

Cheetah, outbound from Harbor System

"Ready?" Thayne asked Lanezi, weeks later, on the morning of the jump to Atikameq.

"Yes!" Lanezi smiled reassuringly and in all honesty, he was excited, and very tired of boosting.

"Great!" Thayne was encouraged. He seemed to have felt Lanezi's change of heart lately and been slightly more relaxed. However, Whisper and Thayne had no change in their mutual antipathy. "Let's cross our fingers about Evan," Thayne continued.

"Well, he was fine this morning," Caspia said, coming in and going straight for the coffee.

"Jump minus two hours," Nkiroo announced, as Thayne joined them in the Command Bay after prayers.

Lanezi smiled. He hadn't expected to hear that for at least a year. They had survived their gravity assists with damage only to the pilots' nerves. The *Cheetah* crew was doing well and the OSRI people had used every flyby for an excuse to party.

Lanezi met Evan's eyes. Focused and happy. It would be good to jump again. Evan's pockets were full of little gifts from the crew, and of course, more podpup treats. The five podpups were safely in the jump box. Tenshi and Zahar were in the Passenger Lounge, finishing the full prep with Team OSRI.

"*Cashmere* is go in 30 seconds," Nkiroo relayed. "They are at JV now."

Lanezi tried to let his mind open up for just a moment to capture the feel of the jump, but there was just a small blue blip and *Cashmere* was gone.

Evan made a small sound like a hiccup. Lanezi turned to look at him and saw he was wandering again. *It's up to me.*

There was a sudden dip, stronger than the one the gravity ball had caused during their test. They all grabbed their seats in alarm.

"What was that?" Lanezi asked.

Thayne worked furiously at his panel. "Our gravity ball is secure—no activity, no readings. It was not internal." They all looked out the window scanning for any clue.

"Jumps don't cause gravity waves," Nkiroo declared, "Something happened."

"What?" Thayne asked this time. "*Cheetah's* not showing any direct measure. Just a slight change in beacon direction."

Lanezi listened with a growing detachment. He knew they would not abort. He let his thoughts settle to a meditative state despite the ominous dip.

As the minutes drifted by, Lanezi became more aware of Evan. *He is still with me.* Nkiroo took care of all the details of the jump, making sure the passengers were in their cocoons and ready and that they were going the right way. "8 minutes. P&P: 28 and 5."

Helmet on; check through screens. Lanezi felt odd without

the a-ring rhythm, but he kept up the screen with the percent of JV and the trajectory and that was familiar. Lanezi could sense Thayne searching quietly for answers to the dip. He focused on a final prayer. Lanezi knew it was about the mystic journey of the soul as it draws nearer to God. But to him, it seemed both mystic and tangibly practical.

And shouldst thou spur on the charger of the spirit and traverse the meads of heaven, thou wouldst complete all these journeys and discover every mystery in less than the twinkling of an eye. [1]

"One minute," Nkiroo reported.

Atikameq, Lanezi reminded himself, blue.

"Ten seconds."

"JV."

There was no burst of freedom as when they left the a-rings, but Lanezi took a deep breath and closed and opened his eyes. Blue path; he barely had to nudge the *Cheetah*. He could feel Evan alert and in agreement. He squeezed the accelerator. Lanezi's heart thrilled as they dived solidly into the path.

17-Speech

Drumheller, incoming to Redrock Station

Twelve-year-old Terina set her podpup carrier down before she dropped it. Her pup was careening around inside like a wild thing. Wearing the spacesuit for the shuttle trip from *Nightingale* and the ride up the lift in this huge ship piled onto her exhaustion of the last few days.

As excited as she was to be aboard the newly-returned *Drumheller,* she couldn't take much more. Had it only been seven days since the news broke? The mysteriously-vanished, long-lost cargo ship *Drumheller* had disappeared jumping out of Redrock over eight months ago. At first, the news people insisted *Drumheller* was on 'assignment,' but the junk news had been jumping with theories. Networks of junkees reported that *Drumheller* was not in their sector. It was off the map, a secret mission gone wrong. And now, here she was, rushed aboard.

Luckily, they had been at Redrock and were able to quickly accept this *Drumheller* mission. It would be a good distraction for her mom, who claimed *Drumheller* just needed a long jump pilot and it had *nothing* to do with getting a new start in life since Terina's dad took her brother to Earth and *didn't come back*. Grandpa Kelson had said "Let sleeping dogs lie" in his usual clear way. But for Terina, this was big. For once, she had a chance to record history from the inside.

The *Drumheller*'s appearance was good news on top of good news. An advance ship out of Harbor had just arrived at Atikameq with the report of their accident and evacuation plan. Relay ships had spread the news.

She braced a hand against the wall as the adults introduced themselves. Her grandfather had to stop and think before saying her mom's name, "Sequoia," as he had 15 living children, *all named after trees*. The *Drumheller* crew knew her Grandfather Kelson. Of course, being 114, he probably knew everyone in the outer sectors.

Terina had been warned that there was a red-banded 15-year-old aboard and that she should "use her best judgment" in dealing with him. Terina cautiously looked up at him; he was very tall.

Images from the junk news flashed through her mind. Exhaustion disappeared. Jarvie Atikameq! Child survivor of *Sunburst*—turned runaway. Discovered on the *Drumheller! How much better could this story get?*

She wanted to look him in the eye, to get a quick sense of who he was; bad boy out of the system, or mysterious teen, key to the secret mission?

But he was distracted, looking down at her podpup carrier. "Um . . . maybe we should let zir out before ze knocks zirself unconscious."

The carrier was almost tipping over. A fuzzy black podpup was eyeing it with suspicion and an excited white one was looking inside. "Oh, right," Terina said, leaning over to unlatch it, but she stumbled, unbalanced in the suit. A wave of dizziness swept over her. Instinctively, the teen grabbed her, catching her before her mother even noticed.

Katie, the doctor, came around to her, "Let's get back to Arc 1 where they can rest," she suggested.

Meanwhile, Jarvie popped open the door of the carrier and there was chaos. Her podpup, his coffee and cream fur all ruffled up, tore down the rimway, closely followed by the white one, who actually kept up. The black pup jumped straight into the arms of the captain, who knocked into Iricana, who knocked into Jarvie and they almost went down like dominos.

"What . . . who . . . is that?" a stunned Iricana asked.

"Ah, sorry," Terina said sheepishly. "That's Rocket . . . because he is one."

The captain closed his eyes, "Rocket," he repeated. "Just what we need." And he turned and trudged up the rimway, shaking his head.

Then Jarvie did meet her eyes, with a touch of wild humor and a quirky smile. "Star," he said, pointing up the rimway after the pups. *The white one is his. We are going to get along just fine.*

18-Speech

The next day, Beezan sat at the formal conference table, in the formal Consultation Hall, with a formal uniform and hair combed. *I used to be a cargo captain.* He scowled down at Sky, who was sitting quietly in his lap. She seemed a bit tense herself. He closed his eyes and breathed deeply. He had not eaten dinner or breakfast with the new crew, even knowing that it might be interpreted as rudeness. He had spent the time reorienting his mind.

Oatah and Reeder were gone, but three new people and a

crazed podpup had come aboard. After surviving a secret mission, untried jumps, first contact with an alien species, and becoming a father to a teenager, he was not about to let his life spiral into chaos again.

The crew settled into the chairs around him. He felt Jarvie to his right and nudged him to say a prayer.

He opened his eyes and scanned the crew. Katie gave him an encouraging smile. Iricana, pad in hand, waited expectantly. Of the new adults, Kelson was quiet and patient, but Beezan wasn't fooled. The twinkle in his eye telegraphed some obscure saying about to pop out. Sequoia, Kelson's daughter, was a long jumper, the sharp intense kind. Her skin was shiny medium brown and her dark hair was pulled down flat with a fuzzy knot at the back of her neck. Her dark brown eyes were distant, but Beezan thought he detected the merest hint of disapproval. *Of the mission? Of me?*

"Terina's sleeping," Jarvie whispered to him. He nodded. No use stalling.

"Thank you for coming," he started. "As you know, the *Drumheller* is under the commission of Special Agent Oatah, his orders being relayed to us through Iricana. However, before we go any further, I would like to clarify one issue of command."

They all looked up in confusion. There had been no outright moves to override him, but there were certain principles in his life that Beezan felt were being tested. "Truthfulness," he said, relying on the power of the word itself. "I want full disclosure. No more secrets. We all need to know what everyone's mission is so we can work together." He paused. "I need to know in order to command properly."

Sequoia studied him guardedly. Katie and Jarvie looked around, worried. Beezan knew that neither of them had secret orders. Kelson nodded slowly and said, "We are here in Iricana's service and have no other agenda." All eyes shifted to Iricana.

She set her pad down carefully. "Very well, Captain. I am confident in oaths already taken."

Beezan relaxed a little as Iricana continued. *Maybe this won't be so hard.*

"These are our mission orders." Iricana continued, "We are to have a thorough debriefing with the Redrock council, repair the ship, stock major supplies, pick up one additional crew: my husband Thunder, who is a master mechanic and robotics expert. We are to proceed to Tektite and inspect the control panel." This much Beezan had already gathered.

"Mr. Oatah may have us test jumps from Tektite, or we may be assigned to some kind of Ramian expedition." There were little gasps from around the table.

"We're not an advance ship," Beezan objected.

"We are now," Iricana said quietly. Apparently, Kelson and Sequoia had been briefed on the aliens, as they didn't seem shocked by this.

"Why us?" Beezan asked again.

"Oatah is confident in our judgment, and with Sequoia, we have the ability to jump where we need to. On the subject of searching for gravity balls—" This time Iricana had to stop and explain for Kelson and Sequoia. "The Ramians had a method of finding gravity balls. It involved locating them in the k-belts and using certain codes to call and command them."

"Codes?" Kelson raised an eyebrow.

"Yes, codes now in our possession, obtained by Jarvie while he lived with the Ramians."

"Lived with the Ramians," Sequoia repeated to herself. Kelson looked at Jarvie in astonishment.

"*Wheel of Fire* is being sent to Tyee to search for gravity balls, but with orders only to note their locations."

Iricana went on to explain several things from their previous mission to Kelson and Sequoia that were classified, but Beezan sensed an inner tension, as if she had not yet come to some key point—and would not, of course, until everything was explained in proper order.

"So for now, our orders do not extend beyond investigating the Tektite control panel." Beezan nodded but kept his gaze on Iricana. Even Katie turned to her in puzzlement as she hesitated.

"There is other news . . . of a troubling nature . . . which has no direct bearing on our orders and is highly classified, but I believe it may influence our future and is of personal interest. I only received this an hour ago."

Beezan took a deep breath. Whatever was upsetting Iricana must be very bad.

"You know that an advance ship, the *Cashmere*, jumped out of Harbor, to Atikameq." They all nodded. Her voice took on a resigned tone. "A second ship also jumped out. There was no PS packet. It is considered an unauthorized jump. They came in silent—no beacon, and they are heading straight for the a-rings, not Atikameq station. *Cashmere* confirms that it is the *Cheetah*."

This time there were even louder gasps from the *Drumheller* crew. Iricana had to quickly explain to Kelson and Sequoia about the unauthorized transportation of the original gravity ball and its explosion, resulting in deaths to the Ramian crew. Kelson squinted at them. Sequoia's disapproving expression turned to disbelieving. Beezan thought Iricana would be relieved to have delivered this information, but now her knuckles were turning white as she clutched her pad.

"Atikameq authority had issued an order for *Cheetah* to come in for questioning." She took a deep breath. "Because

Thayne transported the gravity ball without telling the Councils, I have issued an order for his arrest."

"Good!" Jarvie said angrily. There were nods of approval from Katie and even Sky, mimicking Jarvie.

"Lanezi?" Katie asked tentatively.

"No word," Iricana said sympathetically. "Although we saw Lanezi's name on the survivor list, provided by the *Cashmere*, we do not know if he is aboard the *Cheetah* now. We don't even know if Thayne is aboard. There have been no communications."

"Assuming it is Thayne, where would he be going?" Kelson asked.

Iricana frowned. "The classified report from the *Cashmere* includes information that a mini gravity ball was discovered intact in the wreckage of the alien vessel at Harbor. It was transferred to Thayne's work group at OSRI for study."

"So he got a gravity ball after all," Jarvie concluded. "And now he's taking it somewhere."

"That is my fear," Iricana agreed.

"Where? Why?" Beezan asked.

"Thayne's original orders were to devise a way to help Luminesse."

"Could a person jump from Atik to Luminesse?" Kelson asked his daughter. It wasn't a regular jump.

Sequoia nodded. Beezan agreed. "Yes," Jarvie agreed, "if he's got Lanezi."

"But if they get into Luminesse and can't fix the a-rings, they won't be able to get out," Sequoia worried. "There are no reasonable gravity-assists from Luminesse. *Sunburst* only got out because they had speed from the a-rings already."

Jarvie shuddered beside him. Katie hung her head. "Can I send a message to Lanezi?" she suddenly asked.

Iricana nodded sadly. "I wish we could. We could warn them about the gravity ball exploding, but the *Cheetah* has not been responding. We don't even know if they are processing packets."

"I have a direct override code to Lanezi," Jarvie said. They all turned and looked at him again, this time in surprise. "Remember? Lanezi sent it to me when I was a runaway and trying to find him and sneak aboard."

At this point Kelson dropped his head into his hands and shook it. Exactly, Beezan thought. Time for direction. "Thank you," he nodded to Iricana. "Send whatever messages you think appropriate. Where are we picking up our new crew?"

"Thunder is on Sandune. Then we need to go to Radium Junction."

Beezan nodded. "Sounds like we don't have much time for repairs."

"We have no time to take our time, but we must be ready for anything. I'll arrange a priority team."

"Thank you. I'll leave you to further explanation."

As he got up, Sky said "stay," so he handed her over to Jarvie. Crazy pup. Who'd want to stay at a confused meeting with upset people? Star obviously knew better.

Of course, as Beezan discovered a minute later, Star and Rocket were busy playing with a sock in the rimway.

19-Speech

Jarvie had just finished cleaning up breakfast when Terina staggered into the kitchen and slumped into a seat. Jarvie hadn't even seen her since she'd come aboard. She'd slept for two days and looked like she needed two more. She was not quite as dark as her mother and had thick wavy hair, partly tied back in a ponytail. The escaping hair fell in her face. She looked like a spring that had lost its sprung.

"Food?" he asked, dispensing with unnecessary pleasantries.

"Starving," she mumbled, resting her head on the table.

"Starving!" echoed Star and Rocket, who slowed down enough to come to a wiggly sit in front of Jarvie, looking up at him pitifully.

"Your breakfast," he told them, "is in the bin. You've run past it twenty times." The word "bin" was all they needed. They raced each other over, skidding into the bin and bumping their heads.

Jarvie slid a protein drink in front of Terina to get her started while he made something more substantial. Although he had been nervous about having another kid aboard, she seemed so pitiful he didn't feel intimidated. He even felt a little . . . mature.

"Thanks." Obviously she wasn't a morning person.

Ten sips later, she sprang to a sitting position, alert as the podpups, and grabbed Jarvie's book from the table. "*From Earth to Radium Junction, an Illustrated History of Sector Expansion*," she read out. "You like history?" she asked, excited.

Not wanting to disappoint her, Jarvie didn't mention it was his only real book. "Ah . . . well . . . it's a good book . . . so far."

She rolled her eyes. Then she tried another tactic. "What about exploring?"

"I guess, sure. I like exploring."

She frowned. "Detective work?"

"What's that?"

"You know, looking for clues."

"Like clues about the builders?" He had recently become very interested in that.

She perked up even more. "Maybe, or clues about the past."

"What are you? An archolo . . . archelo-"

"Archeologist? No. I'm a historian." She said it so matter-of-factly.

"I thought you were a kid," he chided.

"Temporary problem."

He laughed. "So what do you need me to like history for?"

"To go exploring with me."

"We're going to explore the mysterious control panel at Tektite. Didn't you hear?"

"Not outside the ship. Exploring inside the ship."

He must have looked blank, but she leaned forward. "How many cabins have you covered so far?"

"We opened the cabins in Arc 2."

"No, no. The old cabins, on the other side. Where no one has lived for what? 100? 200 years?"

"I don't know how long. I haven't been in any of them. They're probably all empty."

She smacked herself in the forehead. "You've never even looked?"

He shook his head, baffled. "What's to look for, giant dust balls?"

She put down the book and grabbed her big pad. "We have work to do." She took the plate Jarvie offered her and stuffed in big bites, signaling him to sit. She pushed her pad over so he could read it.

"'*Searching for Cabin Logs* . . .' Oh, you know, I'm not much for the junk news."

"Umm!" She smacked the table with her spoon this time and gestured at the pad.

"By Terina Coralia. *Jr. Journal of Outer Sector History, Vol. 344 #12.* Oh, this is for real." And he started to read. "You're a published historian? Wow."

"And a semi-expert in cabin logs. Hundreds of years ago, people left guestbooks in their passenger cabins. This happened on sailing ships *and* spaceships. Each person that used the cabin would sign the cabin log and write something about themselves. But over the centuries, the tradition became more secretive. First you had to find the log. Then you could sign it and hide it again. What's cool is to find one that someone famous signed."

"But *Drumheller* is a cargo ship." *Heaven help me, I'm sounding like Beezan.*

"Don't you know your own provenance? *Drumheller* was a passenger ship once!" She twirled her spoon in the air, planning. "We'll get permission from your Captain."

"I don't know."

"Easy. It's educational. It keeps us out of his way. You can do some dumb repairs—like fix the doors," she added, and scooped up her last bite.

Jarvie sighed. This kid was a schemer. "Besides," she gestured with both hands. "It's *Heritage*. Historians have rights, you know."

"What do you need me for?" he asked again.

"You're 15. You've got to mentor me in something. Might as well do some real work, instead of sit around and tutor me in differential equations."

He considered it only briefly, especially since Terina would probably end up doing the tutoring. "*Drumheller* Heritage Project: Cabin Log Search. Deal."

They shook on it.

By lunch, Terina had a formal proposal.

By dinner, it was approved by Iricana and Beezan.

By morning, Beezan had attached a list of repairs and procedures and assigned part of the robot repair team.

Katie suddenly agreed to watch the podpups, as they wouldn't be able to cope with the robots. Jarvie was pleased as he thought that would help keep her mind off Lanezi. Katie really liked podpups anyway. Too bad she and Lanezi didn't have any.

1-Questions

Drumheller, orbiting near Redrock Station

"Well, it can't be helped," Iricana sighed as she collected her dinner. Beezan scooted over so she could sit by him at the table. "They won't allow us to dock. We must do two weeks of quarantine, undocked. That's a law, apparently."

"So no work, even on the hull," Beezan confirmed, although he hadn't had much hope to start with.

"Right," she said. "For now, we can send formal requests and try to organize a schedule."

Beezan nodded, glancing at Kelson, Sequoia, and Terina at the other end of the table. "The vaccines seem to be working," he said to Katie.

"Yes, so far, and Tiati, and the crew with Oatah are also doing well. But remember, the mershla took eight days."

Jarvie rubbed the bridge of his nose where the purple rash had been. "It still itches." They all laughed, including Jarvie.

Beezan couldn't believe it had only been three days since Kelson, Sequoia and Terina came aboard. He was still adjusting to the idea that Jarvie was now his son. He found himself watching Sequoia for clues as to how to be a parent, but Sequoia was so intense, more even than most long jumpers. Perhaps she wasn't the best example.

"Anyway," Iricana continued, "the good thing about not docking is that we don't yet have to deal with the public."

Beezan shook his head in denial. "Do you really think they're that interested?"

"Captain," Iricana said firmly, "we're going to need to call security the first few times we go out, especially you; you're not used to crowds."

He frowned. They were back to Redrock, but he had to face the fact that he was never going back to his quiet life. *Do I really want to?*

"So on the 15th," Iricana continued quietly, "right after we finally dock, the Council would like us, the Captain, Katie, and me, to make a public appearance."

"Why?" he asked, heart starting to pound. "They don't know anything about the Ramians. All they know is that we were gone a long time."

"Exactly. And it's our job to make sure that's all they figure out for now."

"But people do know," Jarvie said.

"Know what?" Iricana asked.

"That something is up."

"Yes," Katie added, "I'm sure the junk news has been wild. And now add the *Cheetah* jumping out of Harbor to the stories."

"We're not officially linked to the *Cheetah,* and besides, the fact that they jumped out of Harbor illegally is classified."

"Sure, but people can see. They will know the *Cheetah* is at Atikameq," Katie argued. "Just wait a few days for personal packets to circulate. People will jump to wild conclusions."

"Like aliens and bad gravity balls?" Jarvie suggested sarcastically.

"Well," Iricana conceded, "depends how much imagination they have."

"Don't you read the junk news?" Terina suddenly chimed in,

her grandfather raising an eyebrow. "They've got more imagination than sense. And no one cares for documentation."

"So why do you read it?" Kelson kidded her.

"Because . . ." Terina frowned, as if caught with an extra cookie, "sometimes, a lot of times . . . the junk news is true."

"No!" Kelson scoffed, good-naturedly.

"Yes!" Terina insisted.

"Well, knock me over with a feather."

"Grandpa! 51% of all breaking news was reported on junk news first. And 14% of all junk news has, so far, been officially verified." They all stared at her. "Of course, that doesn't count classified information."

3-Questions

Jarvie looked down at Terina, her tool belt loaded with items never seen in his teen training, not to mention her peculiar hardhat.

"Are we going on . . ." he searched for the proper historical word.

"Safari? Yes. Seeking rare and hidden beasts, the cabin logs." She glanced behind him at the robot team and at Jarvie's toolbox and belt. "What job did the captain give you?"

"Doors." He rolled his eyes.

"Thrilling!" She threw her hands up.

"So what do you have in your 'tool' belt?" he asked.

"I'll show you while we walk over. Arc 7?" and she started off.

"Umm, sorry, we have to go the long way, Arc 9 is closed."

She stopped, peering back over her shoulder. "Well then, a real *expedition*."

On the way, Terina removed her tool-belt items one by one to show Jarvie. "Camera, of course, all-purpose scanner, multi-field detector, notepad, recorder, paper preserver, flags, search log, reference books, lights, dust masks," she handed him a mask. "Universal card charger, back up cards, and old-fashioned magnifying glasses." She handed Jarvie one. It was one big glass lens on a handle. He looked back at her. She ogled him with one giant copper eye.

"Just how small are these cabin logs?"

"Oh, they can be tiny—the size of a few microbots even. You know how they went crazy making smaller and smaller data storage devices."

Jarvie shook his head no, so she went on. "Well, they overdid it of course. They made them so small people couldn't even pick them up, or in some cases, couldn't even see them. So we have regular-sized ones now." She popped the card out of her pad for example. It was flat, hardly bigger than a square centimeter. "However, mircocards are still useful for one thing —hiding in plain sight."

"So why did they hide the cabin logs if they wanted people to find them?"

"The official reason, which I 80% agree with, is that it was a game, like the older game, geocaching." Again, Jarvie shook his head, mystified. "The idea is that only people in on the game will look or even notice."

"So what's the unofficial reason?"

"That secret information was being passed through the sectors via a network of operatives."

He stopped dead, the robots halting behind him. "What?"

"Like a spy network, yes."

"That's crazy. You're talking about only 500 years ago, not like some pre-unification crime-ridden age."

"Yes, but it did take the councils a couple hundred years to completely deal with the rebel waves, few as they were."

Rebel waves?

"You didn't really read that *Radium Junction* book, did you?"

"I started at Sector 5."

"Ahkk! Because the inner sectors are just Ancient History—an imaginary place, and Earth is but a distant dream." She started walking again, gesturing grandly, but Jarvie had the feeling this wasn't personal. "It's the 'world' view of outer sector people. They are even disconnected from the recent past."

"By recent, you mean . . ." Jarvie said, catching up in two big steps.

"A few hundred years. Jarvie! When people first came out from Earth, it wasn't one big organized project, like it is now. There were still remnants of sub-planetary national rivalries, not to mention the last stand of the mega corporations.

"As the Council cleaned up the mess on Earth, a few waves of rebels got away. It took a couple hundred years to get everyone under the rule of modern law."

"So these cabin logs were left by criminals?"

"Mostly no, but sometimes you find something. Some things were still technically legal for a while, like amassing huge personal or corporate wealth at the expense of the environment or others. That's just not done anymore."

"Whether we want to or not," Jarvie joked.

"Good example really," she explained when he frowned. "In the outer sectors, you just can't exist by yourself, let alone make any profit. If people didn't work together, we wouldn't be here at all."

As they cleared the last double lock into Arc 7, Jarvie checked his door list. How long ago it seemed that he had been out here with Sarcee.

Terina pulled out her recorder. "3-Questions-1083 BE. First search for cabin logs on *Drumheller*, under Captain Beezan, by Terina Coralia and Jarvie Atikameq. First cabin: A7C1."

As she finished she dramatically pointed to the first door. "*Drumheller*, check status inside cabin A7C1," Jarvie instructed.

"Testing sensors non-operative."

Jarvie sighed and added that to his repair list. They both put on their breathers and stood aside. Jarvie put his s'link in the slot and pushed the code. The door started to open and then stopped, stalled until the pressure equalized.

"Air test unit," Jarvie signaled the robot manager, who dispatched a small drone through the crack in the door. "Feed to my s'link," he told the manager.

"Hey!"

"And Terina's, of course."

"I don't see anything toxic," he said, checking the readout and pulling off his breather.

"It's usually safe, unless they had a lot of old plastics."

Jarvie signaled the door again and it opened stiffly. *Too bad, I'll have plenty to do while she's looking.*

By lunchtime, Jarvie was done with the door and the next two. Terina was sitting on a bunk in the third cabin, scowling.

"Is it that unusual not to find anything?" He asked.

"No," she admitted, "but it would have been fun to keep you interested."

He smiled. "Doesn't matter if I'm interested. I have to fix the doors."

"Tomorrow then. Mom was very stern about being back for lessons. She said I better not distract you from your studies."

They went back up the stairs, collected Jarvie's tools, and started back, the robots trailing after.

"It'll be nice to have a classmate anyway," Jarvie said.

"Jarvie, you're three years ahead of me."

"Oh," he cleared his throat self-consciously. "About that. Didn't Iricana tell you? We'll be in the same class. I've sort of missed three years of school."

He expected some mild disapproval from such an obviously educated kid, but when he braved a glance, she was looking up at him with amazed admiration. "Wow, you must have some story to tell."

7-Questions

Cheetah, incoming to Atikameq a-rings

Zahar finished cleaning the EEHAB and slammed the door shut. Not on any paws, of course. *I hate this job!* Her latest favorite little rat that had especially liked to ride in her pocket was gone. The rats were disappearing faster than usual.

Io and Euro came in, agitated. They didn't even come over to check the rats. *They know better.* "We have to talk to the doctor," Euro whispered.

"Are you sick?" Zahar asked.

"No." Io stood straighter. "We have a grievance."

Good luck, Zahar thought as the doctor came out of the radiation lab.

"Doctor," Euro said formally, "We request to be allowed to get off at Atikameq."

Zahar froze. *Get off? Not visit?*

"Euro," Dr. Tenshi said, unconcerned, "there just isn't time for a dock visit."

"No, doctor," Euro was flustered, so Io took over.

"We don't want to go to Luminesse."

"We don't want to see the people suffering," Euro explained in a hush.

"Oh," the doctor said, understanding. "Well, I'm sorry. Thayne isn't stopping at Atikameq. We're going straight to the a-rings."

"*What?*" Zahar and the twins all said at once.

"Didn't you know?" The doctor looked back and forth between them. *How could we know? Nothing is posted on the Cheetah itinerary.* "That's why we took extra food from Harbor. Luminesse is past the terminal point. Every day could make a difference."

Zahar's mind raced. All her plans were ruined if they didn't go to Atik. She wouldn't be able to leave the *Cheetah*.

"We could go in a shuttle," Euro suggested.

"Euro, Io, Thayne will never allow it. And you need to stay with me."

"You can come too. Or come back after Luminesse," Io pleaded.

"Io, it will be fine. You don't have to go down to Luminesse station or even look."

"We would know, though," Io started tearing up, but the doctor was immune to such things, even if sincere.

"You two are being illogical. Whatever is happening there is happening, whether we witness it or not."

"We could be stuck there!" Zahar objected.

"Zahar! Don't make things worse. You're scaring them. Captain Thayne wouldn't take us anywhere with no way to get out. That's the whole point of bringing the gravity ball."

"But—"

"We—"

"Please!" Doctor Tenshi sat down, exasperated. "Try to be

brave. Maybe there will be a way for you to help people. Now go." She shooed the dejected twins out.

"Besides," she said to Zahar, "the sooner we get there and get that gravity ball off the ship, the better."

But Zahar didn't answer. She turned back to the rats to hide her face. *I won't be able to get off.* Scenarios ran through her head: complain to Thayne. *Futile.* Lodge a formal protest with the Council. *No time, even if my message got through.* Escape on a shuttle. *Too much security, thanks to Alesta Eve. How long if I go to Luminesse? Months, maybe forever.* The rats were looking up at her, still and worried. *I might never see my family again. I hate this ship!*

8-Questions Eve

Zahar was tired, frustrated and upset, and didn't feel like sitting alone in her cabin fretting. Now was the time she needed her family. She missed them so much. Just a regular family. Two parents, two younger brothers, two younger sisters, and two podpups. And aunts and uncles and cousins of course. She wondered how her busy parents were doing without her help. At least she'd get some packets now that they were back at Atikameq. She bit her lip, forcing herself not to cry. She had really been counting on getting away.

It was too late at night to visit the twins, so she distracted herself by cleaning up her junk drawer, eating the last of the chocolate she had stashed there. Then she remembered the junk news she'd received from the shuttle pilot.

She spent some time dumping the crazier stuff. She found lots of music that she'd have to go through later and pay for what she liked.

"Mysterious Disturbance in K-Belt" was a new subject with

many items. A couple of them were just copies of ordinary news packets.

15-NAMES: MONITORS MAPPING THE HARBOR K-BELT SYSTEM TODAY NOTICED ODD PATHS OF ACTIVITY IN TWO PLACES. NAVIGATIONAL UPDATES ARE BEING PREPARED, EVEN THOUGH THERE IS CURRENTLY NO INCOMING SHIP TRAFFIC.

. . . they're alien ships, spying on us . . .

. . . they're ships coming to rescue us . . .

. . . it's just to distract us . . .

. . . it's just a natural perturbation . . .

. . . two perturbations at the same time? . . .

18-NAMES: HARBOR INBOUND AUTHORITY MONITORS HAVE BEEN DOUBLE-CHECKING FOR ACTIVITY ALONG THE ATIKAMEQ INCOMING ROUTE, EVEN THOUGH IT'S RARE FOR A SHIP TO DROP INTO NORMAL SPACE OUTSIDE THE K-BELT AND NO JUMPS ARE EXPECTED. HOWEVER, AN ADDITIONAL AREA OF DISTURBANCE WAS DISCOVERED. THE PATTERNS OF ALL THREE DISTURBANCES ARE SIMILAR, AS IF PLANET-SIZED OBJECTS WERE MOVING THROUGH THE K-BELT.

. . . we're surrounded . . .

. . . the disturbances will cause new comets . . .

. . . there's nothing there . . .

3-MIGHT: MONITORS HAVE CALCULATED THAT THE DISTURBANCES INDICATE THAT BODIES MASSING ALMOST 1G ARE MOVING THROUGH THE K-BELT. HARBOR STATION TELESCOPES CANNOT DETECT ANY OBJECTS.

Zahar glanced at the date of the first report, 15-Names. That was . . . six days after Thayne and Melawn had pushed all those alien buttons and turned on the gravity ball.

She studied the charts. One comment did catch her eye. "Harbor Mystery Objects Chart Extrapolation." She opened it up. Someone had attempted to calculate the trajectories that the three objects would follow. She did a double take. The three paths would intersect at the orbit of Hb4. But the person hadn't run the planet positions back. Zahar did, and the point where the objects would meet was exactly where OSRI was on the day they pushed the buttons.

Why didn't the news mention that? She searched for more news reports, but they ended on 12 Knowledge, the day before she'd collected the junk news. Zahar searched through the *Cheetah* packets and didn't find anything. *Who is censoring our news?*

She looked back at the first report, six days after the button pushing. Thayne had pushed those buttons on the alien control panel and turned on the gravity ball. Actually, it had started moving! And they stopped it. *Is it possible?* They called one gravity ball. *Could they have accidentally called others? Or something else? Were alien objects sitting out in the k-belt?*

She scanned through the rest of the junk news. They had a lot of crazy theories, but nothing about extra gravity balls. *They aren't crazy enough.* One thing was alarming people though. More disturbances could lead to an infall of comets, endangering everyone.

Nothing else makes sense. Ignoring potential problems, even if they were someone else's problems, was not one of Zahar's weaknesses. *We need data. Melawn.*

Two minutes later, Zahar was knocking on Melawn's cabin door. He answered in his sleeping clothes, holding his prayer book, obviously a hint, but she braved right past him down the stairs. He stared after her.

"You have to look at something."

"Now?"

"Yes. That's why I'm here." She played the real news without saying anything about her suspicions.

"This is back on Harbor," he said, trying to follow. "Why . . ."

"Just watch."At the end, she put up the chart of data showing the three perturbations.

Melawn stared at it, half asleep. Then a little frown flitted across his face. "You think . . . you're thinking we have something to do with this?"

"Yes. Look at the date."

"You think our experiments with the gravity ball somehow caused this?"

"I think pressing those alien buttons called more than just the one gravity ball."

He stared at her, stunned. "More . . ."

"What else could explain it?"

"Zahar, that's crazy. There aren't gravity balls sitting around in the k-belt."

"How do you know?"

"We'd have seen them."

"How? They are small and non-reflective."

He frowned again, but she could see his data hunting brain had been challenged and now he was actually thinking about it. He sat down, put down his prayer book, pulled out a pad, and did some quick calculations. "Maybe not. Not if we weren't looking for them."

"How long to get a signal from the control panel out to the k-belt?"

"Well, that one's on the other side, maybe twenty hours. Six or seven hours for this side."

Melawn looked back over the charts. "The closer ones started first," he muttered. He shook his head. "I'm not thinking straight. These are still moving. We sent the off signal and the gravity ball stopped."

"Did we send a signal that would stop them all? Didn't Nkiroo say something about using the semi-circle off button, not the master switch? What if he turned a bunch on and only turned the one off?"

Melawn scowled and rubbed his eyes, obviously tired. Zahar leaned over and pulled up the last chart, the one that had sent her to his cabin in the middle of the night, the chart showing the three paths intersecting at OSRI on the day they pressed the buttons.

"It must be something else . . ."

"Twenty pages of reports from monitors and astronomers can't figure it out. Apparently, none of them have access to your classified gravity-ball-calling-button data."

"No. No one has it." Melawn stared at the screen for a long time. "More gravity balls. That's how the aliens have them in their ships. They don't make them. They just go pick them up. That's why the technology is different."

"What about Harbor? *Three gravity balls are going to come flying into the system!* And who knows how many little rocks they'll perturb and send in-system?"

"God in Heaven." Melawn stood up and started pacing around. "They'll figure it out. Jamez will figure it out. And he knows how to turn the gravity balls off."

"If Jamez even knows about it."

"Why wouldn't he? It's in the news."

"News that only came to us in the junk download I got from

your shuttle pilot! This news never came to the *Cheetah*. How do we know it went to Jamez?"

"It will eventually. When it's bigger news. Then he can just turn them off."

"The longer it takes, the more trouble it might cause. Can't we send a ship to warn them? We can't just do nothing!"

Melawn nodded. "Okay. I'll talk to Thayne."

8-Questions

Drumheller in orbit near Redrock

After days of useless searching and tedious door fixing in Arc 7, Jarvie was tired and cold and missing the pups and wishing he could head back early.

But it beats being out here by myself, even if Terina is down the steps. He would sometimes have flashes of the long lonely hours he'd spent on the *Drumheller* when he'd first come aboard. Then he'd be homesick for the *Pearl* and all the warmth and fun he had had there. It had hardly been more than two weeks since the *Pearl* had made the scary jump back to their space. *Did they make it?* He bit his lip. Just knowing if Quay was okay would make him feel better.

Things had been so hectic, and now, after the big adventure was over and they were home, there was not a moment to rest, not a day to even reflect on what would probably end up being the most significant part of his life. *Done at 15.* He tested the door. *It's downhill from here. Nothing exciting will ever hap–*

"That's weird," he heard the muffled voice of Terina from inside the cabin.

Jarvie, ready for any excuse, tromped down the stairs to look. "What?"

Terina was on her back on the deck under the panel with

one of her detectors, scanning the joint in the desk. "I see evidence of defunct microbots, but nothing else."

"Oh, I lost a bunch, but I don't know how they could have gotten in here."

"How old were they?" she asked.

"Ancient."

She crawled out and scowled at him.

"Oh, I mean, maybe 50 years old."

"Fifty! Well, these are more like 500 years old."

"How can you tell?"

"Even if they're not on, they have a signature bar."

"Well then, some other clueless person lost them."

"Sometimes, rarely, people set microbot guards around especially sensitive cabin logs. That meant only they could get to them."

"But if they stopped charging the bots . . ."

"Exactly, no more guard. But I don't see what these bots were guarding."

"Let's look from on top," he suggested.

"Can't hurt."

Terina had already scanned the top, but now, together, they activated all the pop-ups, removed them, and checked inside. "Nothing," she sighed.

Jarvie did not want to go back to the door. "Let's take it apart."

"That would be overdoing it for hiding a cabin log."

"Maybe, but we might find some more old microbots. We could collect them."

She looked dubious, but let Jarvie and the bot team disassemble the top. Carefully, she scanned again. "There, more microbots."

Jarvie got out his tools and started picking up the microbots, carefully setting them in the gel of the micro box. Some were especially small. Terina got out the big magnifying glass and took a close look at them. "Can we charge them?" Jarvie asked.

"These don't match my charger," Terina said. "There's more than one kind here. This one doesn't even scan. It's smaller too."

"Can you find more?" Jarvie asked. He'd feel a little better about losing so many if he could collect a few extra.

Terina handed the scanner to him. Slowly, he ran it across the top of the panel. "There," he said, pointing down the furthest of the pop-up slots. Terina climbed up on the desk, shining a light down the narrow slot.

"There is something down there."

"Bots?"

"No. Yes! No!" She sat up, excited. "Bots and something else. We need an extractor." She looked at the robot manager. It came over, couldn't bend over the desk in its configuration, so it dispatched an investigator. Terina pointed to show the manager what she was after. "Carefully!"

The investigator morphed into a long extractor, and after several tense moments pulled out a small flat card, smaller even than the one Terina had pulled from her pad to show Jarvie.

She gasped and took it. "It's old. Oh, this is a good one!"

"Get the microbots, please," Jarvie told the extractor, setting down his box, while Terina put the card in her universal reader.

Slipping on her recorder, she breathlessly summarized the operation, then made a safety backup of the card. She glanced at the hiding place and made a second backup, handing the first one to Jarvie.

"Hunch?" he asked.

"No hunch. This is big. Old and well hidden."

"Can we look at it?"

"Oh, yes. Finders' privilege."

Terina slipped the backup into her big pad. They settled down on the deck to watch. A white background came up with a simple text headline.

For a second after he read it, Jarvie almost laughed. Then some feeling, something like when Oatah was rearranging the future, draped over him. He looked at Terina. The color had drained out of her face. She read the headline in a whisper. "I Have Seen the Builders."

8-Questions

Cheetah at Atikameq a-rings

Lanezi tried to clear his mind for the jump. He'd given up last night, frustrated by having to leave Atikameq with no packets from Katie. The whole crew was unhappy and confused about their continued packet silence. Thayne had given them plausible reasons at Harbor, but now Lanezi was growing suspicious again.

Supposedly reluctant to speak ill of the Council, Thayne hesitantly explained that the Atikameq Council wanted them to come into station instead of proceeding directly to the a-rings. They would not accept Thayne's higher orders, so Atikameq was withholding packets.

"That's illegal," Caspia said. But Zahar, the former monitor, commented that it wasn't illegal if someone on the *Cheetah* command crew had been issued an arrest warrant.

"Ridiculous," Melawn had said. "What would we be arrested for? It's just confusion, orders lost. Who knows what's been happening since we left?"

Melawn was right. It had been over 15 months, nearly a year, since Harbor's a-rings had gone down. But it didn't help morale any that no one had news from loved ones and they would be gone for months again. They all sent out messages, trusting in the system that they would be delivered eventually.

Lanezi was also understandably bothered by the destination itself. The last few nights, he had been troubled by flashbacks of those final fatal moments of his exit from Luminesse, of the last words of his shipmates and the desperate instructions of the Luminesse monitor, knowing their station was doomed.

"Something's happening at the rings," Evan said, worry in his voice. Evan was just to Lanezi's left, with Thayne on the far left and Nkiroo on his right. The others were safely in their jump chairs with full cocoons. Lanezi studied the screen. They were only 90 minutes away, calculating to come in at speed to join the others. Nkiroo had sent their intention directly to Atikameq Outbound Authority and the ships. They would know to leave space for them whether they were officially jumping or not.

"New outbound order maybe?" Nkiroo suggested, as the ships appeared to be moving around. But there was no way to know, as they were not receiving the jump instructions or the ship tracker feed. Lanezi didn't like it. What they were doing could be dangerous.

"They should have started," Nkiroo complained. "We'll have to recalculate if they don't start soon."

Lanezi frowned. Their fuel was good, even if they had to slow down and then speed up, but it was a waste.

"Is there any way to pick up the monitor's instructions?" Thayne asked.

"I can't think of any," Nkiroo answered. "They must be sending them on private channels."

They had a clear view when they got within 50 minutes

travel time. The ships, instead of remaining in a line, had spread themselves out, across the entrance to the rings.

"I don't understand," Nkiroo muttered.

Evan was piloting the run-in so Lanezi could rest for the jump. "Hmmm," he said quietly.

Nkiroo asked, "What if they don't move?"

Lanezi looked up with a snap of his head. An image and a word came to him from some long ago place. "Blockade," he whispered.

"What?" Nkiroo asked.

"No!" Thayne said, suddenly angry.

"It's to tell the pilot—" Evan started to explain.

"No!" Thayne overrode him. "They are misinformed."

"Calculating deceleration program," Nkiroo said.

"No!" Thayne almost yelled this time. "Don't decelerate. We're going. They'll just have to get out of the way."

Blockade . . . the memory filtered back to Lanezi. He'd been sitting at licensing school, right next to Bannezi. Blockade was a message to the pilot, not the owner, the captain, or the monitor, a message for the pilot to stop. It was a message that ships had sometimes sacrificed for, not just their jump, but their safety. It was a direct-to-pilot order to stand blockade. Others didn't even know much about it.

"It's been 210 years since this has been used," the instructor had said. Bennezi had rolled his eyes. He hated learning the old stuff. "It is a sacred duty to comply."

Lanezi didn't know what was going on. He didn't know if it was confusion or if there really was an emergency. "Don't worry about your license," Thayne was saying. "We'll straighten it out."

This wasn't about his license. It was about doing the right

thing. About being trustworthy, about being honest. "Deceleration program," he ordered Nkiroo quietly.

Thayne yelled at him, "No! I'm the Captain. We are going! Those are your orders!" Lanezi sat rock still and stared at the blockade. Nkiroo's helmet turned as he tried to look at Thayne and Lanezi.

"We are supposed to stop," Evan said mildly.

"We'll explain later. Luminesse needs us. We must go now!" Lanezi continued to stare at his screen, thinking of his duty and his connection to all the other pilots. Then Thayne's voice took on a flattering tone. "It's up to you now Evan. Take us to Luminesse." Lanezi closed his eyes. It was unfair pressure. Evan would give anything to jump again.

Move. Move, for your own sakes, Lanezi willed them. *Cheetah* was obviously committed. Nkiroo had resent their intentions. Thayne had announced his status and orders but the blockade did not disperse. "It's just symbolic," Thayne insisted. "No one wants an accident. They'll move."

At ten minutes, with helmets on and ready, the ships suddenly fanned out. Lanezi took a huge breath. *Thank God.*

"The path is clear," Nkiroo said quietly.

"Lanezi?" Thayne asked, with barely controlled anger. Lanezi had no voice left. He could barely shake his head no.

"Evan," Thayne asked carefully, "are you ready to jump on your own?"

"Yes," he answered, unable to hide his excitement. "If it's okay."

Suddenly, something poked Lanezi on the wrist, where the jump drug would normally be administered. Lanezi felt sluggish. He gasped. "What was that? What did you do?"

"Evan can't be distracted. You understand," Thayne said soothingly. *He planned for this possibility.*

. . .

Drumheller, in orbit near Redrock Station

Sitting beside Terina on the deck, Jarvie read the hidden cabin log.

Dearest Miranda, I must write quickly. I don't know how long I have. I'll try to explain from the beginning, but if I run out of time just know that I love you, I would have been the happiest husband and I'm so so sorry. It breaks my heart. They are saying we can't go back. I don't even know if you will ever get this message. I will pray for you every day. Please don't hate me—there is nothing I can do. We can never come home.

"Oh my God," Terina said, "What could have happened?" But Jarvie was racing ahead.

We jumped out of Cove on the 5th as planned, and arrived in safety at 5E.

"Where's 5E?" Jarvie asked quickly.

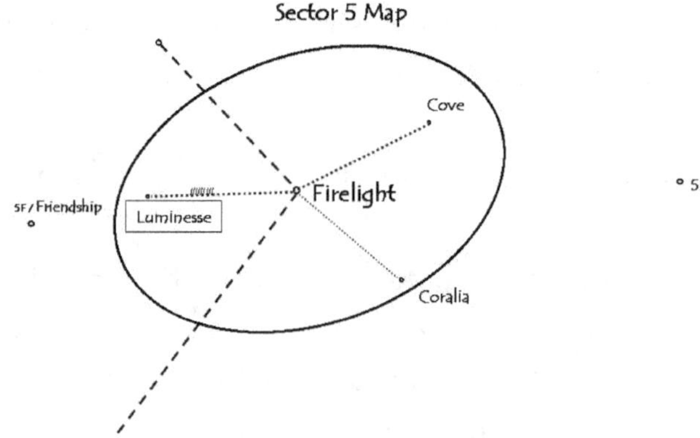

"It's outside of Cove, on the opposite side from 5F. I've seen it on old maps."

We were right. We found a system with a-rings, life planet, everything—including spaceships, stations, big energy torus, other structures, and people. And the people were not happy. They are more advanced than we are. They guided the *Ultrasoar* in. We cooperated, just like they asked. It took two weeks. We were excited. We thought it would be well, but it wasn't. They came aboard; they are gecko-people, only big. They were so stern. They had long poles. They already knew our language. They said 'Why did we come/intrude/defy again?' and 'Why didn't we follow/heed/obey their advice/order/warning?' Mom and dad and Aunt Kumi and Uncle Kayzann didn't know what they were talking about. Everyone was embarrassed and disappointed. Since mom was captain, she said we'd go, but they said no, not this time.

Then they took all the pilots! They used their poles to prod them, walking them to the hangar and putting them on their shuttles. Only Izann tried to run. They zapped him with a pole and he just went unconscious and they put him on a floating sled and took him. They are very strong for their size. We never tried to hurt them or touch them. We begged them to stop, but they did not. They said the pilots were safe but we couldn't talk to them. But they didn't get Zeezann. She's tiny even for a

9-year old. We thought we could escape with Zeezann and use the a-rings, but Mom said we wouldn't leave the pilots and Uncle Kayzann said we'd never get away if they didn't want us to. We talked to them a lot. Dad got them to explain some things. They are called the Chike and they are one of eight species of the Gentoo. I don't know what that means except that there are more of them out there! We think they are the Builders because they said we were not supposed to have the a-rings and they would turn them off.

Dad pleaded with them that we would go and never return, but they said it was already a broken promise. Then they told us to pack, we have 2 hours. They are taking us off the ship. They say we will be happy, but how can we ever be? They said we were willing to sacrifice or we would not have come here in the first place. They are sending the *Ultrasoar* back as a warning!

Dad says we must cooperate for the sake of humanity. Show that we are civilized. He says at least we're together, but you and I are not together! I wish I would have stayed with you or your parents would have let you come. I have to hide this good. They are cleaning the ship, but I know you can find it. I love you forever. I beg you to pray for us always. For eternity, Azann

. . .

Jarvie and Terina could not speak. Tears leaked down their faces. It was heartbreaking on a personal level, but far worse was the shattered delusion of a safe and peaceful galaxy.

Terina stood up and looked at the mess. "We have to take this to the Captain."

Jarvie nodded. "Number 9, reassemble the panel, stow and secure, and bring the micro box to me when you're done. We're going back to Arc 1 now."

"Understood."

Luckily, they had their skates.

Cheetah incoming to Luminesse

Normal space. Lanezi felt it. It always woke him up, even with the drug. *Evan!* Evan had made the jump to Luminesse. He took in deep breaths and toggled through his screens. All chairs had green lights, but it was quiet. He fumbled through removing his brackets, unsealing the cocoon, and removing his helmet.

"*Cheetah*, status."

"Multiple beacons. No a-ring beacon."

Well, at least they hadn't programmed the ship to ignore him. "Main screen." They had to face the situation now and quickly inventory what they'd flown into.

Thayne's standing orders were to proceed directly to the a-rings, or what was left of them, at L4. Lanezi wasn't sure why *Cheetah* would be confused. A picture blinked on the screen and Lanezi squinted at it. *What is all that?*

"*Cheetah*, show the planet."

He traced an arc around to where the a-rings should be, but —there! A standard location beacon. No wonder the computer was confused. "Use beacon 7. Run incoming program."

He worked the ship through two burns while everyone else was still asleep and strapped, doing his job, despite how Thayne treated him and despite his fear of what that blockade had really been about.

"ETA: 19-Honor."

Four weeks. Not terrible for someone who hadn't jumped for a couple of years.

Lanezi was increasingly distracted by all those beacons. This was supposed to be a dying system. *Robots?*

There was one station, the a-rings, and the outbound authority mini-station. But there were hundreds of other beacons, some with prefix codes he didn't recognize. "*Cheetah*, hide ship beacons."

That cleared up quite a bit. Now Lanezi could make out an arc of beacons slightly starward from the station. There was a huge structure out there. He had a junk news moment thinking that some alien race had come in and set up the infrastructure to save Luminesse. *No, it's all human. They haven't been saved. They saved themselves.*

A great pride and warmth spread through him. Humanity had prevailed. The Council had not panicked and given up. They had saved the system.

Team OSRI was stirring. "Please stay seated," he cautioned. "All is well. ETA at Luminesse a-rings in four weeks."

"Lanezi?" It was Evan, pulling off his helmet, dazed but clear thinking enough to glance quickly at the still asleep Thayne. "Lanezi, what could I do?"

"Evan, I'm not mad at you. I'm not even mad. Just very, very worried that there was some miscommunication. It doesn't even look like Luminesse needed a big rescue."

Evan studied the screen in astonishment.

· · ·

Drumheller, in orbit near Redrock Station

"It's fiction, sweetheart," Sequoia was saying to a distraught Terina. But Beezan didn't think so, especially as Iricana was frowning in deep thought. The entire crew sat in the Rec Room around the big screen. They had read and reread the message.

"It feels real," Terina said, still in tears after two hours. Sequoia looked to Iricana for help.

"Even if it were classified, Iricana would know. She's the expert on these things."

"I will attempt to extract verifiable facts," Iricana said neutrally.

But facts already resonated in Beezan's heart. The Zann family names. He stared at the old sector map Terina had pulled up. *My family is out there.*

9-Questions

Beezan sent Jarvie and Terina back to Arc 7 to look for more bots. While they were gone, the adults met in the Med Bay. Beezan called the meeting without sharing any of his personal concerns, assuming that no one else would notice the names.

Iricana, who had obviously slept very little, explained, "So far, I've been able to verify the existence of all those people named, plus the *Ultrasoar* and their disappearance out of Cove in the year 645."

"So it's true?" Sequoia asked, stunned.

"That much is true. There is no evidence of the return of the *Ultrasoar* or any person on the original crew list. They disappeared for good. From the scant history in the summary database, Miranda was a person of some import. She became a Council Member and an outspoken opponent of advance ships."

"Which makes it seem all the more possible," Katie said.

"None of it makes any sense if we can't explain how this message, supposedly hidden on the *Ultrasoar*, would turn up on the *Drumheller* 438 years later."

"There is only one way it makes sense," Kelson chided gently, nudging at Iricana's resistance to the unlikely.

Iricana looked to him but Kelson only gazed at Beezan, who squirmed and hugged Sky. "It seems obvious to me that the *Drumheller* is the *Ultrasoar*," Beezan admitted.

Sequoia and Katie gasped. "No," Iricana said, shaking her head. "I checked the records." She called up a file and read it. "*Ultrasoar* was built from 507-517 in Sector 2, *Orca* class, commissioned in Sector 3 in 520 and lost out of Cove in 645. That's all documented. *Drumheller* was built from 635-642 in Sector 2, *Timpano* class, commissioned in Sector 4 in 650. And *Ultrasoar* was the first ship to jump to 5E, not the second, as in the story. Also documented."

Kelson contemplated the ceiling. "Perhaps a document is just so many . . . words."

"False documents? In official records? That's hardly a first assumption!"

"And" Kelson continued mildly, "in those days, people did tend to jump wherever they wanted on occasion, without telling anyone."

"There are no records of any unofficial losses out of Cove."

"But" Katie shook her head, confused. "If *Ultrasoar* came back, someone must have come with it. Who was it? What happened? Why would they change the name of the ship and bury the story?"

"Why would an advanced civilization return the ship and not the crew?" Sequoia asked.

"Captain," Iricana appealed directly to him. "Have you ever

seen anything in the computer or on the *Drumheller* to make you think it once had another name?"

"No."

She nodded.

"But . . ." He paused. Iricana's blue eyes flashed at him as everyone else looked back. "Did you notice the names of the sister ships?"

"You mean the ones built with *Ultrasoar*? There were only four more of that class." She looked back to her screen and read them off. "*Orca, Komodo, Emperor,* and *Mammoth.*"

"Five were built at a time."

"Yes. They had five hangars."

"But *Drumheller* had five sister ships, meaning six were supposedly built," Beezan pointed out. Iricana had sent her file to the rest of them so they were all looking at the same thing.

"Yes," she agreed. "*Circle of Life, Star Hoop, Pi Surfer, Timpano,* and *Wheel of Fire.*"

"But," Beezan continued, committing himself, "we know that *Wheel of Fire* is smaller than the *Drumheller.*"

"No, they are the same class. Same specs." Iricana pointed to the screen.

"The gravity ball in that big container did not fit on *Wheel of Fire.*"

"Perhaps one or the other has been modified," Iricana suggested.

"No," Beezan protested. "We have seen them side by side. *Drumheller* is bigger."

Katie nodded. Iricana paused, likely thinking back. Vexed, she continued, "Captain, you seem convinced beyond reasonable evidence. What is it?"

"The names. The *people's* names, not the ship names."

He could see them mentally reviewing. "Zann, yes, variations on a family theme, that was common then in ship families."

"Way out of fashion now," Sequoia added, sending a scowl toward her father.

Katie gasped. "Zann! Beezan. It's your family name. Of course you would feel a connection."

"Do you know something you're not telling us?" Iricana demanded.

"I only know two things. My family was not rich and yet they ended up with a supposedly new ship. And despite all those family names about that time, I have been told I am the last of the family."

Kelson nodded solemnly.

"We need more data," Iricana declared. Everyone nodded. "But let's not mislead the children. This could all be fiction still."

"Or it could be true," Beezan insisted. "And Oatah could send us jumping out of Tektite into this 'Gentoo' territory. And we'll never come back."

"I will advise Mr. Oatah."

"Thank you." It was all he could hope for with the information he had.

9-Questions

Cheetah, incoming to Luminesse

Twenty hours after the jump, after dinner, sleep, breakfast, recorded greetings from the Luminesse Council and downloads from the station, and no apologies from Thayne, Lanezi stood with the *Cheetah* crew around the screen in Consultation Hall, looking at close-up pictures in amazement.

"What is all that?" Io asked.

Nkiroo explained, "This arc-like structure is a series of giant hydroponic platforms, each section anchored by a cargo ship and serviced by both robots and people. Shuttles run between the arc and the station. Additional energy is collected at the platforms. These smaller installations are robot mining stations. These clusters are ships linked together to make manufacturing plants. It's all quite ingenious."

From Nkiroo, that was saying something.

"So, they're not starving?" Io asked.

"No."

"How?" Caspia asked. "I thought they had minimal resources here and that we were in a big rush."

"Well," Nkiroo considered, "true, in traditional terms, only one planet, a few moons, no asteroid belt, and a scant seven Trojans at L5 is not much. But they have a stable star, the atmosphere of the giant planet and—what saved them, the most advanced engineering university in the outer sectors."

"They're not dying," Euro said.

"No," Nkiroo repeated.

"I guess we won't be heroes," Dr. Tenshi joked with Io and Euro.

"We didn't want to be heroes," Io said innocently.

"They may have technology here to help the outer sectors," Nkiroo speculated.

"It's the best possible situation," Thayne said, excited. "We won't be distracted by rescue factors. We can get the gravity ball up and running—which I assure you, they will still need. We can test the a-rings and be on our way."

Of course, at the time, Lanezi thought Thayne meant be on their way back to Atikameq.

10-Questions

Zahar sat on the one comfortable foldout couch in the Med Bay, holding a sick mutant rat in her lap. The rat's days were numbered, but Dr. Tenshi was still doing tests on her. Zahar tried not to be angry, or at least not to let the rat sense her agitation.

Lanezi's four little pups were playing with the healthy rats, but would occasionally come over to look sadly at the sick one.

Zahar contemplated getting off the ship with Team OSRI, but that might mean an extended stay at Luminesse. She wanted to go home. Unless she could think of something else, she'd be stuck here a long time.

And she didn't want to talk to anyone now. Things were tense again after the jump, with no explanation. Lanezi was sticking to his cabin most of the time. Thayne seemed annoyed and Caspia and Evan were walking on eggshells. Something had happened during the jump. In fact, she'd overheard that Evan had made the jump.

What was up with Lanezi? He was obviously unhappy aboard. Zahar was sure he missed Katie, but there was more to it. As much as he tried to hide it, Lanezi was angry—*like me*. He probably wants off too. *An Ally.* The word popped into her head. Allies were opposites of enemies. *Enemies?* Like an old movie? She shook herself. "Oh, sorry little one." She resettled the disturbed rat.

People against you. Bad guys. The others weren't bad guys. They were crew. She could not think of Evan or Caspia or Nkiroo as enemies. Maybe Thayne and Tenshi, but they were doing their jobs. She just didn't happen to like it. She gazed down at the poor rat. Although Tenshi assured her that it was in no pain, it was still dying. Tenshi didn't wish any harm to the rat, and the work was for the good of humanity, but Tenshi was still the enemy of the rat—no good or bad to judge. Doctor against rat.

Zahar took a deep careful breath. *Who is throwing my life away? Thayne and whoever follows him! I will not be a suffering rat! Good or bad, they are my enemies.*

15-Questions

Drumheller at Redrock docking ring

Beezan, Iricana, and Katie, all in their best uniforms, two

sand and one sky blue, hung anxiously by the lock, waiting for their escort.

Beezan automatically went to push his hair out of his eyes, but it wasn't there. Cut short and proper—again—and shockingly grayer than the last time. Of course, Iricana and Katie were beautiful. He planned to be invisible between them.

He wished he could disappear altogether and not have to deal with crowds and reporters. He'd already refused to answer questions, knowing he couldn't tell much, but there was one sad duty that was his, and he was honored to complete it. Lander's possessions needed to be delivered with due respect to the Pilot Center. Since Lander had no next-of-kin on Redrock, the Pilot Center would send a representative to the family.

Iricana and Katie carried Lander's large cases. Beezan held the specially folded pilot's jacket showing all Lander's pins. Beezan studied it. So many ships, and in the center front, *Drumheller*, last service.

Through the dock cam they could see a crowd gathered outside. Beezan took a few extra breaths. "Gerit, Gery . . ." He was too jittery to remember the name of their escort.

"Jerrod," Katie whispered, "special assistant to Redrock Council. We've seen his photo and we'll verify his ID before opening the door."

"So much fuss," Beezan complained.

Iricana nodded and patted his arm. "It'll die down."

"When?"

"In a couple of years—or when the next big story hits." She and Katie laughed, but he couldn't.

Exactly on time, Jerrod hauled himself expertly up the ramp.

Drumheller was docked at the docking ring, repair arc. Some outside repairs were already started even though they'd only docked this morning. The main Pilot Center was here.

Iricana turned up the volume as Jerrod approached.

"Noisy crowd," Beezan fretted. Big crowd too. People must have come over from the station.

"They won't bother you, Captain," Iricana assured him, and he believed her, but his mind flashed back to the *Pearl* and the stifling, strange-smelling, overcrowded ship.

"ID verified," Iricana whispered, squeezing his arm again, harder. "Ready?"

He made sure he was upright and adjusted Lander's jacket to show—even while swimming around in nogee. He nodded minutely and Katie opened the door.

Different air. Smells of machinery, of humans, of the Red Ribbon special wafted over him. Beezan took a deep breath. Jarrod, so human with his brown eyes and skin, was saying "Welcome to Redrock, Captain Beezan," in a perfectly normal outer sector accent.

Although Beezan had felt a sense of relief arriving safely in Redrock system and a great sense of satisfaction hearing the *Drumheller* hard dock this morning, it did not compare to this overwhelming blast of humanity.

People—humans—lined both sides of the ramp, down to the dingy cargo bin. At the bottom of the ramp he could see the lights of the Red Ribbon Restaurant. His eyes filled with tears.

Home. He swallowed and pressed his lips together.

He offered to shake hands with Jerrod, who seemed to be the sensitive diplomatic type. Jarrod shook hands and greeted Iricana and Katie. "Shall we proceed, Captain?" he asked quietly.

Beezan nodded again. The three of them waited for Jerrod to take off and then followed. Katie and Iricana stayed close to him the whole way down the ramp, past Red Ribbon and onto the main dock.

"It's not far," Jarrod reassured, but Beezan knew exactly where he was now. His dock. His home.

People lined the dock, holding to everything that was bolted down. Beezan almost had a sigh of relief when they turned onto the Pilot Center ramp—only to discover it was lined with pilots—for Lander, of course. He held the jacket out in front and moved as decorously as he could.

Besides the word *Lander*, he also heard his name, whispered, *welcome home Beezan* and *God is Most Glorious*. Some of the faces he knew, and they nodded at him in the serenity of the moment. It was then that he started to shake.

Inside, they set Lander's things for display and strapped themselves loosely in the front row of chairs. The pilots filed in for a quiet memorial, with prayers and music.

Beezan was allowed to say a few words, but passed, knowing he could never do Lander justice. Instead, Katie read the eulogy that Reeder and Iricana had written, and that seemed to capture some small part of who Lander was.

After the memorial, the Council members were escorted out, followed by Beezan, Iricana, and Katie. They were all going to a secure room for the *Drumheller* debriefing. Normally, Beezan would be nervous about it, but today he had no hesitation, as the Council was one place he could tell the whole truth.

They got separated. The crowd had grown and now they were not protected by the Lander memorial. Questions murmured though the crowd and sometimes broke out in small shouts.

"Where were you?"

"What happened?"

"Why did you quit Solo Journey?" Beezan cringed. And beneath all that, did he hear other words? *Jarvie? Aliens? Gravity ball?* He wondered if he was hearing things again or if the junk news people were just looking for any reaction. The crowd, the noise, so human, yet so outside his experience. He started to cover his ears, but Iricana found him and took his arm and they casually continued.

Beezan rigged his sleeping sack and crawled in. He would sleep well tonight. Sky was making her last rounds, stowing Jarvie's prayer book, which floated off when he fell asleep, towing Star to the sleeping sack with Jarvie, zipping them up and turning off the lights before burrowing in with Beezan. She was so responsible. She remembered, even when they hadn't been in nogee for a while.

He could finally stop worrying. They were docked. He'd survived the crowds. He'd made his report to the Council and they were one-hundred percent on top of things, although extremely distressed about the gravity ball exploding and killing the Ramians. They thanked Beezan, answered every question he had and assured him that all councils would be fully briefed. A great burden was lifted off him. That part of the journey was done. That segment of his life, "Nocturne and the Ramians," could be labeled and separated. He could start anew.

Ship repair. Regular jumps. Educating a teenager. That's new. Taking care of a podpup. Having a crew. Cargo. So, they would check out the control panel at Tektite. Fine. Interesting even. By then, people would come to their senses and realize that *Drumheller* obviously couldn't jump into unknown, possibly occupied space. No worries.

Sky suddenly stirred. "Tell!"

"Tell what?" He supposed he'd been quiet after all that talk with the Council. He hadn't given her the daily rundown. He didn't realize that she even paid much attention to his usual evening chatter with her.

"Today," she insisted.

"Well, we said prayers for Lander."

She thought about that for a while. She had been so young when Lander died. "Good. Lander good. Miss Lander."

"Me too."

"Prayer Sarcee?"

"I did."

A lot of sad and scary things had happened in the "Nocturne and Ramians" part of life, but also one of the happiest. Sky had been born and bonded to him. He gave her a little hug.

He almost wished he could stay awake to enjoy the whole luxury of falling asleep without so many worries, but as he drifted off he puzzled over why Sky was still awake. She was normally snoring contentedly within minutes. What could keep a podpup awake? Thinking of her mother? Worries? What could she possibly be worried about? What treats they would get tomorrow?

18-Questions

Cheetah, incoming to Luminesse

Melawn and Nkiroo waited in the Command Bay for their first official message from Luminesse Inbound Authority. Melawn was amused at Nkiroo's obvious excitement to see the engineering wonders of the Luminesse system. He searched and scanned, delighting in each new discovery of innovative design.

"Kiro, a person might think you were in love," Melawn kidded him.

"Oh, I am!"

Melawn laughed. "Are we going to be able to drag you away from here?"

"Not without a good look."

"Doesn't seem like Thayne is going to stay around once we get the a-rings up and running."

"No, he seems so anxious to move on, but it will take a few days at least, even for the amazing Team OSRI," Nkiroo said sarcastically.

"A few days," Melawn laughed again.

"Well," Nkiroo said more seriously, "once they see that we really do have a gravity ball and we're not some rogue ship, I think we can expect concentrated help."

"I hope so. At least some communications. Everything is so quiet. Maybe we'll get some things sorted out when the monitor calls."

Of course, the monitor's communication would be prerecorded, so they wouldn't have an opportunity for questions. He smiled when his panel beeped. "L.I.A. to *Cheetah*, God is Most Glorious." His screen lit up, revealing a pleasant, if slightly pale, young woman, efficient and friendly, speaking as routinely as if there had not been a two-year absence of incoming ships. "My name is Harmony, and I will be your monitor. Welcome to Luminesse. We have received your messages regarding your incoming trajectory and intention to repair the a-rings. L.I.A. approves both, with thanks, pending the approval of the Council. Your trajectory is approved. In-system communication is restricted to point-to-point coded transmissions. Please refrain from any general broadcast aside from ship beacon. Your point-to-point protocol will be forwarded at lag time one hour. Please check in at that time. Until then," she smiled and looked up at the camera, unconsciously scratching the bridge of her nose, "Have a safe journey."

"Why the communications restriction?" Nkiroo asked. But Melawn was distracted. Something about the monitor. He ran the last part of the message again. "Too much packet traffic?" Nkiroo speculated when Melawn didn't answer. Melawn froze the woman's picture and magnified it. "Who's in love now?" Nkiroo asked.

"Look."

Nkiroo unstrapped so he could see Melawn's screen. "What are you looking at?"

"Her nose." Just slightly visible, long healed, was a pattern of dots across the woman's face. "Same as Lanezi."

Nkiroo straightened up so fast he shot himself back and hit the wall. "The alien fever!"

"Survivors." Melawn agreed. "Why didn't we think of it?"

Nkiroo maneuvered back to his chair. "It might explain some of the engineering." He sounded disappointed.

Melawn's heart was pounding. "Maybe that's why they're so quiet. They don't know that *we* know about the aliens."

"We have to talk to Thayne."

"Yes, but you know the first question he's going to ask."

"What?"

"What happened to the gravity ball from the alien ship?"

Dinner was a ruckus that night after Melawn explained the possibility of aliens. "They could have contracted the disease without any aliens surviving," Caspia argued.

"But they would have had to examine the ship," Nkiroo argued, "which means that some remnant of the ship survived."

"Yes," Tenshi agreed. "And if they suffered a rapid spread of the fever, or any other diseases, things here may not be as happy as they appear."

"Lanezi survived and Zahar didn't even get it," Euro argued hopefully.

"Too small a sample," Tenshi declared.

Lanezi scratched his nose. "I thought the scars would fade, but Harmony must have had hers for two years."

"We do not know," Tenshi insisted.

"You can always have your scars removed," Caspia commented.

"No!" Io objected.

"Why not?" Lanezi asked.

"Because it's awesome," Euro said.

"The mark of the purple aliens," Io said dramatically.

Melawn couldn't help smiling. Tenshi shook her head at them. "Regardless, we should tell Luminesse what we know. They have to share vaccines anyway. It's good news really. We won't have to worry so much about keeping Team OSRI quarantined."

"Yes, excellent," Thayne agreed. "We won't even have to take them with us when we go." *Thayne's going to leave them here?* Melawn didn't think that was the deal. But Thayne seemed unconcerned. He turned to the doctors, "A report from you would be most appropriate. Please prepare one. Give it to Melawn to send as soon as we have our codes."

Caspia and Tenshi nodded.

"Meanwhile, Nkiroo, see if you can improve our long range scanning. We need to take a closer look at their engineering."

"Well, we know one thing," Melawn offered. Everyone turned to him so suddenly, he continued more shyly. "You know, the aliens can't be more advanced than we are. They couldn't fix the a-rings."

"True," Thayne agreed. "So we have nothing to be afraid of."

"Except the fever," Lanezi complained.

Zahar watched from a distance as Nkiroo went over the last details of their transmission to Luminesse.

"A photo would convince them," Nkiroo said, looking over the doctors' packet of vaccine specs.

"We don't have one. The DNA team was very thorough. We left Harbor before the babies' existence was made known, so we don't have a news packet."

"Nothing? The twins don't have a random photo in their p'links?"

"We checked." Tenshi said. "They were quite offended."

Lanezi scowled over his painting. He was not used to drawing people—or aliens. *Aliens are people.*

The strongest image in his mind was of the grayish-sick baby looking up at him. He had tried to draw two babies and two purple podpups, but there was no focus, no personality. He struggled to remember a clear happy moment, healthy purple with strong white headband.

I wonder how they are now.

"It's not art!" Thayne had complained when Lanezi told him he wasn't done. "It's just to prove we've seen the aliens."

"What do you think, Whisper?"

Whisper floated over, the pups tumbling after her, so Lanezi had to block them from bumping the wet paint.

"Chu-eff."

"What?"

"Chu-eff. That one," she pointed.

"That's ziz name?"

"Yes."

"What does it mean?"

Whisper looked puzzled at the question. "Name."

Okay. "What is the other one's name?"

Whisper made a podpupish gurgle-puff sound that Lanezi couldn't really capture. "Oh." He looked back at the painting of Chu-eff. Suddenly the nuances that made Chu-eff Chu-eff came into focus. Lanezi quickly painted in the slight details. *How igno-rant we were to not give them names, it only made them less in our minds.*

He took Thayne's fancy camera, took a picture of the painting, and then, as an afterthought, took a picture of the pups in their colorful splendor. How much more proof could they want?

3-Honor

Drumheller, at Redrock docking ring

Beezan tethered himself to his chair in the Command Bay so he could interact with every panel and see every one of the 20 pop-ups he'd activated. He'd been in repair and cargo mode since returning from the public appearance, only twice leaving the ship to sneak down to the Red Ribbon Restaurant. Crowds were thinning and he would soon be able to go farther. Meanwhile, he coordinated repairs from the Command Bay, leaving the hull crew to their expertise with vague explanations of what in the sectors might have happened. He didn't think they'd believe him if he told them that purple aliens had smacked their starfish shuttle onto the side of the torus. He still shuddered at the memory.

Iricana was in charge of mission planning and loading supplies. Jarvie continued to supervise the robots searching for cabin logs and microbots in Arcs 7 and 8. Beezan expected the engine inspection team next week. They were the most specialized group and could not be rushed around. Kelson kept up the garden, thank heavens, and Sequoia coordinated the kids' education, another huge relief. Katie supervised the Med Bay and generally looked after podpups all day.

The repairs were always a distraction to Beezan's regular work, cargo. He studied the markets, supply lines, and requests along the route they would take to pick up Thunder and then jump to Tektite, figuring out what cargo would be most useful.

Beezan now had a generous stipend from Oatah to buy

supplies and pay his crew, so profit was of no importance. He even asked Terina to check the junk news to see what sort of things people really wanted out past Radium Junction. Requests for trade sometimes didn't take official routes.

His s'link beeped.

"Yes."

"Jerrod here, honor, at your dock hatch with a VIP."

Beezan froze. He wasn't expecting anyone, especially not some important official. "I'll be right there." At least he was in his uniform.

He pressed his p'link. "Jarvie, where are you?"

"Arc 8."

"Stay put. We have a visitor."

"Who?"

"I don't know." Beezan chided himself. He could have asked. He was the Captain after all.

At the airlock, there was a blinking blue light, request for override to open both locks at once. Luggage. *Someone is coming aboard to stay.* Beezan's heart started to pound. Another of Oatah's surprises? He pulled out his s'link for the override and opened both doors.

Beezan floated back instinctively when he saw the newcomer, with a flash of the huge Kazorbot in his mind. But he was not a robot; he was a man, possibly the biggest man Beezan had ever seen. The smiling Jerrod seemed boyish beside him.

"Captain Beezan, this is Thunder Terrace," Jerrod announced.

Beezan blinked in surprise. Thunder was Iricana's husband. He hadn't waited to be picked up. He'd taken the first ship out to meet his wife.

"Oh, ah, God is most Glorious. Welcome to the *Drumheller*."

Thunder smiled warmly. "God is Most Glorious, Captain. Thank you. Permission to come aboard?"

"Yes, of course," Beezan swung aside while a troop of robots towed in a large supply of luggage and equipment. As soon as the last robot was through the outer lock, Jerrod gave Beezan an encouraging wink and shut the door.

"Wait," Beezan said, flustered. "Aren't these Jerrod's robots?"

"Mine, Captain. At your service of course." He smiled gently down at Beezan, who blushed and looked away. Iricana had probably confided all of Beezan's hesitations with people. Giant people didn't help.

Thunder was taller than Jarvie and as wide and muscular as the Kazorbot. His skin was the same color as the brown tool belt he wore. His hair was completely black and robust even though he was probably in his late fifties. Beezan bravely offered to shake hands and found his hand engulfed, but unharmed, by Thunder's warm, friendly handshake. He told himself to relax and that anyone married to Iricana must be a wonderful person.

"Oh, ah, I guess Iricana doesn't know you're here."

"No Captain, I thought I would surprise her. Forgive me for not confiding in you."

"It's okay, I just . . . your baggage . . ." There was so much of it.

"I took the liberty of assembling some equipment. With your permission, most of this can go to your work tower."

"That's fine, but the robot niches there are already full."

"Perhaps the tower in Arc 9?" Beezan glanced up, somewhat alarmed. Thunder had studied the ship specs—or just knew them by heart?

"Arc 9 isn't pressurized."

"Oh, technical problem?"

"Yes." Thunder gazed down at him expectantly. Beezan let out a tense breath and gave up all attempts to appear calm and in control. "I have no idea what's with Arc 9. It's been that way since my grandfather's time, maybe longer."

Thunder rubbed his large hands together. "Sounds like a challenge."

Beezan nodded absent-mindedly, eyeing the robots. "Maybe I can send the robots to the kids to sort out for now."

"Kids?" Thunder asked. "I was only aware of one child, Kelson's grand—oh, the classified passenger X is a child."

"My son."

Thunder gave Beezan a searching look. "How long have you had a son, Captain?"

"Two months."

"Please tell me he's not an alien."

"No! Well, no more than any other teenager."

Thunder laughed heartily at that, but fortunately refrained from slapping Beezan on the back. So Beezan sent the robots off, located Iricana in her new cabin and directed Thunder there, and called Jarvie and gave him the all clear. Of course, as soon as Terina and Katie heard, there was a party in the planning. Even Sequoia descended on the kitchen to help. Kelson, probably in self-defense, wandered up to visit Beezan in the Command Bay.

"Did you meet Thunder?" Beezan asked him.

"Oh, I know him." *Figures.* "Great small craft pilot. Excellent with troublesome technical stuff. Raised with robots, rock relocators, and mining tugs. Smartest mechanic in the outer sectors."

"Biggest too."

Kelson laughed. "Big hands, big heart."

• • •

At dinner, Beezan was inclined to believe that Kelson's saying was true, at least regarding Thunder. He seemed immediately at home. Everyone liked him. The kids were sitting close to him, completely engaged. Jarvie joked that he'd have someone to look up to. Terina gushed, hands over heart, about the romance of surprising Iricana. Iricana and Thunder took it all in stride, laughing and eating cake with the rest.

Sky, Star, and Rocket were the most hesitant to embrace Thunder, no doubt suspicious of anyone who dared bring so many robots aboard. Thankfully, the robots had vanished. *I hope they're secure.*

Star boldly poked Thunder in the chest pocket.

"This?" Thunder asked innocently, pulling some gadget out of his pocket. "Just a little something I've been tinkering with." All three pups floated over to give him the stare. "It's not part of a robot. Really." The pups glared. "It finds small things, maybe even crumbs," he appealed to their hungry nature.

"Humph," Star spurned him. "No need."

"Yeah," Terina agreed. "With these three, there are no crumbs."

Everyone laughed. "Actually, it finds very small anomalies—breaks—in wires or nanocable. Things like that."

Sky gave a slight nod then and the pups went to approval mode, landing in Thunder's lap and 'sharing' his dessert. He seemed perfectly at ease with them, especially for a robot person.

"Thunder," Jarvie asked, as if he'd known him forever, "do you think that thing might find uncoded microbots?"

"That's exactly what I think," Thunder said conspiratorially.

5-Honor

Cheetah, at Luminesse a-rings

Zahar had just finished checking the last healthy rat when Caspia came in, excited.

"Tenshi, have you seen it?" she asked.

"What?"

"The vaccine data has been forwarded from Luminesse."

"Already?"

The two doctors strapped in at the big screen, Caspia pulling up the files. Zahar floated over to look.

"No," Tenshi studied it a moment. "The vaccines are not exactly the same. We'll have to give boosters."

"And they have four other vaccines."

"What's that file?" Zahar asked, pointing to one that said "Ramian Summary."

Caspia sent it to another pop-up for Zahar, who gasped when she opened it, distracting the doctors. It was a photo of an adult, bluish-purple alien. His light headband was dark grey with a streak of black. Zahar's first impression was that he didn't look good, either healthy or happy.

<u>Three survivors of the wrecked ship.</u>

Toranor: Adult Male. Doctor. Sustained concussion and whiplash injuries. Still in observation at Luminesse main Med, but concurrently training in human medicine.

Torashone: Son of Toranor. Approximately 19 years old. Male. Uninjured, but languished badly until given a guitar. Sent to music school and is now improving.

Keen: Approximately 12-year-old male. Uninjured. Has no specific training. Sent to teen training and is doing very well.

All three are suffering from grief and anxiety.

None have knowledge of gravity balls or engines.

Vaccines have been developed.

Translators have been developed.

At this time we have only minimal information on their home planet, named Ramia, and it remains classified above the level of this report.

"Ramia," Zahar repeated. "That's the name of the planet. They're not aliens anymore. They're Ramians."

21 / MISCALCULATION IN ARC 9

7-Honor

Drumheller, at Redrock docking ring

Terina unconsciously patted her waist where her tool belt would normally be, but she'd left her tools behind, except for the camera. She was in her pressure suit for their excursion to Arc 9. She was so excited that Thunder had allowed her and Jarvie to go with him.

Thunder asked the Captain to over-pressurize Arc 9 with a tracer gas so that crews on the hull could help track down the leak. So far, they had narrowed down the problem, but Thunder thought it wasn't going to get fixed until they got the old microbots out of the system.

The pressure was still high, but Thunder said they could go in and try the Robot Recharge Relay, as long as they wore their suits. *Worth the trouble.* Beezan's investigation of the repair log didn't find any mention of work in Arc 9 for over 300 years. Jarvie was anxious to find old microbots. Terina was anxious to see where they came from, holding out a hope there was more to Azann's story.

The lock cycled and let them into Arc 9. Jarvie took a holdbar and pulled ahead slowly.

"Okay," Thunder said, "Go ahead."

Thunder had taught both of them to program the recharger, but Terina let Jarvie do it so she could watch for bots. She had her camera ready.

Jarvie floated down to the middle of the rimway, attached the relay box to the deck, swung open the lid, and turned it on. About twenty fully charged microbots were ready to search out their defunct counterparts. "Starting." Jarvie opened an access panel on the wall by a cabin door so that the bots could have easy access to the inner workings of the ship.

Terina took a "be patient" breath. The departing bots would track down old decharged bots and give them instructions and just enough charge to get back to the relay box.

Thunder and Jarvie watched the screen on the inside lid of the relay box. It showed a real-time diagram of bot progress behind the walls. Terina watched as Jarvie magnified so they could see the stream of bots climbing up the wall to the access panel.

"Gecko pads," she said. "Creepy, huh?"

"What?" Jarvie asked.

"That's what the sticky feet used to be called, on the bots and on the suits, because geckos were little creatures that could walk on ceilings. Now we call them nanopads, because no one in the outer sectors knows what geckos are."

"Well, I never heard of geckos until I heard of the Chike, so it doesn't sound good to me," Jarvie complained.

"I lived at a station that had geckos," Thunder said. "Very sweet creatures."

"Wow, do you think we could get one?" Terina asked, totally sidetracked.

"Recharge!" Jarvie exclaimed, pointing to his relay screen. There was a blue mark. As Terina looked, there was another small blue burst and another. Jarvie set out the main charger and turned it on.

"Look how many!" Terina said, as whole lines of blue lit up the screen. She focused on the access panel. "I don't see them coming out though."

Suddenly, the access panel at the next door popped open. She grabbed a holdbar and swung around. "That's them! They're coming back that way."

"So they return on a different pathway and don't get in the way of the recharge supply chain," Jarvie said.

"Good programming, Jarvie," Thunder said in an odd voice.

"I didn't program that. Maybe it's a default."

Terina looked up at Thunder. He scowled and floated down to the access panel where the bots were coming out. The screen was practically all blue now. "Why don't you zoom out, Jarvie?" Terina suggested. Jarvie did, but the screen was still blue.

Terina looked back through her camera. "There are hundreds! They're swarming around the charger!" She picked up the charger and restuck it a little further away from them. "Good thing it's nogee or we'd step on them."

Another access panel popped open near Thunder. "More!" Terina exclaimed. This was more fun than she had ever expected, but by his occasional hmmms, Terina didn't think Thunder was happy. Terina took photos as another panel popped open, and another. "How many can there be?" This would make a great story if she could trace their history. "Jarvie, could they reassemble into their original config?"

"Maybe." Jarvie typed a few commands into the relay box. Thunder was still down the rimway, looking at the access panels, which were now opening on the opposite side. "There must be thousands," Jarvie muttered.

"Hundreds of thousands. More than a person would need to guard a cabin log," Thunder commented.

"Depends what you're guarding it from, maybe," Jarvie contemplated.

Suddenly, the cabin door right next to Jarvie and Terina opened, startling both of them into spastic rolls. A partially assembled robot unit, too big for the access panel, rolled out.

"Look!" Jarvie recovered first, pulling himself back to the relay box while Terina groped for a holdbar and reeled in her camera. The bots were coming in bigger and bigger configs.

"How can they open the doors?" Thunder asked. "Surely the door codes have been changed since 500 years ago?"

"Umm, maybe not," Jarvie mumbled. "*Drumheller*, how long ago were these doors recoded?"

"No record. Doors are not being opened by code. Bots are tampering with override mechanisms."

"What?" Jarvie asked, confused.

"Microbots are triggering the door opening mechanism directly so that the bigger units can get out," Thunder explained, which didn't really explain it to Terina, but she knew that doors were always a big issue. They were the only thing between them and the vacuum.

"Maybe we should stop them," Jarvie suggested.

"Yes. Try, Jarvie," Thunder agreed, sounding a bit strained.

"Sending stop code."

Nothing obvious happened. Units kept appearing, blue bursts kept happening on an almost blue screen, access panels hung open, and more doors started to open, completely unnerving them, even in their suits.

"Captain," Thunder called over his s'link. "We need to secure airlocks immediately."

Jarvie reached over and turned off the charger. A robot arm immediately assembled from one of the bigger units and turned it back on.

"Hey!" Terina gasped.

"Oh no! I think we have an emergency," Jarvie whispered. "They seem to have minds of their own."

"Agreed," Thunder said. "Go to priority channel," he ordered. Captain and Med Bay, along with the rest of the crew, would now be able to hear everything.

Thunder floated back towards them. "*Drumheller*, can you command the microbots?"

"Attempt will require #9."

Attempt?

"What is going on?" Beezan's worried voice came over the s'link.

"Captain," Thunder reported, "There are more bots than expected and they are operating on an independent program. They are opening cabin doors manually. We need to put extreme security on airlocks."

"Got it."

"Kelson here. I'm bringing #9 from the work tower. It'll be a few minutes."

"Thanks," Thunder said, distracted.

Two large units were beginning to form, a recognizable spider shape that just got bigger and grew longer legs as more robots joined, and another unit, shaped more like a large flat loaf of bread.

Terina backed away instinctively. Jarvie again reached out to turn off the charger, but this time the loaf robot sprouted short legs and moved to intervene. Jarvie tightened his grip on the holdbar and pulled back.

Thunder, who was on the other side of the spider and loaf bots, signaling them to move aside, so he could sail over safely and join them.

"The blue is decreasing," Jarvie pointed.

"Good. We're getting to the end," Thunder said.

"What is that one?" Jarvie pointed. "It looks like a lizard."

Terina looked at the long body, short legs with little rounded fingers and had a sudden burst of fear. They were just talking about it . . .

"Gecko," Thunder said. "Must be an old config."

"Can we get a visual?" Beezan was requesting. Terina steadied herself, linked her camera to the feed and started sending. "*Drumheller*," Beezan was asking, "is that a standard config?"

"No."

Thunder had his new gadget out and was scanning the gecko from a meter away. Terina was continuing to slowly back away. "It's not a gecko! It's a Chike—like in Azann's message!" Even more nerve-wracking was that no one chimed in to disagree with her.

"The gecko-bot is entirely assembled from non-coded bots," Thunder reported.

"Antique ones?" Beezan asked.

"Well, that's what I thought before," Thunder said grimly. "but they could also be illegal or—

"Alien!" Jarvie finished for him.

"I see no other logical explanation," Thunder admitted.

"It's a Chike robot! We have to stop it!" Terina insisted.

"Maybe we could put it in a box—#9 could do it," Jarvie suggested.

"Katie here. I don't have a nano box that big."

"We only need a micro box, I think," Thunder replied.

"I'll look. I'm closer," Kelson chimed in.

The relay box beeped loudly. "Sequence complete," Jarvie reported.

Terina gave a little sigh of relief. At least it wouldn't get any bigger. The Chike-bot was over a meter long. It turned to face the spider, which was half again its size. The spider's multi-eyes swiveled ominously to the Chike-bot. "Jarvie!" She called out, but he had the same instinct and had shoved himself back, just as the spider put one leg on the charger and jabbed the Chike-bot with the other. An arc of power ran across the spider and blasted the Chike into the wall. The spider, braced by six other legs, rocked back and forth from the blast. The fire alarm went off and red lights started flashing.

"To the lock!" Thunder ordered, pointing.

Both bots had fried some of their units, which flew off like dust.

"What's happening?" Beezan called.

"Captain, one robot attacked the other using power from the charger. They're reassembling!" Thunder warned, urging them to the lock.

Now, the reassembled, slightly smaller Chike bot grew two electrodes, formed a power ball between them, and shot it at the spider, resulting in similar damage, but only to the spider this time.

Terina and Jarvie were in the lock. Thunder was almost there when the Chike seemed to take a step after him. Terina bit her tongue to not shout 'hurry.' Then she stuck her camera on the deck as Thunder maneuvered into the lock. As the door shut they could see the spider grab the Chike, pick it up, and slam its tail down onto the charger. The charger blew up, along with part of the Chike.

"Maybe we could just let them destroy each other," Beezan suggested, when the spider reached over to the open access panel and tied into ship power directly. "*Drumheller!* Override! Shut down access panels in Arc 9! Shut down power—wait—Thunder, are you out of the lock?"

"Not yet. 20 seconds."

Terina watched through the window as the spider extended a leg, telescope-like, and jabbed the Chike again, even as it tried to evade. Power from the *Drumheller* surged through the spider into the Chike causing a double explosion.

Beezan was shouting for Iricana and Sequoia to get to the Command Bay. The Arc 8 door opened, revealing Kelson, #9, and a big micro box. "Switch!" Thunder ordered.

Kelson transferred the box and #9 to Thunder and then guided Terina and Jarvie into an open cabin door. "Secure yourselves."

"Why?" Terina asked, reaching for her helmet.

"Leave that on. Strap." He helped them into the chairs with their big suits. "Better safe than sorry."

"Captain," Thunder's voice came, "I've sent #9 in with orders to link to the spider and see if it can override the attack program."

"Who's going to override the Chike program?" Jarvie objected. Then he reached for a pop-up and tied into Terina's camera. They could see the two bots still going at each other, now drawing power from the *Drumheller*. #9 entered the view using the rail to travel down the rimway.

"Captain," Thunder called, "you can try to power down now."

"We've lost access to Arc 9," Beezan warned.

"Look!" Terina pointed to the screen. #9 had sent a stream of bots to communicate with the spider and now, #9 was morphing into some kind of armored, knight-like shape.

Beezan, in the Command Bay, tried desperately to route power out of Arc 9, but the entire system was scrambled. Arc 9 had been bypassed for so many centuries, he had no direct access. Iricana had her s'link at level 1 in the master command slot and was trying to help #9 override the rogue program. Suddenly, #9 turned on the Chike, using a lightning-like power beam to stun it repeatedly. "The spider program has taken over #9!" Iricana called.

"It'll take over the *Drumheller* next!" Thunder declared. "Captain, you're going to have to vent them out of here!"

"*Vent them?*"

"We're still over-pressurized. Open the Arc 9 dock hatch and blow them out!"

Beezan was stunned, realizing the magnitude of what Thunder was suggesting. "We are DOCKED!"

"We better undock fast!"

God in heaven! "We have a work crew on the hull!"

There was another round of blasting, with bigger charge balls coming from the gecko. "Captain," Thunder said more calmly, "we can no longer control #9."

Beezan was panicked into action. "Sequoia! Emergency undock! Iricana, talk to the dock people! Emergency secure!"

Beezan tried to keep track of it all, the secures, the counter-vent, what were the workers likely to do? "We need clearance!"

"Working on it," Iricana said. "A team will seal the ramp. Work crew will secure on the hull."

Katie's voice came during a lull, "Katie and three pups secure."

Jarvie's voice, "Terina, Jarvie secure."

"*Drumheller*," Beezan ordered, "estimate venting thrust. Be ready to use multiple thrusters to compensate."

Beezan could see flames in Arc 9, but he couldn't be distracted. He forced himself not to look. The venting would take care of it. He hoped someone was saying a prayer, because he sure didn't have time. He couldn't even think straight from the constant stream of alerts and overrides.

"Work crew secure. Dock says go!" Iricana reported.

"Wait!" Beezan's mind reeled. Someone's not secure . . . Oatah, Neah, no, no, too many people. "Kelson?"

"Kelson secure."

I'm forgetting. "Repeat sequence by name!"

They hadn't practiced. It was a system that only worked for very small crews. They were supposed to go in alphabetical order, but no one said anything.

"You! Captain, Iricana, secure!"

"Jarvie, secure."

"Katie and pups."

"Kelson."

"Sequoia."

"Terina."

"Thunder."

"Go!" he shouted to Sequoia, but she had already thrown the locks and burned back from the dock.

"Give me 1000 meters," Beezan said.

"No time!" Thunder warned. "They're linking power circuits together! They'll blow a hole in the hull!"

Stupid bots! "*Drumheller*, confirm Arc 8 airlock is closed.

"Confirm, closed."

I've got to calm down for this. Beezan took a big breath. *If I get the wrong doors, I'll vent the whole ship.*

"*Drumheller*, confirm Arc 9 outer access hatch on screen." It blinked. Beezan signaled Iricana to hold the level one override. "*Drumheller*, open both doors of Arc 9 outer access as highlighted and use thrusters to counter estimated vent thrust, now."

Both airlock doors opened immediately. A rush of air, with an amazing amount of moisture, dust, and blasted robot debris spewed out the door. The ship rocked slightly with the difference between the all-out vent and the controlled burns on the other side. The robots tumbled down the rimway, still attempting to blast each other.

"Not enough air!" Thunder said. The bots were now attempting to grapple onto holds and door jams, although they slid to within two meters of the hatch. "We need to open the cabin doors to blast them again, before they gain a good foothold."

Sequoia was struggling with the ship. Iricana was ordering #9 to find a way to dislodge the Chike-bot. Carefully, carefully, Beezan spelled out the next command. "Confirm Arc 8 lock will remain closed."

"Confirmed."

"Execute."

A bigger blast of air, but uneven, buffeted the bots, as the cabin air vented into the rimway and then out. #9 and the spider were dislodged and almost out when the spider caught the door with its legs. The Chike-bot hunkered down onto the rimway, its paws grown huge against the deck.

"It's a gecko!" Terina fretted. "It sticks!"

Almost as if #9 comprehended the whole situation and the desperation of the crew, it grabbed the spider. The two robots morphed together, giving the spider long shovel-like legs to sweep the Chike-bot off the deck and tumble out the door with it.

"*Drumheller!*" Beezan was going to say, shut the doors, but they were shutting.

"Is #9 under our control?" Thunder asked.

"No," Iricana said, "but it seems to be on our side."

"*Drumheller*," Beezan said with a tinge of regret, "ignore input from #9."

"Acknowledged."

Iricana arranged more screens showing the outside view while Sequoia still struggled with the ship, continuing to slowly back away from the dock.

The giant spider had flung itself and its prisoner upwards. It wouldn't get to the dock. But the struggle wasn't over. The Chike reached out a bot line, snagging onto the hull of the *Drumheller*, mere inches from a suited worker.

"Oh, no!" Iricana exclaimed. The worker was small, but workers knew bots and she seemed to understand her danger. She opened her tool kit and pulled something out.

"Flash welder," Thunder said.

"She's too far!" Kelson objected, but she bided her time as the bots reeled in towards the hull. Locking her boots, she suddenly stood to full height and started firing at the bots, zigzagging the narrow beam across both bots, and circling around as it came apart. The blasted pieces started tumbling back up and away from the hull. She paused to switch to wide beam and raked it back and forth against the whole area, sweeping all parts upward.

"The particle shield will finish them," Thunder explained quietly.

. . .

Beezan couldn't calm down. The workers had looked for any bot units on the hull, but nothing large enough to be identified had been found. Then the workers had jetted back to the dock safely.

The *Drumheller* was freeparked now, repairs abandoned. The dock monitor had told them "No possible way!" when they'd requested to redock. Beezan had spun up, partly just so he could collapse in his chair, but it didn't stop his heart from pounding. Everyone else had checked in at the Med Bay and had gone to the kitchen.

Finally he stopped being stubborn, and admitted he was embarrassed. There was no need for him to stay here and he had to check on Sky.

He walked shakily down the rimway and weakly climbed the stairs to the kitchen, feeling awkward about being so shaken. As soon as he came in, Katie handed over a keening Sky, who burrowed into his jacket. "I'm sorry Sky. Really bad bots." He started to tear up then, extremely embarrassed. Some captain. But then he was gently shoved into a seat, food appeared, a tea bulb was in his hand, Jarvie had an arm around his shoulder, Star nuzzled him, Rocket said something like "Yea Cap," and the crew was apologizing for all the little things they hadn't done right. Their warmth and support were medicine to his pounding heart. He had a few sips of tea. He took the offered bottle for Sky, who turned her head to spurn it and then grabbed it a second later.

"I'm so sorry, Captain," Thunder said.

Beezan waved it all away. "Who would have thought?"

"It was kind of exciting," Jarvie said. They all looked at him in horror.

"Twenty generations of teenage boys and they still have the shooting instinct," Kelson muttered.

"What about the woman on the hull?" Jarvie complained.

Katie shook her head. "Sixteen-year old boy."

"Not to mention Azann," Iricana said. "He's probably the one who programmed the bot."

"So you believe?" Terina asked.

"It seems a *possible* explanation," Iricana conceded.

"Do you really think he programmed the bot to fight?" Jarvie asked.

Kelson nodded grimly, rolling out one of his sayings, "If you start a war, you don't know if it will end in peace or pieces."

"We are not at war with the Chike!" Iricana objected. "Even if all this speculation is true, we must not let a couple of unhappy events prejudice us. After all, we had a rough start with the Ramians, Captain. You thought they were crazy, but we worked peacefully with them."

"Sure, I love the Ramians, but they're still crazy."

"And if the Chike do exist," Sequoia said, "they could still be dangerous."

"Our own ignorance is our biggest danger," Iricana insisted.

"There is only one cure for ignorance," Kelson offered.

Sky peeked up at him and scowled. Beezan was afraid he knew what that meant. They were all about to get an education.

4-Sovereignty

Luminesse Outbound Authority Station

The Luminesse Outbound Authority Station orbited L4 at a safe distance from the destroyed a-ring system. To stay oriented towards the a-rings, it didn't rotate. Melawn came to the L.O.A. station with Nkiroo in the shuttle *Spring Azure;* then they made their way in nogee to the conference room, where they tethered at the table and waited.

Melawn swallowed nervously, wishing Thayne had come himself. The two Council Members were showing great courtesy by coming out from the main station. Although, this way, they could take a personal look at the new gravity ball and Kanika's operation with Team OSRI.

It would be more appropriate for the captain to meet with them, but Thayne had claimed illness and sent Melawn and Nkiroo. They had done their best to show respect. They wore their nicest uniforms, but Melawn feared that Thayne's fancy uniform demands might be too much.

A light over the door blinked green. They straightened up to greet the Council Members and present the gift of the model a-ring. Melawn knew the Council Members by reputation only. Sanichi, an elderly man, was small but strong and rumored to actually speak Japanese. Pandeen, a middle-aged woman, was said to be a visionary and charismatic speaker. Melawn had no doubt that the survival of Luminesse was at least in part due to these two Council Members. To be met by such esteemed people only put him more ill at ease.

The view out the observation window was a perfect background for their talk as the manufacturing units and still-collapsed a-ring segments were being hauled into place.

"Forgive us please," Sanichi said, after a prayer, "if we have many fundamental questions. We've been out of communications for a while and this technology is new to us."

"The technology is new to everyone," Nkiroo assured them. "Your system will be the second to have human designed tori and a mini-gravity ball."

"Harbor being the first," Pandeen clarified, "after a similar accident there."

"Yes," Nkiroo confirmed, explaining the details of the engineering with such enthusiasm that Melawn understood why Thayne had sent him. Both Council Members listened attentively, even to complex details.

"Do we have any idea why these gravity balls are smaller?" Sanichi asked.

"Not really," Nkiroo answered. "We suspect there may be a variety of models. Team Leader Kanika will be staying here with some of her staff to interface with L.O.A. Commander Maxwell until he's completely comfortable with the new gravity ball and commands."

"Commands?" Sanichi asked at once.

"Yes, the alien ship at Harbor had a command panel that we were able to interpret."

"But no explanation from a Ramian?" Pandeen asked.

Nkiroo faltered for a second. Melawn was sympathetic. They had read that the aliens were called Ramians, but to hear Pandeen say it, like they were regular people, was so strange.

"The only survivors at Harbor were babies."

"And our survivors have no knowledge," Sanichi mused quietly.

"Would you like to hear the schedule?" Melawn said the first thing that popped into his head, and then kicked himself. Of course, they would be fully briefed by Kanika.

"We would be most interested," Pandeen said politely.

Nkiroo launched into his explanation. "Tomorrow, Team OSRI will finish expanding the segments, as in the model." Nkiroo picked up the gift to demonstrate. "Meanwhile, the tori are being formed in the manufacturing unit. From the 8th to the 11th they'll be finishing the tori and attaching them to the segments and testing them. On the 12th we'll release the gravity ball and tow it to position. On the 13th we'll turn on the gravity ball and check positions and feedback of the segments. On the 14th we'll run test objects. If all goes well, our pilot will run a shuttle test on the 16th."

"And after that?" Pandeen asked cautiously.

"We'll do the test jump ourselves, aboard the *Cheetah*," Nkiroo reassured them.

"We see," Sanichi said. "So you'll jump somewhere and come back."

"Come back?" Nkiroo repeated, caught off guard.

"Well, how else will we really know it works?" Pandeen asked.

"Certainly you did that in your test at Harbor," Sanichi added. It was uncanny how they never interrupted each other.

"Oh," Nkiroo explained. "Actually a pilot jumped out using the new system, but the *Cheetah* had to bring the gravity ball, so we used a gravity-assist to get out."

"After the other pilot sent word back."

Nkiroo shook his head slowly.

They looked at Melawn as if to confirm such a crazy idea.

"Why didn't you wait for confirmation?"

"To come here as soon as possible. Our Captain was extremely concerned," Nkiroo said. "We thought the situation was urgent."

"Too urgent to wait for a relay ship to come back?"

"Well, yes. We thought you were starving," Nkiroo said.

"On your Captain Thayne's word you did this, and never questioned him?"

"We don't question," Melawn admitted.

There was a long pause, and the two Council Members calmly gazed at each other before Pandeen continued. "We do honor your heroic efforts to assist us, but you are saying that this system remains untested."

Nkiroo was turning pink under his dark skin. Melawn could think of nothing to say that would help. It wasn't like they could explain that Alesta Eve had jumped unexpectedly and they had no expectation that she would ever send a message back. Obviously, they should have sent a ship to Atik and back before dismantling the new a-rings. It was an embarrassment. "Well, in this case," Nkiroo said quietly, "I'm sure our Captain can send word back so you'll know we arrived safely."

"We would like to speak to your Captain," Pandeen said in a slightly firmer tone of voice.

"Of course," Melawn agreed.

"In person."

Now Melawn was caught in a really tight spot, between the Council Members and Thayne, who had insisted that it would be too stressful for him to meet them. "I'm afraid he's not feeling well."

"Perhaps the tests can wait, then, until he is better," Pandeen said in that same tone of voice, and when a Council Member said *perhaps*, that was as good as an order.

"We'll relay your wishes," Melawn said meekly.

The briefest of looks passed between Pandeen and Sanichi. "Proceed with your project and your shuttle test, but we will speak with Captain Thayne before you jump," Sanichi declared.

"Yes, Council Members," both he and Nkiroo replied instantly.

"Very well," Pandeen said formally. Melawn reached for his tether. They were dismissed.

Melawn's heart pounded, but he was silent all the way back to the shuttle. Inside, Nkiroo sagged and said, "They're right about the testing. Alesta Eve could have jumped to the eighth dimension for all we know."

"What were we thinking?"

"We weren't," Nkiroo shook his head, as if to clear it. "We were blindly following Thayne."

<<LUMINESSE COUNCIL CODE 17>>
ORIGIN DATE: 4-SOVEREIGNTY-1083
SENDER: PANDEEN
TO: LUMINESSE COUNCIL
[MEETING WITH *CHEETAH* REPS]

MET WITH MELAWN TAHIR PATARICK ATIKAMEQ AND NKIROO MELE NAMBU CANYON OF THE *CHEETAH*. NO PS PACKET WAS DELIVERED IN PERSON. NO HARBOR PASSWORD WAS GIVEN. AUTHORITATIVE DOCUMENTS LACKED EXPECTED CODE MUTATIONS. WE ARE EXAMINING THE GIFT FOR POSSIBLE MESSAGES. BOTH MELAWN AND NKIROO SEEMED SINCERE BUT NAÏVE. THEIR TECHNOLOGY IS SOUND, BUT TESTING NON-EXISTENT. ALL PARTIES DEFER TO CAPTAIN THAYNE WHOSE ULTIMATE AUTHORITY IS DEEPLY QUESTIONED. WE HAVE ALLOWED THEM TO CONTINUE THEIR TESTING BUT WILL MEET WITH CAPTAIN THAYNE BEFORE THEIR TEST JUMP. -P

7-Sovereignty

Drumheller, at Redrock a-rings

Terina waited for the Captain in the rimway outside the Command Bay. The rest of the crew was already there, in various states of sleepiness. All were in uniform except Katie, who had dressed in a beautiful red satin suit with hummingbirds on it. Jarvie was juggling both Star and Rocket as he'd thought to bring them bottles, even though it was before breakfast.

"What exactly are we doing?" Terina asked, but her mom didn't answer. It was jump day. The *Drumheller* was in line and they were technically on countdown. Her mom's focus was already on Sandune.

"We are circumambulating," her grandfather pronounced, smiling and making a grand circle with his hand.

"Why?"

"The Captain wishes to celebrate the opening of Arc 9 by circumambulating the *Drumheller* and saying a prayer in each section."

"Oh." *Figures. Any other Captain would have had a party.* But then Terina smiled. She had come to like the prayerful, shy Captain.

It had been a month of hectic, noisy, round-the-clock repairs. The whole crew was tired from lack of sleep. Beezan had offered to transfer them to the station, but everyone had refused. The restoration of Arc 9 had come as a last minute victory, thanks to Beezan, Kelson, and Thunder, along with Thunder's robot team. But no bots were to be seen this morning. They were carefully secured for the jump. Terina checked her p'link, hoping they would have time for breakfast before they had to go to their jump chairs.

Just then, Sky and Beezan floated out of the kitchen to join them. Captain Beezan was entirely serene. Terina glanced over at Jarvie, who was supposed to be doing jump training. He wasn't even pretending to be serene. Of course, with two pups, it would be futile. Rocket launched off Jarvie, pushing him into the wall, in order to intercept Sky, but Sky tucked herself under Beezan's arm for protection. Rocket would have sailed right by if Beezan hadn't snagged him.

"Thank you for coming," Beezan said. Even his usually somewhat-stressed voice was calm. He handed Rocket to Terina and passed out prayer cards to them. Sky had a couple of words with the other two pups to get them with the program. The prayers were numbered, so the crew lined up in nogee.

Jarvie went first. His chanting was so beautiful that even Rocket settled down, burrowing into Terina's jacket, with head out so he could see, of course. ***"O Thou forgiving God! These servants are turning to Thy kingdom and seeking Thy grace and bounty. O God! Make their hearts good and pure in order that they may become worthy of Thy love. Purify and sanctify the spirits that the light of the Sun of Reality may shine upon them. Purify and sanctify the eyes that they may perceive Thy*** *light. Purify and sanctify the ears in order that they may hear the call of Thy kingdom."*[1]

One of Terina's favorite pieces from the Mars Desert Symphony started to play. *Who else on this crew, besides the Captain, would even know that piece?* Jarvie led their floating procession down the rimway to the double locks at Arc 2. He was about to put his s'link in when Beezan whispered, "Lock them open."

There were tiny gasps from the crew, but no one objected. Captain Beezan would be the last person in the universe to be careless with doors. Jarvie opened both doors and stood aside for Terina to enter first. Her turn. When they were situated, she swallowed. It suddenly seemed so serious. A historic moment for the *Drumheller*, of course. She didn't need to read her prayer. It was a well-known favorite in the outer sectors. *"O God! Refresh and gladden my spirit. Purify my heart. Illumine my powers. I lay all my affairs in Thy hand. Thou art my Guide and my Refuge."*[2]

Terina led them to Arc 3. Just as they got there, Iricana, behind her, handed up her s'link—a level 1! Of course, Terina's s'link would not override the door safety. Her hands shook as she opened the doors, passing the s'link back to Iricana as she let the crew go by.

Iricana read with confidence and conviction, *"We must purify ourselves from the mire and soil of earthly contact until our hearts become as mirrors in clearness and the light of the most great guidance reveals itself in them."*[3]

In Arc 4, Katie chanted, *"O Lord! Render our tongues eloquent so that we may become engaged in Thy commemoration. O Lord! Sanctify and purify the hearts so that the effulgence of Thy love may shine therein."*[4] The wait at each set of double doors was longer as the *Drumheller* double-checked the override against the standard orders.

In Arc 5, Beezan himself chanted, practically whispering, he was so overwhelmed with emotion. ***"This divine and ideal power has been bestowed upon man in order that he may purify himself from the imperfections of nature and uplift his soul to the realm of might and power."***[5]

The Arc 6 doors opened right away, surprising them. *The Drumheller has figured it out!* Her mom read the next prayer with all the serenity and strength of a long jump pilot, making Terina shiver. ***"O God, my God, and my Desire, and my Adored One, and my Master, and my Mainstay, and my utmost Hope, and my supreme Aspiration! Thou seest me turning towards Thee, holding fast unto the cord of Thy bounty, clinging to the hem of Thy generosity, acknowledging the sanctity of Thy Self and the purity of Thine Essence, and testifying to Thy unity and Thy oneness."***[6]

At Arc 7 Jarvie had another turn. ***"This is the station of searching after truth and seeking the knowledge of the real—that station wherein the sore athirst longs for the water of life and the struggling fish reaches the sea, wherein the ailing soul seeks the true physician and partakes of divine healing, wherein the lost caravan finds the path of truth and the aimless and wandering ship attains the shore of salvation."***[7]

Kelson read at Arc 8, ***"Purify me of all that is not of Thee, and strengthen me to love Thee and to fulfill Thy pleasure, that I may delight myself in the contemplation of Thy beauty, and be rid of all attachment to any of Thy creatures, and may, at every moment, proclaim: 'Magnified be God, the Lord of the worlds!'"***[8]

Beezan must have given the Arc 9 prayer to Thunder for his role in fixing it. There was no sign of the robot fight. It was even hard to imagine that it had happened here, that Azann had come through here in his desperate hour, or that alien geckos had ever drawn breath on the *Drumheller*.

Terina suddenly understood what Beezan was doing. It wasn't about the repair; it was about purifying the *Drumheller* from its unhappy past. Not erasing the past, but claiming the *Drumheller* as their own and taking them into the future.

As he chanted his prayer nine times, Thunder's deep voice rolled up and down the rimway, rattling their bones. Now even Rocket was having little shivers. ***"Purify, O my God, the hearts of Thy creatures with the power of Thy sovereignty and might, that Thy words may sink deep into them."***[9]

The music faded away. They proceeded to the Arc 9 double locks. The rimway where they had started was just on the other side. As they completed the circle, opening the last two doors, the pressure equalized, the usual small breeze increasing suddenly as the air circulated all the way around the ship for the first time in centuries. Arc 9 was free. The *Drumheller* was whole.

Beezan looked at them, tears in his eyes. "Thank you," he whispered. "Please come to the kitchen."

Terina was tired after the long pulling in nogee, but she pulled herself up the kitchen stairs and stopped. The table was full of treats. The pups puffed in delight, circumambulating the table. "It's a party after all!" Terina blurted out. Everyone laughed, even Beezan. Even her mom. Good. Because in less than four hours, her mom was going to jump the new *Drumheller* to Sandune.

12-Sovereignty

Cheetah at Luminesse a-rings

Zahar's heart pounded all the way from the Entry Lounge to the Observation Bay, where she found Caspia already staring out the window.

"The gravity ball is off the ship?" Caspia asked.

"Yes. Off. It should come into view soon."

"The twins went with them?"

"Yes, off tether. Somehow they charmed Kanika into bringing them."

Tenshi came in, quickly going to the window. Now they could see the lights of two tugs swinging around from the cargo area, towing the still-netted gravity ball between them. "Did you need me to spell you Doctor?" Zahar asked, knowing Thayne was having one of his mindstorms.

"No. I've seen enough. That thing is off the ship." Tenshi spun around and was back out the door. Caspia turned to watch her go with a deepening frown.

It was a relief that the gravity ball was off the *Cheetah*, but Zahar was still concerned about Euro and Io.

"I don't understand Dr. Tenshi," Caspia admitted quietly. "She dedicates her life to finding a cure that will save the twins, yet allows them to go out there."

"I think her dedication is to isolating the radiation resistant gene combination so we can *all* go out there safely," Zahar explained.

"I'm sure she doesn't wish them harm—and they are necessary for her work," Caspia said.

"Well, as Dr. Tenshi reminds us, they are qualified," Zahar added.

Caspia shook her head and Zahar felt guilty for repeating what she disagreed with herself. "Can you tell which ones are Io and Euro?" Caspia asked.

"They have the purple cuffs, but it's hard to tell from here." They watched as the tugs maneuvered between two of the a-ring segments, one original and one human made, and settled the gravity ball into the central position.

"This isn't even what I'd call standard EVA work," Caspia said, frustrated. "What did we bring Team OSRI out here for anyway?"

"I know, but what can I say?" Zahar wasn't sure why Caspia was complaining to her.

"You've been with Dr. Tenshi a while. Don't you have any influence with her?"

"None. I'm not sure anyone does. Except the Captain, of course."

"The last person she should listen to."

Zahar glanced over, shocked at such a statement of no confidence in their Captain, but Caspia was staring out the window.

The first of six nets was floating off. It was probably the twins doing the tricky release work.

"He is the Captain," Zahar said half-heartedly.

"That I can't figure. Or why Tenshi hasn't declared him unfit."

"Well, the others take care of things during his mindstorms."

Caspia frowned directly at her this time. "I know you don't support him any more than I do. The crew is a mess. There's disunity, suspicion, lying, non-compliance issues to the hilt," she looked back out the window. "Not to mention questionable risk, and tampering with packets."

Zahar gasped. Another net floated away to be rolled up.

"It was Lanezi that was doing the lying." *Why am I defending Thayne?*

"There's more trouble than that going on, but forgive me, it's not your doing, and you couldn't possibly be expected to solve these problems."

"There's nothing any of us can do. We swore oaths. Tenshi, Melawn, and Nkiroo were specifically charged to keep Thayne contained and help him."

"I think they're in over their heads." Another net came free. They both cringed as a corner of the net with a little too much momentum came within meters of a worker.

Zahar kicked herself for being stubborn. She had been looking for an ally. Either Caspia was testing her or she was on her side. The Observation Bay was a Tee Free Zone. They could not be recorded or overheard in here. Zahar decided to take a chance. "My contract is up. As soon as we get back to Atik, I'm leaving."

Caspia turned to look at her, general frowning changing to personal concern. "You should get off here, at Luminesse."

"Why?" Another net floated away.

"I fear it will be a long time until we see Atik again."

Now Zahar was getting unnerved. *What did Caspia know?* "Why?"

"I've spent the last two years living with the deluded—pilots who think they 'know better', who would risk multiple lives on their conviction of improbable jumps. Pilots who think they can do what others couldn't do. Pilots that think they will be heroes."

"And you think Thayne is one of the deluded?"

"Yes. Except he isn't confined to a retirement center. He's the Captain of a ship on a secret mission."

"But he's obviously a genius—and they did make the new segments."

"Which just feeds his ultimate delusion," Caspia said.

"What is his *ultimate delusion*?"

"To be the hero of humanity. To reconnect the sectors. We'll go to Firelight next."

"No! We don't have another gravity ball."

"He'll get one." Caspia grasped her arm as the fifth net came away. "Try to get off, with Kanika or if the council visits or something," she whispered fiercely.

"Won't you get off?"

"No. I'm in this with Evan." Caspia's voice faltered. "I'm in it to the end." The last net came away, seeming to reveal nothing. It was a dark orb in a dark place.

18-Sovereignty

Melawn shook himself, chagrined to drift off while praying. It was hard to stay awake in the dim Med Bay when Thayne was quiet. The whole Med Bay had been especially quiet with the twins on EVA and Zahar closing up the OSRI cabins. Caspia would go to the observation deck when Melawn came to visit. Tenshi was busy with the rats in the radiation lab. They seemed to be disappearing faster than ever—which might explain Zahar's mood.

Melawn wished he could go to the observation deck to watch too. He felt for Nkiroo, obviously anxious to redeem their engineering reputation after the meeting with the Council Members. So far, everything had gone perfectly. No torus flew off to embarrass them. Test objects ran and were recovered without incident. Lanezi did the shuttle test without disappearing into the cosmos. Evan was resting for the jump, day after tomorrow. The manufacturing plant and shuttles would be reloaded later today.

He glanced down at Thayne, sleeping restlessly. Thayne's mindstorm had run longer than usual. The two Council Members were scheduled to come today, regardless of Thayne's condition, which didn't help his mood any.

But Melawn had confidence that the Council Members would see how hard it was for Thayne, how he sacrificed, and how brilliant he was. They would give their blessing for the jump.

"We don't need them!"

Melawn jumped and grabbed a holdbar. Thayne was suddenly wide-awake and sweating. "Sorry, what?" Melawn asked.

"I have seen it!" Thayne reached over and gripped Melawn's arm, turning his feverish black eyes on him. "We don't need the tugs *or* the plant *or* Team OSRI. We can get all that at Firelight."

As practiced as Melawn was at tamping down his reactions to some of Thayne's wild ideas, a gasp escaped him.

"Yes, Firelight. We will reconnect the sectors. We don't need help. We have the plans. Our test run was perfect. We will jump today."

"You're to meet the Council Members today."

"I don't need too!" Thayne's eyes flashed angrily and Melawn instinctively pulled his arm away, but Thayne only gripped it harder. "No," Thayne shook Melawn's arm, unstrapping with his free hand. "I've had a vision. I've seen our future."

Melawn shook his head ever so slightly.

"Yes! People do have visions!"

"People have dreams," Melawn dared to whisper.

"No! This was a vision, not a mindstorm. I've had enough mindstorms to know." He stared off, eyes intense now, still gripping Melawn with his right hand and gesturing with his left as if to show Melawn a faraway scene. "I saw Firelight. We will rebuild their a-rings. It will happen. But we must go today. We don't need to wait." Melawn gently tried to pull his arm away and this time Thayne let him go. "Melawn, we will save them."

Melawn smoothed out his sleeve where Thayne had wrinkled it. "We thought we were saving Luminesse."

"And we have! Now we must—must!—save Firelight, because that will save the outer sectors. It will save us all!" Melawn tried to think clearly. Thayne's intensity and anger could be distracting. "Melawn! Don't you believe? Don't you trust me?"

"Of course I trust you." His mind searched for a delay tactic. "But . . . we don't have a gravity ball."

Thayne drifted back, eyes darting as if reviewing his vision. "Yes. Yes, you're right. We had one in my vision. That means we got it somewhere else—you told me! There were extra gravity balls at Harbor!"

"That doesn't mean there are extra gravity balls everywhere!"

"Yes, of course it does, Melawn."

What? "We can't-*can't* disturb this system by calling them."

"No, of course not. And we can't disturb Firelight." Thayne reached out and gave his arm another shake "That's why 5F has been on my mind."

That sudden chill came back to Melawn, his own version of a vision. *We will go to 5F.*

"We'll get the gravity ball at 5F." Thayne calmed down. He nodded to himself. "We'll go today," he said decisively.

Today? "The Council Members are coming to see you today. And someone has to jump back to prove to them the jump worked."

"Melawn, don't trouble yourself with mundane matters. You must learn to unleash your mind. I'll just call the Council Members and explain. Another ship will jump out once they see it works. They can come back for proof. We have more important work. Go tell the crew. Prepare to jump. By tonight we'll be in 5F."

"*What?*" Caspia gasped. "He really has lost his mind."

Melawn swallowed nervously, not that he had expected the others to understand. Nkiroo frowned, alarmed. They were clustered outside the radiation lab where they found Tenshi. Tenshi shook her head. "This is normal behavior for him."

"The Council shuttle is already on the way," Lanezi added. "It'll be here within the hour."

"We're to leave in 40 minutes. Evan's gone to prep the Command Bay."

"We can't go today." Nkiroo said. "We agreed to take some of Team OSRI back on board, even if he doesn't want to load the manufacturing plant. And I promised to take Zahar to the station."

All turned to look at him. "Why in the world would Zahar go to the station?" Tenshi asked.

Nkiroo looked confused. "Didn't she tell you? Her oath is expired. Her contract is up. She has the right to deboard. She showed it to me."

Melawn's chill became a sick sinking feeling. Thayne would never let her off.

"Well, she can't leave now. Everything is still classified. And we'll be understaffed," Tenshi declared, moving as if they were done and she would go on to work.

"We can't hold her prisoner," Caspia said, gesturing for Tenshi to wait. "Why don't we let her go with the Council Members?"

"We're not to rendezvous with them. Thayne's orders," Melawn added quickly.

"They're coming. Are we supposed to just leave?" Lanezi asked.

"Yes. Thayne said he'd talk to them." Caspia, Lanezi, and Nkiroo looked at Melawn as if he were crazy. "What can I do?"

"You can tell him no!" Caspia declared with more force than they had heard from her.

"He's the Captain," Melawn said in defense.

"He's unfit." Caspia turned to Tenshi. "Doctor, you must declare him."

"He's the same as always. What would I declare that is different this time than any other time?"

"That he thinks he has visions and he's disobeying a Council Member!"

"There's no law against having visions," Tenshi said. "And

he's talking to the Council. He'll work it out with them. He always does."

"What about Zahar?" Nkiroo asked.

"I don't see how to help her unless we defy Thayne," Melawn said sadly.

"It's time to defy him!" Caspia said quietly.

"Listen people, this is very simple," Tenshi explained in her impatient voice. "Thayne has ordered that we go, so we go, unless you are prepared to mutiny."

There was a very long moment of consideration. Caspia, angry. Nkiroo, confused. Tenshi, impatient. Lanezi, scared. One by one they all turned to look at Melawn. He shook his head, automatically. He could never turn on Thayne. Never.

"Very well then, can we carry on with our work?"

Melawn took a few breaths. "Countdown. It's on your s'links. Someone please tell Zahar. Tell her sorry. Please Nkiroo, tell her I'm sorry."

Zahar hung tensely in the Entry Lounge of the small hangar, watching the shuttle trajectory on the screen. Another 33 minutes. Alerted by the countdown message, she knew that Thayne had ordered that they leave before the shuttle arrived. She also knew it would take her 20 minutes to get to the Passenger Lounge and strap in. They would send someone to get her in the next few minutes.

She would have to defy whoever they sent. *Nkiroo.* He'd be the one that knew where she was. And they'd count on her to be nice to him, since he wasn't good at conflict. But she could simply refuse. They couldn't go anywhere while she was unsecured. She'd wait for the shuttle and then go with them. All she had to do was not lose her nerve. She had never been a rebel.

The door slipped open. She didn't mean to look, but instinctively she checked. Nkiroo. Looking upset. "I'm so sorry," he said. "Melawn begs me to tell you he is sorry. There's nothing we can do. I promise, I'll get you off when we come back."

"You can't promise. I'm getting off now, while I have the chance. He's crazy and he has no right to hold us."

"You must come to the Passenger Lounge while it's safe."

"He can't go if we stay here and wait for the shuttle. You'll only be delayed an hour."

"The shuttle can't dock. He's locked the hangar door."

"What?" Zahar turned in alarm.

"He warned them, of course. He wouldn't endanger the ship."

Surges of anger and fear now alternated with wondering how stupid they all were. "The shuttle is still coming!"

Nkiroo frowned. "He said that he warned them."

They have to come. I have to get off.

"I . . ." Nkiroo trailed off, looking at the screen. Suddenly the ship tracker opened.

"UPDATE: NEW INCOMING: *CASHMERE*, ETA 8 DAYS, 14 HOURS 6.3 MINUTES."

"What is *happening?*" Zahar yelled at him. He cringed. "Why is the *Cashmere* here? Why would they risk coming when they're not sure they can get out? What are you *doing*? Are you *all* lying? Was Lanezi right and all of you are doing something crazy?"

"No. No, of course not." Nkiroo seemed as baffled by the appearance of the *Cashmere* as she was.

"Nkiroo, Zahar, come to the Passenger Lounge immediately. Countdown moved up 5 minutes." It was Thayne himself.

"No!" She shouted at Nkiroo—then pressed her s'link and tried to sound calm and firm. "I'm not coming. I'm waiting for the shuttle. You'll just have to let me go."

"No one is going," Thayne responded. "You'll just have to stop your tantrum and—"

There was a rumble. Zahar felt it through the holdbar. The hangar doors were opening! She shut off her s'link.

"A suit!" She said to Nkiroo. "The hangar might not pressurize. At least help me get into a suit." She pushed off for the suit closet, but Nkiroo hung there, frozen.

"Nkiroo!"

"I don't understand," he said. "They couldn't possibly override Thayne's level 1."

Zahar's personal panic went on hold. This was bigger than some personal craziness. "It's a level zero override."

"That's a myth!"

"*Kiro!* I was in special monitor training on Canyon, remember? If a majority of Council Members use their level 1 override, it goes to level zero, the highest override in the sector. They can take over *any* ship. They have the power to shut down the engine."

"Why?"

"To stop us from disobeying their orders!"

"But we're not."

"*He locked them out!*"

"But he's not . . ." Zahar could see that Nkiroo was too confused to decide against Thayne. She opened the suit locker and grabbed the legs.

"They're turning," Nkiroo whispered.

"What?" Zahar hung on the suit locker door swaying as she looked at the screen. The Council shuttle was turning around. They could feel the hangar door rumbling shut.

"The *Cashmere* must have sent them an official update on Thayne," Nkiroo speculated.

Zahar stared. The *Cashmere* hadn't come with any approval

for Thayne. It was something else. *The Council decided not to risk two of their members coming aboard.* She let go of the suit, stunned.

I need Allies. Is Nkiroo on my side? "A shuttle. Take me to them. Stay if you want to."

"What? No. That's impossible. Zahar, what are you thinking?" He shook his head, confused.

"This is our last chance! He'll drag us God-knows-where in his insane heroics!"

"No, it's not like that. Everything will be okay. You just need to be patient."

Her last hope was gone. She was stuck with them, abandoned to their genius delusions. "*Nothing good will come of this!*"

"Peace, please." He held up his hands, shaking.

She shoved the suit back in the locker and slammed the door. There was only one way to take action, she thought. *'They' aren't against me anymore.* She pushed ahead of Nkiroo to lead the way back to the Passenger Lounge. *Now I'm against them!*

18-Sovereignty

Cheetah incoming to 5F/Friendship

Melawn unsealed his cocoon and dragged himself out of the passenger chair. Hard jump. It wasn't good to jump when the crew was upset. It made the depression even worse. But of course, nothing would stop Thayne. Melawn checked Thayne's icons on his wrist p'link. Good and conscious. He pushed off for the Command Bay and noticed Lanezi look that way and hesitate, embarrassed about being banned from the Command Bay.

"Come on," Melawn took his arm. "Let's see if we made it to 5F."

In the Command Bay, Evan was looking very pleased and coherent. Thayne smiled. "Ten weeks out of 5F. Evan was perfect."

"A-ring beacon confirmed," Nkiroo said. "And two additional beacons." He turned to Melawn with a puzzled expression. "One of the beacons is on your alien frequency."

Melawn and Lanezi dived for chairs, strapping in and

bringing up pop-ups. "The Ramians?" Melawn wondered. *Are we in a Ramian system?*

"Well, the other beacon is ours. I'm getting the location signal, but if there's a message, it's not coming through."

Thayne frowned. Melawn switched to his alien receiver program and tied in the translator he'd received from Luminesse. "Well, there's some kind of repeating message on the alien beacon," Melawn said as the others came in. "I don't know how good the translator is, but let's try."

WELCOME AT FRIENDSHIP — A TOGETHER RAMIAN/HUMAN SYSTEM

There were gasps all around. "We have treaties with aliens?" Evan asked.

IN THE ATTRIBUTE OF ONE SPIRIT WITH ALL MERCY.

NAME: DIEGO LOYAL OATAH, PERSON OF HUMAN FROM PLANET EARTH AND ALL HUMAN PLANETS (SEE LIST 1) NEXT CALLED HUMAN AND NAME: NEAH SME COLLI-ELL, CAPTAIN AT ZHARTA OF RAMIA AND SISTERS OF RAMIA (SEE LIST 2) DID TRAVEL AND SING AND TALK THIS TREATY NOW:

DECIDE 1: PLANET SYSTEM MANUA (HUMAN NOT CONCENTRATING) (SEE LIST 3) IS MADE COMMON SYSTEM TO HUMAN AND RAMIAN TRAVEL AND LIVING.

DECIDE 2: PLANET SYSTEM ##UNKNOWN## (HUMAN 5F) (SEE LIST 3) IS DECIDE COMMON SYSTEM.

DECIDE 3: NO MATERIALS CAN BE TAKEN AND NO STATIONS CAN BE MADE ON MANUA OR ##UNKNOWN## UNTIL MORE TALK DECIDES.

DECIDE 4: STARS HUMAN SPACE CLOSED RAMIANS UNTIL TALK DECIDES.

DECIDE 5: STARS RAMIAN SPACE CLOSED HUMANS UNTIL TALK DECIDES.

DECIDE NOW: MIST 1409:14:2 (HUMAN 2-MIGHT-1083)

EXTRA: MIST 1409:14:7 (HUMAN 7-MIGHT-1083) ##UNKNOWN## DECIDE QUARTIL (HUMAN FRIENDSHIP)

The crew crowded around the panels. Melawn sent the 'lists' up to the big screen. "This is the first one," he said, "that they call Manua." It was a copy of a physical document. He enlarged it. There was human handwriting on it in the bottom corner.

"Look, signatures," Caspia said.

Melawn focused on the corner. "Oatah. And witnesses. Look 'Beezan.'"

"I know him," Evan said. "Captain of *Drumheller*. He's a Solo Journey pilot."

Nkiroo pointed. "The coordinates written there are human."

"It says Manua/Daydream," Caspia said.

"Well, even this translation gives us the basic meaning," Nkiroo said. "Yes, we do have treaties with the Ramians."

"That's clearly this system," Melawn said. "They renamed 5F Friendship."

They all adjusted handholds to look outside. Nkiroo pointed to the star, just slightly brighter than the others.

"But we can't take the gravity balls," Evan said innocently. "The treaty says, 'no materials.'"

Thayne spoke for the first time. "It's an emergency," he soothed. "We'll just report it so they can keep track. What's one gravity ball among friends?"

Tired, shivering, and embarrassed to still be in his suit underwear, Melawn hovered in the Operations Bay with Thayne and Nkiroo, waves of jump depression still crashing over him. *A little food would help.*

Yes, alien messages were exciting, but now Thayne was doubly intent to call the gravity ball, without even letting them clean up first.

"We can't call it from here," Nkiroo was trying to talk sense. "We need it to go to the a-rings so we have to call from there."

"I know that! But you said there was a standard human beacon at the a-rings," Thayne replied.

"So . . ."

"So! It will have a repeater. *So* we tightbeam the code to call the gravity ball to the beacon, and it repeats on broadcast from there. Then the gravity balls go there. We'll keep broadcasting so it will track on it."

Nkiroo considered. "I suppose that's possible. We should try it with a test signal though."

"That would take . . ."

"Three hours. Round trip lag time." Melawn said.

"That's too long!" Thayne argued.

"Three hours is too long?" Nkiroo said, shaking his head. "We won't even be there for ten weeks!"

"Yes," Thayne answered. "And if we wait, it'll be another 10-12 weeks for a gravity ball to arrive. If we send the signal now, we'll get there at the same time."

"So we can still wait three hours to test it," Nkiroo insisted.

"Fine! Send a test signal. In the morning, we can call the gravity balls."

Melawn and Nkiroo exchanged a quick glance. *Balls?*

"We only need one," Melawn said quietly.

"We don't know which code will work," Thayne answered.

"Right," Nkiroo agreed. "So we'll have to call one and wait to see if there is any disturbance in the system."

"And first we have to map the system better," Melawn added. "There's a lot of stuff here. Five gas giants and three asteroid belts."

"But there are no habitations, so it's no danger to anyone if we call a few more."

"What's the rush?" Melawn knew he was risking Thayne's anger by pressing him. "We shouldn't trash the system just to save a few weeks." *Why is he so adamant?*

Thayne rolled his eyes. "You two are so grumpy after the jump. Fine! Send the test signal. In the morning, we'll take a wild stab in the dark about which of the 18 call signals to use."

Okay. Melawn and Nkiroo both nodded. *Thank heavens. At least one problem averted.*

19-Sovereignty Eve

Lanezi's mind whirled with the excitement of discovering the alien treaty. So of course, the pups whirled around the cabin, more crazy than usual at their bedtime. He pulled off his p'link and noticed that he had a message.

```
Outside origin: 1
```

Outside? The only messages he'd received lately were from aboard the *Cheetah.* And 5F couldn't have sent any messages. It must have come before the jump.

```
To: Navigator, Cheetah
From: Jarvie, Drumheller
```

Jarvie! Drumheller. That's the same ship as in the treaty . . .

```
God is Most Glorious

If you are aboard the Cheetah and get this
message it is because I am using the override
code you gave me. I am on the Drumheller with
Iricana and Katie.
```

Katie! Lanezi raced ahead.

```
We have been traveling with Honor Oatah,
the new leader of Project Restore. He was sent
by Sector 1 Council. Thayne has not responded
to any of Honor Oatah's orders sent through
```

Iricana. Maybe you do not know that Thayne is under arrest.

Arrest?

The gravity ball Thayne sent blew up and killed some people.

God in heaven. What people? What happened?

I hope you are okay and I miss you and I have so much to tell you. Official orders follow. I hope to see you soon. Love, Jarvie

Lanezi choked up at the last part, the only part that sounded remotely like the Jarvie he remembered. *What is he talking about? Arrest?* Lanezi's mighty effort to trust Thayne crumbled with no resistance. He'd been right all along. *The blockade!*

To: Lanezi — please read and forward

To: Thayne and Crew of *Cheetah*

From: Iricana, Project Restore Deputy, on behalf of Sector 1 Agent D.L. Oatah

1) Thayne is removed from Project Restore, immediately.

2) Thayne is under arrest. He is ordered to turn himself in to the nearest Council, immediately.

3) All operations with gravity balls will cease, immediately.

4) If a gravity ball is aboard your ship, you must get it off and put it in a safe place away from stations or planets, immediately.

5) The most qualified person is ordered to take command of *Cheetah* and reopen communications, immediately.

To: Lanezi
From: Katie
Yes.

Much love. Please be careful. K

Yes? *Yes, she'll marry me!* Lanezi jumped out of his chair, scattering the podpups and hitting the ceiling. A surge of pure joy, overriding all the other confusion, surged through him. *She got my package. She's with Jarvie. Explosion? But she must be safe. Her message had come through with Jarvie's.* Via the *Cashmere!* Direct override, Jarvie had written. Lanezi suddenly realized how serious this was. The *Cashmere* was sent to follow the *Cheetah*, just to deliver this message to him. And probably a separate message for the Luminesse Council.

Lanezi maneuvered back to his chair and strapped in, huddling in a blanket. He was ordered to forward the packet. What would happen? The idea made him sick. He should have listened to Dr. Obala. He should have left the *Cheetah* that day! He should have left even before, before the lying, before he became someone he didn't want to be.

Whisper floated over to him. "Sad?" she cocked her head. "Happy? Scared?"

"Yes." He hugged her. "All three. Katie will marry me!" He held her up and then hugged her again. "Oh, my God, Whisper. What am I going to do?" She looked at him, perplexed.

Reopen communications? What has been going on? Before he lost his nerve, he stuck his p'link in the slot, selected the message and pressed send all. Then he turned off the screen and dived for his sleeping sack. Maybe he would have until morning.

19-Sovereignty

Zahar's p'link beeped while she was doing the dishes. The message was from Lanezi, who'd missed breakfast, although the podpups had all showed up.

What's happening?

Zahar frowned. What was he on about? If Thayne had been mad at Lanezi again, he didn't show it.

Nothing. Why? She sent back. She just restarted the dishes when it beeped again.

Where are you? Who is there?

She went to the panel and hit the s'link. "Lanezi, what's the problem?"

He appeared on screen, looking around behind her and hesitating. "No one's here," she assured him.

He shut off. *This is crazy.* She wasn't going to get involved in Lanezi's trouble, but when he showed up at the door and beckoned her to follow, she did, along with five pups.

They pulled all the way to Arc 2 and through the lock. It was freezing. He held a finger to his lips until they got to the Prayer Room in Arc 2.

"What is going—" She stopped when Lanezi grabbed her by the arms.

"Didn't you get my message?"

"What message?" She pulled out her s'link as he let her go. "Just now?"

"Last night." He seemed so agitated.

She looked. "No. Why don't you just tell me?"

He pulled out his own p'link. "You have to read if for yourself." He frowned. "It's—oh, my God." His face went very pale. "It's gone."

"Lanezi! Just tell me."

"It was from Jarvie, about Thayne being arrested," he whispered, "about the other gravity ball exploding and killing people and how someone else is to take command of the *Cheetah* and reopen communications."

"Lanezi!" Was he dreaming? She took his p'link from him

and looked for the message herself. Nothing. But when she popped into the manager tool, the count said one. There had been an external message. "But how could you have any message?"

"Jarvie." Lanezi was shaking now, from the cold or his internal panic or both. "I gave Jarvie an illegal override code, a long time ago, when he was a runaway. The packet must have come direct from the *Cashmere*. Jarvie said he was on the *Drumheller* and that Iricana and Katie were there.

Zahar told herself to stay calm. "What happened to the gravity ball?"

"He didn't say any more than it exploded and killed 'some people.'"

"How could the message disappear?"

"I plugged it in the slot to send everyone the message."

"And we didn't get the message and . . ." She stopped. The Prayer Room. Lanezi himself must suspect. Prayer Rooms were completely T-Free. Even Thayne could not monitor them here. "You think the *Cheetah* erased your message?"

"He programmed it somehow."

"How could he?" she asked.

"Maybe he's monitoring everything and blocking our external packets."

"But he would have been angry this morning. That's something he's not good at hiding. And he was fine."

"Maybe he just stores them and reads them later."

We might have some time. "Tell me everything you remember."

He did remember. Almost word for word. "And from Katie," he hesitated, suddenly shy. "She said 'yes.'"

"Yes?"

"I asked her to marry me."

Zahar smiled despite the other news. Then she shook her head in confusion. He wouldn't have made that up. "Oh Lanezi, now what?"

Zahar and Lanezi left the Prayer Room, collected their shoes, and rounded up the frolicking pups, whose excited breathing made tiny cloud puffs in the freezing air.

"We can't stay here," Zahar said. "Let's write a note for Caspia and see what she thinks we should do."

"I don't want a conspiracy. Let's just tell everyone."

Zahar put her s'link in the lock to Arc 1 and considered Lanezi. "Maybe if I just asked her advice." The door buzzed.

Error – unauthorized.

"What?" She pulled out her s'link and frowned. She'd been through this lock a hundred times while setting up for Team OSRI.

"Here," Lanezi put his s'link in.

Error – unauthorized.

"God in heaven," Lanezi breathed, holding his head. "He knows. He's locked us out."

"Lanezi!" It was too paranoid. "That's not possible." Zahar pulled out his s'link and tried hers again.

"We got through ten minutes ago. What could have changed unless he overheard?"

"Be sensible. He's going to lock us out to freeze us? We could just turn on the heat."

A fleeting expression of hope crossed his features. "Let's try."

Zahar pressed off the door and floated to the Arc 2 control closet. It didn't have a lock. Lanezi and all the pups tumbled after. She opened the door and adjusted the heat control.

Need authorization.

She stuck in her s'link.

Error – unauthorized.

Lanezi gasped. She frowned and looked back at him. He was shaking hard now. "He knows!"

"Shhh! He can't! There's no monitoring in the Prayer Room —and you think he's spying on everyone all day? He doesn't have time," she whispered, trying to talk sense to him.

"Some kind of automated program. The *Cheetah* could do it." He looked over his shoulder.

Zahar took a big breath. The first priority was to determine if Lanezi was paranoid, or if she wasn't paranoid enough.

Outside the Prayer Room, she kicked off her shoes, just letting them float down the stairs. She left the door open, letting the pups in. She turned to look at them.

"Whisper, listen." They all floated over to her. She pulled out her p'link and s'link. "Find."

Whisper cocked her head, confused.

"Find, please."

Summer pointed to the p'link.

"Another. Find another one."

The pups turned in unison, pushing off each other and spinning around to point at Lanezi's p'link pocket and then at the s'link in his hand.

"Good pups!" Yes, a game. "Another one!" And then they were all over. Lanezi gripped a holdbar, closing his eyes to the pups tearing up the Prayer Room. "We'll clean it up," she assured him quietly.

Kiwi got under the rug and Summer and Blue followed, little bumps crisscrossing the room. Dusty looked at the few small art items stuck on the meditation shelf. Zahar carefully took the pictures off the walls and ran her fingers around them.

Whisper settled on the rug in disgust. "Find people!"

Lanezi snapped out of his cringing. "It's okay. Just a game." He started to go to her, but she was bumped by a pup under the rug and went tumbling the other way.

"Humph!" she declared.

Zahar would have laughed if she weren't so unnerved. She stuck the last picture back up as Whisper started going through the prayer books, tossing them aside to sail all over. Lanezi cringed again and collected them, holding them to his chest. Then the other pups started helping Lanezi.

"Find!" came Whisper's satisfied cry.

Incredible. In her paw she held a small receiving device designed to look like a common p'link. Zahar held a finger to her lips. Even pups understood that. They all floated over to Whisper, who pointed to the bottom of the bookrack where she found it.

Zahar gently took the device and went down the stairs, signaling the others to stay. She went back to the control closet and left the device in the equipment pouch, still turned on. She spent a few seconds collecting herself. *There's more than one way to get a door open.* She went to the storage closet to get the door opener.

Need authorization.

No! Monitoring the Prayer Room. Completely illegal. Locked out. Temperature dropping! *Lanezi is not crazy.*

Back in the Prayer Room, Lanezi and the pups were almost done putting it right. She closed the door.

"Okay," she admitted. "Something bad is going on."

He was holding his head now. "Originally, we were going to put Team OSRI in Arc 2. Maybe, *maybe*, he was just monitoring them," he said.

"Totally unthinkable. Face it. He's not under arrest because he exceeded his mandate. He's up to something that he knows he has to keep secret."

"I know. I know." He shook his head more. "I guess I've known ever since the blockade, but I felt so guilty myself and I couldn't find any evidence ..."

"Blockade?"

"At Atik."

This was news. "You ran a blockade?" She was appalled.

"No!" He hunched over as if in pain. "Evan did."

Lanezi was now just trying to control his shaking.

"Cold," said a little voice.

"Oh, sweetie," Zahar looked down at the shivering Kiwi. "We have to get out of here. I'm calling Caspia."

Error – unauthorized.

"He's insane," she said. "We could freeze before someone thinks to look for us."

"Maybe it's just to teach us a lesson. He'll open the door soon."

"Not if it's an automated program and no one even knows!" Her mind started to run through scenarios, thinking of all the actions they might take. "Slow down. Let's not panic," she said to herself.

"Well, what should we do?" Lanezi asked.

"Let's go bang on the door."

She tried the s'links again. They made a noisy business of banging on the door and the rimway walls. But unless someone was near, or really paying attention, they probably would not hear.

"Okay," she had banged some sense into her mind. "Here's what we have to do. One of us will stay here and bang and the other must try to go around."

"No!"

"Yes!" She handed his s'link back to him. "Maybe he only locked this door. One of us must make it to save the other."

Melawn hung back as Dr. Tenshi hovered over Thayne, scowling at the diagnosis screen. Melawn had had to turn off his wrist monitor it was blinking so wildly.

"His scans are swinging more extremely than usual," the doctor said. "Maybe it's more than a mindstorm."

"He was fine at breakfast," Melawn said, wondering if he had missed some small sign. "He went back to his cabin and about twenty minutes later, my alarm went off." He'd had to get Dr. Tenshi to help him bring Thayne to the Med Bay.

"Something must have triggered it. Maybe you should go to his cabin and see what he was looking–"

"Melawn?" Nkiroo's anxious voice came over the s'link. They could hear Lanezi and Evan in the background, tensely trading information.

"I'm in the Med Bay with Thayne," Melawn answered.

"Is he conscious? We need a level 1 right now."

Melawn glanced down at Thayne. "Impossible. What's happening?"

"We can go around," Nkiroo was saying, "the way you came."

"No time!" Lanezi insisted.

"Melawn," Nkiroo said, "We have a life support emergency. Zahar is trapped in Arc 2 and freezing."

"Hurry!" He heard Lanezi's voice, sounding panicky.

Thayne was only partly conscious, thrashing on the exam bed and babbling nonsense. Tenshi shook her head.

"Patient is not rational," Tenshi said.

"Can you promote yourself?" Nkiroo asked.

He didn't need to convince Tenshi. She fished through the drawer of Thayne's possessions for the s'link. "Here," she handed it to Melawn.

Melawn put the s'link in Thayne's hand, which was restrained on the bed. It blinked on—already on level 1. With one hand holding Thayne's hand around the s'link he joined his s'link to it. "Promote," he ordered. The red override light blinked on. "Override."

Nothing happened. "Thayne has to say it," Tenshi reminded him.

"Thayne," he started talking gently, calmly. "We have an emergency. There's a problem—"

"Logic is useless!" Tenshi hissed. "Thayne, say 'override.'"

"What?" He responded! And jerked his hand. Melawn hung on.

"Override." Tenshi repeated and then chanted "override . . . override . . ."

Thayne froze and opened his eyes. "Override?" he asked with a half-second burst of clarity, but it was enough for the voice recognition in the s'link. Melawn's s'link bleeped, the light panel flashed white and changed to level 1.

"Got it! Nkiroo, where do I go?"

"Command Bay."

"I thought she was in Arc 2."

"We must fix it from here. I'll explain later," Nkiroo said with a strange tone of voice.

As he spun for the door there was a commotion as Evan and the twins came in with Whisper and three pups. "Just a little chilly," Evan said brightly and sent a perfectly different and lucid look to Melawn. *Hurry. Trouble.*

He did hurry.

The Command Bay doors were blocked open with a deactivated sweeper bot. Lanezi was half strapped in a chair, crying and shaking, with a blanket around him. Nkiroo held up a piece of paper with handwriting: AI crash. Must shut it down.

Old nagging fears leaped to the surface. Thayne's constant talking with the AI must have scrambled something. Melawn put his s'link in the slot and nodded to Nkiroo. "Command interface reduction, Cheetah N111. Execute."

The override light went on. "Override," Nkiroo said.

Insufficient.

Two layer security.

Melawn checked that his s'link now said level 1. "Command interface reduction, Cheetah M97437291. Execute. Override," he ordered.

There was a very long pause. Melawn glanced at Lanezi, who shook his head. No third code. In the background, they could hear Caspia ordering a medical team, asking for the manual door opener. She couldn't open the storage door to get them.

WARNING! Formal command interface now in place.

It was a slightly different voice.

"Open the Arc 2 airlock. Both doors. Execute."

"Opening!" They heard Caspia shout over the s'link. "Very cold in here—I've got her! Unconscious. God help us. She is cold."

They held their breaths. "Alive. She's breathing. I don't know about the pup."

Lanezi looked up as if to heaven. "Kiwi," he whispered.

"Voice interface off," Nkiroo ordered.

He looked at Lanezi then. "What has happened?"

Lanezi opened his mouth and then shut it, glancing at

Melawn's s'link, seeming to go from panic to prudence. He looked at Melawn with mistrust and fear. "Promote Nkiroo."

There was a long silence. Melawn could not imagine that Lanezi would not trust him. The AI was under control and Thayne would be better in a couple of days. But he knew that stubborn Lanezi look. Calmly, he held his s'link out to touch Nkiroo's.

2-Dominion

Cheetah, heading for Friendship a-rings

Zahar's eyes flew open. *Med Bay. Alive. I'm alive!* She gasped for air. *Thank heavens. Thank you, for my family. Thank you. Otherwise my dying thoughts in that freezing airlock would have been angry ones.*

Another chance. She had tried to find some peace in it, in those last moments, but now, wondering what happened, she felt a strange change of heart. For whatever insane thing Thayne was up to, God had spared her to have some influence on it. Maybe her whole time here was not just a waste, but a preparation for something yet to happen.

Thirsty. *Kiwi!* "Kiwi?"

"Fine. He's fine," Caspia was beside her, taking her hand. "We piled him in with the others on the warming bed."

"Lanezi?" she felt guilty for not asking about him first, but he must have made it around or she wouldn't have been rescued.

"He's extremely agitated," Caspia whispered. "Spouting talk

about arrests." She glanced into Thayne's alcove. "As soon as you're up to it, we're going to say some prayers in the Prayer Room. Zahar started to sit up in alarm. Caspia shook her head. "Eat first. You've been sleeping over a day."

On the way to the Prayer Room, escorted by Tenshi, Zahar noticed that several doors, including Lanezi's cabin, were blocked open. "Why?"

Tenshi gave a little shake of the head.

Aside from being tired and sore from pounding on the door, Zahar didn't seem to have any other ill effects from the cold, but she couldn't believe she had slept for a full day.

The Prayer Room was also blocked open. Evan, Caspia, and Lanezi were already there. "Nkiroo's gone to find Melawn. He was supposed to be here ten minutes ago," Caspia said.

Find him? They can't just call him? Something is still going on.

Lanezi had a pad of art paper and pen.

Already searched in here. P'link found.

Zahar scowled. *Hope they searched twice.* There was a commotion in the rimway, all the more noticeable because of their silence.

"Okay. I'm okay," they heard Melawn say, but he obviously wasn't. He floated into the Prayer Room, holding a handkerchief over his face with a shaking hand, unable to hide his red eyes and tears. Erratic breathing turned to sobs as Lanezi helped him stick to the rug. Zahar's heart sank. *Whatever it is with Thayne, Melawn will go down with him.*

Nkiroo nudged the bot out of the door, letting it close. A couple of the others swallowed nervously. "It's true!" Melawn sobbed again, hunching over, even in the nogee, as if in terrible pain. There were gasps from Caspia and Evan. "I didn't . . . know." Melawn shook his head as if he still could not believe.

"What exactly is true?" Tenshi asked severely.

Melawn was gasping for air and holding Nkiroo's arm. "Program . . . tell them, please."

"That big program, which was taking up computer space, was a router," Nkiroo explained soberly. "All message packets were routed through a private AI network that Thayne devised and implemented. He had asked me to develop remote navigable routers, for use in case of invasion, he told me. I had no idea that he would use them both outside *and inside* the ship, on us."

"Everything," Melawn started again, but couldn't speak.

Nkiroo continued, "Every message, incoming or outgoing, has passed through a filter in the AI which has rewritten it to Thayne's specs—or just held on to it. All our personal packets too."

"How long has this been going on?" Tenshi asked.

"Don't know," Melawn shook his head. "Over a year. It will take time to sort it out—weeks. I can't . . . believe," he whispered.

They all nodded. Thayne's deception would be hard on Melawn. "We'll help you," Zahar said, seeing in her mind exactly what had to be done. Nkiroo would take command, return to Atik, turn Thayne over to the council, release the rest of them. Meanwhile, they could reconstruct some of the packet history.

"We need to deal with the AI first," Caspia said. "They can be dangerous."

"What's happening?" Zahar asked. "I thought you restricted the command interface."

Nkiroo sighed. "We did, but either the AI has taken autonomous control of some functions or the native programming has been corrupted, and we cannot tamper with that out here."

"How do you know?" Zahar persisted.

"The computer is not responding correctly to Lanezi, even if he's with someone else. You got your s'links mixed up in Arc 2. He was able to get through the doors with your s'link. But the computer thought you were Lanezi and wouldn't open the doors."

A chill went down Zahar's spine, reminding her of the freezing rimway. The computer was after him. "Computers don't have . . . enemies."

"The native programming," Nkiroo explained, "the operating system that learns from its exemplars—captains, owners, top officers, and so on—starts its layering from when it's first installed on the ship. People can be added or deleted from the exemplar list, but the past learning can't just be deleted without damaging the AI. It takes an AI expert to do anything. And we can't access the exemplar list, even with our level 1 s'links. There may have been some tampering. Historic or recent, we have no idea."

"You're saying the AI had bad examples?" Evan asked.

"Worse. The corrupted programming has filtered down from the AI to the foundational programming. Even with the AI leashed, the ship has decided that Lanezi is some kind of threat. It's now learned to identify him by sight and attempts to prevent his movement."

God in heaven. Zahar cringed. *It's us against the ship, like a bad movie.* "So protecting Lanezi is a priority," she added to her mental list and looked at Nkiroo. With a jolt, she realized he was not processing. Overwhelmed. Confused. Lost in technical details.

"Someone needs to take command. That was in the orders," she reminded them.

"Well," Nkiroo shrugged, "we can just operate as usual."

"No!" Zahar said. "We need a leader! We need command decisions! We need direction! We need action!" With each need, another person lifted a bowed head to look up at her. "We have muddled through, hoping for the best, for far too long!"

Melawn held up a hand as if to push away the thought. "I'm sure Thayne had good reasons to do what he did. If I could just talk to him."

The others scowled and some shook their heads. "There is a lot to sort out," Nkiroo agreed.

"No!" She was fuming now. They were incapable. She looked to Lanezi, fearful and hopeless. Tenshi, frowning, but still looking to Nkiroo. Evan, lost. They drooped their heads down again, except Caspia, who gazed intently at Zahar, waiting.

With a surge of clarity, Zahar realized her purpose. There was the one big action that needed to be taken. "I'm taking command," she said firmly and knew it to be instantly true. Heads snapped up again to stare at her. "I'm taking command, and I'm going to tell you right now what to do."

Caspia and Tenshi nodded. Nkiroo and Melawn looked at her in disbelief. Lanezi and Evan made small sighs of relief. Zahar held out her s'link to Nkiroo. "Promote me. To level 1. Promote everyone—everyone!—to level 1. We're in charge here, not some wayward computer."

6-Dominion

Melawn hadn't slept for days. He had hovered in the alcove by Thayne's side until Tenshi sent him out. Told him to sleep.

He couldn't sleep. He couldn't eat. He couldn't start rebuilding the packet database 'immediately' as he'd been ordered. Caspia had tried to talk to him. But he couldn't talk. He couldn't listen. He couldn't even think. He could only cry. Caspia had told him to pray and that they would all pray for him. He tried. He tried to make his prayer from the heart and not through the head as he always had. His whole world was in upheaval.

That Thayne had done wrong was devastating enough, but that he hadn't confided in Melawn, who would have guided him, helped him, kept him from being confused, was the ultimate heartbreak.

Thayne was just confused. His mind didn't focus on trivial things. Whatever he had meant to do was really for the best. If only he had trusted Melawn.

Melawn pulled the blanket up over his head, but he couldn't shut out the pain and sick feeling. Trying to work only made it worse. Just trying to sort through the most recent packets had left his head spinning with conflicts. How to know? How to sort truth from untruth when you don't know when the last truth was? Should he weight each field with a truth probability and sort? Would that give them likely truth? Should he attempt to traceback every packet? They couldn't do that here. He couldn't face it. If he continued down this path, his data-mining brain would be broken. Heart and mind both broken by lies.

"Melawn!" There was a clomping on his stairs. The noise of gravity was back thanks to Zahar spinning the ship. Caspia and Zahar knocked and came in through the blocked-open door. He just looked up at them from his bunk, pushing down the blanket. Caspia leaned over him, breathing a sigh of relief. She attached a monitor to him, rattling off a disclaimer that he paid no attention to.

"Didn't you hear your p'link?" Zahar asked. "Or the s'link?"

He shook his head dully. He felt so shaky.

"Okay," Caspia said as Euro and Io shyly came in. "Euro and Io are going to be your helpers. One of them will always be with you."

"No. I'm all right."

"No. You're not," Caspia said firmly. "They understand what needs to be done."

Zahar and Caspia gave him some food and left, leaving a tool box wedged in the door. Io sat with him while he forced the food bar down.

Melawn puzzled over the tool box. "Have we run out of cleaning bots?" There were a hundred of them.

"Hiding," Io whispered.

As crazy as it seemed, Lanezi felt a sense of relief in having a teenager in command. After all, she was a high-level monitor, trained in the new 'Teen Training' system, and most of all, she wasn't Thayne. She was also determined to take them back to civilization.

Lanezi and Evan had agreed to jump to Canyon. It was Evan's home station and he claimed he could find it from anywhere.

Lanezi reached his cabin. The door was blocked open with one of the few remaining cleaning bots. He couldn't fit through the slot with all the pups, so he had to hold the bot down with his foot so it wouldn't run off while he opened the door wider. They had turned the bots off, but rogue bots skittered around and turned them back on. Luckily, they couldn't figure out how to cooperate to escape the door. At least not yet.

The bot wiggled around, but Lanezi got through and jammed it in the door again. He set the pups down, and they tore around, happy to have gravity, except Kiwi, who was pouting for Zahar. "I'll take you to her later," Lanezi assured him. "Hey!" he shouted to the rest, who were bumping up and down the stairs near the open door, "Stay in the cabin!"

Fwup. The door shut. He clomped back up the stairs. The bot was gone. Blue was gone. *The rascal.* He pressed the door open button, knowing it wouldn't work. *Stupid computer.* He had to fish around for his s'link, stick it in the slot and say, "Open. Override." Nothing happened. Visions of his long haul around the freezing rimway came back to him. "*Cheetah!* Open the door!" The lights went out. There was an air hissing sound. Kiwi whined.

Lanezi's heart pounded. He grabbed the rail. *Think.* "Whisper, get the pups back in the box."

Podpups couldn't see in the dark even with their big eyes, but Whisper was a finder. She'd figure it out. He heard her herding them down the stairs.

He carefully followed, using the holdbars. At the bottom of the steps he realized he was an idiot and fished out his p'link. He turned on the small emergency light and checked his environmental readings. It was a little low on air and the temp was dropping. *The computer wasn't going to suck the air out of his cabin, was it? But what was with the lights?* "Lights," he said. Nothing. *It's personal.* He sealed the pups in the box and turned it on. Being more cautious by the moment, he pulled out his breather. He jumped when there was a knock on the door—then more. The emergency knock code. He had learned it when he was 8 and never used it. And of course, he had no idea what they were saying. Back up the stairs, feeling a little winded this time, he could hear a door opener being attached. He reached for the breather switch, but before he could get it, a crack of light appeared in the doorway and little rush of air blew against his face.

"What was that?" Evan asked, jamming another toolbox in.

"Equalization," Nkiroo said grimly.

"It's only been a few minutes," Lanezi said.

"Any module could depressurize," Nkiroo warned them, "to recycle air. There's an override required though."

A jolt of fear went through Lanezi. The ship had just tried to suffocate him.

"The ship . . ." Evan trailed off.

Zahar was holding Blue, who announced, "Blue help."

"Good Blue," Zahar agreed whether Blue had done anything or not, "but this isn't just a glitch. Since we can't get an AI expert out here, we need to get Lanezi off the ship."

Nkiroo, Evan, and Lanezi looked at her in astonishment.

"Umm, *Captain*," Nkiroo said mildly, "Where exactly is he going to go?"

Zahar set down the pup, pulled out a pad and wrote:

Dr. Tenshi's shuttle. Independent Med computer. Pack your stuff.

Zahar was in the kitchen, organizing food for Lanezi when Nkiroo and then Melawn came in for a snack. Evan trailed in behind them, gesturing with his pad. "There are perturbations in the outer asteroid belt!"

"Great! Nkiroo said. "A gravity ball is on the way. That should make him happy."

"Actually," Evan said, "it looks like several gravity balls are on the way."

"What?" Zahar gasped, and turned to listen. Then she remembered she was the Captain. "Show us."

Evan sent his file to the main screen. He pointed, "Here, here," and ran his finger along another arc, "here. Maybe here too."

"At least four," Nkiroo agreed.

"But we only called one," Zahar said.

"Well," Melawn answered. "We only sent one code. But what if multiple gravity balls answer to the same code."

Zahar scowled. "Or what if he called more?"

Melawn shook his head. "No, he agreed to just call one."

Evan and even Nkiroo scowled. "What he says is . . ." *meaningless*, Zahar was going to say . . . "unreliable," Evan finished.

She dried her hands. "Come on. Let's have a talk with him."

In the Med Bay, Thayne was awake and seemed coherent. Tenshi gave a warning shake of her head, but Zahar and the others went on in to Thayne's alcove.

"We need to know how many of those call buttons you pushed," Nkiroo said quietly.

"All," Thayne said hoarsely, "I pushed them all, of course." Melawn cringed silently.

"All? We only needed one!" Zahar complained.

"Well, how many gravity balls could there be in one system?" Thayne asked reasonably.

"We don't know, do we?" Zahar scowled at Melawn. "We'll have to turn them off."

"We don't know which codes turn which ones off," Nkiroo pointed out.

"Right, so you're going to have to figure that out, one at a time."

Thayne frowned at her. "Since when are you giving the orders?"

She paused. "Since I took command four days ago."

Thayne looked at the others in disbelief. But they all nodded. "Yes, she's the captain now," Melawn said very carefully.

"That's impossible," Thayne said with barely controlled anger.

Zahar left, leaving the others to catch up. To explain or not, to tell him he was arrested or not. She had bigger worries. She wanted to get home, but she wasn't quite ready to abandon the idea of collecting a gravity ball after they'd come so far to get one.

9-Dominion

Zahar frowned. How could it be a year since the Harbor accident? It seemed only weeks ago. Things were just happening so fast.

She dispensed with the details of command in a decisive, orderly way. To their immense relief, the a-ring gravity ball seemed unaffected by messing with the off codes. All of the balls were stopped now. Judging by the graphic on Evan's screen, it seemed that one of the gravity balls was very close. Nkiroo was now trying to calculate if it was the safest one to call.

The computer glitch against Lanezi had inspired Melawn to focus. He was now feverishly hunting down the problem. Tenshi was busy dealing with a still-irrational Thayne, now under arrest, leaving Caspia and Evan to be her main assistants. Euro was still with Melawn, so Io was helping to ready the shuttle.

"But Lanezi can't go without us," Io complained.

"What?"

"He promised. He said he would take us if he left the *Cheetah*."

Interesting promise. She leaned over and whispered to Io, "He's not leaving. He's just riding behind in the shuttle until we jump. Besides, you have to help Melawn."

"Only God can help Melawn." *Oh, scary.*

"Io, we'd have to stock more food and water and it would reduce the safety margin and use more fuel. He's not going anywhere," she whispered again.

"He shouldn't be alone."

"He's got *five* pups."

"He promised!"

That Lanezi! "We'll talk to him." *Mistake.* In the back of her mind, she knew it. She was too soft on the twins. She should have just said no, not this time.

But they calculated that it was possible with resupply, and loaded the shuttle. There was no time for big consultations. They had to get Lanezi off the ship.

10-Dominion

Enkindler heading to Friendship a-rings

With Nkiroo in the Command Bay, Evan at the hangar, both with their level 1's engaged, and cameras covered, they managed to get Lanezi, the twins and four podpups on the shuttle without mishap. Kiwi had refused to go, clinging to Zahar. "It'll be a long time," she had warned him, but he would not part from her.

"It's okay," Lanezi whispered. "Five is too many for anyone. He needs you."

She watched on the screen in the Entry Lounge as the shuttle maneuvered to a safe 'following' distance, which was actually to the side. "Well, it'll be weeks, but I'll be glad to get them back on board and get out of here," she said.

"Me too," Evan replied. "It won't be the same without the twins and all those pups."

"Kiwi here!" he proclaimed. Zahar hugged him. So she had her wish now. A green podpup. And her own command. And somehow none of it seemed right.

14-Dominion

Drumheller at Sandune a-rings

Jarvie tried to relax in the copilot chair. His only job was to scout the jump path. Beezan would do the actual jump out of Sandune and Sequoia was monitor. All he had to do was demonstrate that he could locate the path to Hamada and not send them to RJ. It did happen that new pilots would sometimes jump to the wrong place.

Jarvie toggled through his screens. Two laps to go. He tried to say a few prayers, but knowing that the Ramians jumped without the prayers somehow made him less devout. He had mixed feelings about returning to Hamada. He had not been happy at the Teen Training Center there. But he'd also met Beezan, so it all evened out.

"One lap," he heard Beezan whisper. *Bump. Bump. Bump.* "Exit." The *Drumheller* shuttered a little. Jarvie looked at the overlay on his helmet screen and then refocused on the view to space—and saw nothing. *Nothing! Don't panic.* He felt the ship drift to the left very slightly. *Beezan sees something.* He looked harder. *Close your eyes. See with your inner eyes.* After all, it was the implant helping him see the path. *Nothing.* He opened his eyes again, and saw a ghost of a shimmer. It was not like the strands or threads they were trained to see. It was more like an aurora. *That's not the path,* Jarvie was just telling himself, when Beezan hit the thrusters and they were going that way. Jarvie was forced back in the seat, his eyes closing by reflex. Even then, he saw the shimmer tip and collapse into a diffuse wide path and then they were in.

The acceleration stopped. He could breathe. He could relax. Well, at least he had seen *something*.

Jarvie awoke with a start just in time to glimpse the fuzzy spots against the utter blackness of jump space before they dropped into normal space. Then the noise of *Drumheller* talking, cocoons unsealing, and quiet voices slowly brought him back to reality.

"ETA Hamada, 10 days, two hours, 3 minutes."

Jarvie popped off his helmet and smiled. "Ten days! Great!"

Beezan laughed quietly, politely not asking if Jarvie had seen the path. But Sequoia did.

"Well, it was more like a shimmery veil than a path."

She frowned. Beezan rolled his eyes. "Just like the Ramians. Install alien implants without giving you the instructions."

"Maybe they did," Jarvie mused, cocking his head while he tried to visualize his implants and if there might be some mental trigger for instructions.

"Heaven help us," Sequoia sighed.

"Otherwise okay?" Beezan asked.

"Yeah. I mean yes, honor." He felt good, without the jump depression even.

"Good," Beezan said. "Welcome back to Hamada. Now we can pick up two years of your homework."

3-Loftiness

Drumheller, heading for Hamada a-rings

Beezan and the crew lingered after dinner during the fast, enjoying an extra cup of tea. Beezan had spun up the ship so they could have gravity as they headed directly for the Hamada a-rings, deciding not to stop at the station. It was only the third day of fasting, but, so far, Jarvie was doing fine. When Beezan remembered last year's fast and Jarvie's condition, he couldn't believe everything that had happened. He marveled at his extended kitchen, two six-person tables. His crew had gone from zero to seven. His world was expanding.

News of the reopening of Harbor and Luminesse had energized the outer sectors. Loved ones would be reunited. People were delirious with happiness. Hope for Firelight and the reconnect to Earth ran high, but Iricana's classified packets were more troubling. *Cheetah* had disappeared in the direction of 5F. Councils had ordered that no one was to follow. The junk news, Terina informed them, was running in favor of the *Cheetah* being a heroic mystery ship.

Beezan tried to stay calm and focused in his new role. He looked around, pleased with his crew: Jarvie, Terina, Katie, Iricana, Thunder, Kelson, and Sequoia. He had gone from running cargo to exploration, from humans to aliens, from alone to a crowd of people and podpups. Would his orbit continue to expand out to the vast empty regions or was it just the last large ellipse of his own life, hurtling back towards some supermassive destiny?

"I wish we could get a language expert," Iricana was saying.

"We did fine when we met the Ramians," Jarvie said.

"Yes," Iricana agreed, "but the Ramians are very much like us. I don't think the Chike will be so easy."

Beezan was suddenly alarmed. "*What?* Who says we're going to talk to the Chike?"

15-Loftiness

Cheetah, heading to Friendship a-rings

Melawn wasn't purposely breaking the fast. He didn't eat for long periods and then he gulped down available food. He didn't even know if it was officially day or night. He had one purpose—to find the monster routing program that Thayne had hidden in the computer. Zahar had asked Thayne. He refused to tell her. He had refused to stop it himself or even admit it was there, even though they had proof. There was no time for prayer and reflection. There was only the program to find.

Melawn carefully snapped his pad back together, minus its s'link and any other part he thought could be influenced by the *Cheetah.* He needed a safe place to track the files he was quarantining on the *Cheetah* computer. So far, his level 1 override was at least making the computer obey. He could examine files, decide they were clean, move them, and try to go deeper into the nesting. But there were millions, and files would mysteriously move around.

"It's not a small file" he reminded himself again. He wasn't looking for a nanobot in a pile of microbots. He was looking for a shuttle in a pile of microbots. But the more he dug through the small stuff, the more fell in to cover its tracks. *I'm chasing something, and Cheetah knows it.*

Melawn put as many file restrictions on the *Cheetah* as he dared, concerned for the safe running of the ship. Still, just as he thought he was getting to a deeper level, he'd pop back out. *I need a worm.* But the *Cheetah* was too smart, too quick. For every maneuver Melawn tried, dodging, faking, sending worms and spiders and hunters, he could not dig down to the foundation level, the only place where that big program could be hiding.

He tried every back door, sending traps through the routers Nkiroo had installed on the hull, back when he believed in Thayne. Melawn watched six screens at a time. One of his worms suddenly turned red—breakthrough to another level—and then it was just gone.

I need more. But how many more? He couldn't really use *Cheetah's* computer power to overcome itself. He reached for a snack, but the food was gone. He looked over at his empty plate and frowned. His wrist p'link, with Thayne's icons, was sitting by the plate, flashing. Not like a mindstorm, but in sequence. Busy and directed. Thayne was doing something that required a lot of mental concentration.

Zahar was right. He should get rid of it. Get rid of all his attachment to Thayne, but it was just so painful. Melawn tore his gaze away. He sent more worms. A thousand. Five thousand. The screens became meaningless blurs of blips. He took a deep breath. He really didn't mean to check Thayne's icons. But now they were even more active.

Melawn increased the worms. About 4 seconds later, Thayne's icons blazed. More worms, more mental activity. It wasn't *Cheetah* that Melawn was trying to beat. It was Thayne. He must be at a panel in the Med Bay. *How many worms to overcome the human mind? Ten thousand? But Thayne's mind?* And then Melawn knew it was hopeless. Already Thayne had turned the worms against themselves, reprogramming them to seek and destroy. He was battling Thayne, and he could never win.

15-Loftiness

Drumheller, at Hamada a-rings

Beezan's s'link buzzed. One hour countdown.

They were ten minutes from entering the a-rings at Hamada when Iricana got a classified packet.

"Captain," she told him over a private channel, "Unofficial announcement of Ramian presence has unexpectedly come out of Luminesse. We'll be carrying news of aliens to Radium Junction."

16-Loftiness

Cheetah, heading for Friendship a-rings

Before she even got up the rimway to the kitchen for breakfast, Zahar had already collected folded notes from a frowning, tired Melawn, heading for his cabin, and a distracted Nkiroo, headed for the Command Bay. After she sat down with her food, she opened the notes. Nkiroo's was short and puzzling;

All the cleaning robots are missing.

Zahar looked. The kitchen doors were closed again, robot

gone. When she unfolded Melawn's, one sentence was under-lined: <u>He must be moved to a tee-free zone.</u> Zahar skimmed the rest, a bite of breakfast unchewed in her mouth.

When I called Dr. T to ask that she get Thayne away from the computer, she told me he was not at a panel or using a pad, p'link, s'link or anything. He was just lying there, eyes closed, occasionally babbling. But she agreed that he was awake and his mind was very active. Somehow he is accessing the Cheetah through non-conventional means.

Zahar scowled. *Thayne probably has some experimental implants we don't know anything about.* She stuffed another bite down. She should be just in time to catch the doctor. She called on her s'link, "Nkiroo—meet me in the Prayer Room, please."

"No record. No implants show in the scans." Tenshi insisted. "I've done enough brain scans on him."

"He's connecting somehow," Zahar said.

"If he is, I don't know how. Moving him to a tee-free zone would mean not being able to monitor him in any way. As his doctor, I would object to that for medical reasons."

"Nkiroo, where do you recommend for a completely tee-free zone?"

He glanced at Tenshi. "But . . ."

Zahar was getting frustrated. *Patience.* "It's the doctor's job to object. We're going to move him anyway."

"Well, the only truly tee-free rooms are the Prayer Rooms, but even they have ports for s'links."

"Could we isolate one for special monitoring?"

"Probably," he sighed. "But it may not do any good."

"Why?"

Nkiroo shrugged with his hands. "He is Thayne. He is brilliant. He is a manipulator of both machines and men. He's most likely behind the disappearance of the cleaning bots. He may even be using them to communicate. Can he reach through the bulkheads somehow? I don't know." He was shaking his head, defeated.

"Based on what we know, would it be enough?" Zahar pressed.

"We do not yet know the depth of his deception. I suspect it will not contain him entirely."

"But even if it slows him down . . ."

Zahar kept her s'link in hand. She had a coat, water, food, a door opener, survival blanket, and extra air in her pack. But she still couldn't shake the cold fear of those moments in the freezing airlock.

She was on a mission to find the cleaning bots. They had managed to free all their comrades from door-block duty. Even more alarming, they had stolen everything else being used for door-blocks.

Arriving at the work tower, she had no idea what she'd find. She took a deep breath and pressed the door open button. Nothing. *As usual.* "Override." The door slid open. "Lights." The lights went on, revealing a deserted room. The charging towers were empty. Storage bins, repair station, empty. A chill went up her spine. "Where are they?"

Hiding . . . but where? There was a map of the *Cheetah* on the wall, so she studied it. *Where would hundreds of robots hide?* She scanned the Arcs of cabins between the work tower and Caspia's nano-lab in Arc 9. There was no reason to think they would favor one cabin, one library, one Prayer Room over another.

She focused on the map. In the work tower, there was a room marked **Prayer Room H.S.** She turned and looked. It was right beside her. *What's H.S.?* All the other Prayer Rooms were marked T.F. for tee-free. She looked closer, holding up her s'link. "Magnify."

High Security

"*Yes!*" Good for the ship designers. She'd just found Thayne's jail cell. She was half way back to the kitchen before she remembered that she hadn't found the robots.

1-Splendor-1084 BE

Enkindler, heading for Friendship a-rings

Lanezi sat in the Command Bay of the *Enkindler,* with a full stomach, grateful that fast was over. He had tried to make it as uplifting as possible for the twins. And they had done their best to make their exile on the *Enkindler* seem like fun. It was difficult, but not boring. Euro, Io, and four podpups could never be boring, but the constant worry and responsibility had no outlet in snacking.

Now he was fretting over the twins, suited up and sealed in the back of the shuttle, unloading the resupply vehicle. He listened for their required check-off responses between the excited chatter of how much stuff there was. *I thought we were going back soon.*

"Resupply door secured," came Euro's voice. "Green light on aft hatch."

On the screen, Lanezi could see them clamoring around. *Almost done.* Lanezi had no rational reason to worry. Whisper wasn't even worried. She was sleeping. And snoring—the loudest sound Lanezi had heard from her. The three little ones were bouncing around, excited at the voices, but jumping at every clang. "*Enkindler* doors secure," Euro continued.

Lanezi checked his panel. "Confirmed. Permission to suit out."

"Yes Captain!" they said happily.

Lanezi opened his command door and stared, befuddled. There were containers of all kinds floating around the passenger area.

"We must secure these," he ordered, automatically.

"We ran out of space in the storage cabinets," an excited Io explained. "They must be full of New Year's presents!"

The podpups hurtled through the door to investigate.

After making sure suits were checked and boxes were stowed, Lanezi went back to the Command Bay and released the resupply vehicle. "*Enkindler* to *Cheetah*. Resupply back to you in 18 minutes."

"Thank you." Zahar came on the screen.

"That's a lot of food and water, and fuel. What's going on?"

"Just in case. We still plan to bring you back in a couple of days. But if we can't, that will keep you until we get to the a-rings and have some to spare."

"Shuttles aren't meant to jump," Lanezi whispered so the twins would not hear.

"I know." Zahar leaned toward the screen and spoke quietly. "We've found a high security Prayer Room to isolate Thayne from the computer. We're moving him today. But I want you to stay there a couple more days to make sure the programming sorts out. I'm sorry. I know it's hard for you."

"We're okay," Lanezi hastily added, not wanting to be a complainer. There was more commotion at the door as the twins came through towing a box and three pups.

"Oh, Happy New Year, by the way," Zahar said.

"Thank you, Captain," they coursed, while the pups started chanting to open the presents.

8-Splendor

Drumheller, at Radium Junction a-rings

Jarvie was supposed to be saying his prayers, but he was preparing for the jump from Radium Junction to Tetra in a more practical way, by huddling in the kitchen with Terina, fortifying himself with more food. Rocket and Star were highly approving, doubling their breakfast too.

"So what's the big history of Tetra?" Jarvie asked, knowing he could read his book, but far preferring Terina's take.

"Tetra!" she exclaimed, instantly opinionated. "You know there was a big controversy over whether Radium Junction or Tetra would be sector hub? But RJ was already built up and no one wanted to take the time to establish Tetra, even though the pilots favored that route."

"What was the rush?"

"Stations were already being abandoned, even in Sector 7. Advance ships feared the order would come to stop jumping to new systems."

"But why keep jumping?"

"It was like a fever. Almost like gambling. They wanted so much to find a life planet. They thought they could establish minimal stations and go."

"Which explains why those stations are barely more than a few habitats stuck together."

"Right. And now it's a big strain to keep them supplied."

"So why do they keep them now?"

"Well, Terrace has some serious precious metals. And Tanuki is a good mid-jump point to get there."

"And we know that Tektite has the control panel."

"Yes, with Tundra for a mid jump."

"And Tyee would have been abandoned long ago, except *81 Petals* jumped from there."

"And disappeared. Forever?"

"Who knows? It's only been 15 years. But that's why they have to keep it open. In case they come back. But with population dropping and the number of pilots declining, they'll have no choice but to abandon all but the biggest stations."

Jarvie frowned and stashed both their plates. "Maybe we'll find something amazing in that control panel at Tektite."

"Jarvie! Holding out for a miracle is what got us into this mess."

But Jarvie couldn't help but hold out. And later, in those last few breathtaking seconds of the jump, freed from the RJ a-rings, he hoped, or imagined, or maybe really did see the whole pattern of promise, the threads to Tetra and Tyee, Tanuki, Tundra, Terrace and Tektite, and maybe even beyond.

19-Splendor

Cheetah, heading for Friendship a-rings

Dr. Tenshi sat down next to Melawn at breakfast, nodding curtly. The crew was impatient with him, even untrusting. Their anger at Thayne eclipsed the anger they once had for Lanezi and even rivaled Thayne's own anger. And it inevitably spilled out on him, for his loyalty to Thayne. *So much anger.* The ship was even angry at Lanezi. Evan and Zahar slid into their seats, Evan squeezing Melawn's arm gently. Melawn sent him a thankful glance.

"Five days to the a-rings," Zahar reminded them. "If all goes well, we'll take the *Enkindler* back aboard on 5 Glory and go straight to the a-rings. We'll release Thayne, take him directly to a jump chair, and give him the jump drug. Evan will jump us to Canyon. She nodded at Evan and he responded with a shy smile.

"Zahar," Dr. Tenshi said, "Thayne's been asking for Melawn." Melawn's heart leaped, even as Zahar scowled.

"No."

"Please," Melawn said quietly, "I'd like to see him."

"You're in no condition," Zahar said bluntly.

"He needs me."

"He's using you, Melawn. Just like he's used all of us."

"No. I—"

"Zahar—Captain," the doctor interrupted. "There are compliance issues regarding isolation."

"Fine. You and Caspia and Kiro can visit. Two at a time."

"He's not using me," Melawn whispered. But they all looked sadly at him. At least Evan tried to hide his pity.

1-Glory

The next morning, when Melawn didn't show up in the Prayer Room, Zahar took Kiwi and went looking for him, starting with Thayne's high security room. Melawn was sitting outside, saying his prayers.

She felt a little bad. She startled him and he jumped up, tugging on his sleeves and tunic.

"Sorry Melawn. I was worried."

"I just thought I would be near him."

She sighed. "Go inside. Ten minutes."

He was surprised, and suddenly nervous. "I'm going to be right here," she continued. "Just tap on the door if there's a problem."

"Thank you."

There was only one door, but it wouldn't open if anyone was standing near it, inside. Melawn pressed the enter button and it immediately slid open. Zahar didn't see Thayne before it closed again. She checked the time, sat down with her back to the door, set Kiwi down beside her, took a big breath, and surveyed the work tower.

Maybe I should have thought this through. What if Thayne is mean to him? Or tries to use him? Zahar fretted over the ways Thayne could use Melawn. Tell him to release him later? No. Melawn could have freed Thayne any time. *I shouldn't be so nice.* She scowled at Kiwi. Maybe he was making her too soft.

There was a *chink* and *whirr*. The lift was coming down. *What?* Zahar slowly got to her feet. She had just seen everyone at breakfast. Who could have gotten to the lift without her knowing? It must be automated. As the lift hit the bottom and stopped, she got a very bad feeling.

"Melawn!" She knocked on the door. She pressed the open button. Nothing. *Don't panic! It's just the stupid lift.*

But her instincts were good, if not her judgment. As the lift doors opened, a liquid sea of gleaming microbots tumbled across the deck toward her.

"Bots!" She yelled. Poor Kiwi rocketed towards the rimway in primal fear. *I'm human. I'm not afraid of bots!* She stood her ground, but they reached her feet and started climbing. "No!" she screamed. She tried to brush them off and stomp them, but there were too many and they were too fast. They swarmed up her legs in a thick layer. She pulled out her s'link, but they engulfed it, turning it off. Her strongest instinct was to cover her eyes. She tried to cover her ears at the same time. They pressed against her. She flung herself to the deck, trying to crush them, but it was useless. She could feel them massing and moving over her, inside her clothes. She curled up in a ball, but realized they were not going above her neck. She was getting them on her face with her hands. She flung her hands away, fearing her heart would stop from the panic.

There was a sudden *whoosh* of air and someone grabbed her. For a second she thought they would help, but they just rolled her into the Prayer Room. *Thayne's voice. That babbling.*

"*What?*" Melawn's voice was so startled and puzzled, Zahar only wanted to scream more.

Melawn recoiled from the sight. Zahar, covered with swarming bots, uselessly trying to get them off. *And Thayne.* Pushing her with his foot. To get rid of the bots, of course. *He's helping her.* Melawn reached over to brush the bots away. Thayne grabbed Melawn's wrist, ripped his sleeve open and wrenched off his wrist p'link, cutting his arm. He threw it out the door. Then he grabbed Melawn's regular p'link, his s'link and Zahar's, reaching into the writhing bots with no hesitation.

"I convict you of mutiny," he raged at her imperiously, "and imprison you for the duration of the voyage." Melawn cowered away from the voice. Thayne made a disgusted sound at him and calmly turned to stand in the doorway.

Melawn looked up at Thayne. Thayne wasn't helping. Thayne did this. He looked down at the thrashing, gasping, terror-stricken girl. *Thayne. Did. This.* A surge of anger propelled him to the door, which slid shut in his face, except for a tiny crack, held open by a s'link. More babbling. The bots started out the crack in a thin line.

"Thayne! *Why?*"

"You!" Thayne continued in his angriest, craziest voice. "You are convicted of mutiny too. You could have released me any time. You are not worthy! *You are nothing to me!*" As the last of the bots streamed out the door, Thayne yanked out the s'link and it closed.

Zahar was breathing in ragged sobs, shaking her hair and clothes as if to rid them of imaginary bots. "They're gone," he whispered, reaching to help her.

"You!" she hissed. Melawn cringed and backed away.

Zahar staggered to the door and ran her hands up the wall. "No s'link!"

Melawn shook his head. "I'm so sorry. It'll be hours before they find us."

She glared at him, eyes burning with indignation and anger. "No it won't. Kiwi got away."

Her knees collapsed then and she sat, leaning against the wall gasping, occasionally shivering as if a bot was crawling on her again.

Melawn searched the room for food. There was none, but he brought her a cup of water from the facilities. For a moment he thought she wouldn't take it from him, but finally, she reached out and shakily grasped the little cup. "Thank you."

Melawn scooted back away. They sat in silence. He looked down at his bleeding arm. Never before had anyone touched him in violence. Except for the *accidents* with Thayne. But there was no question of intent this time. Melawn tried to say prayers but ended up calculating. Apparently, so was Zahar.

"Where will he go?" she asked.

"Command Bay, no doubt. He will take over the ship."

"And then?"

"Firelight."

"Lanezi won't jump," Zahar said.

"Evan won't resist."

"He hasn't got a gravity ball yet, and he can't get one aboard by himself."

"I think we've just seen that nothing will stop him. He'll get a gravity ball at Firelight."

"The shuttle . . ."

"*God in heaven.*" Melawn dropped his head into his hands and started to cry. *It's all my fault. And Lanezi and the twins will have to jump in a shuttle.*

"Maybe they can stop him," Zahar finally said.

No one can stop him.

"How did he call the bots?" she asked.

He slapped his hands on the deck with a burst of realization. "The babbling! I am so *stupid*! I should have recorded and analyzed it. It must be a programming language. He must have modified my wrist p'link. He's using his med monitors to access it remotely."

"That wrist monitor! I told you to take it off!"

"I know. I'm so sorry." He fished a handkerchief out of his pocket to wipe his face.

She glared at him. "He uses you. You worship him and—you're not supposed to worship people!" she complained. Her hard look continued. "And I don't want you transferring your worship to someone else! We're just humans. Even Thayne."

Melawn rested his arms and head on his knees. He was horrified at Thayne's behavior, but still. Thayne's last words, *You are nothing to me!* just cut into his heart.

"All crew to blue zones!"

"Oh, no!" Zahar jumped up. "He's taken the Command Bay already."

Melawn felt along the walls until he found an emergency restraint. He folded out the straps. "Here." She hesitated at his offer. There might not be another in the cell. "Captain," he insisted. She took the straps while he felt the wall for another. Yes. He folded it out and shrugged into it.

"Thirty seconds."

Slowly, the spindown routine completed. Gravity was barely gone when they started accelerating.

"Same direction," Zahar noted. "He just wants to get there faster."

"He's going to use the hot start."

"He must have Evan. He must." She willed that Evan would cooperate, if only to save their lives.

For hours, they were strapped against the wall, praying and sleeping. Zahar awoke with a start every time a little hair or gust of air touched her, setting off the creepy feeling of the bots. She would have rubbed her arms and legs, but they must have been over two gee.

She awoke again when the boosting stopped.

"Remember the last time he did this?" Melawn asked.

"Yes. Three hours boosting, 10 minutes break." He gestured towards the facilities and she scrambled. She also got a drink. Melawn did the same. Without a p'link, s'link, or clock of any kind, they couldn't judge the time. But she realized that Melawn was counting. At his 9-minute-mark they got back in the straps. Five seconds later, the 30-second announcement blared.

Zahar groaned when the acceleration started again. "There's no way to rescue us while this is going on."

"No," Melawn agreed. "Assuming he didn't lock the rest of them up somewhere."

On that happy thought, Zahar tried again to sleep. She focused on storing up her energy. Thayne might be brilliant, might be devious, but he was wrong, and she would marshal all the forces in her possession to stop him.

Enkindler, heading to Friendship a-rings

Lanezi leaned back in the pilot's chair and closed his eyes. The twins woke him up early yesterday, kept him up late last night, and asked a never-ending series of questions. They kept the podpups running and generally frayed his nerves. All day. For yet another day. And now, they were up early again, working in the small kitchen to make a secret breakfast for Feast day. With four podpups helping.

He tried to remind himself of all the bad times in his life, and how this was really a good time. And away from Thayne. And would be over in a couple of days. And praise the Lord, they were going to jump back to Canyon. Civilization, almost.

He loved the twins dearly. Their innocence and quirkiness only increased their natural good nature. Lanezi did his best with their material education, and figured that spiritually, they were teaching him.

Whisper floated in and settled on his lap. "Too much."

"They do have a lot of energy," he agreed. "How are the pups doing?" He asked on a whim.

Whisper considered. Lanezi was amazed that she seemed to grasp the question. "Missing Kiwi. Like twins. Too young."

"Too young for what?"

"Cooking."

"Oh—hey, Euro, Io, keep those pups away from the cooker."

"They're okay," Euro called back. Lanezi frowned.

"Whisper says," he added.

"Oh! Io, tether them, so they'll be safe."

Lanezi looked down at Whisper. "I guess you're really in charge here."

"Humph."

"Auto NAV alert."

What? "*Enkindler*, report."

"Target is moving out of stationkeeping."

Lanezi tapped a pop-up. The computer wouldn't bother him for normal variations or corrections. The *Cheetah* was moving steadily away from them. "How fast are they going?"

"Acceleration is still increasing. They are now at .27 gee."

Oh, no. There was no way the shuttle could follow if they kept increasing. "*Enkindler* to *Cheetah*." He exchanged a worried look with Whisper.

"Lanezi to *Cheetah*. Urgent."

"*Cheetah*, please respond."

Lanezi checked over his shoulder to make sure the twins couldn't hear. Too late. Supersensitive, they were already floating in to see what was happening.

"*Enkindler*, are there any hazards they could be avoiding?"

"Nothing detected."

Besides, they would warn us. "Can you consult with the *Cheetah* computer?"

"I am blocked and secured by order of Captain Zahar."

To make sure the *Enkindler* didn't get infected with *Cheetah*'s computer troubles, Lanezi realized.

"Why are they leaving us?" Io asked plaintively.

Euro grabbed his brother's arm. "It's him," he said sadly.

"No, Euro," Lanezi explained. "It can't be. Thayne is not allowed in the Command Bay anymore."

But Io looked from Lanezi to Euro and nodded. "What else could it be?"

"Why don't we catch up?" Euro asked.

Lanezi leaned over and did some quick calculations. "Depends when they stop accelerating. We may not be able to reach them by the time they get to the a-rings. Not in the shuttle."

"We'll be stuck here?" Euro asked.

"No! No, I can jump in the shuttle. We'll be okay. But we need to secure and start boosting."

Suddenly Io lunged over and hugged him. Lanezi grabbed

the panel to stabilize and hugged him back with one arm. "Thank you," Io said. "Thank you for keeping your promise."

2-Glory

Cheetah, heading to Friendship a-rings

Zahar woke with a start. "Someone's here," Melawn whispered.

She'd fallen into a deep sleep after the boosting finally stopped. "Sounds like people," she said nervously. Then the door slid open and Tenshi, s'link in hand, came in. A frantic Kiwi sailed out of her arm toward Zahar.

"Thank heavens," Tenshi said, as Caspia moved in behind her.

"Wait!" Zahar called out as she caught Kiwi. "Someone has to stay outside."

"Yes, please," Melawn whispered. He looked like he hadn't slept at all.

Zahar hugged Kiwi. "Good Kiwi! Good rescue!"

"He was very helpful, once he calmed down," Caspia said. "He kept saying bad bots."

Kiwi hissed and hid his head under Zahar's arms. "He's not kidding."

"Are you injured?" Tenshi asked.

"No," they both answered and hauled themselves out the door as quickly as possible. But Tenshi snatched at Melawn's sleeve where he was bleeding.

"It's minor."

Zahar took a deep breath, relieved to be out of there.

Tenshi touched her s'link. "Nkiroo, we've recovered the Captain. And Melawn."

"Good. Thank you. Nothing has changed here."

"What time is it?" Zahar asked the doctor.

"3:20."

No wonder we're so tired. "Where is Evan?" she asked Caspia.

"In the Command Bay, with Thayne."

"He's taken over the ship, by force," Tenshi added quietly.

"He attacked us too," Zahar confirmed. "He's using Melawn's wrist p'link to control the bots." Both of their eyes widened. There was a gasp over the s'link as Nkiroo heard. Tenshi and Caspia cast involuntary, scowling glances at Melawn.

Zahar pushed over to the tool cabinet, opened it, and considered. "No," Melawn whispered, aghast. "No weapons."

"I'm not crazy, Melawn. But we need something we can use to interfere with the bots."

"Micro boxes," Caspia said. "That's all we need. "Nkiroo got the nano intervention kit from my lab. It'll work on the bigger bots too."

"Okay, grab the boxes and let's get back," Zahar ordered, accepting a food pack from Tenshi. "Thank you."

Enkindler, heading to Friendship a-rings

Lanezi's nerves were finally starting to settle. They had their Feast, although subdued, and ate the special breakfast in a break between boosting. He complimented the food, and praised the twins and the pups—and nearly launched into the ceiling when he heard—

"NAV alert!"

They crowded back into the Command Bay. "*Enkindler,* report."

"Possible hazard detected."

A pop-up appeared showing a fuzzy dot.

"Beacon detected. Ramian frequency."

Lanezi gasped. *Not again! Just like Luminesse. Just like Harbor. How can this happen to me three times?* He pictured the ship crashing into the a-rings, destroying their only chance to get home. They would die. He stared at the screen in dismay.

"They are far," Euro said tentatively.

Denial. But he looked at the screen. And Euro was right. At Luminesse and Harbor, everything had happened so fast. But not here. The ship was very far away. "*Enkindler*, can you calculate the trajectory?"

"They are on an a-ring intercept course."

"Will they get there before or after the *Cheetah*?"

"*Cheetah* has stopped accelerating. If neither ship changes velocity, *Cheetah* will arrive 14.3 hours ahead of the Ramian vessel."

"Enough time to jump," Euro said.

Cheetah, at Friendship a-rings

"We've set up a secondary command center in the kitchen," Caspia explained as they hauled themselves into Arc 1. Melawn was lagging behind, exhausted, but could still hear. "We've disabled the cameras and all other links we could think of."

"Why not Operations?" Zahar asked.

"Locked out," Tenshi answered, scowling.

"What about the door openers?" Zahar asked.

"I think you need to see," Tenshi said darkly.

So they stopped at the kitchen door just long enough to send Kiwi up the stairs. Melawn, near the not-even-caring point, pulled along behind. They went almost all the way to Operations, just one door before the Command Bay, when

Tenshi slowed and put up her hand, allowing Caspia to go ahead.

"It's gone!" Zahar gasped. Melawn blinked in confusion. The door to the Command Bay was *gone*. There was only a wall. But then Zahar gasped in fear and pushed back down the rimway. A shimmer of movement rippled through the wall. *The bots!* They'd assembled themselves across the door of the Command Bay in a solid wall.

"Operations too," Caspia pointed calmly. Zahar had a hand pressed over her mouth as if trying not to cry out. Tenshi looked at her, puzzled.

"The bots attacked her," Melawn explained quickly.

Tenshi nodded grimly, gripping Zahar's shoulder. "Evan too. Thayne used the bots to force Evan into the Command Bay."

"Monster!" Zahar gasped, eyes filling with tears. And then she turned, holding the wall. "Caspia! Be careful!"

Caspia was almost to the bots. "Did Caspia see what the bots did?" Zahar asked.

"Oh, yes," Tenshi said. "But she has no fear of them. Watch."

As Caspia carefully approached the Command Bay door and reached for the controls, a layer of bots swarmed out and created a block on top of the controls, so she couldn't touch them. She reached as if to put her hand on the door—

"No!" Zahar called out. "Caspia, please come back. Please. We need a different plan. We need to try the micro box."

"We need food and rest," Tenshi said. Heads nodded in agreement.

But as they all turned to go back to the kitchen, Zahar held up a hand to Melawn, stopping him. "Wait. Once and for all, for the record, with witnesses, Melawn, you will decide whose side you're on."

"Captain," he objected. "There are no sides! We're in this together. Thayne isn't an enemy."

"He is under arrest. He took the Command Bay by force. I declare him a mutineer. I know you were not involved. But you must choose now. You're with him or you're with us."

"I . . ." *can't* . . . he almost said. How could she ask such a thing?

All three of them glanced at him sharply.

"No more doubt. No more hesitation. I must know where you stand."

"I didn't . . . I'm not . . ." His mind spun. Thayne was the center of his universe. Everything he had done for 10 years was all for Thayne. Even if Thayne was wrong, he would still need Melawn's help.

"Fine!" Zahar said, sounding like a teenager. "Go to him then." And she pointed to the wall of bots.

Caspia and Dr. Tenshi cringed.

The image of the bots swarming over Zahar, her screaming, the evil look on Thayne's face. "I'm sorry. I'm confused," he confessed.

"You've been confused for too long," she said sternly. "I don't think I can ever trust you. Go to him!" She ordered, pointing.

It was a direct order. She had chosen for him, seeing that he was too weak to do it. Slowly he turned, and hand over hand pulled himself to the wall of bots. Would Thayne let him in? Or would the robots swarm him? Up close, the bots shivered. Could they kill him? But Thayne wouldn't let that happen. *You are nothing to me! Thayne needs me. You are nothing to me!* He looked down at his bleeding arm. *Thayne did this.* He lied. He hurt Zahar. He disobeyed the councils. But loyalty was supposed to be a good thing. *And without Thayne, I'm no one.*

He'd just spent hours in the cell, convincing himself to forgive Thayne, because forgiveness was good.

He hung there forever, his life passing before him, the years he had given to Thayne, the ideas, the love.

He turned on his data hunting brain, sorting through every action of Thayne's, every gesture of attachment, every unreasonable demand, every flattering compliment, every burst of anger, every disobe—no. Yes. Thayne disobeyed a council. He lied. The facts could not be hidden from Melawn's brain once he decided to see them. And the database of good transferred over to the bad. Thayne may have loved him, but he had used him, betrayed him, and worst of all, allowed and encouraged Melawn to worship him.

He reached out to the wall of bots and they parted in front of him. His hand touched the control box. He choked back a sob. Thayne had programmed them to let Melawn in, thinking he would come back to him, again.

"No. Never again," he whispered. "I was wrong to worship you." He didn't know how he could ever face the others, but he turned to push away from the wall and was startled by Nkiroo, who had floated up right behind him. Nkiroo's sympathetic eyes welled with tears and he hugged Melawn fiercely. "We don't want to lose you. It would be unbearable."

Enkindler, heading to Friendship a-rings

"Zahar to Lanezi."

Lanezi gulped his bite of protein waffle. "Lanezi here!" The twins dived to his side, stabilizing against the chair.

"Sending packets while I can," Zahar said quickly. "We've rigged a transmitter from a shuttle and the Hangar Bay door is open. We may not have much time."

"Zahar . . ."

"Listen first please. Thayne has taken over the Command Bay, using the bots. He has Evan. We believe he means to jump to Firelight. The attempt to use the nano-return kit to box up the bots failed. We . . . I have decided not to take the Command Bay by force. It would be an act of violence." She stopped and swallowed, lifting her hands in supplication. "We put our trust in God."

Everything that Lanezi had planned to say left him. "Zahar," He interrupted.

"Wait! I formally relieve you of any responsibility to the *Cheetah*, Project Restore or this crew. You are appointed Captain of the *Enkindler* and guardian of Euro and Io. Make the best jump you can for your survival." She took a breath. "Okay, go."

"The ship? Do you know? There's a Ramian ship," Lanezi told her.

"No. Where?"

"I'm sending you a packet. You'll get to the a-rings first."

Zahar adjusted the camera control to wide angle so they could see. Crowded into the shuttle with her were Tenshi, Melawn, and Nkiroo. She brought Kiwi into her lap so he could see the screen. The tears started down Lanezi's face. No matter what happened, this was goodbye. The four podpups on *Enkindler* piled into Lanezi's lap. The twins reached out to touch the screen.

"Euro, Io," Zahar said formally, "I appoint you special assistants to Captain Lanezi."

"Summer!" Summer insisted suddenly.

Tears came to Zahar's eyes. "Yes. Summer, Dusty and Blue are appointed . . . mascots of the *Enkindler*. Whisper is official Teacher of Podpups.

Kiwi looked at the screen and frowned, as if he was getting

the idea of what was happening. He gave a little worried whine and looked at Zahar for reassurance. "Kiwi is brave," she whispered. He sat up tall.

"Zahar," Lanezi struggled to get the words past his choked up throat, "Tell them all, I'm sorry, and I love them, and God Protect you all."

"I bid farewell to you all, seeking for you the divine mercy, the eternal glory and everlasting life; and I pray that you may attain the highest station of humanity."[1] Euro said quietly.

"Although our bodies may be far apart, in spirit we shall always be together."[2] Io added and put his hand over his heart.

"The jump," Lanezi added. "It's doable. Have faith."

"Well, goodbye for now, then."

"Goodbye! We love you!" The twins shouted.

Choruses of "We love you" echoed over the speaker when the connection was suddenly broken. And Whisper buried her head in Lanezi's chest.

4-Glory

Cheetah, approaching Friendship a-rings

Melawn dreamed of the bots, woke up sweating in fear, fell asleep in exhaustion, and dreamed again. The bots were everywhere. He touched a table and it dissolved into bots. They chased him down the rimway. Hand over hand, he tried to escape in the true slow motion of nogee, but then he grabbed a holdbar and it disintegrated into bots.

They swarmed him. They pushed him into an airlock. They opened the airlock to vent him and he was falling. Somehow Thayne was there in the airlock. Melawn reached out, but Thayne did not. Thayne just looked, and smiled that sweet smile. "Thank you Melawn. I don't know what I'd do without you." And then Melawn slammed against . . . space? *What? I'm awake.* He was gasping. He ran his hands over his face and hair, panicking. *No bots.* He was swinging in his sleep sack.

"All crew! Report to the chairs—NOW!" came Zahar's voice.

"Oh my God. Lights," he gasped. He pulled his sleep sack

apart. Before he could get out, he swung against the wall again. *Are we accelerating? Are we in the rings?* Nothing made sense.

He didn't pause for the facilities. He checked his pocket for his s'link and pushed for the door. Being double sure to have at least one hand on a holdbar at all times, he struggled to the Passenger Lounge.

Just as he pulled up the stairs and into the Passenger Lounge, he heard Zahar yelling for him. There was a small surge and he started to fall down the stairs, but he reached out and, unlike in his dream, Zahar braced against the wall, grabbed him, and propelled him to an empty chair. She slammed the door control with her other hand and pushed off hard from the wall.

The others were already in their chairs. "Strap!" Tenshi yelled, unnecessarily, as he was already doing it, but then he realized that she was talking to Zahar, who had no time to put Kiwi in the travel box. Melawn finished his last restraints when there was a tremendous surge—sideways.

"Zahar!" Tenshi and the others cried. She had only tethered herself to the chair, with one leg hooked around it. Now she strained not to break loose, holding desperately to Kiwi.

There was a sickening lurch and somehow she got in the chair and got one belt on. "Kiwi hold on tight!" she ordered him. "Stay with me, Kiwi" Then it was as if they were not just falling, but speeding downhill, completely in the wrong direction for a jump.

What are they doing in the Command Bay? But as he faded to unconsciousness, Melawn realized the ship wasn't doing this under its own power. Something was happening outside. He was falling into blackness, just like the dream. And Thayne was not going to save him.

• • •

Enkindler, approaching Friendship a-rings

"Auto NAV alert!"

Lanezi woke from his fitful sleep. *Now what?* He was in the Command Bay chair. He reached for the controls, but his arm was thrown aside, hitting the next chair painfully.

"Lanezi!" Io cried from the chair. Lanezi's stomach whirled as the shuttle careened up, sideways and then began a sickening roll.

"*Enkindler!* Stabilize! Auto-stabilize!"

What vague thoughts he had beyond *What's happening? Don't throw up,* and *Thank God we slept in the chairs,* ran along the lines of *Where are the podpups?* and *It's probably the aliens.*

Enkindler made a correction, only to be slammed again. Lanezi cringed at the waste of fuel. *What's happened to the Cheetah?* And with a horrible conclusion, he ordered, "*Enkindler,* stop corrections! No corrections until there are no more bumps for five minutes!"

Lanezi could hear Io and Euro sucking in big breaths, trying not to be sick. God bless them for not asking questions. And then four podpups were wheeling around the cabin. He hoped they were as squishable and resilient as podpups were rumored to be.

Cheetah

Zahar breathed a prayer of thanks that she had been able to strap before the huge surge of acceleration. She held Kiwi as tightly as she dared. It was making her arm hurt. How much acceleration would it take to actually hurt a podpup? She struggled to get him into the part of her podpup pocket that wasn't covered by straps, and he helped. Finally she zipped it up, just in time. As her hands flung away and she faded into unconsciousness, she prayed that Kiwi would be safe.

Enkindler

Lanezi gripped the panel, still gasping and willing his stomach to behave, even though they had stabilized minutes ago. Both twins were subdued, from fear, not the wild ride. The pups had settled into their laps. He couldn't make sense of *Enkindler's* position. It was as if they'd been thrown back several weeks of travel, but that sort of acceleration would have killed them.

"*Enkindler*, recalculate trajectory to a-rings."

"Course correction required. ETA 11 weeks, 6 days 5 hours, 3—"

"What? That can't be right."

"See for yourself."

A screen popped up with their position data. "*Enkindler*, you're showing our position of weeks ago."

"This is our current position. We are moving away at high speed. Suggest immediate course correction."

In a panic, Lanezi checked to make sure both twins were strapped. "Yes. Yes! Do the most efficient one now!" He was thrown back in his chair before he even finished his order. How was it possible that they could have been accelerated so far, so fast?

While they were doing the burns Lanezi had Euro search for the *Cheetah*.

"Nothing. No Ramian either," Euro reported.

"*Enkindler*, confirm a-rings are still there."

"A-ring beacon detected."

With a sinking feeling in his stomach, Lanezi ran the playback in fast speed, stopping when he saw a huge white flash. "Something happened," Io said plaintively. Lanezi forced himself to go back to 2 minutes before the flash and they all watched with dread.

They could see the *Cheetah* and the Ramian ship. Then both ships seemed to jerk. Several times they jerked, as if someone had pulled the fabric of space out from under them.

"Gravity ball malfunction," Euro speculated.

"But they're still half a day away from the a-rings," Lanezi objected.

"Who knows how dangerous—" Io said.

There was the flash—a blinding ball of white, which dissipated instantly and was followed by a smaller ball of blazing light. A plasma jet went up, away from the plane of the planetary system. And then that was gone. Only after several playbacks and enhancements could they track the *Cheetah*, which seemed to get sucked in the opposite direction of the jet. The Ramian followed a second or two later. And then they were gone. And then the picture jerked and started to spin wildly.

"Exploding gravity ball," Euro said.

"A second gravity ball. One that Thayne called, and the *Cheetah* never even saw it coming." Lanezi nodded. And then he remembered. "Jarvie's message said that the other gravity ball blew up and killed some people, but he didn't say how."

"What happened to them?" Io asked.

"Whisper," Lanezi asked. "Where did they go?"

Whisper closed her eyes a moment. "Kiwi gone."

"The others?" Lanezi asked.

"Gone."

"Ramians?"

"Gone." She looked at Lanezi, puzzled.

"They jumped," Euro said. "They must have."

Lanezi agreed it looked like they had jumped. There was no wreckage of any gravity ball or the ships. And thank God, the a-rings and that gravity ball were intact.

"We're stranded," Io said.

"No. We can jump in the shuttle," Lanezi said calmly. "*Enkindler*, ETA?"

"12 weeks, 3 days, 7 hours, 4 minutes."

"We'll starve," Io said.

"No, we won't. Captain Zahar gave us extra food. We'll go on rations, right now."

Later, when the twins were sleeping again, Lanezi reviewed supplies. They could make it to the a-rings alive, but after that, how many weeks to be rescued? How severely should he ration? He ended up dividing their 3 week supply into 16 weeks. Food would be the least of their troubles. Fuel to keep life support going would be the hardest part. They couldn't ration breathing.

Cheetah, location unknown

Everything happened so fast. Melawn sensed the jump, but only for a second. Then they were back in normal space. He heard the gasps of Caspia and Nkiroo, meaning that Tenshi and Zahar were unconscious. Then Evan's voice came over the s'link asking for help. Melawn didn't hesitate. They were no longer accelerating. He threw his straps off. In nogee, he maneuvered to the Command Bay, still covered by the wall of robots. He was aware of Nkiroo and Caspia coming behind him.

He reached for the door control and the bots moved away. "Hold on," Caspia said, but he didn't wait. He pushed the controls. Bots fell away and disappeared as the door slid open to a scene of standoff.

Evan was backed against the panel, preventing Thayne from reaching the controls. His look was completely rational and determined. Thayne turned gracefully as the door opened, speaking even before he saw who was there. "Melawn, move Evan out of the way. He's lost his mind." Then Nkiroo and Caspia appeared and Thayne's expression darkened. Melawn had a stab of fear, and a second later, there was a thwang and a med-dart was sticking out of Thayne's chest. Melawn and Nkiroo gasped. Thayne's angry eyes narrowed on Caspia, who was holding a spring loaded gadget.

"A weapon? Barbarian," Thayne hissed at her, before his eyes rolled back and he hung uselessly in nogee.

They all turned in shock to Caspia. "What is that?" Nkiroo asked carefully.

"Tranquilizer. He'll only be out for 15 minutes, so we need to restrain him in the Med Bay immediately." She reached for Thayne's arm, but no one else moved.

"You need a license for that," Nkiroo said with careful mildness, but Caspia was fed up.

"Of course you do! I have one! What do you *think* I've been *doing* at the pilot retirement center for years? *Making cookies?* Half of those pilots are irrational, but not nearly as dangerous as Thayne!"

They recoiled at her annoyance. "Sorry," Nkiroo said. "Just checking. Melawn, stay here and help Evan."

Next to Melawn, Evan, already agitated from Thayne, had looked down in distress when Caspia made her 'irrational' comment. Before she left, she made sure Evan was okay and gave his arm a quick squeeze.

Evan looked at Melawn in all innocence. "Am I crazy?"

"No," Melawn answered. "She wasn't talking about you." He gripped Evan's shoulder. "Let's stabilize and see where we are."

But it wasn't that easy.

Evan, exhausted from his ordeal, Melawn, Nkiroo, and Zahar gathered in the Command Bay in disbelief. Evan and Melawn's frantic work at the controls had given way to Nkiroo's focus and thoroughness, but it made no difference.

"No beacons," Nkiroo confirmed. "All our equipment is working properly. There are no stations, no a-rings, no ships. No *Enkindler*. No Ramian vessel, either."

"We'll have to do a gravity assist," Zahar suggested.

"No," Nkiroo shook his head sadly. "There are no planets. We don't seem to be in a planetary system, but we're still checking. We can't even confirm the usual navigational stars."

An icy cold settled over Zahar. If she'd thought things were tough before, that was nothing. "We can't be stranded," she breathed. Nkiroo stared at his screens, but Melawn looked up at her, despair in his eyes.

"Evan," she asked, "how did you jump without the a-rings?"

"I'm so sorry." Evan rubbed his face. "I was scared. That gravity ball was suddenly right there and I just wanted to get away. I don't know what happened."

"It's not your fault, Evan," Melawn consoled him. "But do you have any idea where we are?"

Evan shook his head forlornly. "I'm so sorry."

"Melawn, take him to Caspia," Zahar ordered, slipping around to strap into a chair.

When they were gone, Zahar and Nkiroo shared a long look. "Even the stars seem strange. Wherever we are," he said, "we're not in the same part of the galaxy . . . maybe not the same universe."

"No," she breathed. But then she remembered she was captain and refused to give up. "Evan got us here. He can get us back."

Enkindler, heading back to Friendship a-rings

The problem of life-support power vexed Lanezi. "You understand, we must conserve fuel in every possible way," he told the twins gently. They nodded somberly. "No cooking. No showers." They frowned. "And I'm sorry. We have to turn down the heat. You can keep the pups with you to stay warm."

He turned the heat down even more at night. The twins took to sharing a sleep sack and stuffing the pups in with Lanezi. At first, he thought they would keep him awake, but they were quiet and seemed to be slowing down. And one morning he woke up and the three babies were still. "Summer?" He grabbed her.

But it was Whisper who answered. "Summer sleeps."

"Sleeping?" Lanezi tried to confirm.

"Long sleep," Whisper explained.

"Hibernation?"

But Whisper just looked at him, puzzled. "Whisper soon." It must be, he thought, holding Summer to his ear. Her heart still beat, but so slowly.

Lanezi spent three minutes of power on the med scanner to prove to the twins that the pups were hibernating. All the specs matched the podpup medical database.

"Pups okay," Whisper repeated, miffed that he had checked. The twins and Lanezi took turns hugging Whisper until she slipped into hibernation later that day.

But it wasn't enough. After a week of reduced usage, life support numbers could not be extended to the necessary remaining weeks. And life without the lively pups was all the more grim.

15-Glory

Cheetah, location unknown

Zahar floated into the Command Bay to find Evan, Nkiroo, and Melawn in a state of excitement, for the first time since the jump. "Something good?" she asked.

"Yes, Captain," Nkiroo answered. "We've been able to verify our speed—.89 JV."

"What?"

"Yes," Evan explained, smiling. "Our mini-jump didn't knock off a lot of speed, as jumps usually do. We'll be able to regain JV with no a-rings or gravity assist."

A flood of relief went through Zahar. "Thank God." They nodded.

"In twelve days we'll have enough fuel," Nkiroo added.

"But we're lost," Zahar said, puzzled. "How will we know where to jump?"

"I'm hoping to pick the strongest path," Evan said. "It may not get us to Canyon, but anywhere with a-rings is better than here."

"Will Thayne be well enough to jump?" Melawn asked quietly. A flicker of anger and determination crossed Evan's usually compassionate face.

"Yes," Zahar said, but was glad to see that worrying about Thayne wasn't going to hold Evan back.

· · ·

17-Glory

Enkindler, heading for Friendship a-rings

The two fields were the biggest drains on their energy. Lanezi checked the number of hits on the particle field. Too many. Turning that off would be a quick end.

But radiation levels were average. Maybe he could turn the field down. And they had radiation tents listed in the supplies. *Zahar thinks of everything.* The twins and podpups were known to be radiation resistant. He ran through medical records to get estimates, which thanks to Tenshi's work, were the most reliable available.

During his late-night calculations, he realized, and was ashamed to be saddened by it, that he only had to survive to the jump. After that, Euro could bring in the ship. He could even program *Enkindler* to do it. Whisper would die with him, but the twins and three pups would be saved. They could survive in the suits for a few days as a last resort.

Finally, the numbers balanced. He turned the radiation field down. Cold, hungry, tired, and visualizing his cells being mutated by radiation, Lanezi contemplated how to spend his final weeks in joy instead of sorrow.

6-Beauty

Drumheller, incoming to Tundra System

"Tundra beacon located. ETA 8 days, 3 hours, 12 minutes."

Beezan struggled out of his cocoon and called Katie, trying to keep his voice calm. "Something's wrong. Jarvie has a green light, but he's thrashing around. He's gasping, but conscious."

Jarvie grabbed his helmet and pulled it off in a panic. "Don't throw it!" Sequoia warned. Beezan pulled over to Jarvie and snatched the helmet from him.

The just-completed jump from Tetra to Tundra had not been difficult. In fact, Beezan feared to hex himself by even thinking it was easy. But it was. Prayers, JV, look, see the path, jump. Routine. And they were only eight days out. He would have been thrilled if not for Jarvie's wild reaction. Beezan stowed the helmet and put his hand on Jarvie's forehead, mostly to get him to be still enough to look at his eyes. "What's wrong?" He asked casually.

"I heard him!"

"Heard who?"

"Quay!"

Quay, *one of the Ramians*, Beezan remembered, and relaxed a bit. Sequoia nodded and said, "Jump dream."

"No! I heard him. Three times! It was so strange. But so real. He was calling for help."

"You're learning to jump. It's just a dream," Beezan said, squeezing Jarvie's shoulder.

"It wasn't like a dream. It was as clear as if he were calling on my p'link."

"Well," Sequoia asked, "was he speaking Ramian?"

"Yes. No." Jarvie frowned. "I don't know. I understood."

"No worries, then," Sequoia soothed. "You were probably thinking about him. People who jump together form bonds."

"He needed help," Jarvie appealed to Beezan. "They were desperate. Please. We have to help them. Please believe me."

Something in Jarvie's eyes, some conviction of things seen only by pilots made Beezan doubt that it was all a dream.

"I'll send a message back through. Maybe someone can jump out to Friendship and see if they've come back."

"Thank you," Jarvie whispered.

8-Beauty Eve

Cheetah, lost

Melawn clipped on the chair at the conference table, glancing down at his wrist out of habit. He clenched his jaw, exasperated with himself. That was the 87th time today he had looked for Thayne's icons. He'd had no idea how often he checked on Thayne until Zahar destroyed the wrist p'link for good. He tugged his sleeve down sharply. The others didn't seem to notice, except Tenshi, who frowned at him, and Kiwi, who started to come over, but Zahar held on to him.

Zahar finished the pre-jump briefing, going over their path and timeline. No question, this was the most important jump of their lives. If they couldn't escape this weird empty space, they would die. "Evan," she said quietly, "please start the prayers." Evan would be considered their pilot. *He is our pilot, Melawn reminded himself.* No thoughts of desperation pilot, last-chance-only pilot, he's-crazy-and-he'll-kill-us-all pilot. The pilot had to have the confidence of the crew.

I trusted Thayne—and look what happened. And now I have to trust Evan.

Evan's whisper of a voice, tremulous, didn't inspire confidence. And it wasn't one of the usual pilot's prayers. He chanted a long prayer, from memory, never faltering, but heart-breakingly beseeching.

Finally, they filtered out, leaving Caspia and Evan to say their last prayers together. Melawn held his hand over his wrist willing himself to transfer some of that betrayed trust he'd had for Thayne to renewed trust for Evan. Wherever they went in tomorrow's jump, they would go together.

8-Beauty

Tenshi, passenger monitor, came in the Command Bay to give Melawn his jump drug. He was sitting to the left of Evan, with Nkiroo on Evan's right. He had his brackets on and was about to put his helmet on when Tenshi floated in.

"Not Melawn," Evan said quietly.

"What?" Tenshi asked. Melawn held his breath. He was as surprised as Tenshi, but you weren't supposed to question a pilot. Melawn was usually considered a distraction in the jump.

"Melawn, this side. Nkiroo, that side," Evan pointed each way. "That's how it should be," he said mysteriously.

"Yes, Evan," she nodded and turned to go without giving Melawn the jump drug.

Evan smiled serenely at him and said, "Like wings," and then it was back to business.

Tenshi reported passengers ready, apparently not having the heart to announce their reduced P&P. Nkiroo put up the acceleration map, showing the small burns they would be making to mimic the PAT bumps. Helmets went on and they were in final countdown.

Melawn calmed himself, rerunning a few lines of Evan's chanting from the night before, finding it stronger in spirit than it had been in volume.

The *Cheetah* hurtled toward JV, making powerful burns, first every minute and then every 15 seconds. "Two to go," Nkiroo said.

Melawn closed his eyes and tried to clear his mind. *Nkiroo and me, two wings of Evan's bird. Accept data only. Blank.* A big, painful, burn.

"Five seconds," Nkiroo reported. A tremendous burn pushed them into their chairs. He knew Evan would be searching for the path. Melawn didn't have implants, so he didn't see anything, but he opened his heart, his mind, and his spirit, giving himself up to be of any assistance at all. He waited for Evan to use the thruster to put them into the path—except he didn't.

Instead of a nudge, they were violently whipped into a leftward spin. Melawn felt the grab of the path then. His head rocked even with the reinforced helmet. They were spinning in the path! Tighter and tighter, he spun terrifying circles around himself, being crushed into his own spine. His breath froze inside him and, thankfully, he spiraled into darkness.

· · ·

By the time Zahar got to the Command Bay, Nkiroo's light had just gone green and he was wrenching off his helmet.

"What—" she asked, but he was white-knuckled and anxious.

"Evan!" he called.

"He's yellow."

"Get him out. We need to talk to him."

Zahar preferred to wait for the green light, but obviously, something had happened. All four of the conscious jumpers had gone yellow. She wasn't feeling so good herself. Her quick glance outside revealed nothing, but a screen ominously flashed "auto-stabilize."

She unsealed Evan's cocoon and Nkiroo gently dealt with the arm brackets, which woke Evan up. He groaned and opened his eyes. He was completely rational just long enough to say, "Loops. The paths were loops. Paths to nowhere." And then he was wandering.

"Did we jump?" Zahar asked.

"We did something," Nkiroo answered.

She got Melawn's helmet off. "Sick," he groaned—and she managed to get a bag on him in time.

"*Cheetah*, Elapsed time during jump?" Nkiroo asked.

"Twelve minutes."

Twenty minutes later, Zahar drank her restoration drink in the Med Bay with the others. Caspia also gave them a motion sickness booster. Kiwi was fine, of course, nuzzling around Evan's pockets.

"Our position is here, compared to where we started the jump," Nkiroo pointed out on the big screen. "We didn't exactly jump, so we didn't get far. The good news is that we still have

.78JV—and, we're going almost the opposite direction. We're headed back the way we came."

"We're going backwards?" Tenshi asked.

"No. Loops, Evan said. I believe we looped around." Nkiroo turned to Evan. "Were they closed loops?"

"Hundreds of them . . ." he murmured.

"What made us spin?" Zahar asked.

"I did," Evan said calmly, and then drifted off.

Caspia let out a slow breath. "I've heard the pilots talk about it—spin the ship just as you enter the path and you'll pop out automatically. No need to wait to pass a large mass, or dump the speed."

"Why would anyone do that?" Tenshi asked.

"The pilots weren't always rational."

And then Evan was back in focus. "I just wanted to see where it was going without committing," he explained.

"Did you?" Zahar asked.

"Yes. It was going nowhere."

Zahar frowned. "We got here. We can get back. Melawn!"

He jumped. She chided herself to be patient with them. It had been a rough jump. "Melawn," she said more gently, "correlate all the cameras and nav data we have from just before we jumped and just after. Forget the paths. We need to pinpoint the exact direction that we entered this . . . space."

He nodded, already thinking how to do it.

"It won't help," came Thayne's rasping voice from the alcove. There was a beat of silence.

"Why?" Tenshi asked calmly.

"Mini universe, non-inflating dimensions. Fool pilot jumped us to a pocket."

They gasped, half from the insult and half from the idea of jumping to a place of no return. Sweat broke out on her forehead, but Evan didn't even seem to hear. Thayne was intolerable. It was a mistake to even be in the room with him. "Don't listen to him, Evan. You, Melawn, and Nkiroo are going to find our way home." She motioned them all out of the Med Bay. They were already sick to their stomachs. No need to make them heartsick as well.

8-Beauty

Drumheller, incoming to Tundra

Two days after arriving in Tundra, Jarvie sat in an Arc 1 classroom looking over his new class schedule for the next couple of months. He'd be with Terina and have multiple teachers. He was embarrassed to be so thrilled. No trying to fit in with the kids on Hamada, all staring and knowing his history. No more lonely hours in his cabin trying to stay ahead of Beezan.

A Day: Ship repair with Thunder.
Consultation skills with Iricana
Exercise/Rec/Music
B Day: Hydroponics with Kelson
Podpup care with Katie
Exercise/Rec/Music
C Day: Shuttle Duty with Sequoia
Physics with Beezan
Exercise/Rec/Music

"Shuttle Duty!" Terina was jumping up and down, pumping a fist.

"Oh, historians don't like to pilot shuttles," he teased her.

She jabbed a finger at him. "*You* are inaccurate. Many historians were great adventurers." He laughed, but she turned serious. "Jarvie, what are you going to be when you grow up?"

"Taller," he said.

"You're tall enough!"

"He's going to be a pilot," Thunder answered, coming in with a robot team carrying boxes of extra tools.

"Well, I hope so," Jarvie said quietly.

"Have no doubt," Thunder said. "But if you're going to be flying *this* ship, we need to learn some serious repair skills. That Arc 9 business was just the beginning."

Jarvie and Terina went over to the table. "Where are you going?" Thunder asked. "We're off to the work tower. I don't sit at tables."

"Unless you're eating," Terina clarified.

"Only when I have to."

"Or saying prayers," she added.

"Only when I have to." And as they started up the rimway, Thunder started singing "We Have Come to Sing Praises." Jarvie and Terina joined in enthusiastically. They sang all the way to the work tower. Jarvie didn't know all of the songs, but Terina did. Maybe she was a music historian too.

And no table for lunch either. They sat on the deck of the work tower. "Thunder," Jarvie asked, trying to make it sound like an engineering question, "how long do you think it would take to make a-rings from scratch?"

Thunder and Terina stopped chewing and looked at him, sympathy crossing Thunder's expression. "Well, it took about two and a half months, according to the Luminesse report, to put two pre-assembled a-ring segments into place with a new gravity ball."

"With a pre-trained team of workers," Jarvie added.

"Yes, so engineers have estimated that working from blueprints only, building everything from scratch, would probably take a year. Provided they have what they need."

"Oh." Jarvie frowned. He'd been worried that there was no word from Lanezi.

"If the *Cheetah* went to Firelight, we don't expect to hear anything for a long while," he said. "A backup plan is in the works."

Jarvie looked up in surprise.

"They're making more segments at Harbor. If there is no return ship from Firelight in a year, they'll ship in new segments. Then they'll start manufacturing segments for each sector to keep in reserve."

"Oh, good plan," Terina said.

"So the sectors could be reconnected in a year," Jarvie said. It was almost too much to hope for.

"And," Thunder added, "thanks to your mission with the Ramians, they will no longer be jumping into our space to cause the accidents. Things are truly looking good for the outer sectors."

"Well, I'll feel better when it happens," Jarvie admitted.

"In the meantime," Thunder said, "Let's get this ship into shape. Who knows what exciting missions might come up."

"I don't think Beezan would go for exciting missions. He seems happy things are calm again," Jarvie said and Terina nodded.

Thunder smiled and stood up. "Your Captain, bless his soul, may think it's calm, but *I* think we're just in the eye of the storm."

"You sound like Grandpa!" Terina laughed, but it gave Jarvie a twinge of worry.

. . .

9-Beauty

Beezan sat in the corner of the Rec Room, eating cake and trying to create a zone of calm. Sequoia sat down somewhat near him as if to expand the calm zone, and Kelson joined on the other side. He wondered if it was even remotely sane to have a big birthday party for two podpups. Actually three, as Star and Sky were officially one year old, but Rocket could not be left out.

There were presents, treats, games, and silly songs that Kelson insisted he didn't make up.

Beezan tried to let go of the serious issue on his mind, which crew member to add to the *Drumheller's* role model list. He supposed it was the point of parties to relax. Besides, at the moment, he couldn't imagine adding anyone to the list. Except for Sequoia, they all seemed a bit wild.

The current game was rolling a ball across the deck with your nose. Podpups vs. humans. Human teens anyway. The loud cheering unnerved Beezan, but they were all having so much fun. The champion, Sky, was awarded an extra treat. She brought it over and gave it to him. "For Bee."

"Oh, Sky, you're so sweet to share." He patted her on the head.

"Huh! Win more," she said wickedly, and got back in the game.

Sequoia laughed. "What a funny pup."

Beezan watched Sky have her way with pups and humans. He wondered what the *Drumheller* thought about all this. "What exactly does the AI learn from human exemplars, anyway?" he asked, aloud, apparently, as Kelson and Sequoia turned to look at him in mild surprise. He looked down shyly, embarrassed to be caught considering other people's virtues.

"Well, you know," Sequoia answered seriously, "that 97% of the programming, both technical and ethical, is locked in. However, the

3% flexibility in communication, empathy, and ethics application is plenty of room for wide variation in AI reaction and personality."

Kelson nodded, "They are conscious, but must acquire a conscience."

"Yes," Sequoia agreed with his old saying, "if you're looking for exemplars, you don't need to bother with intelligence, or logic. They have that. You need to give them the human side of the traits. They need role models for wisdom, benevolence, obedience, risk assessment."

"They have the brain," Kelson said, "but we must give them the soul."

"But they don't really have a soul." Beezan said, feeling self-conscious of the *Drumheller* overhearing.

Sequoia answered, her father nodding, "They retain the impression of the souls who have gone before—in *Drumheller's* case—your ancestors."

"A great AI," Kelson added, "will carry the love and care, the spirit and hope of generations."

Beezan shuddered, "What would happen if a ship had a bad role model?"

"I've heard about that," Kelson answered. "In the old days, of course. A ship was co-owned by three families. The head of each family was an exemplar. They fought constantly. The ship became paralyzed. They had to erase the AI."

"But they don't erase these days," Sequoia said. "AIs are considered *unique personalities*. They have special AI doctors."

Kelson laughed at the pups. "We have some unique personalities on this ship. But seriously Captain, you could not go wrong with anyone on this ship being a role model."

"Unless you want it to have a saying for everything," Sequoia added dryly.

Kelson laughed so hard Beezan couldn't help joining in.

Much later, under excuse of his bedtime, Beezan left Sky at the party and went to the Command Bay. He worked through the long security process to get to the exemplar program. He had never thought much about it before. He had never even read the full list. He did now for the first time. The original exemplar was Jazon Kahale, over 400 years ago. Jazon, Jazann, and an old-fashioned last name. Beezan skimmed a long list of names of strangers until he recognized his great-grandparents, grandparents, parents, and former crew. His own name was added when he was only 9 years old. And his name was all that remained for the past 10 years. He took a deep breath.

"*Drumheller*, add exemplar."

There was a very long delay, almost as if *Drumheller* were reluctant.

"Name?"

"Thunder Marima Alrik Terrace."

"Added. Update with stored data?"

"Yes."

There was a long, long pause.

"Name?"

"That's all."

"Closing program."

"*Drumheller*, can you tell me anything about Jazon, the first exemplar?"

Several pictures and small movie clips appeared on the screen. In one photo, a dark-eyed man of Polynesian descent stared into the camera.

"Jazon Kahale, born—"

"I mean something personal, not his bio, what you thought of him."

"Jazon was a strong and courageous captain, an inspirational leader, and had great composure and humility. He was generous in servitude, kind to the crew, and just in settling human matters."

"Do you miss him?"

"He is with me, always. As you are, Captain."

11-Beauty

Cheetah, in the pocket

After recovering from their loopy jump, Melawn combined the pre and post jump data and visuals. A series of gravity waves at Friendship, right before the jump, had distorted data, so he'd had to sync it up.

Now he was just fretting, waiting for Nkiroo to watch the run-through for the first time. At least he'd been able to do something useful for the crew. There was a clattering at the door that had to be more than the quiet Nkiroo. Evan was with him.

Evan's eyes were red and swollen. His dark skin looked sickly, if not exactly pale. *He feels as bad as I do. Except the bad jump wasn't Evan's fault.* Instinctively, Melawn got up and hugged Evan, or tried to, with all the hard pocket items poking him. They settled into the chairs. "It's just now compiled. I haven't seen it yet. I'll start with the forward view, real time," Melawn explained.

Starting from the Friendship side of the jump, the advanced

graphics allowed them to see the NAV stars in the distance, as well as their nearly 90° swoop under the doomed gravity ball. "Why weren't we killed?" Melawn asked Nkiroo.

"I suspect the gravity flux may have allowed the ship to change direction without so much force."

"There are two more NAV stars," Evan pointed to the screen.

"Yes," Melawn said. "We were lucky to ID those in the three seconds we had before jump." Then the screen went blank.

"Do you remember anything?" Nkiroo asked Evan gently.

"I didn't do it. I mean, I didn't mean to dive under. That just happened. But as far as remembering the jump, I . . ."

Melawn ran it back a few times so that Evan could see the pre-jump angle again. "I was so panicked," Evan whispered. "I was so afraid of the gravity ball. We were so close and I knew something bad was happening to it. I just wanted to get away and then I saw a path, a white path. I should have known better, but it was too late."

"And later," Nkiroo asked, "when we tried to jump out of this space, were there any white loops?

"They were all white." Evan hung his head.

The picture on the screen blinked back to life as they entered this weird space. There were no regular NAV stars.

Melawn pointed. "These are NAV2 stars. *Cheetah* started a new system for this space. The best we can do is make a proba-bility chart for our exit." Nkiroo and Evan nodded, frowning. Melawn checked the computer. "The rear camera view is ready. I'll run it in real time."

Again, he started at the Friendship side. This time, they could see the *Enkindler* behind them. There were major jerks, first as the *Cheetah* and then the *Enkindler* were hit by gravity waves. But each time, the camera, led by the beacon, refocused on *Enkindler*.

"*Enkindler* looks like it's getting hit harder than we are," Nkiroo said, puzzled.

"Look!" Evan pointed to the side of the screen. "The Ramian. They're also being sucked under the gravity ball."

Another couple of jolts and they lost the view of the Ramian. "NAV stars," Melawn whispered as they were identified by the computer. The image locked on the *Enkindler* again and then something catastrophic happened to the gravity ball. And the picture froze. All three of them gasped.

"It exploded!" Nkiroo said.

"There's some kind of jet there," Evan pointed.

Melawn went back and slowed it down. The gravity ball did explode, sending a white jet bursting from the top as the *Cheetah* was propelled the opposite direction.

"The *Enkindler*!" Evan exclaimed. Melawn refocused on the shuttle, ran enhanced graphics, and slowed it down.

"It's been hit by a huge gravity wave," Nkiroo explained, "the last of the gravity ball."

In the last microseconds of data they saw the *Enkindler* tumble away, hurtling out of control with what looked like incredible force.

"No," Melawn whispered.

"Oh, my God," Nkiroo said.

Evan was sobbing into his hands.

Lanezi, the twins, the pups . . . Melawn's heart denied it. "Maybe they survived. We did."

Nkiroo snatched a pad, wiping his eyes on his sleeve. Melawn shook his head. "There's not enough data to calc the gees." Melawn put his hand on Nkiroo's arm. "Even if they survived the main kick, they would have been thrown back weeks." Evan hung his head.

"The Captain did put extra food," Nkiroo whispered. "We

must tell the crew, and pray for them," he added. He grasped Evan's arm. "It wasn't your fault. Whether you jumped or not would not have changed things for them."

But a cold dark feeling came over Melawn. It was not Evan's fault. But none of this, not being at Friendship, not Lanezi in the shuttle, and not that stray gravity ball would have happened if not for Thayne. He looked to his wrist by reflex and then, furious with himself, pounded his arm down on the panel, hoping to break off that part of himself. Pain streaked through his arm. Before he could do it again, Nkiroo grabbed him and Evan was calling for help. "Let me go! Thayne did this! And it's my fault, because I believed in him! All this time. I believed in him!"

The pain in his arm was not near enough to stop the pain in his heart, but Evan and Nkiroo held him tightly until Caspia got there. He remembered the trank dart and tried to control himself. "I won't hurt you. I promise," he sobbed.

"Promise not to hurt yourself," Caspia said calmly, hand under his chin, making him look her in the eye.

He jerked his head away, but slowly, with Caspia telling him to breathe, the crazy urge to do painful things drained out of him and he slumped against Nkiroo. "I promise."

Alone in the conference room, Zahar stared at the screen. She'd watched the replay of the *Enkindler* 40 times, trying to convince herself that Lanezi had somehow survived. The crew had said prayers and drifted off, leaving her to ponder the *Enkindler's* fate.

She never should have let the twins go—but when she considered their own situation, it may not make any difference. So sad. So useless. If they couldn't escape this space, she would be the captain of a doomed vessel.

The stars were far away and strange. They might not even have planets, let alone habitable ones. They could live for years on the ship, but any hope for a rescue was slim, and relied on the *Enkindler* being found first, then figuring out what happened to *Cheetah*. But if no one knew how to get out of these pockets, no one would jump in. That was a given.

The crew was already full of anger and disunity. They couldn't even enjoy their last years together. How could she ever fix that? *Were there some groups of people that just couldn't get along, or some problems too much to overcome?*

She tapped off the screen with a stray thought, *what happened to the Ramians?*

12-Beauty

Melawn woke up to the ethereal chanting of Nkiroo. Heartbreaking thoughts crowded his mind, but he held them out, floating in the serenity of the moment.

But he had strength only until the end of the prayer before the cascade of fear, despair, grief, and hopelessness overcame him. He was in his own cabin, on his bunk, unrestrained. Slowly, he sat up. Nkiroo sat at the panel, eyes closed, quiet now.

Melawn felt his arm. It was tender, but not even bandaged. He pulled up his sleeve. His arm, from the back of his hand to his elbow, was covered in black writing. *We Love You Melawn!* was surrounded by the signatures of the crew, embellished with virtues and phrases of support and hope. He burst into tears and hugged his arm against his chest, now cherishing what he had yesterday hated.

· · ·

Zahar arrived at the Med Bay for her meeting with the doctors, but only Caspia was there. "Where's Dr. Tenshi?"

"I'm sorry Captain. She's had some sort of breakthrough and hasn't left her lab. I thought we could let her continue."

Zahar peered at the screen showing Thayne in his secure alcove in the Med Bay. "Who is in charge of Thayne?"

"I am."

"Are you qualified?"

Caspia gestured for Zahar to sit at the table, joining her in the adjacent chair. "I may be more qualified than Dr. Tenshi," she said, without boasting, "but the situation is unique, especially if we remain separated from advanced facilities."

"What would normally happen to him?"

"We have to figure out if he's rational. It takes time to discover what's really going on in the mind. Sometimes it isn't possible. Take Evan for example. He doesn't know where his mind wanders. He only has a vague idea."

"But Thayne isn't a pilot."

"Right. And Thayne doesn't have the same thing. But he still has some sort of delusion, along with a tremendous disconnect from his fellow human beings."

"Does he know what happened to the *Enkindler*?"

"Yes." Caspia indicated a screen and tapped it. A view of Thayne's alcove appeared. He was sitting up, dressed, thin, stormy-looking. He had no panels or controls, just a screen on the wall. When the screen went on, he turned his back. But since there was no sound, he eventually glanced over. It took only seconds for him to understand the graphics and data ticking across the bottom of the screen. Then he paid full attention. When the *Enkindler* was kicked back he gasped and took several steps toward the screen. He stared, defiantly, a long time.

Caspia turned the replay off. "Twenty minutes he stands there, fuming. Then he sinks into the chair shaking his head, like how could we be such fools."

"You've cut back the sedative."

"Way back," Caspia confirmed. "I can't judge his grasp on reality until he's completely off. And it prevents him from reconnecting with humanity."

"I don't see ever letting him out of there."

"Solitary confinement makes people worse, not better."

"We can't just let him loose."

"No. He has to earn his way back. And it has to be real work. But first—he has to want to."

11-Grandeur

Enkindler, heading for Friendship a-rings

Lanezi straightened the survival tube tent at the end they used for makeshift Prayer Room. It kept them warmer and protected them a bit more from radiation. He smoothed down the stick-and-stays and reaffixed the bolsters and hold straps. The twins had done their tent organizing chores, moving the pups to a safe side area where they could stay warm together. As they had not much else to do besides exercise and eat their tiny rations, they spent three hours a day on devotions and readings. Sometimes it turned into storytelling, and sometimes, accidently, naptime. The twins stirred, coming out of their semi-dreamy state of meditation.

"Lanezi," Euro asked, "why are you so tired?"

"Yeah, we don't do anything all day."

"I'm not tired of the days," he sighed. "I'm tired of the years."

"Why?" Io asked. "You're not so old."

Lanezi laughed. "I'm sorry. It's fine. I'm fine."

"You are sad," Io declared.

"I'm happy to be here with you two. It's just that every time I think I know how my life is going to go, it changes."

"Tell us!" Euro said.

"Oh, like my life is a story."

"Yes," Io insisted. "It will be good."

"It will be a long and boring story that doesn't go anywhere."

"Where did you want it to go?" Io asked.

Lanezi paused to really consider the question. "All I ever wanted was a family," he whispered.

They settled closer to him. "Tell us," Io whispered back.

These could be his final days. It would be good to tell his story. Lanezi took a breath. "My parents are still alive."

Both twins gasped. Lanezi-the-artist was highly promoted as an orphan. Another lie, he realized. "They were long jumpers —very long jumpers. They made the test jumps into sector 8. They were so good at jumping that they didn't fear it in any way. They never lost passengers. When I was born, they didn't sedate me. They put me in a padded chair and jumped. I was 12 days old on my first jump." They gasped again. "It was on the *Solstice*."

He smiled. "Of course, I don't really remember specifics. They didn't even pray much. They just seemed to know where they were going. Until one day when I was four years old . . ."

Hungry and scared, four-year-old Lanezi sat patiently for many hours, as he was forbidden to get out of the jump chair until someone released him. But eventually, he figured out how to toggle through the screens, discovered that his parents were both yellow-lighted, and battled his way out of his brackets and cocoon.

He cried, he screamed, he pleaded, but his parents were gone. Alive, but gone. They did not know him, or even acknowledge his existence, although, once released, they held hands with each other. He didn't know where the food stores were and they didn't care.

He was four. But he became the parent. He asked the *Solstice* for help and was able to feed the three of them. And there was one other thing he knew how to do—jump. So he became the pilot and jumped them back to civilization.

"You jumped when you were four?" Euro asked.

"The ship took me to the a-rings and I jumped from 8C to Sandune."

"That's a long jump," Io said.

"I had no idea where I was going. Sandune Incoming Authority sent a rescue ship, but it was another three weeks alone with my parents."

"So they're at the Pilot Retirement home, on Harbor?" Euro asked. "We just came from there, why didn't you visit them?"

"They're not there. They're in private care. Many long jumpers wander, or have short periods of disorientation. But they can still function in the world. My parents never came back. They never knew me again. I'm not allowed to visit them for more than a few—I'm sorry. This isn't a good story."

"We want to hear," Io said softly. "What happened to you?"

"I went to a station orphanage, at Azure. It was a dependency. I was pretty happy, well-cared for, lots of attention from the people at the senior home next door. I went to school. But people come and go. You make friends and then they're gone. And besides, you know, once you've seen the paths."

They nodded. "I wanted to go back to space. I started

painting then, when I was five or six. When I was seven, I was placed with station family. Their teens had gone off to school and they were lonely. But they gave me back after a year."

"Why?" Io asked, shocked.

"I might have been too much for them. But the series of abandonments was starting to wear me down. Finally, though, I was placed on a family ship—my dream. The *Emerald Bay*." Lanezi paused to let the wave of grief roll past. "Inner sectors. So much adventure, excitement. Earth, Mars, the Moon. Have you been to Earth?"

"Yes," Euro nodded.

"On Pilgrimage," Io added.

Lanezi nodded, trying to savor the good memories, the amazing planets, the home of humanity. "They loved me. I had a younger brother and sister even. When I was 15, they left me at pilot certification training for two months." He stopped.

"The *Emerald Bay* was lost," Euro whispered.

Lanezi nodded, unable to go on. Io chanted a prayer.

"Well, you know about *Sunburst*," Lanezi went on. "I thought I would never pilot again. Every ship I'd been on had been lost. And for some reason, I survived. But I was sent to *Cheetah*. And met Katie. And thought things would be better. But now the *Cheetah* might even be gone."

"But Katie is okay, and you will be together again," Io declared. It was a sweet idea and he would savor it until the end.

"Anyway," Euro said, "we're your family now and we're not going to give you back." Lanezi was going to start crying if they kept on and he didn't want them to suspect that he didn't expect to live, so he tried to lighten up.

"Well, Zahar made me your supervisor, but I'll never take

the place of your parents. And that's where we're going next, God willing, to take you home."

"Okay," Euro said, "Until then, we'll be *your* parents."

"Yeah!" Io declared. "Time for bed!"

"Did you do your exercise?"

"No more rough-housing!" The sudden emergence of the strong S-Tro accent could only have been the voices of their parents. It sent the three of them laughing.

"Stop fussing!"

"Do your math!"

"They always got us mixed up," Euro said, wiping the tears from his eyes.

"Calli! Gany! Euro! Io!" Io laughed. "I was always last."

"Even though it was always your fault!"

Lanezi put his arms around them and they laughed and cried together. "Okay," he said. "I'll be your family until you get back to them."

"No!" Io declared.

Lanezi looked at him, startled. And Euro clarified, "You'll be our family, *always*."

31 / COLD DARK MATTERS

14-Grandeur

Cheetah, in the pocket

Melawn hesitantly entered the Command Bay. It had been weeks since he'd seen Thayne. He hadn't been allowed—hadn't wanted—to see him, but Nkiroo had called him.

"Hi Melawn," Nkiroo said distractedly, "Thanks for coming."

Melawn grabbed the back of the empty chair left of Thayne and Thayne turned to look at him, but Melawn didn't meet his eyes, not after everything that had happened. Not after *you are nothing to me*, which still echoed in his mind. Thayne reached out and put his hand over Melawn's on the chair. "Melawn," he said softly, "so good to see you," so sweet and friendly as if he was no relation to the monster who'd set the bots on them.

Melawn slid his hand free and turned to the panel, managing to whisper a neutral "Good morning." Thayne brushed his arm, but Melawn turned away.

"In the case we aren't able to jump out this attempt," Nkiroo began, "the Captain wants us to consult about whether we could send a message out."

"*What?*" Thayne turned sharply towards Nkiroo. "Is she crazy? The greatest minds of humanity have been working on that for 200 years."

"You are one of the greatest minds of humanity, and you have not been working on it," Nkiroo replied calmly.

"If we can find the thread that goes out, we don't need to send a message, we can just jump out," Thayne said, exasperated.

"The question is, if we can't find the thread out," Nkiroo clarified. "She suggested that now that we know the gravity ball frequency, that might be a starting point."

"We're not trying to communicate with a gravity ball!"

"The captain suspects that other, more advanced races, whoever built the gravity balls, for example, might know how to send messages through jump space."

"Sure, they probably do. But that doesn't mean that we know."

"We need to figure it out," Nkiroo insisted.

Thayne turned toward the screen, folded his arms and sunk down in his seat, frowning. Nkiroo glanced at Melawn as if he might offer a suggestion, but he wasn't about to. Except he couldn't stop his brain from considering it. "Well . . . we know that the Ramians jumped into our space during our jumps."

"Four times. And the *Drumheller* info confirms that they were homing in on active jumps," Thayne said.

Melawn was stunned by this information. So was Nkiroo by his expression. "How do we know this?" Nkiroo asked.

"Oh, it's in the classified packets," Thayne waved his hand dismissively.

"Maybe it would help if we saw those," Nkiroo suggested, not able to keep an edge of annoyance out of his voice.

Thayne, who had been strongly warned to cooperate for his

freedom, entered some command into the computer, so fast, and a bunch of files popped up.

"The Ramian implants can somehow detect an active gravity ball," Thayne explained. "That's why they've jumped into our space and, consequently, crashed into our a-rings. And since the fact that they were destroying themselves didn't get back to them, because no one ever came home, they somehow concluded it would be sensible to keep doing it."

Nkiroo ignored his attitude. "They can detect active gravity balls during a jump?"

"No, once they reach jump velocity, then they jump in that direction."

"How is that different than what we do?" Nkiroo asked.

Thayne frowned. "Maybe the path is more obvious. We would need to ask Evan."

Nkiroo and Melawn exchanged a frown. "Evan's afraid of you," Nkiroo said.

"That's ridiculous. Call him," Thayne said

"He won't come," Nkiroo said.

"Why?" Thayne asked.

There was a strained pause. Melawn took a deep breath and squeezed his own arm where all the supportive writing was.

"Why?" Nkiroo repeated. Thayne looked at Nkiroo, thoroughly puzzled. "Do you remember setting the bots on him?"

"Oh. That."

Melawn was starting to breathe heavily. Like there was not enough oxygen in the Command Bay. *The nerve. The insanity. The supposed innocence.* He remembered the bots and Zahar screaming.

"*Oh that!*" Melawn couldn't help himself. He was out of his chair. "You have no care for your crew that you terrified and abused and . . . forced to—" he could not even choke out what he meant to say.

"Melawn," Nkiroo had grabbed him gently and was guiding him out the door.

"You're a monster!" Melawn yelled at Thayne. "I can't believe I ever defended—" The door shut. Nkiroo let him go, hands up in peace, shaking his head sympathetically.

"Sorry. Sorry Nkiroo. I can't do this."

Nkiroo sagged. "I don't think I can either."

"He doesn't care what he's done to us—oh my God—we've left him alone in the Command Bay!"

Nkiroo spun and hit the door control and it opened, to their great relief. Thayne was exactly as they left him, hands in the same place even, but with a slightly different expression. The element of calculation, of how stupid are you people, was back.

"Go," Nkiroo told him, patting Melawn on the arm.

15-Grandeur

Zahar and Nkiroo looked up as Melawn peeked in the Conference Room, checking left and right.

"He's not here," she reassured him. "Although he made it through lunch today, before we had to escort him back."

Nkiroo nodded. "I'm grateful Dr. Tenshi is sharing the load with me, Captain. It's very challenging."

She squeezed his shoulder. "It is beyond challenging, but you've been so patient, and Caspia says it's helping. She says the fact that he is up and ready to come out every morning is a sign that he wants to be with other human beings."

"Maybe he just needs his pawns," Nkiroo said. "How do we get him to stop using us?"

"We don't let him," Zahar insisted.

Evan hung his head. "I'm sorry I'm not helping."

"Caspia insists that you don't," Zahar said. "You, Melawn and I are too emotionally charged to interact at this first stage. Don't have a worry about it. Besides, you have a more important job." At first, she'd felt awkward patting their shoulders or reassuring them, as she was so much younger, but she saw now that they really looked to her as Captain, that they were all hurt, all scared, and needed support. When Thayne was not around, Zahar was determined to build unity with the rest of the crew. They settled down and she nodded to Nkiroo.

The main screen went on with a map of their current position. "These are NAV2 stars of course," Nkiroo said. A blue ellipse blinked. "That's the best I can pinpoint our target. We entered this space within .001 lightyear of this spot."

"About the width of a star system?" Zahar asked.

Nkiroo nodded. "That's the best we can do."

Evan blinked at the map. "So you want me to just . . . aim for that spot?"

"Yes," Nkiroo explained. "We hope a non-looping thread will appear to guide you."

"And if not?"

"I've written a return program optimizing our turning time without dumping more speed than we have to—but it's possible we will loop around again."

"How will I know?"

"We'll get a fix from NAV2 stars which will trigger one of two different return programs. We'll save what speed we have and try again."

"But that will take . . ."

"Months. Yes. Possibly years if we lose too much speed," she nodded. "There are no other options."

Evan swallowed hard, lifted a nervous hand as if to indicate himself.

"Hard jump," Nkiroo sympathized. "We know. Whatever happens, the crew won't blame you."

"Thayne blames me—for jumping here."

"Thayne is Thayne," Nkiroo shrugged, nothing positive to say.

"I'm not counting him in the crew," Zahar said, a little angrier than she meant to, "at least not until he earns it. So either we'll get out, or we'll loop around and dump out, and try again. What else could happen?"

16-Grandeur

Drumheller, in the Tundra a-rings

In the last moments of the jump, Jarvie tried to focus on Tektite.

"Unlock, then, to their hearts, O my God, the portals of Thy knowledge, that they may recognize Thee as One Who is far above the reach and ken of the understanding of Thy creatures..."[1]

BUMP. Breathe. Two more, Jarvie thought.

"Alone, We communed with Our spirit, oblivious of the world and all that is therein. We knew not, however, that the mesh of divine destiny exceedeth the vastest of mortal conceptions, and the dart of His decree transcendeth the boldest of human designs."[2]

BUMP. His chest hurt. He wasn't sure about this piloting business. *Please, just get a breath.*

"The birds of men's hearts, however high they soar, can never hope to attain the heights of His unknowable Essence."[3]

Thank you, Jarvie prayed, relaxing in relief. The bumps were over. He floated his mind as if he had finished the most grueling exercise routine.

With Beezan as jump pilot and Sequoia assisting, he had no worries about finding the path—and they suddenly appeared. Yellow and brighter yellow, greenish yellow and several lesser paths. Beezan had warned him there would be several.

Jarvie!

He jerked out of his serenity. *Quay?*

Jarvie. I call on you. Hear me. Come to Friendship. The monster devours us.

Quay's dear preschooler voice sounded so different. Intense, yearning, but still with that element of trust.

Jarvie's mind tentatively reached for his friend. And was gently pulled away.

Jarvie!

Quay! Jarvie threw his mind towards Quay, striving to hear, to communicate, even if it was only a strange vision.

The gentle force, Beezan, he recognized, started to pull him back again, and then *Wham!* He was jerked away.

Jarvie!

Quay? Where are you? What's happening? But it was too late. They were in a path, and Quay was gone.

Beezan felt a planet-size mass behind them as they dropped into normal space. He struggled to orient himself. They did not jump to Tektite. That he was sure of. It had been more of a tug-of-war than a jump. A wave of annoyance washed over him, but he sent it away. *Be calm. We are where we are meant to be.* Even his 17-week disaster jump with Jarvie had turned out to be for good.

He popped his helmet. Sequoia, on his right, did the same. Not so serene. "Where are we? What happened?" she demanded. Then she frowned and stopped, realizing that she had overcorrected and pulled them off the path. She had not trusted Beezan to correct for Jarvie, as he was always prepared to do. "My fault," she whispered.

She did not trust him. She doubted him even for a mid jump. He recognized it and her disregard for him as pilot of the jump. He was saddened and discouraged, but he didn't have to say anything. She knew.

"I'm sorry, Beezan. Captain. I'm so sorry. We are not at Tektite."

"No," he agreed. Though disappointed, the jump had not been too deep, so depression wasn't terrible. But now he was worried. "*Drumheller*, report."

"Searching for beacon."

Beezan checked Jarvie and the crew in the Passenger Lounge, all green. "All crew, remain seated." Jarvie wasn't moving, which concerned him. "Jarvie?" Meanwhile, he and Sequoia stowed the cocoons and helmets and he let Sky out, who let Star out and then climbed in his lap. "*Drumheller?*"

"No a-ring beacon."

Beezan froze. Sequoia gasped. *Not possible.* They just jumped to the wrong station. He couldn't accept any other answer.

"We did jump," he confirmed.

"Yes. We're no longer at Tundra," Sequoia confirmed.

"We must be near Tektite." But away, towards—he almost said it, *Chike space.* "*Drumheller!* Search for the nearest star, for Tektite, NAV stars or any beacon. Scan behind us!"

What's wrong with Jarvie? He reached over and shook Jarvie's arm gently. Jarvie jerked and started thrashing around.

"More dreams!" Sequoia said. "He was pulling us off course."

"Jarvie. Calm. *Calm.* Sky, check Jarvie."

Sequoia frowned and shook her head. If she had no confidence in him, she certainly had none in a podpup. "No obvious star system," she said. "We must be a long way out."

Stay calm. I've done this before. Long run in. That's all. More company this time.

Sequoia pounded the panel, scaring him. "Captain, I'm so sorry." She hung her head and shook it back and forth.

"Sequoia, I forgive you. Things happen. I only ask you to trust me next time."

"You should put me under next time."

"We all must learn to work together."

She nodded, tears starting. But she angrily wiped them away and went back to her scanning.

Beezan put the main screen on in the Passenger Lounge. "I'm sorry," he told the crew. "We are not at Tektite. Stand by."

With Sky's help and prodding, Jarvie finally stirred. "It was Quay!"

"Again?" Sequoia asked in frustration.

But Jarvie looked imploringly at Beezan. "He was calling me. They need help at Friendship. Did we jump to him?"

Oh my God. "No," Beezan said. "At least I don't think so. We don't know where we are."

"We're not at Friendship," Sequoia said sternly. "That's on the other side of human space."

Jarvie seemed confused, upset, and although it hurt for Beezan to admit it, Jarvie seemed disappointed in him.

"It was a dream, Jarvie," Sequoia insisted.

Beezan scowled to himself. *Maybe I should put them both under next time.*

A map, mostly of empty space, popped up. **"Tektite located."**

"Thank God," Sequoia breathed.

"ETA?" Beezan asked.

"17 years, 5 months—"

YEARS? God in heaven! He gripped the arm of the chair, forced himself to stay calm. "Nearest star? ID and ETA?"

"8J is the nearest star. ETA 12 years 7 months."

8J was historically known as a jump of no return. Probably in Chike space. Beezan's chest hurt. He forced himself to breathe. Sky brought him a protein pack as he hung in his chair, just trying to think.

"*Drumheller?* Could there be a-rings with no beacon?"

"We are not in a planetary system. A-rings are not expected."

"What's the mass behind us?"

"Rogue planet. Gas giant. No moons."

Great.

The nearest star had at least the hope of a-rings. He could take the time to consult with the crew. It would only cost them a few months. But he was the Captain. He switched to a visual of the Passenger Lounge. They were biting their lips. He reached for the microphone button—

"Ship beacon detected."

A new screen took priority. A red mayday beacon flashed on the screen. "Heaven help us," Sequoia said. "Another ship is stranded here."

Beezan checked the location. "It's orbiting the rogue planet."

"Quay?"

"I don't think so," Beezan said, not willing to say anything was impossible. "*Drumheller*, ship ID?"

"High power mayday and location broadcast only."

"ETA?"

"2 weeks, 6 days—"

"Stand by for boosting! Sky, Star, heads up."

"Ready in the Passenger Lounge."

"*Drumheller*, burn for the beacon. And send a query."

17-Grandeur

Drumheller, heading to the rogue planet

Terina sat with the others in the Prayer Room for the final few minutes of contemplation. The Captain had spun up for gravity and called them for prayers early. Beezan was anxiously awaiting the ID from the ship. Terina didn't know whether to hope for a rescue or be the rescuers. Her mom had explained to her that they had already lost their outbound speed. It was too late to take the 12-year option to 8J. They were in this for 20 years now. Kelson's life for sure. Maybe Iricana and Thunder's and most of Beezan's. And Katie separated from Lanezi. She thought of Azann. It was his story. And now it was their story. Except without the Chike—she hoped.

She and Jarvie would make it home, maybe alone. It was too soon to see him in a whole new light, but it was comforting to know that her gut reaction wasn't outright horror.

For his part, Jarvie seemed completely distracted, asking several times about Quay. She'd shamelessly used the opportunity to document the whole Quay story. It had taken him three hours to tell it last night, the whole saga of his time on the *Pearl*. First person source. Thrilling.

Whatever missing ship that was, and there were so many possibilities, finding it would be a piece of history. Her mom was agitated. Mad at herself, impatient with Jarvie and being careful not to cross Beezan, who was in a state of forced calm.

Beezan asked them to come to the Observation Bay after prayers, where he'd had breakfast set up. No one was ready to eat, but they got their drinks and sat down.

"*Drumheller*, how much longer?"

"3 minutes, 10 seconds for response from the beacon."

They sat quietly, nervously sipping.

Slowly, Beezan reached across the table and put his hand, palm up, in front of her mom. Sequoia blinked in confusion for a second, but Jarvie reached out and took Beezan's hand. Then Sequoia took a deep breath, nodded and gripped hands with both of them. The rest of the crew reached out, like a sports team. Terina had to get out of her chair and slip in beside Jarvie to reach, setting her hand on top of Katie's, who gave her a brave smile.

"10 seconds."

Ten seconds passed. Fifteen. Twenty. A few seconds processing could be expected. They all turned to the screen. Twenty-five seconds.

"Beacon ID: Double-checking."

There were small gasps of consternation.

"Beacon ID: The *81-Petals*."

Terina threw up her hands and shrieked with excitement. There were exclamations around the table. She met her mom's eyes. Her unhappiness was tempered with amazement. Jarvie just looked more confused, but Beezan was nodding his head.

"You were right Captain," Thunder said. "We are here for a reason."

"And *81-Petals* must have sent a light-speed distress call 15 years ago! Only 5 years to go." Iricana added.

It was more than history, Terina realized. *It was destiny.*

1-Light Eve

Enkindler, approaching Friendship a-rings

Dear Katie, Lanezi wrote,

I hope this journal gets to you. I fear all the messages I sent from the *Cheetah* were deleted, or are still with the *Cheetah,* wherever it is.

I'm on the shuttle *Enkindler* at 5F, now known as Friendship. On 3-Light we are going to reach the a-rings and jump to Canyon. I have no worries about the jump. However, we're now approaching the area where the extra gravity ball blew up, so I turned up the particle and radiation fields. Also I'm going to order full rations, starting tomorrow, to prepare for jump. I just can't jump in this fuzzy state of mind.

The twins have been so good. Inspiring even. I am tired and hungry, and sick of wearing the vapor mask, and getting claustrophobia from being in the survival tent. But I can't complain. It would be so low of me and I don't want to let the twins down.

Euro and Io look almost normal-size in their layers of sweaters and blankets. They do their chores, say their prayers, fix the food, play quiet games, and don't complain about the minimal washing. We have water, but you know, it's really cold and we don't want to spend the fuel to heat it and recycle it any more than necessary. I told them they could have tea once a day, but they drink it cold. They have been vigilant about conserving energy. They don't even listen to music. They say it plays in their heads. They never fuss with each other. I suggested they spend some time apart for variety, but that made them unhappy. They help me and take care of me. After I go to the cold hold for food, they put their warm blankets around me. It's so touching.

They keep me focused and mindful of my command. I am ridiculously excited about eating more tomorrow. We'll have a special Feast. And soon we'll know if we have a long run in and have to go back to rationing or can eat again. And I hope and pray that I'll survive long enough to see you.

Lanezi saved what he wrote, fingers too cold to go on. He put his gloves back on and tightened his restraints, pulled Whisper and Summer closer, and settled down to sleep. In the dark dark of a ship in survival mode, with not even a panel light, he tried to imagine himself somewhere else. Somewhere warm and bright. The twins were murmuring together.

"Euro, do you think praying burns calories?"

"Dr. Tenshi says the brain takes a lot of energy whether you're thinking or not. 'So you might as well think!'"

"If our souls get energy from praying, where does it come from?"

"That's spiritual energy, not physical."

"So where does spiritual energy come from?"

"From God, I suppose."

"So maybe if we pray enough, we can equalize our energy."

Lanezi smiled to himself. He was never sure if he was in touch with his soul. Like now. He tried to let his mind go and see if there was something more, but maybe the mind and soul were so interconnected you could not tell them apart. Maybe the brain took extra power to connect to the soul. Maybe it was like jumping. It would be so nice to let the soul take over. At least it wouldn't be hungry.

3-Light

Cheetah, preparing to jump out of the pocket

"Friendship," Zahar whispered to Kiwi, just in case podpups had any mystic influence. After hugging and stowing him, she got in her cocoon and started on the brackets. Next to her, Thayne was complaining about being put under early.

"Don't do it," he insisted.

"Your doctor's orders. And the Captain's," Caspia explained. "Next time maybe."

"There may not be a next time!"

"Exactly the attitude we don't need. I'll give you two more minutes." Caspia left him to say whatever prayers or make whatever peace with himself he could. But Zahar knew he was far too troubled to do that in two minutes.

Caspia set the helmet on Zahar and they tested links. "You're good," she said, with a light rap on the helmet.

Tenshi was already under. If there was more discussion with Thayne, she didn't hear it. But as Zahar flicked through her helmet screens, she saw that he was under. That left Caspia to be passenger monitor. She had requested to ride this one out with Evan.

"1 minute."

They settled in for the one hour run. Piece of cake compared to the usual six hours. Friendship, she chanted to herself. Anywhere actually. Regular space. A-rings. Something familiar. She thought of her family. *I just want to go home.*

She had great faith in Evan. Better to have a wanderer when you didn't know where the path was. *I must banish all doubts, oppose any thoughts of anger.*

"Strive ye to banish that darkness for ever and ever . . ."[1]

Evan got us here. He can get us home. That's the straight logic of it.

"Banish discord from this world and illumine it with the light of concord."[2]

After 45 minutes she started to fret, did some deep breathing, and checked through her screens. She could trigger her jump drug at any time, but if they were going to die, she wanted to be awake for it.

Nkiroo was counting down the fake PAT bumps. Fake as there were no a-rings, but equally painful bursts of acceleration. "Six more," he announced, calm as could be.

She focused on Friendship as she heard the countdown. She could not see paths, and was hesitant to imagine, so she focused on supporting Evan, as if her hand was on his back, ready to run with him.

"Two. One."

There was a feeling of surprise and amazement, like recognizing your room upside down in nogee, and she felt a faint tug. *Got it!* There was a thrill from the crew. They were going somewhere, but the thrill warped into puzzlement and alarm.

Melawn had learned, in his years with Thayne, when something hurt, didn't make sense, or was breaking up orderly data, just shut down and observe. And this made no sense. Usually there was no feeling of time or space in the path, even if you went too deep. But he felt pulled, as if on the edge of a whirlpool of time. *Blank, blank. Don't distract Evan.*

There was something in the path, another ship. *The Ramian!* Had they been here for months? What would happen? But it was already happening. In the strangest, scariest moment of his life, he felt himself, the ship, and the space around them surge and push through the Ramian ship. People, as terrified as he was, were standing all around their ship. He glimpsed one Ramian in particular, arms up as if he were an old-fashioned preacher, calling his people to him. *Why aren't they in their jump chairs?* And at the center of their ship—a black pulsing menace.

Somehow the *Cheetah* kept going, now with the Ramian ship bobbing behind it. And then they dropped into normal space with a horrible lurch. Alarms were blaring. His cocoon was pressurized.

"Proximity alarm."

"Venting alarm. Arc 6."

Melawn flicked through his screens with one finger. Evan, next to him, had taken manual control. On the tactical display,

Melawn could see the tumbling Ramian ship, perilously close behind them. Blasts of acceleration in different directions were rocking him in his chair. Someone he didn't know had taken command. A calm decisive voice was giving orders. "*Cheetah*, program best trajectory to avoid the ship behind us."

"Venting alarm. Arc 7."

"Increase particle field. Increase radiation field. Cancel venting alarms. Crew! Stand by for maneuvers!" And even as he heard it, the ship flipped end over end in a sickening roll meant for far-smaller vessels. On the tactical, Melawn could see that Evan had just turned them so as not to blast the trailing ship with their radiation.

Evan, Melawn realized, coming to his senses. Evan's voice was somehow changed, more grounded, in command. Despite their situation, hope surged through Melawn.

"Nkiroo!" Evan said. "I feel something from the a-rings."

"Checking."

Evan again, "Debris field is clearing. Prepare to reorient."

Another sickening lurch flung them around to their regular orientation.

"Robots, report to damaged areas," Evan ordered. "Crew, stay put, please. *Cheetah*, scan for beacons."

"A-ring beacon confirmed: Friendship. Ramian beacon on the ship behind us. Human and Ramian treaty beacon located. *Enkindler* message beacon located."

"*Enkindler* live beacon located."

There was a gasp from the crew. Everyone must be awake now. Someone was crying.

"Location of *Enkindler* live beacon?" Evan asked.

"In the a-rings. They are near jump velocity."

"Jump crew, report in."

"Nkiroo, alive and well."

"Melawn," he meant to say with cool efficiency, but it came out as a whisper, "alive and well."

"Passenger monitor, report."

The crying stopped with a great sniff. "All green in the Passenger Lounge."

"*Cheetah* to *Enkindler*: All alive here. Godspeed to you."

"*Cheetah*, condition of Ramian vessel?"

"Severe venting. Radiation leaks. Recommend avoidance."

"Stay in range. Contact them using the Luminesse translator."

Melawn's heart started to calm and then realized, with tremendous joy, that they had survived, they had made it to Friendship, and that Lanezi must have survived.

"*Cheetah*, venting report."

"Vents are sealed. Arcs 6 and 7 are depressurized. Cargo hold is breached. The ship is stable down to tertiary resonances. Arc 1 and its auxiliary rooms are safe."

"All crew, you can get up now."

There was a tremendous cheer over the s'links. Melawn pulled out of his brackets, unsealed his cocoon, and yanked off his helmet. He and Nkiroo could barely contain themselves, reaching to gently help Evan. When they pulled off his helmet, a new person looked up at them. Melawn grabbed the side of the chair, puzzled. The same easy-going smile, the same bright eyes, but someone was home. "Evan," he whispered as they helped him out of the cocoon.

Melawn was about to hug him, when Evan looked behind them. "Caspia?" He didn't get a meter away from his chair before she was there and they were hugging each other so tightly Melawn feared for their ribs.

Through tears of joy, Caspia laughed, "Evan, Evan, you are back."

Then everyone but Thayne grabbed on, hugging the both of them, delirious with joy. Even Thayne was smiling and saying, "We made it!" And in the moment, Thayne seemed one of them again.

Enkindler, in the Friendship a-rings

"NAV Alert."

"We're in the rings!" Lanezi protested uselessly.

"*Cheetah* Beacon detected."

"What?"

"Ramian Beacon detected."

Oh my God. The Cheetah is back. They're alive! I should have kept the twins awake to deal with this. I can't be distracted.

"Seven laps."

Should I abort? "*Enkindler,* show visual," but it was useless. He couldn't see more than a bright dot.

Another surge, bump. *Keep breathing. Concentrate. They may need help.* But he could send help from Canyon. He had every reason to jump.

"*Enkindler* to *Cheetah*: We are alive, but low on supplies and power. I'm going to jump and send help back for you. Full report on my message beacon—"

He didn't get a breath in before the surge, and had a little panic. He couldn't even remember what he was going to say. *Breathe.*

"*Enkindler,* send the message. Show only the jump screen."

He didn't live through everything in his life, through Luminesse and Harbor and this starvation run just to get distracted at the last minute. *FOCUS!*

He became one with the surges, every one taking him closer to the jump.

"NAV alert."

He nearly jumped out of his seat.

"Ramian vessel has exploded."

Good God. How horrible. "No more NAV alerts unless they're ours!"

"NAV alert! Navigation error." And they were kicked to the side.

But after all these years, Lanezi was getting a sense of when things were about to go wrong in the a-rings. His hand was on the manual control and he was already avoiding the misaligned-next segment. They shot out of the a-rings.

NO! He did not want to abort. He wanted out. All that practice at honesty was forcing him to be honest with himself. He did not want to go back to the *Cheetah*. He looked at the screen: .99JV. So close! They had a little fuel. Now that he'd broken free of the circle of a-rings, he would risk all their lives to be free of the *Cheetah*.

He held his finger down on the thruster. *I need that .01! I need a path.* Canyon was totally the other way. No close star was even in their direction. He didn't care.

I am a long jumper!

"JV."

Lanezi threw the power and experience of his mind behind the desperation of his heart. *Yes!* A very clear, strong path appeared. Blue. Where it went, he had no idea. And he didn't care. *I'm taking charge of my life.* And he boosted the *Enkindler* into the path.

Goodbye Thayne.

Good luck everyone.

It was a deep, deep path. He and the twins were weak from their rationing. But they were strong in spirit. And the pups were strong, even Whisper. They surged along. The sentries hovered, but Lanezi willed them away. *We're going to live.*

Cheetah, near Friendship a-rings

What is that knocking? Zahar looked at the tactical screen.

She didn't see any debris coming their way from the Ramian. Maybe it was small stuff. She wished the Ramians would answer.

Suddenly, there was a flash of blinding white. Zahar gasped. The others, still hugging each other, grabbed holdbars and each other and turned to the screen. Their happiness froze on their faces as they realized that the Ramian ship had exploded.

"I think we should secure—" she tried to say, but too late. They were kicked to the side and up, everyone flailing for holds at the last second. But it was more like a big wave than a sharp smack.

"Okay? Okay? Is everyone okay?" she asked.

"Yes, yes," they answered, sorting themselves out.

"We better strap for a bit . . ." But there was that knocking again. And her mind flashed back to being trapped and freezing in the airlock.

"*Cheetah,* report on *Enkindler.*"

"Still in the a-rings."

Now the others heard the knocking. Subdued again from the destruction of the Ramian, they exchanged worried looks. "Let's just check that out before we settle down," Zahar suggested.

Evan and Caspia stayed in the Command Bay to watch over things. She and Tenshi led the others, hand over hand to Arc 2 and opened the door. They squeezed in the airlock. Zahar peeked through the window and didn't believe her eyes. She shook her head and thought she was having a delusion. "I. You. Better just open the door."

Tenshi did, and there, lining the rimway on both sides were at least a hundred Ramians. "How is this possible?" Thayne asked.

And the Ramians all turned toward them, waves of blue and purple people in colorful clothes and jewels. But they were tired, strained, faded. One of them floated to the center. He was younger, a teenager maybe. "I saw him," Melawn whispered, "when we passed."

"Somehow they came here," Zahar said. And realized, "They're not dead!"

"Praise the Lord!" Tenshi agreed.

And then the teenager, bright, almost pure blue, with the eyes of a visionary, raised his hands in friendship and called out, "Greetings. I am Quay."

To be continued . . .

Chapter 1: Coming Apart

3-Light-1084

Enkindler, outbound from Friendship

Aboard the shuttle *Enkindler,* Lanezi gripped the arms of the pilot's jump chair as he slipped into the one clear thread leading away from Friendship System.

The shock of learning at the last moment that the *Cheetah* had survived turned to despair as he realized that Friendship system was coming apart. The *Cheetah* may not have time to jump to safety.

The thread, the elusive jump path between the stars that they were riding, to whatever desperate destination Lanezi had sensed, was just about to drop them into normal space, when something catastrophic happened behind them, at Friendship. The thread snapped up, away from their destination, threatening to whiplash the *Enkindler* into oblivion. Vulnerable in their makeshift jump chairs, with tremendous gees crushing them and the shuttle, Lanezi hung on to the thread as it rebounded back down near the star. With his last conscious effort he tipped the *Enkindler* into normal space, praying for a rescue that they would surely need now.

"Venting alert!"

"Auto stabilize complete."

"Medical alert: Lanezi."

"Medical alert: Euro."

"Medical alert: Io.

"Suit alert: Io."

"Suit alert: Euro."

"A-rings located. Course optimized."

The calm voice of the *Enkindler* contrasting with the terrifying venting alarm, the cries of Euro, and the silence of Io dragged Lanezi back to consciousness. Pain. Panic. His ribs were burning. *No. No. It wasn't supposed to be like this.*

"Venting damage temporarily repaired. Command Bay doors sealed. Venting alarm canceled."

Lanezi gasped for air. First things first, but the pain scrambled his mind. "Pain meds, non-drowsy," he whispered. A sting hit his arm, but it gave no immediate relief. *The ship is working. Trust the ship. Trust the suits.*

He just hung there in his restraints, trying to slow his heart and partition the panic. Through his helmet visor, he realized that debris was drifting around. He flicked through the screens on his helmet. *Still working, thank God. Air in the Command Bay. The computer is working. We jumped in a shuttle and we're still alive. Thank you. Thank you,* Lanezi prayed. *And if it's not too soon for another request, please help us stay alive.* But the shuttle was badly damaged. Despite the pain and confusion, he summoned some primitive parental strength to save the twins. *I need to take command.*

"Euro," Lanezi whispered, knowing Euro wouldn't speak first.

"Lanezi! Lanezi—Io, I can't see—my helmet is broken."

"Euro, Io is okay. His suit has been punctured, but repaired and he has air. He's breathing, but unconscious. He has lost some blood, but that's stopped. His light is yellow."

"Can I open my helmet? It's dark. I want to see." His voice was so scared and plaintive, Lanezi almost said yes. But his good sense was coming back.

"No. Not yet. I'm sorry. A few minutes. Close your eyes and I'll tell you everything." Lanezi slowly, carefully, got out of his chair, and holding one arm against his apparently-broken ribs, he started snagging the bigger debris while continuing, in gasps, to let Euro know what was happening. "Pups all have green lights. *Enkindler*, where are we?"

"System unknown. Multiple beacons, Ramian and other unknown signals."

"Engage Ramian translator. Send mayday in Ramian."

A schematic of the system appeared on Lanezi's helmet screen. Multiple planets, a-rings. "Ships! There are all kinds of ships, Euro. They're heading for the a-rings, like . . . like they're running away."

"From us?"

The *Enkindler* answered. **"Ramian ships are all en route to the a-rings at high speed. Ships from the third planet appear to be chasing them. Human beacon detected."**

"Attention human vessel. You have entered Seven system. This is a restricted system in Ramian space. Send messages only during blackout periods for the third planet. Instructions follow. Cooperate with Ramian command."

Well, the *Enkindler* had been blasting their mayday for all to hear. Lanezi scowled. And didn't turn it off. "What have we stumbled into? *Enkindler*, view of the third planet."

The main screen was broken, but a popup slowly emerged

from the panel showing a view of the third planet. Lanezi gasped, unable to put it into words. "Euro, open your helmet."

"Earth," Lanezi whispered in his confusion.

"No," Euro said, sensibly. Lanezi shook himself. "There's no moon," Euro explained. Of course not Earth. But some planet so much like it. Lanezi opened his helmet. He could see tears on Euro's face. He got vapor masks for the three of them and helped Euro out of the chair so he could go to Io, who was waking up.

"*Enkindler*, how much air, counting tanks?"

"**35 hours.**" *Oh my God. That's not much.*

"Time to a-rings?"

"**64 hours, 12 minutes.**" He stopped. Repeated the numbers to make sure he heard them right. *After all this? We can't make it? Stay calm. Think of it as a math problem.*

"Time for two people? No podpups."

"NO!" Euro cried, turning to Lanezi in shock.

There was no answer. "*Enkindler!*"

"**52.5 hours.**" *Okay. I won't have to make that decision, thank God.*

"*Enkindler*, add to mayday and focus broadcast to the Ramian ships. 'Human shuttle requesting rescue. Damaged. Not enough air to make it to a-rings. We need a pickup. Please. Two children aboard. Please.'"

"**Sent. 1.3 minutes lag time.**"

There was a spark of orange light on the screen. "**Explosion near Ramian ship,**" *Enkindler* reported.

"Another one!" Euro pointed with his suit finger.

"**Old records indicate this type of explosion is caused by weaponry.**"

"No," Lanezi whispered. A war is what they had stumbled into. Humans believed that any species advanced enough for space travel would have overcome its warring stage. They had always trusted that the universe, aside from being deadly in itself, was a fairly friendly place. But here was the contradictory evidence. And, he realized with a final bleakness, if the Ramians were running, no one would come back for them.

The Sundering Series, Book 1:

Far in the outer sectors, the supply chain from Earth is stretched to the breaking point. Ships can only jump between stars using an ancient alien transportation system called the a-rings. But now, someone or something is jumping into human space, destroying the a-rings, and trapping people on rundown space stations.

Cargo captain Beezan Mirage, one of the few people that can jump, has sacrificed eight years as a solo pilot delivering critical supplies to keep space stations operational. For Beezan, it's better to be alone than suffer the loss of another crew.

Runaway Jarvie Atikameq makes a desperate move to get away from teen training school, onto a ship, and back to his last surviving shipmate. He may be the only person with a clue to what's really happening with the mysterious a-ring accidents.

They never meant to change history.

Non-violent - First Contact - Science Fiction Adventure

What You Win: Stories for the Whole Family

• How can Mica compete at the science fair when parents are helping the other kids?

• Niccolo doesn't want to play in the symphony this summer, but can he bring himself to blow the audition?

• How will Jenna and Abby ever become astronauts if they're stuck on the farm, and lost in the maize?

From silly to serious, here are sixteen hopeful stories about walking your own path, finding friends, and fighting everyday battles.

ACKNOWLEDGMENTS

Thank you so much to the readers who got this far. I think you will find that it's a wild ride to the end, so I hope you'll stay tuned.

Special thanks to proofreaders Jeff Price, Brian Burriston, and Raeleigh Price, as well as early readers Shirlie Burriston, Doug Krotz, Amy Renshaw, and James Schwartz.

Thanks to the Brilliant Star Crew for your support, past and present: Amethel Parel-Sewell, Amy Renshaw, Susan Engle, Annie Reneau, C. Aaron Kreader, Heidi Parsons, Katie Bishop, Foad Ghorbani, Lisa Blecker, Darcy Greenwood, and Dr. Stephen Scotti.

I've just seen the Tom Edwards cover today. Wow! Thank you for bringing more spaceships to life!

And to Don Burriston, Jordan Price, and the rest of my far-flung family, thank you for all your support and encouragement over the years.

-DRP

NOTES

2. CIRCLE OF LIES

1. 'Abdu'l-Bahá, *Paris Talks* www.bahai.org/r/728570642
2. 'Abdu'l-Bahá, *Paris Talks* www.bahai.org/r/232471605
3. 'Abdu'l-Bahá, *Selections* www.bahai.org/r/445636918
4. 'Abdu'l-Bahá, quoted by Shoghi Effendi in *Advent of Divine Justice* www.bahai.org/r/293314070
5. The Báb, *Selections from the Writings of the Báb* www.bahai.org/r/065828247

3. BROKEN CONSTRAINTS

1. 'Abdu'l-Bahá, *Some Answered Questions* www.bahai.org/r/228364906

4. FRACTURING PATHS

1. Bahá'u'lláh, *Gleanings from the Writings of Bahá'u'lláh* www.bahai.org/r/568533901
2. 'Abdu'l-Bahá, *Promulgation of Universal Peace Peace* www.bahai.org/r/864288420

14. JUMP DISCONTINUITY

1. Bahá'u'lláh, *Gleanings from the Writings of Bahá'u'lláh* www.bahai.org/r/487380847
2. 'Abdu'l-Bahá, *Additional Tablets, Extracts and Talks* www.bahai.org/r/807710579

15. OUTBOUND

1. Bahá'u'lláh, *Gems of Divine Mysteries* www.bahai.org/r/731075255

22. COMPLETING THE CIRCLE

1. 'Abdu'l-Bahá Compilations, *Promulgation of Universal Peace* www.bahai.org/r/014236147

2. *Bahá'í Prayer, author unknown*

3. *'Abdu'l-Bahá, The Promulgation of Universal Peace www.bahai.org/r/ 021995680*

4. *'Abdu'l-Bahá, The Promulgation of Universal Peace www.bahai.org/r/ 838170951*

5. *'Abdu'l-Bahá, The Promulgation of Universal Peace www.bahai.org/r/ 437467020*

6. *Bahá'u'lláh, Epistle to the Son of the Wolf www.bahai.org/r/270933711*

7. *'Abdu'l-Bahá, Some Answered Questions www.bahai.org/r/307669381*

8. *Bahá'u'lláh, Prayers and Meditations by Bahá'u'lláh www.bahai.org/r/ 705115639*

9. *Bahá'u'lláh, Prayers and Meditations by Bahá'u'lláh www.bahai.org/r/ 458879931*

27. DEGREES OF SEPARATION

1. *'Abdu'l-Bahá, The Promulgation of Universal Peace www.bahai.org/r/ 792941907*

2. *'Abdu'l-Bahá, Paris Talks www.bahai.org/r/568565770*

31. COLD DARK MATTERS

1. *Bahá'u'lláh, Prayers and Meditations by Bahá'u'lláh www.bahai.org/r/ 905622579*

2. *Bahá'u'lláh, Kitáb-i-Íqán www.bahai.org/r/848851360*

3. *Bahá'u'lláh, Gleanings from the Writings of Bahá'u'lláh www.bahai.org/r/ 998881880*

32. NEW DIMENSIONS

1. *'Abdu'l-Bahá, Selections from the Writings of 'Abdu'l-Bahá www.bahai.org/r/ 159531595*

2. *Bahá'u'lláh, Tablets of Bahá'u'lláh www.bahai.org/r/694735299*